SHE HAD WAITED LONG ENOUGH

"I don't care anymore, Jon. I don't want to think anymore. I just want to feel."

He kissed Elizabeth then, his mouth coming down with a hard force that pushed aside everything but the feel of his lips. Gone was the gentleness of every other time he had touched her, swept away by a greedy desperation that left no room for anything else.

Jon wasn't kind. He wound his hand in her hair to hold her head still, and the instant she leaned against him he demanded she give him everything. And she did.

Also by Susan Kay Law

Journey Home

Available from HarperPaperbacks

Traitorous Hearts

⊰ SUSAN KAY LAW ⊱

HarperPaperbacks
A Division of HarperCollinsPublishers

This is a work of fiction. The characters, incidents, and dialogues are products of the author's imagination and are not to be construed as real. Any resemblance to actual events or persons, living or dead, is entirely coincidental.

HarperPaperbacks *A Division of* HarperCollins*Publishers*
10 East 53rd Street, New York, N.Y. 10022

Cover illustration by Jim Griffin

First printing: March 1994

Printed in the United States of America

HarperPaperbacks, HarperMonogram, and colophon are trademarks of HarperCollins*Publishers*

❖ 10 9 8 7 6 5 4 3 2 1

1

1774

He was the most beautiful man in the world.

It was a pity he was an idiot. Even worse, he was *British*.

Elizabeth knew who the man was even before he lumbered into the Dancing Eel. She should; she'd been hearing about him for weeks, ever since the company of British troops had been stationed just outside New Wexford. Every patriotic colonist was outraged at the indignity of Crown soldiers camping so near their village. However, the town's women couldn't help noticing that the over-aged, stupid lieutenant looked like a baffled angel.

Elizabeth handed a tankard of hard cider to a ruddy, middle-aged farmer, a regular customer, and slipped into the shadows cloaking the kegs near the back of the taproom.

She would watch, and wait.

It was one thing she was good at.

* * *

The Dancing Eel seemed perfectly suited to its location. If it was small, rough, dark, smoky, and insular, nobody seemed to mind. It was also snug, the diamond-paned windows shut tightly against the frigid wind of a Massachusetts autumn. The tavern was convivial, sometimes boisterous, and relentlessly, passionately colonial.

There were two things everybody knew about the Dancing Eel: it drew a good beer, and the British never bothered with the place.

Until now.

When the small contingent of British soldiers had entered the tavern, it had gone silent—dead silent. The air, which had smelled of ale, whale oil from the lanterns, and good roasted meat, now smelled of anger and mistrust, of arrogance and fear.

No one laughed, no one sang, no mugs were clanked together. No one was having fun anymore. Worse still, no one drank.

The owner, Cadwallader Jones, couldn't let that happen. He scrambled forward, hoping to dispose of his newest customers as quickly as possible. He planted himself in front of the men, his big feet spread wide, his arms crossed in front of his still-formidable chest, and looked down at the man wearing the silver insignia of a captain. Pretty tall, but skinny, Cad thought. Turkey-necked. The floppy wig perched on the top of his head made him look like a mop.

"You are not welcome here."

Francis Livingston, captain of the Light Company, 17th Regiment of Foot, gulped slightly at the size of the man blocking his way. But he had plenty of support, the captain reminded himself. Besides, this fellow was old, as the solid silver of his wildly wavy hair attested. Livingston adjusted his meticulously curled wig—the only one worthy of his station that he'd been able to find in this godforsaken place—and stepped forward.

"I am Captain Livingston. We, as the military representatives of this area, are welcome anywhere," he said, holding his head at what he assumed was a regal angle.

"Ah." Cadwallader scratched the bridge of his nose and tried another tactic. "How silly of me. Of course you are. We, however, are simple colonists. We prefer to take our entertainment without worrying about disturbing such exalted personages as yourselves. Surely you would not be comfortable in such ordinary surroundings, *sir*." The customers snickered at the sneer that had crept into Cad's voice.

Livingston was momentarily perplexed at their chuckles, but then smiled, gratified at the respect the owner obviously had for him. Perhaps he was not the troublemaker the captain had been led to believe.

"I appreciate your concern, my good man. But I must insist. We will stay for a drink. As I am the new commanding officer here, I deem it necessary to become familiar with the area."

Dropping his arms to his sides and clenching his fists threateningly, Jones straightened to his full, impressive height. A half dozen men, equally as large as he, gathered behind him in implicit threat.

"I'm afraid *I* must insist," Cad said, a thread of steel running through his voice.

The captain nodded in acknowledgment. "Ah. You must be Cadwallader Jones."

"I am," he affirmed proudly. "You've heard of me?"

"No one else would be foolish enough to threaten a British officer and his men over such a trivial thing as a tankard of beer."

Cadwallader stiffened. No one had dared call him foolish, not in a very long time—no one but his wife, of course, and he would allow her almost anything.

"This post can be a very simple one for you, Captain, or a very troublesome one. I suggest you save yourself some trouble and leave now. We only want one thing from Britain: to be left to our own devices."

"I have no wish to make things difficult, Jones. I merely wish to test the waters, as it were. I have heard it rumored that anyone who can best one of your sons wins a free drink. Have I been misinformed?"

"No."

"Then I accept the challenge."

Cadwallader glanced pointedly at the Captain's thin arms, encased in spotless red wool, and snorted derisively. "You're not serious."

Captain Livingston smiled genially. "Oh, I don't mean to compete myself, of course; I have long outgrown such games. I am the intelligence of my company, not the brawn. I had thought to have one of my men contest."

Cadwallader shook his head determinedly. "No, we have no business with the likes of you."

Livingston gave an exaggerated sigh. "Pity. I hadn't heard you were one to back down so easily."

"A Jones never backs down!" Cadwallader shouted, his face going purple with the effort to control himself.

One didn't just haul off and strike an officer of the Crown, no matter what the provocation.

"Then it is a wager?"

"It is."

"Good." The captain inclined his head to one of the privates accompanying him, who leaned out the door and beckoned to someone outside. "Allow me, then, to introduce the muscle."

The man filled the door, blocking the pale light of the setting sun. He had massive, solid shoulders that looked like he could support the weight of the world as if it were a load of swansdown. His features were a unearthly blend of perfect symmetry and exceptional strength. His hair was simply brown, a color that on anyone else would look ordinary, but on him took on the depth and richness of a whitetail's coat.

Stumbling over the doorjamb, he crashed into the nearest trestle table, sending the tankard of cider on it flying toward the floor. The dark golden liquid spewed out in a high arc, drenching nearby men. He reached to catch it, missed, and overturned the rough-hewn bench.

"Sorry," he mumbled, clumsily righting the bench. He retrieved the empty tankard from the planked floor, setting it gingerly in the center of the table; the large pewter mug looked unusually small in his huge hands. He swiped at the table-board with his forearm, succeeding only in spreading the puddle of cider and thoroughly dampening his sleeve.

Apparently satisfied with his efforts, he straightened somewhat and turned to face his captain, hunching his shoulders slightly as if afraid that if he stood to his full height he would hit the ceiling—and it almost seemed he might.

Grinning foolishly, he tugged at the uneven hem of his crimson coat, obviously unaware the tarnished buttons were pushed through the wrong holes.

The giant bobbed his head. "Cap'n? You asked for me?"

Livingston chuckled indulgently. "Yes." He turned to face the stunned owner and patrons of the Dancing Eel. "Allow me, Jones, to present Lieutenant Jon Leighton."

"Lieutenant?" Cadwallader asked incredulously.

"Yes, well, Leighton received his rank before he had a rather unfortunate episode with a horse. Kicked in the head, I'm afraid. He should have been drummed out of the service, of course, forced to sell out, but his commander took pity on him and allowed him to keep his commission. Despite his rather obvious shortcomings, however, he does have his uses."

Snickering laughter and a low, astonished murmur rumbled through the taproom. *This* was the best the British army had to offer? A pompous captain and a muddle-headed hulk of a lieutenant?

Lieutenant Leighton smiled more broadly, stretching his lean cheeks and showing gleaming, even white teeth.

Cad shook his head sadly, feeling a twinge of sympathy for the boy, who didn't even seem to know when he was being made sport of. No one had the gall to make fun of a Jones, thank God, and Cad could hardly imagine what it felt like to be the brunt of such ridicule. Ah, well, the lieutenant was clearly too stupid to be hurt by it all.

"I take it you mean for Lieutenant Leighton to be your champion?"

Captain Livingston lifted his chin smugly. "Yes.

Unless, of course, you wish to simply concede and save us all the bother?"

"No one bests a Jones once he hits four-and-ten years," Cad asserted, his hazel eyes glowering beneath bushy silver brows.

"Good." Livingston waved at one of his men, who scurried to pull out a nearby bench for his captain. Settling his lanky frame onto it, he glanced around the room. The colonial ruffians were watching intently, ill-disguised hatred on their faces. Livingston preferred to think of it as respect.

"How many . . . offspring do you have anyway, Jones?"

"Nine. Healthy and strong, every one of them."

"Of course. Well, nine drinks will be sufficient, I should think. There are only five of us, after all, and we rarely allow Leighton here to drink—I don't think it wise to befuddle his wits any further."

"Nine? But Bennie can't—"

The captain cut off Cad's protest. "I will accept no excuses, my good man. Let's start with the eldest, shall we?"

Cad braced his fists on his hips and bellowed, "Adam!"

"Right here, Da." Adam stepped from behind his father. Taller than Cadwallader, he was a brawny man, muscular from his work as the town's blacksmith and just past thirty years of age. His blunt-featured face was roughly good-looking, his hair a sheaf of the pure gold his father's must once have been.

"Adam?" Captain Livingston's mouth curved wryly. "How appropriate for a first-born son."

Cad placed his hands on his son's shoulders. His

voice was low, so only Adam could hear. "I don't want you to just beat that lobsterback, do you hear me? I want you to humiliate him."

Adam gave a confident grin. "When have I ever done anything else, Da?"

Cad clapped him heartily on the back. "True enough, son. True enough."

Going to the nearest table, Adam turned a bench sideways and straddled it. Once he had braced himself to his satisfaction, he plunked his elbow on the table and looked expectantly at Lieutenant Leighton.

Leighton brightened. "Hello. I'm Jon."

"Uh, yeah, I know that." Adam gestured at the opposite seat. "So are you going to sit down, or are you going to just stand there like a lump all night?"

"Sure." The lieutenant bobbed his head. "Thank you." He plopped down, a little off center, and wobbled for a minute before finding a precarious balance.

Adam looked up at the man across from him, realizing he hadn't had to look up at another man since he'd reached his full growth. It was unsettling—or it would have been, if the man didn't have such a friendly, vacant grin on his face, like a puppy who didn't realize the wagon he was so happy to see was just about to run him over.

Leighton didn't have a clue what to do, Adam realized. "Look, first put your elbow on the table, all right?"

"All right." The lieutenant did as he was told.

"Then put your forearm up in the air, and we're going to clasp hands."

"Uh-huh." He obligingly grabbed Adam's hand.

Adam gave a deep, exasperated sigh. How was he supposed to work up the appropriate anger and concentration? "Listen carefully now, Leighton. When Da says 'Now,' I'm going to try and push your arm down to the table, and you're supposed to try and push mine. We can't lift our elbows. Do you understand?"

"Uh-huh."

Adam tried again. "It's a game."

"I like games."

He gave up. "Da, go ahead."

"Just a moment," Captain Livingston interrupted. "Why should Jones be the one to begin the competition?"

"Do you object to this?" Cad asked.

"Well, actually, yes. How do I know the two of you don't have some secret signal worked out, giving your son a head-start, and thus the advantage?"

"Are you questioning my honor?" Cad raged, taking a step toward the Englishman.

"Da, wait!" Adam nearly came off his bench in protest. "What does it really matter who starts us?"

Cad forced himself to relax. "It doesn't, I guess. You'll win anyway. Rufus!"

"Yes, Cad?" A thin, bespectacled man, anxious for this chance to get a better view, hurried forward from his place in the back of the room.

"If I can't start them, you can't start them, Captain. Same reason." There was steely determination and barely suppressed anger in Cad's voice. "Rufus can start them. He's the shopkeeper, and he depends as much on your business as ours."

"Agreed."

"Start them."

Rufus nervously pushed his spectacles up his thin nose. "But, Cad—"

"Start them!" The shout resonated off the ceiling.

"Fine." Rufus scuttled to the table where Adam and Lieutenant Leighton sat, their beefy fists wrapped around each other. "Are you both ready?"

"Yes. Are we going to play now?" Leighton asked excitedly.

Adam rolled his eyes. "Would you just get on with it, Rufus?"

"Yes. On my count of three. Ready? One . . ." All the spectators, their drinks forgotten, leaned forward in anticipation. "Two . . . now!"

Muscles strained. Biceps bulged. Tendons tightened and veins stood out in bold relief. Adam grunted, then groaned. Turned red, then purple. Sweat trickled down his face and dripped onto the table. Still the hands remained upright, locked.

And through it all, Leighton grinned.

Finally, slowly, almost imperceptibly, the hands inched toward the table. Adam's eyes grew wide with disbelief, and he pushed himself, taking a deep, gulping breath that bulged his cheeks, but to no avail. The back of his hand dropped to the planked wood.

"Good game. Next?" Jon said brightly.

The crowd was silent, stunned. Since Adam had been twenty-three, when he'd finally managed to defeat his father, they'd never seen him lose. Hell, no one had even bothered to challenge him for four years.

Adam, his face rigidly set, shoved his bench back from the table and stomped out the door, giving the wall a thunderous kick as he left.

Captain Livingston applauded enthusiastically.

"Rather good showing by your son, there, Jones. That's one. Shall we work our way down the list?"

Cad clenched his fists. "Adam's just a bit out of practice. The others will do better."

"If you insist. Well then, where is your second son?"

"Ah, well." Cad shuffled his feet. "Brendan's—"

"I can speak for myself, Father," said a young man standing a bit away from the rest.

"Brendan . . ."

Brendan faced the captain. He was of average height and slender build; in no other place but among a collection of such outsize men as the Joneses would he look small, but here he undeniably did. He was dark-haired, had graceful, almost delicate bones, and looked nothing like any of his brothers.

"What my father is trying to say, Captain, is that I don't have the, uh, heft of the rest of my family. If you'd consider turning to a test of wits rather than strength, I'd be happy to oblige you."

"You don't look much like your father, do you?"

"I favor Mother. Now, what do you say?"

Livingston shook his head. "No, I'll stick to the original wager. It will be a contest of strength. Do you concede this match, Jones?"

"I concede nothing!" The men closest to Cad flinched at his bellow.

"But I do," Brendan said calmly. "I see no advantage in wasting my energy on a cause I cannot hope to win. It is something you might consider, Father."

Father and son stared at each other, the argument clearly an old one, but, equally clearly, neither was ready to yield to the other.

"Sometimes I wonder how I ever produced you," Cad finally said.

"I often wonder the same."

"There will be time for family squabbles later, Jones. I'm here to win some drinks. Who is the next one?" Captain Livingston asked.

"Carter."

"Carter. Good God, man, you can't mean you named them alphabetically?"

"I most certainly did."

The captain chuckled. "Well, then, bring them on."

Carter proved no better than Adam, nor did David, nor Frank. By the time Jon met George, the consensus was that the lieutenant must be tiring. They were wrong. One big, strapping blond man after another was defeated, giving way to strapping blond adolescents. Through it all, the lieutenant grinned and laughed and generally seemed delighted with the whole process. By the time Henry and then Isaac lost, Cad's anger had faded into weary resignation. This man could best his sons. He was mightily tempted to give it a shot himself, but he knew deep down, bitter as it was, that he would not fare better. Besides, Mary, his wife, would make sure he regretted it if he did something so foolish.

"Well, that's it, then." Captain Livingston leaned back, crossing his thin legs at the knee, his booted foot swinging. "You may as well bring us some beer."

"No E," the lieutenant put in abruptly.

"What?" Livingston asked.

"No E." Leighton pointed to the door. "A—Adam." He gestured to Brendan, who was propped comfortably against a far wall as he watched the proceedings. "B."

He pointed to the remaining Jones sons in turn. "C, D, F, G, H, I. No E."

"That's right, isn't it?" Captain Livingston clicked his tongue against his teeth. "We may as well make this complete. Where's the fifth one, Jones? Hiding him? Perhaps he's not quite up to snuff, eh?"

"I told you, Bennie can't—"

"Bennie? We're looking for the E one. Lose track of your letters, Jones?"

Cad ground his teeth together. "I most certainly did not! Bennie's a nickname."

"Well, then, bring him out. I'm sure Lieutenant Leighton wouldn't mind humiliating another one of your sons."

"I'm Bennie." At the soft, musical voice, Jon leapt to his feet, tipping his bench over in his haste to stand rigidly at attention.

"Dear God!" Captain Livingston's boots thunked on the plank floor as he abruptly sat up. "He's a woman!"

"How brilliant of you to notice, Captain. I am Elizabeth Jones," she said.

The captain stood and circled her slowly while she stood comfortably tall and waited. She was clearly a Jones: tall, strong-boned, and clean-featured. Her hair, wayward curls escaping from the tight braid down her back, combined all the various shades of her brothers': sunny gold, pale wheat, and a few strands of the dark, warm brown that matched her eyes. And, despite the loose, concealing fit of her flowing white shirt and baggy, gathered brown skirt, she was also clearly a woman. She had broad, square shoulders, generously rounded hips, and a matching, impressive bosom. The bunched fabric at her middle hid but hinted tantalizingly at a sharply curved waist.

Captain Livingston smiled slowly and reached out to wind a curl of her hair around his forefinger, marveling at his good fortune. This wonderfully proportioned woman was the most intriguing female he'd seen since he'd landed. She was not only a colonial, but she worked in such a place as the Dancing Eel; clearly a woman who'd be flattered by the enthusiastic attentions of a young, fast-rising British officer. "You're rather a lot of woman, aren't you?" His gaze dropped to her breasts. "Ample. I like that."

The spectators drew a collective, anticipatory breath and waited. In New Wexford, Elizabeth held a rather unique position. They didn't think of her as a girl, exactly; she was just Bennie Jones. She didn't really have a gender. But, on rare occasions, a traveler passing through town, intrigued by her curvy figure and encouraged by her quiet manner, would make the mistake of thinking that a wench who worked in a tavern was naturally a tavern wench.

The damage Bennie could do to a man's ego was matched only by the damage she could do to his body—she'd had eight brothers to learn from, after all. And if that weren't enough, any man who was, in her brothers' opinion, *disrespectful* to Bennie could look forward to a painful visit from one or two or several of the Jones boys.

Bennie stared directly down at the captain from her two-inch advantage. She grasped his wrist in one hand, and peeled his fingers off her hair with the other, bending those fingers back, and back, and back.

"Yes, I am a lot of woman. It's too bad you're so little a man, isn't it," she said, so quietly Livingston was the only one who could hear her.

The captain's face blanched nearly as white as his wig. He tried to jerk his hand from her grasp, but her grip was firm. She smiled and released him, giving a careless shrug. "Too bad."

Color flooded back into his face. "Why, you . . . " He stopped. "Lieutenant Leighton, it appears you have another drink to win."

"Now see here, Captain Livingston. I won't be having my Bennie touching that lump you call a lieutenant. I'll *give* you the damn drink," Cad protested.

"Oh, but that wouldn't be acceptable at all," Livingston replied. "We had a wager. One drink for every one of your offspring the lieutenant defeats. I demand that you honor it."

"But you didn't make Brendan go through with it."

"No." The captain chuckled. "But there was no sport in that. This, I think, could be highly entertaining."

"I will not have it!" Cad thundered.

"Da." Bennie laid a calming hand on her father's arm. "I don't mind."

"Ben, he could hurt you."

She shook her head. "He won't."

"You sound very sure."

"I am."

Cad sighed heavily. "But, Bennie, I—"

"I'm going to do it anyway, Da, whatever you say."

"Do none of you ever plan to let me finish a sentence?"

She rose to plant a kiss on his grizzled cheek. "I can't help it, Da. I'm a Jones."

She walked over to her opponent, who, for some reason, was still at attention, his gaze fixed at some point over everyone's head.

Dear Lord, he was a big one, she thought. He was taller than her brothers, who, with the exception of Brendan, towered over her, and *she* was taller than every other man in New Wexford.

Up close, he appeared less like an angel. His face wasn't ethereally perfect and insubstantial. He looked more like her vision of a devil, his face sharply chiseled, strong, seductively appealing. A face capable of drawing her in, luring the unwary into sin and destruction. A fallen angel.

But that was only at first glance, for once she got past the initial shock of that compelling face, she could see it was strangely empty, devoid of life. Blank. His grin was broad, vacant. His lids were lowered over his eyes, making him look half-awake, or half-asleep. She could catch only a glimpse of pale, pure blue beneath them.

"Hello," she said. "I'm Bennie."

He looked down at her. Bennie blinked. Had she imagined it? For an instant, his eyes had opened fully, and she had seen blazing, brilliant blue—intense, aware, assessing. Now there was only that dull, simple expression again.

"Yes, Bennie," he said. "Girl."

She must have imagined it. She smiled back, unable to resist his childlike friendliness. She felt a twinge of pity for this simple, happy man. She had seen the way the other men had ridiculed him, had made him the butt of jokes, how his commanding officer had dismissed him. Simple Jon. Perhaps he didn't notice, but she did.

She knew what it was like always to be the different one, the odd one, to have people see only the obvious. Perhaps it was easier not to know.

"Yes, a girl. It's my turn to play the game now, all right?"

"All right."

He bent, clumsily righting his bench, and plopped down, jamming his elbow on the table and holding his hand in the air. He glanced at her expectantly. "I'm ready now."

She couldn't suppress a small laugh. When she was younger, out of sight of her mother and father and the rest of the town, she had often tested her strength against her brothers. And not just arm wrestling, but sometimes in a full-scale, flat-on-your-back-in-the-dust wrestling match. She'd acquitted herself well, actually, winning her share—at least against her younger brothers. When she was thirteen, her mother had caught them at it. Her mother's obvious disappointment had wrenched Bennie, and she'd given up rough play. She'd missed the exercise almost as much as she regretted hurting her mother.

Now Bennie would get a chance to try again. She knew she wouldn't win, of course, but the thought of competition sent the blood rushing through her veins anyway. Her mother would be disappointed once more, but Bennie had long ago given up the idea of being the daughter her mother wanted. It wasn't that she hadn't tried—and tried, and tried. She simply couldn't do it.

Rolling up the sleeve of her linen shirt, she sat and placed her elbow carefully on the table, arranging herself for maximum leverage. She lifted her hand to place it in his—and froze.

His hand. Dear Lord, he was going to touch her! With that big, strong, male hand. Attached to that big, strong, gorgeous male body. She felt oddly . . . odd.

Stop it! she told herself. She'd touched lots of big, gorgeous men. So what if they were all related to her?

She tilted her arm forward an inch. Her mouth went dry.

That large, warm, male hand wrapped itself gently around hers.

2

"*Are you two* prepared now?" Rufus asked. "Get ready. One . . ."

"Stop!" Bennie licked her parched lips. She couldn't concentrate, could only stare at him. Strands of smooth brown hair escaped from the clumsy club at the back of his neck, falling around his beautiful, unearthly face, those sleepy blue eyes.

"What's the matter, lass?"

"Huh? Oh, nothing, Rufus, nothing. Just give me a moment, please." If they didn't start yet, then it wouldn't end so soon, and then maybe he'd hold her hand for just a little bit longer.

What was she thinking? He was a British soldier. A clumsy, bumbling oaf of a British soldier at that. Maybe if she didn't look at that face . . . She dropped her gaze below his neck.

Bad idea. In the warmth of the crowded tavern and the heat of the struggle, he'd discarded his coat and matching scarlet waistcoat, tossing them over the end of the table. His dingy white shirt was missing a button. The lamplight was dim and wavery, but she could catch occasional, flickering glimpses of . . . skin.

He wasn't hairy. Her brothers were hairy. His chest looked like his hand felt: smooth, hard, warm. She squeezed his hand experimentally. Unyielding. Strong.

He squeezed back.

"Ready to play now, Bennie-girl?" His voice was low, a rumble as much as words, felt as much as heard.

She looked up into those hazy, cheerful eyes. "Uh, yes, I guess so."

Concerned, Rufus peered at her through his lenses. "Bennie, if you're not—"

"Yes, yes, yes. Don't worry about me, Rufus. Let's just do it, please."

"Well . . ." Clearly reluctant, he pinched his brows together.

"Come on, Rufus."

"If you insist. One . . . two . . . *three* . . ."

Bennie pushed. Lieutenant Leighton's hand didn't waver. She pushed harder. Nothing moved. She dared a peek at his beaming face. His smile broadened. Bennie frowned, leaned forward to put her weight behind her arm, and pushed harder. Still nothing. But, surprisingly, her hand wasn't going backward, either.

Gradually, she relaxed her arm. His grip on her hand loosened. Suddenly, without warning, she exerted full force. His muscles tightened fractionally, matching his power to hers. Still, he held her hand gently, almost tenderly, as if he were carefully curbing his overwhelming strength, as if her hand was fragile and precious.

Bennie settled back, her hand still comfortably in his. "You're not going to win, are you?"

He shook his head vigorously, sending wisps of hair flying around his face. "No."

"Then I'm going to win?" she asked hopefully.

He smiled like a proud little boy bringing home his first hornbook and shook his head again. "No."

"Are we just going to sit here all night, then?" Actually, that wasn't such a terrible plan.

His face clouding, his shoulders slumped. "I don't know."

"That's enough!" Cad slammed his palm down on the table next to Bennie. "Let go of my daughter!"

"Now just a moment." Captain Livingston rose from his bench. "This is not over."

"Yes, it is. He's not going to defeat Bennie," Cad returned.

"This is absurd. He could, easily, and you know it."

"And how would I be knowing that? They're just sitting there," Cad said smugly.

"Leighton, beat her now."

"Sorry, Cap'n. She's a girl." Jon lifted his other hand and tried unsuccessfully to push the hair out of his eyes.

"Yes, I know she's a girl. We all know she's a girl. I'm ordering you to defeat her!"

The corners of Jon's exquisitely sculpted mouth drooped. "Can't. Bennie-girl." He thrust out his lower lip, giving a great gust of breath that lifted the strands of hair for a moment before they fell back across his face. " A nice girl."

"Why, thank you, Lieutenant Leighton." Bennie

smiled brilliantly at Captain Livingston. "I guess it will just have to be a draw, won't it?"

"Leighton, you addle-brained oaf." The captain rubbed his temples tiredly. "Ah, you're not even bright enough to insult properly. Jones, bring us the drinks. All eight of them, mind you. I'll be counting. I could go for a nice Madeira, myself."

"Well, there, Captain, we never said what kind of drinks, did we?"

"I assumed the victor would choose, as in any gentleman's wager."

"Well, now, I never claimed to be a gentleman, did I? We'll bring you a nice New England flip."

"A New England flip?"

"Just the thing to warm your bones on a cold November day." Cad smiled, but his eyes remained as frosty as the day he'd just spoken of. "Bennie, would you go get . . . Bennie!"

"What, Da?"

"Let go of that man!"

"Huh? Oh, yes, of course. Sorry, Da." Reluctantly, she slipped her hand from Lieutenant Leighton's, but she didn't move.

"Now, Bennie. Go on and get to work." Cad narrowed his eyes warningly at his only daughter.

"Yes, Da."

"Go get these men New England flips."

Curling her right hand protectively, savoring the lingering warmth from the lieutenant's touch, she floated toward the back of the tavern. "Yes, Da."

In the shadowy serving area behind the cage bar, Bennie pulled out five great solid pewter mugs. She filled them with foamy dark beer and molasses, adding dried pumpkin as a sweetener. Taking the iron poker that was kept in the fire for just this purpose, she thrust the red-hot tip into each tankard, wrinkling her nose at the acrid, scorched-smelling steam produced.

Expertly grabbing two mugs in one hand and three in the other, she returned to the main area of the taproom. The colonial customers had filled the outer ring of tables, leaving a clear space around the two tables the British occupied. Bennie went first to three young privates, their brick red coats appearing dull next to the brilliant scarlet their captain wore. They accepted their drinks with a quick nod, scarcely glancing up at her.

Moving to the officers' table, she placed a mug in front of the captain, whose eyes remained securely fixed somewhere south of her neck, and she wondered briefly if she could get away with "accidentally" dumping the hot liquid in his lap. Probably not.

She handed the last mug to Lieutenant Leighton. He took a great gulp—and promptly spewed it out in a great stream that landed unerringly on his captain's spotless waistcoat.

"Ahhh! Burned!"

Captain Livingston jumped to his feet, wiping at the stain soaking into his clothing. "Leighton, I swear you are the most simple, clumsy soldier I've ever had the bad fortune of having assigned to me! When we get back to camp, I'll make certain you regret this!"

Bennie bit her lip to keep from laughing. "Can I get you a cloth, Captain?" She pulled a length of linen from her waistband and flipped it to him.

"Sorry, Captain," Jon said glumly.

Elizabeth took one look at his face and all amusement fled. He looked like nothing so much as one of her nephews waiting to be punished, fearing the cane less than the hurt of having disappointed his parents. She reached out a hand to pat the lieutenant's shoulder consolingly but stopped herself in time. She couldn't go around touching strange, full-grown men, not even when the action seemed so natural.

"It wasn't your fault," she said. "I should have told you it was hot."

"I'm sorry," he repeated.

"Oh, it's all right, Lieutenant," Livingston said, congratulating himself on his tolerance. "I know you didn't intend it."

"No. I didn't. I'll clean it for you?" Jon asked hopefully.

"Certainly, when we get back to camp. Now, why don't we finish our drinks? And try to be a bit more careful from now on, will you?"

The captain blotted his waistcoat as best he could and returned the rag to Bennie. Settling back on the bench, he took a cautious sip of the drink. His mouth puckered and he gave a small shudder. "It's very bitter, isn't it?"

Bennie flipped the damp towel over her shoulder. "Here we consider it the perfect drink to warm a man from the cold." Her subtle stress on the word man appeared to go unnoticed.

"Yes, yes," Livingston said. "I can certainly see how it would be so. Very warming."

"Bennie!" her father roared from the back of the tavern. He wondered, a frown crinkling his brow. "We have customers here, Ben!"

"Coming, Da."

Hurrying to keep every cup in the place filled, Bennie had no more time to pay much attention to the British soldiers firmly ensconced in the center of the room. Their presence made the tavern decidedly quieter than it normally was. The colonials drank steadily, puffed on their pipes, and stared at the redcoats. The Dancing Eel usually rang with shouted protests against the injustices and indignities the Crown imposed on her colonies; tonight, a wary caution silenced the crowd.

Cad gave Bennie duties that kept her near the back of the room, choosing to serve the Englishmen's second round himself. Bennie couldn't believe her father voluntarily went within ten feet of the men—at least, not with peaceful intent. And yet, he clearly didn't want her near them. He'd always seemed to have faith in her ability to handle herself and any situation she came across. She wasn't used to his protectiveness.

As she wiped tables, drew beer, snuffed wicks and rinsed tankards, she shot furtive glances at the soldiers. She couldn't help it; she could feel them watching her. Captain Livingston, sipping on his drink, appeared to scrutinize the room, and her most of all, with speculation and undisguised amusement. And every time her gaze caught Jon's soft, sleepy one, he grinned at her with pure joy. Much as she tried to look away quickly, she always found herself smiling back. Warm, innocent happiness was impossible to resist.

"Better not let Father catch you smiling at them like that." Brendan's soft voice coming from the shadows in the corner startled her; she hadn't thought anyone would notice.

"I'm not smiling at them."

He puffed on his pipe, the rich scent of tobacco drifting to her. "Oh?"

"Of course not."

Arching one dark brow skeptically, he waited.

"I was smiling at him," she admitted.

"Him?"

"Lieutenant Leighton."

Brendan shook his head in mock sadness. "Elizabeth, Elizabeth. You of all people should be immune to handsome faces, large brawny bodies, and empty heads. I'd thought you'd learned to appreciate finer, more subtle men."

"Men who have some of the same qualities as, say, you have, perhaps?"

"Exactly."

Laughing, she reached for a big pewter tankard. "Can I get you something to drink?"

"You didn't really think I'd say no, did you?"

She carefully poured fragrant hard cider into the mug. "It's not that I appreciate him, you know—at least, not the way you meant. But how can you not smile at him? He's so happy. So simply happy."

Brendan reached around her for a bottle and added the hefty portion of dark rum that turned the cider into a "stone wall." "Simply happy? You think so?"

"You don't?"

He took a long sip of his drink. "Is anything ever really that uncomplicated, Elizabeth?"

"He is," Bennie said with conviction.

"Maybe."

Elizabeth filled her own mug with cider and leaned

against the wall next to Brendan, studying his fine, dark profile. Of all her brothers, Brendan was the one she felt closest to, perhaps because they were the two Jones progeny who were different from the rest.

"I'm sorry, Brendan." She traced the rim of her tankard with her forefinger. "About what Dad said about wondering how he produced you, I mean."

Brendan took a sip and leaned his head back against the wall. "It's nothing new, Elizabeth."

It wasn't. In the Jones family, a man was judged by his size and his brawn. Brendan wasn't exactly small, but he was definitely on the lean side. What no one seemed to appreciate was that his clear, brilliant mind was the equal of anyone's anywhere. Bennie knew he'd wanted desperately to go to Harvard and test himself among others who loved to think and learn but even if Da had had the money to send him, both Bennie and Brendan knew he never would. Cadwallader Jones would consider it a complete waste; a man should be working, not thinking.

"I know it isn't," she said softly. "Still—"

"Never mind, Elizabeth. That wound has been scarred over for so long I scarcely feel the pricking anymore."

"I just wish he would . . . I don't know. Stop expecting you to be like him."

"He's not going to change. I stopped hoping he would a long time ago." He pushed himself off the wall and grinned at her. "Now, enough of the diversionary tactics. Are you going to tell me you're really interested in that big lug?"

"I wouldn't say interested. I just feel kind of sorry for him. I wonder what he was like before his accident."

"Ah. So you're simply picking up strays again, is that it? Mother will be so disappointed. She's only been trying to marry you off for six years or so."

"Oh, stop." She gave him a small shove. "At least that's six years fewer than she's been trying to find a wife for you. After all, you're the only other never-married person over the age of twenty in New Wexford."

"I know." He placed his hand theatrically over his heart. "I'm 'in violation of God's command to multiply,' as Mother so frequently reminds me. But who would want to marry a poor printer like me?"

"Poor? You do a fine business, and you know it. The next nearest printer is all the way to Boston."

"I'm sure the right woman for me is all the way in Boston, too."

"Well, then, I guess we're stuck, aren't we? Mother will just have to do with the grandchildren she gets from the rest of the family." Across the room, Rufus waved for more beer. "I'd better get back to work."

The evening wore on; candles guttered in their holders, and the chill wind screamed outside the Eel. Inside it was tense and quiet; a night of steady drinking, uninterrupted by the customary conversation, left the colonials a little drunker than usual. The equally unaccustomed proximity of British soldiers left them a little angrier than usual, and a little more inclined to try and get rid of these unwelcome interlopers by any means necessary.

Whispers and murmurs simmered around the room. Nerves were stretched taut, and Cadwallader was torn between the anticipation of a bloody good brawl and apprehension that his tavern would get smashed in the process.

The redcoats seemed oblivious to the colonials' hostility. They sipped their drinks, turning to beer after they finished the flips. Finally, Captain Livingston stood to leave, his men scrambling to their feet after him, and Cad and his customers heaved a collective sigh of relief. *At last.*

Livingston waved curtly, signaling Cadwallader. A bit miffed at the abrupt summons, Cad was nevertheless so happy about getting these intruders out of his place he hurried over.

"Yes? What would you be wanting now, Captain?"

The captain carefully brushed imaginary dust from his stained uniform. "First, I'm assuming there will be no charge for the rest of the drinks."

"And just why would you assume that? You owe me four shillings."

"How many of your customers actually pay you in hard coin?" Livingston asked, pointedly glancing around the room.

"Not many," Cad acknowledged. "But all trade me useful goods or services. What have you to offer?"

"You are all ready receiving the services of the British army. There is no need to offer them for barter."

"I say there is."

"We are here for your protection."

"Protection! Bah!" Cad planted his fists squarely on his hips. "You are here for our persecution. The Quartering Act is no longer in effect, and the people of Massachusetts are under no obligation to provide for your upkeep. And we have no need of your protection. We are all perfectly capable of protecting our own."

"Ah." Livingston held up one long thin finger. "That brings me to one more thing: It has come to my attention that it is nearly time for your annual mustering of the local militia."

"Yes." Cad said, wondering why the captain had broached the subject.

"It will not take place."

"What!" Cad drew himself up to his full height. "It most certainly will. There has been a yearly mustering on the common as long as there has been a New Wexford."

"It is no longer necessary. The British army is here to protect you now."

"It is our right as free men and English citizens to see to our own protection. It is a man's business to take care of the safety of his family. I would trust no one else."

"You will trust us." The three privates suddenly formed a solid line behind their captain, standing rigidly at attention, their hands hovering close to the short swords strapped at their waists. A few seconds later, Lieutenant Leighton stumbled over to join them, bumping only one of the soldiers before finding his own spot and stiffening his large body.

"I am ordering you—all of you," the captain said, sweeping his arm to encompass the entire room. "There will be no mustering of the militia in New Wexford."

All the men in the room surged to their feet, their anger palpable in the suddenly seething air.

"There will be," Cad stated with utter implacability.

"It was an order, Jones. You are British subjects."

"We are Americans, sir," Cad said proudly.

A small smile played about the corners of the captain's thin lips. "We shall see." He turned to leave, his men following him in perfect, sharp formation. Even Lieutenant Leighton was barely a shade out of step, and no one doubted he had the strength to use his weapon.

"Oh, yes," Livingston said, as if it was an afterthought. "Any protests from the Sons of Liberty will be dealt with most severely."

"The Sons of Liberty?" Cad asked warily. "Why would you think any of us would know one of them? Everyone knows they are headquartered at the Bunch of Grapes Tavern in Boston."

"Boston is only fifteen miles away, Jones. Not so far for such radicals to travel."

"I know nothing about them."

The captain chuckled softly. "Well, perhaps if you should happen to run across one, you could pass on the message. They but play at politics and war. They are dealing with soldiers now."

His carriage proud and confident, he strode out the door.

Lieutenant Leighton was the last to leave. He whirled abruptly, throwing himself slightly off balance, and grabbed the doorframe to brace himself. The night was black and thick. Cold air crept in around his big body, seeping across the planked floor of the tavern, ruffling the flames of the tallow candles.

He swung his head from side to side, like an animal searching a new clearing, seeking prey or danger. Finally, his gaze fixed on the spot near the back where Bennie waited, watching them leave. His eyes brightened and his broad, happy grin spread once more across his strong-boned face.

"Good-bye, Bennie-girl."

The other men would call him traitor. He called himself prudent.

Thoughtfully, he watched the British leave. So that was the new ranking officer in the area. His contact would not change, of course; in fact, the captain would never know he existed unless it became essential. Still, he was glad to have the opportunity to see Livingston in action. One never knew what necessity would bring.

The captain was pompous, certainly. What he didn't know was whether that pride would become a problem. Could Livingston put it aside and do what needed to be done? At least the captain had intelligence. It could be worse.

He didn't know who could be trusted yet, he decided. It was too soon to tell, and too important a decision to be made quickly and carelessly. He would continue to listen, to gather bits of information and pass them on. He would watch, and wait.

The important thing was to be careful. That, and to stop this madness before it went too far, to stomp out the small, isolated fires before they burst into a wild conflagration that would bring only one thing.

War.

3

Bennie tightened her grip on the handle of her leather case and took a cautious step down the stairs. She paused, listening. It was quiet. She continued stealthily on, placing her weight carefully on the old boards, trying to avoid causing any telltale creaks.

The last thing she wanted was for one of her family to catch her before she slipped out of the house. If her father found her, she'd be put to work instead of allowed to go off by herself. If her brothers caught her, they'd tease her unmercifully. If her mother saw her—well, that didn't bear thinking about.

Reaching the bottom of the stairs, she peered both ways, into the dark, quiet dining room to her left and the silent, meticulously polished parlor on her right. Both rooms were empty. She had only to slip across the few steps to the door and then through the small clearing in front of the house without being seen and she was free.

The door opened. Bennie froze; it was too late.

"Hello, Mother."

"Elizabeth." Mary glided into the house, her market basket tucked over her arm, and quietly shut the door behind her. "I was just down at Rufus's store, and look what I found." She stopped, finally glancing up from her basket and getting a good look at her daughter. "Oh, Elizabeth," she said, her lyrical voice tinged with disappointment. "What are you wearing?"

Bennie glanced down at her loose linen shirt, breeches, and scuffed boots. "Clothes, I believe."

"I thought we decided you weren't going to wear breeches anymore."

"No, Mother, *you* decided. I decided I would wear them only when skirts made things difficult. Besides, think of how many yards of material we're saving by my wearing trousers instead of a dress."

"Elizabeth." Mary reached up, her slender hand elegantly graceful, and gently smoothed one of the disobedient curls escaping Bennie's braid. "I don't understand why you won't even try. You are so statuesque. With the proper clothes, you could really be quite striking."

Statuesque. Striking. Resigned, Elizabeth smiled at her dainty, petite, and utterly ladylike mother. Only a few strands of gray threaded the dark, smooth, shiny mass of her mother's hair, neatly woven into a tight bun. Not a stray hair escaped.

Bennie was nothing like her mother, and she knew it. Her dark eyes were the only feature she could say she'd inherited from Mary; everything else came from Cad.

"I really wish," her mother was continuing, "you would consider going to Maryland. You know your

Aunt Sarah would be more than happy to have you visit for a while."

Maryland again. Bennie didn't know how Maryland had gotten the reputation as a place where even the most desperate of women could find a husband the instant they set foot inside its borders, but her mother clearly believed this to be so.

"I'm not going to Maryland. I have no overwhelming wish to get married."

"Who said anything about getting married?" Mary asked innocently. "I just think you should go visit your aunt."

Bennie shook her head. She knew it would do little good to protest; her mother, gentle though she was, could be as immovable as any of the Joneses. Bennie wasn't the kind of woman a man wanted for a wife; she was too tall, too strong, too much like her brothers. But Mary never seemed to give up.

"Well, if you won't go for a visit, why don't we at least see about making you a new dress for the mustering? I have a lovely forest green wool that would look very stately on you. If you had a beautiful gown, I'm sure you wouldn't feel the need to go running around in your brother's castoffs."

"I'm only wearing these now because I'm going for a walk, and my skirts always catch on the undergrowth. I got tired of mending them, and you know I don't have your talent with a needle. I'll make sure no one sees me."

"You're going out to Finnigan's Wood again, aren't you?"

Bennie sighed heavily. "Yes."

"I'm just concerned about you. Do you really think it's

safe for a woman to go tramping around in the woods alone?"

"I'll be just fine," Bennie assured her quietly. "Who would bother me?" There were some advantages, few though they might be, to being her size. She intended to exploit them fully.

"I suppose you're going out to play that thing, aren't you?"

"Yes."

"Really, Elizabeth, I'd be more than happy to get you a more appropriate instrument, something more befitting a young lady. A spinet, or perhaps a harpsichord? If music is your talent, I think you should explore all aspects of it."

"Mother. I am not young, nor am I much of a lady. The violin suits me just fine. Now, if you'll excuse me, I'd like to go practice." Bennie slipped past her mother and strode across the clearing, choosing the path running behind the tavern and directly into a thick copse of trees.

Setting her basket down, Mary leaned against the doorframe, concern etching tiny lines around her lovely, delicate features. She loved her daughter completely and treasured her in the way only the mother of eight sons could cherish a lone daughter. But she didn't understand her.

Mary's hands fluttered up, checking to see if her hair was still tidy. She had known, back when she was seventeen, that the town had thought it a step down when one of the two daughters of the reverend of the First Congregational Church of New Wexford had agreed to marry the young, blustery giant, Cadwallader

Jones. Thirty-three years later, she was still sure she'd made the right choice.

She'd known even then that Cad had loved her wholly and without reservation. She came first with him, and always would. For a young woman whose father had often put faith and duty above family, it had been a seductive lure, and one she'd never regretted succumbing to.

She loved Cad with a quiet devotion. She understood him, for he was an open man, honest, proud, and uncomplicated. All her sons, too, she loved and understood; seven because they were just like their father, and Brendan because he was so much like her. Brendan, as did she, needed to think things through, to reason, to depend on intellect rather than treacherous and unpredictable emotions.

Bennie, despite her clear resemblance to Cad, was different. She didn't have her father's elemental nature. She hid so much. There was never any anger, any pain, any grief, not with Bennie—at least, not where it would show. She seemed satisfied, perhaps, but never content. Too much turbulence hid in those dark eyes. Too many ruthlessly suppressed dreams.

There seemed to be nothing Mary could do; at any rate, nothing she'd tried so far had worked.

But if there was one thing Mary had learned in more than three decades of being a Jones, it was steady determination always paid off—eventually. And Mary was nothing if not steady.

Finally taking her gaze from the place where Bennie had disappeared into the dark trees, Mary bent and scooped up her basket. There was nothing she could do now, and she had hungry men to feed. Later . . . well, later she'd see.

*   *   *

Bennie walked slowly through the woods, still lugging her case. A few lonely brown leaves clung to the rough, twisted branches of the oaks, maples, and other trees growing in disorderly profusion. The air was cool and fresh, as crisp as the leaves crunching satisfyingly underfoot.

Bennie loved the forest. The ground here was rocky, overgrown, and creased with small ravines; there were many acres nearby which were more easily tilled, and so this patch of growth had been left alone. The area was not vast by any means; but securely cloaked from prying, judging eyes by the accommodating trees, here she could feel comfortable. Here she felt like Elizabeth Jones, and not some freak everyone kept trying to shove into one slot or another, slots she could never manage to squeeze into, no matter how hard she tried.

Reaching her destination, she sank to the ground, unmindful of the slight dampness. A stream meandered through a miniature gorge; trees like tall sentinels marched along its edge. The brook was small. It didn't rush and burble along its bed; instead, it flowed smoothly, the sound quiet and soothing.

For a long time she just stared at the water. Shadowed by overhanging limbs, the clear stream waved the long, slender weeds growing lushly along its bottom.

Like Brendan, she'd thought she was immune to the damage words could do. She'd spent her youth being called gawk and giant and boy-girl. She'd dealt with it by becoming strong and proud and controlled. Yet she couldn't help the small but keenly sharp pain she felt when she failed, once again, to live up to her mother's expectations.

Dragging her case toward her, she undid the clasps, pushed up the lid, and lifted out her violin, trailing her fingers lovingly over the rich, smooth wood, lightly plucking the taut strings, listening to the true, resonant notes produced.

The violin had been a gift from her grandfather to the Jones children. Till the day he'd died, he'd never given up trying to "civilize" his daughter's family, and he considered an appreciation of fine music a gentlemanly trait. To his disappointment, none of the Jones boys had even the slightest interest in learning to play the "fiddle"—a term he considered an insult to the carefully crafted instrument. The lone exception was Brendan, and he, unfortunately, was completely devoid of talent.

After it had gathered dust in a corner for years, Bennie had discovered the violin. Her father considered music lessons a useless frivolity; her mother urged her to try a more ladylike instrument. But Bennie had been drawn to it somehow, fascinated by the process of making a lifeless object sing.

There'd been no one to teach her to play, so she had taught herself. Whenever a fiddler had played at a festival, she'd watched him carefully, studying how he moved his fingers, how he held his bow, how he strummed and plucked and drew music from strings and wood.

Doggedly, she'd practiced, hour after hour; in the winter, hidden in the loft of the barn, her fingers stiff and chilled, and in the summer in the private sheltered depths of Finnigan's Wood. At first she was awful; the violin had squealed and squawked like a tortured cat, but as she experimented, occasionally there had been a single, pure note like the notes she heard in her head. And then, sometimes, there were two notes, and three, and finally, a collection she could call music.

Now the music was hers, the one thing in her life she could truly know belonged to her alone; her fingers flew over the strings, and playing came to her as naturally and easily as breathing air. And it was nearly as essential. She could play any song she'd heard, never missing a beat or a note, but mostly she just played, matching the music to scenes in her head, creating a mood, giving voice to an emotion.

Tucking the instrument firmly under her chin, she drew the bow across the strings once, letting the rich note fade, absorbed into the forest. Satisfied the tone was good, she sent her fingers flying in a series of quick notes that loosened her joints and reestablished her easy acquaintance with the instrument.

Closing her eyes, she willed herself to relax, to concentrate only on the violin, searching herself for the music she would try to express.

Loud, enthusiastic applause startled her from her comfortable isolation. She jumped to her feet and whirled, automatically hiding the violin behind her back.

Jon Leighton, grinning hugely, clapping wildly, leaned against a stout tree. When she faced him, he straightened abruptly and snatched off his dusty, silver-trimmed tricorn, nearly crushing it in his hands.

"Hello, Bennie-girl," he mumbled.

"Hello, Lieutenant Leighton," she said, relaxing slightly. "What are you doing out here?"

He shuffled his feet awkwardly, sheepishness creeping into his deep, husky voice. "I saw you go into the woods. I followed." He rolled his big shoulders. "I listened. Sorry."

"That's all right." She found, to her surprise, that she meant it. She knew there would be no judgment from Jon. "Why aren't you with your company?"

"There's no work today. The captain said I should go have fun."

"Surely there's something you could do that you like better than tramping through the woods."

"The others were playing cards, gambling." He frowned, distress written clearly on his handsome features. "Captain told them they shouldn't play with me. I'll lose all my money."

"Oh," she said softly. Clearly, he was hurt by his fellow soldiers' refusal to allow him to play, and she had an absurd desire to soothe him.

"Besides, you need me. Girls shouldn't be out alone." He thumped his chest. "I'll protect you."

"But I don't . . ." Her voice trailed off. She had been going to answer, as always, that she didn't need protection, but what would it hurt to let him think she did? "You're absolutely right, Jon. It was silly of me. I would certainly appreciate your looking out for me."

He beamed immediately, and Bennie was caught off guard by the beauty of his smile. He belonged in a painting, or on the ceiling of a church—or in a woman's dreams.

"I can stay?" he asked hopefully.

"You can stay." What was she going to do with him? She'd never played for anyone else, and she wasn't sure she could do it now. Her music was private, not for sharing. "What do you like to do?"

"Everything."

"Everything?"

"The woods." He waved his arms at the trees encircling them. "I like to watch. To listen." Dropping his gaze, he stared at the violin she held loosely against her side. "I like music."

Like an offering, she extended her instrument. "Would you like to try my violin?"

Beneath his half lowered lids, something light and unidentifiable flared briefly in his pale eyes. "No." He looked sadly at his hands. "Too clumsy."

"Oh, no you're not. Try it," she urged.

"I might break it."

"You won't."

He tossed his hat aside and it sailed away to land at the base of a twisted oak tree. Nervously, he rubbed his hands on his breeches, then tentatively reached for the instrument. As soon as he touched the dark wood, he snatched back his hands as if he were afraid that that slight touch would do irreparable damage.

His pleading expression was irresistible. Bennie didn't even try.

"Would you like me to help you?"

Jon nodded eagerly. Bennie went to stand behind him, placing her arms around him, and found she had to stand on tiptoe to reach the proper height. For the first time she could remember, she felt normal-size. Almost small.

With her left hand, she lifted the violin and placed it

snugly beneath Jon's chin, where he could cradle it securely with his neck and shoulder.

"Now you should hold it," she suggested.

"Wait a minute." He rolled up the loose sleeves of his shirt, exposing thick forearms, solidly sculpted muscle traced by prominent veins. Carefully, gently, he wrapped his hand around the neck of the violin. She was amazed at the delicacy of touch his big hands were capable of, and she was reminded of the similar way he had held her hand in the tavern the evening before.

Concentrating on placing his fingers on the strings, she tried to ignore how close she was to him, how the muscles in his back bunched and shifted as he moved. It was almost an embrace, and Bennie wondered if this was how it would feel if he held her—this heat, this almost breathless anticipation.

She could scarcely reach around him, and she needed to get closer to find the proper fingerings. She pressed herself even more tightly against him, conscious of the nearly painful but completely wonderful sensation in her breasts as they pushed against the solid wall of his back.

She took a great gulp of air to clear her head; the air was tinged faintly with drying grass and distant smoke, leaves and fall, warmth and Jon. When she exhaled, her breath stirred the loosely gathered hair at the nape of his neck. His right hand held the bow, and she curled her hand around his. His wrists were supple, powerful, tendons standing out boldly.

"Here," she murmured. "We draw the bow across the strings, like this."

A single, clear note sang from the old violin. Jon turned in her arms, grinning at her boyishly.

"Pretty," he said.

He was close against her, and Bennie suddenly wished for the bulky protection of her skirts. "Oh . . . yes, it was pretty."

"No." Her hands dangled limply, the bow in one, the violin in the other. His arm was around her back, holding her in place—as if she could move!—and he lifted his other hand to her cheek.

He stroked the curve softly, tracing her cheekbone, and once again Bennie was struck by the amazing delicacy of his touch. There was so much gentleness hidden in his giant frame. What other things lay undiscovered and unlooked for in him?

"No," he whispered. "Not the note. You."

Pretty. Pretty was a word for tiny, elegant, feminine women. Bennie had never been any of those things. She was tall and striking and strong. Statuesque. But when this handsome man looked at her with such tenderness in his face, she almost believed it.

"Too pretty for a boy's name. Do you have another name besides Bennie?"

"Elizabeth."

"Elizabeth." He slid his fingers over the tendrils of hair at her temple. "Yes. Beth."

"Beth," she repeated, the word almost a sigh. It was a small, feminine name. "No one calls me Beth."

"Then I will." He lifted his head, so suddenly alert Bennie started in surprise. "What was that?"

"What?"

"I heard something—a sound in the bushes."

Bennie glanced around. The undergrowth was still, and she heard only a faint rustling. "It was probably just an animal."

"Maybe." His intent awareness vanished as quickly as it had come, and he again looked sleepy and vague.

"How about you?" she asked. "Is your full name Jonathan?"

"No." He stepped back abruptly, dropping his hands, and Bennie acutely felt the absence of his touch. "Just Jon. Only Jon."

"Then Jon it is."

He bobbed his head in acknowledgment. "Play for me?"

"You really want me to?"

"Please."

"All right," she agreed.

He beamed, fetching his discarded hat, and settled himself on the ground, lying back and cushioning his head with the crushed tricorn. "I'm listening."

It was much easier than she'd thought, to play for someone else—at least, to play for Jon. Somehow she knew he'd love anything she played. She lifted the violin to position, closed her eyes, remembered the way she felt when he'd touched her, and began to play.

This was a mistake.

He was supposed to be discovering what was happening in New Wexford. There was too much information flowing in and out of this small town, information vital to both sides, and it was his job to find out why.

When Jon had seen Bennie Jones slipping into the forest, he'd at first told himself that he was following her because she was a possible suspect. Truthfully, he still was; he knew nothing that eliminated her.

But that wasn't why he'd followed her, even though—for a moment—he'd deluded himself into thinking that it was. He rarely was anything less than candid with himself, and it bothered him deeply that not only had he been dishonest, he had done it over a woman.

She intrigued him. She had layers, he could tell. Things hidden beneath the surface. He was always compelled to dig beneath the obvious; it was one of the things that had led him to his job in the first place. He wanted—too much—to strip away a few of her layers.

Intense concentration puckered her forehead as she played, stray golden curls bobbed wildly around her head, and, Lord, did she have legs. He was suddenly sure why women were supposed to hide underneath skirts: the sight of legs like hers could cause a man to do stupid things. Her calves were smoothly molded; he felt sure they would be delightfully firm to his touch, and her thighs were womanly. Her limbs were incredibly long; it would take a man several deliriously happy days to kiss his way up their length.

His job did not allow extended, serious involvement with women. It had never mattered to him before—but now he hated it. He could care about her, but there was no time, no way to let himself get to know her, no way at all to let her get close to him.

It was simply too dangerous. He came too close to slipping when she was near, his concentration broken by the distraction of her mere presence. He couldn't afford to make any mistakes now; too many lives depended on it, including his own.

Yet he couldn't seem to stay away from her. She drew him in a way that was both completely unexpected and wholly irresistible. He wanted her to know what was beneath his act, an act he'd lived for so long even he was unsure what she'd find beneath the surface—if there was anything left.

Frustrated, Jon tore his gaze away from her, looking up through the black, skeletal boughs of the tree at the pale blue sky, and listened. Her music was nothing like any he had ever heard before; it was fluid, changeable, easy, mimicking the gliding soar of a hawk, then the quiet, meandering flow of a stream. It shifted again, becoming slow, subtle, intense, a fierce, beating undercurrent of passion.

He had to leave before it was too late. . . .

It already was. Jon closed his eyes and let the music flow through him.

4

Holding her skirts high above her ankles, Bennie made a small leap over the puddle of icy water as she skirted the New Wexford Common. Last night's rain had left the low areas wet and muddy, although the distant sun was doing a fair job of drying out the high spots. After all the residents of four villages had tromped through the common for the mustering, the place was going to be a black, sloppy mess.

Well, at least somebody liked it; a half dozen hogs were squealing happily, rooting and snorting in the hollow next to the schoolhouse. The pigs ran free in the town, earning their keep by devouring all sorts of garbage and waste, but in wet weather they could always be found here, burying themselves in the abundant mud.

"Watch out!"

"Get it before it ends up in the hollow!"

A blown-up pig's bladder rolled toward her, followed by four puffing, red-faced boys. Bennie stuck out her foot to stop it, giving it a sharp kick in the direction of Adam, her oldest nephew.

"Hey, thanks, Bennie. I didn't want to have to go in after it."

She reached out and ruffled his blond hair. Although he was only ten, his head already nearly reached her chin. "If I were you, I'd choose a little less crowded place to play football. You know Rufus thinks the game is a menace."

"Yeah, well." Adam tossed the ball from hand to hand. "Father said we should go off behind the school to play. But Ma's making gingerbread, an' it's almost ready, an' you *know* if Father gets there first he'll eat the whole thing, an'—"

"And nothing, Adam. If you charge into someone and bump them over while you're playing, you're not going to get any at gingerbread at all. Besides, your father will be too busy today to eat any gingerbread."

"Oh, sure," he grumbled, his eyes wide with complete disbelief.

Bennie laughed. "All right, maybe he'll find a bit of time. But he won't get more than half of it, I'm certain. Now you all go off and play and I'll make sure someone comes to get you when it's time to eat."

Adam darted off, trailed by his three smaller friends.

Tightening her shawl around her shoulders, Bennie continued around the square. Although the day was clear, the sun bright, the air had a definite bite, and Bennie thought she caught the crisp, metallic tang of approaching winter. The blue of the unclouded sky was pale, as if the color had been washed of intensity, a hue that reminded her of Jon's eyes.

His eyes. Why was she still remembering his eyes? It wasn't as if she'd seen him since that afternoon in the woods when he'd listened to her play. The weather had turned colder since then, and she'd only been able to get back there once, practicing in the stables the other days. Yet every time she'd brought out her instrument, she'd found herself looking for him. Missing his presence.

How absurd. She'd played thousands of times alone, only once with him there. She couldn't have become accustomed to him so quickly. Still, it had felt good to share the music. To have a friend who seemed to like it as much as she did.

A friend. Oddly, that's the way she thought of him— as if she knew anything about having a friend. She had more family than she knew what to do with, but she'd never really had a friend. She'd always been too different, too awkward, too . . . something, to be close to someone who wasn't related to her.

It was impossible: he was a soldier, he was British, he was a man. He was beautiful and simple and completely out of her realm of experience. He was many things, but he couldn't be her friend, and she'd do well to remember it.

The common was already crowded with people. The annual mustering was as much an excuse for all the residents of the area to gather as it was a military exercise. Bennie wended her way through the peddlers selling books, patent medicines, and hats; candy, sweetmeats, and cutlery. She inspected a particularly fine collection of twig baskets and pretended not to notice the men, carefully out of sight of their wives, gambling with homemade playing cards.

Betsy Grout, Rufus's wife, along with a number of

other women, was selling a tempting array of sweets arranged on tables in front of her husband's store.

"What will you have, Bennie?"

Bennie rubbed her stiff fingers together. "Mmm, tea, I think."

"Yes, it is a little brisk this morning, isn't it?" Betsy poured the steaming liquid. "Sugar?"

"Absolutely." Bennie grinned. "Lots. And you might as well make it two teas. I'm going to stop over at Brendan's."

"It's a fine day for the mustering, despite the chill." Using a sharp pick, Betsy chipped several large tan chunks off of the hard, beehive-shaped lump of sugar. "I just hope everything goes well."

"It always does."

Betsy pursed her plump lips. "So far it has."

"Why wouldn't it?"

"Rufus said there may be a bit of trouble with the redcoats."

"Trouble?" Bennie accepted the two mugs. "Because the captain told us not to hold the mustering? Oh, I'm sure it's nothing to be concerned about. After all, what could they really do?"

"They're well-armed, well-trained soldiers." Betsy pinched her brows together. "I would think they could do rather a lot."

"Soldiers under orders not to fire on any colonists without orders from a civilian authority," Bennie reminded her.

"I hope you're right," Betsy said skeptically. "Orders can be changed, Bennie. Or disobeyed. Has Brendan heard anything about there being any potential trouble?"

"Not that I know of." Bennie sipped her tea, shuddering

slightly at the bitterness the sugar couldn't quite disguise. Pine needle tea might be better for her digestion, and it was certainly the patriotic thing to drink, but her tongue still preferred a good imported tea. "Not yet, at any rate. I'll go ask him now if he knows anything."

Betsy caught Bennie's wrist, her grip nearly painfully tight. "Will you let me know if you hear anything?" Tension radiated from Betsy's round body. "My sons . . ."

"I'll let you know. I promise," Bennie said, laying her hand consolingly over Betsy's.

A tent, for God's sake. Field quarters. Tapping a folded ivory paper on the table in front of him, Captain Livingston glanced around in disgust. He couldn't believe he was in field quarters again. For all the disadvantages of being stationed in Boston, not the least of which was a hostile and abusive populace, at least they'd had decent quarters. Castle William wasn't exactly a palace, but it certainly was better than a cold, worn, and clearly well-past-its-prime tent.

Winter was coming. He was stuck out here in the country, and he couldn't even commandeer a place to stay. There was no place within ten miles big enough to hold all his troops, so they'd been assigned to this sorry, half decayed excuse for a fort midway between Lexington and New Wexford. He'd taken one look at the place and known it would take his men weeks of work to make it marginally habitable—weeks that *he* was going to have to spend in field quarters.

A gravelly voice outside called for admittance.

"Come in." Livingston settled back in his chair.

Sergeant Robert Hitchcock barely needed to duck to enter the tent. He gave a perfunctory but snappy salute, then dropped into the chair his captain indicated.

The only word for Sergeant Hitchcock was rumpled.; his face was rumpled, his hair was rumpled, and the uniform hanging on his spare frame was rumpled. No matter what time of the day or night, the sergeant always looked like he'd just rolled out of bed after sleeping in his clothes.

He was also the best sergeant that Livingston had ever had. Every inch of his small body was pure toughness, overlaid with a solid, impenetrable layer of undiluted loyalty. The man was Army, and that said it all. His loyalty was first to his men, his officers, and his company. His allegiance to his country and ruler came after his duty to his regiment; it might not have been the accepted order, but it made him one hell of a soldier.

"Well? How are the repairs going?" Livingston asked.

"Bloody slow, Cap'n." Hitchcock shoved a hand through the limp strands of his mixed gray and pale blond hair. Damn, he'd lost his hat again. "Goin' t'take at least two more weeks, probably more like three."

Livingston's thin lips twitched. "As soon as possible, let's start transferring the troops into the parts of the fort that are completed. It'll be a bit crowded, but there's no reason to have every man freezing. Then we'll shore up the rest as well as we can." He traced the edges of the stiff linen paper with his fingers. "Not much we can do about it today, though. It's nearly time to go."

Hitchcock's gaze dropped briefly to the paper. There was no curiosity in his expression, simply acknowledgment. He'd been in the army too long to indulge in curiosity. "Got the information, then?"

"Yes. We received it this morning." The captain dropped the folded paper to the table. "I don't know where they got it, but they're bloody efficient."

"How much time we got?"

"Not much."

"Exactly what're we supposed t' do about it?"

"Good question. I believe they expect me to 'think of something.'"

The sergeant snorted. "Somethin' that doesn't involve shootin' anyone, I suppose."

"That was one of the requirements, yes."

The sergeant mentally ran through his impressive vocabulary of oaths. One of the frustrations of army life was that the men who gave the orders often didn't know or had forgotten what it was like out in the field. As a result, the orders they gave were frequently impossible to follow to the letter.

The captain wasn't a bad sort, as captains went, Hitchcock thought. Oh, he wore his wig just a little too tight, but what officer didn't? At least he didn't whip a man half to death for dropping a little swearword now and again. And he'd somehow picked up a good, practical grasp of military tactics. Seemed to be able to move all the troops around in his head and figure out where they should go.

Hitchcock decided it was going to take most of the captain's overeducated brains to figure out this one. "So what are we goin' t'do, Cap'n?"

"Good question." Livingston wasn't entirely sure himself. He'd been ordered to stop any and all military drills and maneuvers by the local militia. At the same time, he'd been reminded in no uncertain terms he was not allowed to fire on civilians without civil authority.

He'd been here long enough to know things didn't always work precisely as his superiors planned. He'd been among the first thousand troops sent to Boston in 'sixty-eight. A newly frocked lieutenant, he'd been shocked when seventy soldiers deserted in the first two weeks, lured by the freedom and vice of the colonies.

He'd been equally surprised at the Bostonians' treatment of the soldiers: he'd had rocks, chunks of ice, rotten vegetables, and various unidentifiable types of animal dung flung at him on a regular basis. There'd been little he could do in retaliation.

And now this. What did it really matter if the colonists played around in the square with their guns and their bayonets? It didn't make them soldiers. One afternoon of drilling would never make a crack unit—it wouldn't even make a lamentable unit. If he'd been giving the orders, he would have seen it as an opportunity to discover just what kind of shape the colonists' defenses were in.

But he wasn't giving the orders. Not yet, at any rate. And the only way he would ever get that opportunity was to continue to do his job flawlessly. He had no doubt he would do precisely that. Then he'd receive his promotion. Perhaps if these little squabbles with the colonies were settled once and for all, he'd finally be sent back to blessed England, where he belonged.

"Tea, sir!"

"Enter."

Jon bent over nearly double as he came in, carrying a

precariously balanced tray laden with cups, a steaming pot, and a large assortment of tiny cakes.

Livingston held his breath as Leighton served him, hoping that—this time—he'd get his tea without getting drenched, scalded, or otherwise injured in the process. But there were few jobs the man was at all suited for, and he seemed to be especially proud of doing this one.

The tea was served without incident. Livingston took a careful sip of his, sighing with pleasure. A strong, lovely Ceylon blend.

His gaze fell on the paper on his desk. "What am I going to do? Well—"

"Er, Cap'n?"

"Yes, Sergeant."

Hitchcock cocked a ragged brow at Jon, who was trying to stand rigidly at attention with his back bent at what surely must have been an extremely uncomfortable angle.

"Lieutenant, why are you still here?" Livingston asked.

"Didn't say I could go, sir."

"You are dismissed, Leighton."

"Yes, Cap'n." The lieutenant ducked his head and clomped out the door.

Livingston tsked and shook his head. "He's hopeless, Hitchcock."

"Yes, sir." Hitchcock hid his grin behind his teacup. "But he does make one helluva cuppa tea."

"True. Now, then," Livingston said, returning his attention to business. "What else can we do?" The captain rose from his chair, and Hitchcock scrambled to his feet. "We will gather the troops. And we will stop the mustering."

* * *

Brendan's printshop was in a small trim brick building next to Grout's store. Carefully holding both cups, Bennie pushed the door open with her elbow.

"Hello? Brendan?"

"A moment, please. I'll be right with you," he called from the back room.

Three shelves just inside the door held a sparse selection of merchandise: writing utensils, ink, chocolate, coffee, a few assorted bottles. Setting down the tea, Bennie picked up one bottle.

"'Elixir Vitriol,'" she read. "'Miraculous remedy for fever.'" The next bottle was dark and irregularly shaped. "'Dr. Walker's Jesuit Drops.' What are they for?"

"Never you mind what they're for." Brendan plucked the bottle from her hand and returned it to the dusty shelf.

"Do you always have to sneak up on people, Brendan? It startles me every time. I never hear you coming."

"Can I help it if you're not observant?"

"I'm extremely observant. For instance, I observe that you don't want to tell me what that remedy is for."

"Not to worry." He wiped his stained fingers on his equally inky apron. He certainly wasn't going to tell her it was for any one of a variety of diseases a man could pick up from a loose woman. "It's nothing you'll ever need to know."

"Oh." Bennie picked up his cup of tea and offered it to him. "A manly thing, huh?"

"Ah, she comes bearing gifts." He accepted the tea. "My thanks. And yes, it is something for men."

"I'm going to find out eventually, you know. One of you always lets it slip."

"It's not going to be me. Not this time, at any rate."

"It's never you." She gave him a mock scowl. "What do you keep all this stuff here for, anyway?" Bennie gestured at the decrepit shelves of dusty merchandise, most of which had been there for years. "You never sell any of it."

Brendan rolled the mug between his long, elegant fingers. "People expect it."

"And of course you always do what people expect."

His grin flashed suddenly. "Absolutely."

Bennie dragged her forefinger along the edge of a shelf and frowned at the grime that darkened her fingertip. "Business is good, then?"

He shrugged noncommittally. "About the same as always. Paper is still hard to come by. People seem to find other uses for their old linen than sending it to the paper mill."

Drawing her brows together, Bennie contemplated her brother. Along with printing contracts, deeds, and other legal papers, he produced *The New Wexford Journal and Weekly Advertiser*. In this capacity, he often learned of any news, controversies, or legal problems, both in and out of New Wexford, before anyone else in the village.

"Have you heard anything lately?"

"About what?" Brendan reached behind his back and untied his spattered apron.

"The mustering, the British. Whether there will be trouble."

"If you ask me, there's almost bound to be." He yanked off the apron and tossed it over the counter.

"But the redcoats have orders. They *can't* fire."

"Elizabeth, any time you get that many men with that many guns and that much anger in one place, I'd be more surprised if there wasn't trouble than if there was."

Suddenly cold, Bennie rubbed her arms to warm herself. "Things have been strained between the Crown and the colonies for such a long time; sometimes worse, sometimes better but never *here*, Brendan. And never *now*. It could all fall apart, couldn't it?"

"I think you should be prepared for it," he said evenly.

Bennie stilled. The threat had always seemed distant and vague; there seemed no chance of its ever touching her. But now it was taking on form and substance. "I don't understand why Britain can't just leave us alone."

"Elizabeth, think." Brendan lifted a leather jerkin from its hook on the wall and shrugged into it. "The Crown made a huge investment in the colonies. They fought the French for years to protect these territories. From their perspective, are they asking so much? A few pence in taxes?"

"Taxes we had no voice in, Brendan. No control over."

He frowned, his eyes dark and remote. "How much in this life do we really have control over? Or, perhaps I should ask, how little?"

Bennie drifted her fingers lightly over the odd collection of bottles, their smooth curves and familiar solidity strangely reassuring. "You think it is wrong for us to want our independence?"

"Not wrong, Elizabeth. Foolish, perhaps. I'm not sure we've really thought through how slim the chances are of our winning it by force, nor that we've understood what the price will be. I don't like waste, and I don't relish the thought of any of us dying for nothing." He took his powder horn from the hook and slipped it over his shoulder.

Bennie blanched. "Dying?" she repeated softly.

Against his thigh, his hand clenched. "I'm sorry, Elizabeth. I didn't mean to . . . I really don't think anything is going to happen today. It wouldn't be worth it, not for either side. I just want you to be prepared for the possibility—the probability—that something soon will."

She closed her eyes and swallowed against the sudden thickness in her throat. Her life had been so simple. There had been her music, and there had been her family. She hadn't wanted anything else, hadn't needed anything else. But, oh, how she needed that. She couldn't lose part of her family, had never even seriously considered that she might. Her father, her brothers, even her steel-under-softness mother, all had seemed indestructible. They'd always been there, and always would. Even when she'd been a child, and her oldest brother and, briefly, her father, had gone off to fight the French, she'd known they'd come home safely. Of course they would. They were Joneses; they'd come home without a scratch.

But this would be different. It was too big, it was too much.

It couldn't happen. She didn't want it to happen, wouldn't let it happen, and so it wouldn't.

"Elizabeth?"

"Yes?" Bennie squared her shoulders and opened her eyes, forcing the disturbing thoughts away. Today would be wonderful, her family was safe, and everything would go on as always.

"Did I tell you're looking especially pretty this morn?"

She glanced down at her new dress; her mother had prevailed, after all. Bennie liked the deep, forest green color; it reminded her of the few rare pines hidden in Finnigan's Wood. The dress was more fitted than she was used to, snug at the waist, close over her chest. It made her feel exposed, but she couldn't very well not wear the thing after her mother had gone to the trouble of making it.

"A stork in peacock feathers," she scoffed. "Why don't you buy me something to eat before the mustering?"

"Can't." Brendan grinned. "I can't afford it."

Bennie frowned at him in mock severity. "I don't eat that much."

"Uh-huh—compared to a horse, maybe. Or Adam. But compared to the rest of the world—"

"Three sweet buns at most. I promise."

"I really can't, Elizabeth. It's almost time for the mustering."

She glanced out at the square; several dozen men were already milling about in loose groups. "But it's scarcely noon. The mustering never starts before two o'clock."

"It does this year." He grabbed the musket leaning against the wall near the door.

"But why?" His grim look was all the answer she needed. "Oh, in case the British decide to show up?"

"We'll be all done."

"Why didn't someone tell me?"

"We didn't tell anyone who didn't need to know." He opened the door and motioned her through. "Let's go."

*   *   *

The Jones women stood together at the mustering. Bennie, Mary, and the wives of the four married sons all watched with pride puffing up their breasts and bringing broad smiles to their faces. There was no question that the Jones men were the finest of the lot.

Cadwallader strode up and down the raggedy rows of soldiers, his silver-gilt head high as he performed his last inspection as the elected captain of the troops. After today, Adam would take over as leader. It was time.

But that didn't mean Cad was any easier on the men on this occasion. Though they were clothed in a wide-ranging conglomeration of tans, rusty reds, browns, dark greens, and even an occasional purple, it didn't matter. They might not be garbed like soldiers, but they had the equipment.

Each man was required to present his flintlock musket for inspection. Cad made sure it was perfectly oiled and ready to fire; if not, he made sure the man was out of the line until it was. Each man also had to deliver two spare flints, a priming wire, and a brush. They knew Cad would never let them get away without having all the proper tools, so they all did.

At the same time Cad was marching up and down the rows, the selectmen were presenting the other officers with money for the military banquet.

Banquet, hah, Bennie thought. It was simply an excuse to seriously deplete the stores of the Dancing Eel.

Her father stopped dead between the rows, an oddly questioning look on his face. Something was wrong.

Bennie began to go to him but paused, seeing his brows draw together and his eyes darken with rage.

The relaxed men suddenly drew together, their hands tightening on their weapons. Cad looked at Adam, seeming to find satisfaction in his answering nod.

What was it? Bennie wondered in bewilderment.

Ba-dum-dum-dum. Ba-dum-dum-dum.

Drums. But all the towns expected were already here.

Ba-dum-dum-dum. Ba-dum-dum-dum.

Relentless, rhythmic, unstoppable. Almost eerily regular. The drums of soldiers marching to battle.

Ba-dum-dum-dum. Ba-dum-dum-dum.

Louder. Closer. A drumming that seemed to set the pace of her painfully pounding heart.

Ba-dum-dum-dum. Ba-dum-dum-dum.

They were coming.

5

There weren't as many of them as she'd first thought.

Bennie huddled a little closer to the other silent women. All around the square, small groups of women and children drew together, quiet and watchful, as their men were confronted by the redcoats.

When the lines of soldiers had first come into sight, they'd seemed endless. Long, evenly spaced columns, their marching flawlessly synchronized to the beat pounded out by the Negro drummers, resplendent in vivid yellow. Now, with the initial shock over, Bennie could see there were no more than thirty or so men, not much more than half the number of colonial militia.

It didn't seem to matter. These were soldiers. Their bayonets gleamed malevolently in the sun. Their cross-straps were so white they must have been freshly daubed with pipe clay. Their posture was straight, their grip on their weapons sure, their bearing arrogant.

The lone exception was Jon. His size alone would have made him conspicuous. A half step out of line, spoiling the sharp, perfect rows, he fumbled with his musket and nearly lost his hat before he jammed it back on his head. Earnest seriousness darkened his sculpted face as he sidled forward more closely into alignment with the soldiers flanking him.

Quickly Bennie turned her attention back to her father. He was nearly ready to explode. Even from this distance, she could see that his eyebrows were quivering, the way they always did just before his temper erupted onto one of her brothers.

Soon as they'd known what was coming, the colonists had rapidly moved to a better defensive position. Now there were four solid rows backed against one side of the common, protecting the women and children. Behind them were the tavern, the store, the printshop; places their families could quickly retreat to if it became necessary.

But what choices did the militiamen have, really? They couldn't shoot, not without provocation or threat. And they *wouldn't* turn tail and run—that was what the British wanted.

Cadwallader Jones stood proudly in front of his men. If the damn English wanted to push this issue, he would oblige. There'd be better days and places than this, but if this was what was to be, then he was ready.

Captain Livingston sauntered slowly, almost casually over to Cad. Planting his feet slightly apart, Livingston linked his hands behind his back.

"So, Jones, you couldn't see your way clear to make this simple, could you?"

"It could be very easy. You march your men back to

your fort, and we'll continue as if nothing had happened."

The captain shook his head regretfully. "Well, no, I don't think that would work. I've been ordered to stop you from conducting any military maneuvers, you see."

"And just how do you plan to stop us? You can't shoot us."

"No? It would be a bit messy, I will admit. All that blood and everything. Still and all, it's a rather expedient way of doing things, and my men haven't had much chance to practice on moving targets recently. Might do us some good."

Cad's hands tightened around the stock of his musket. "You can't shoot first."

"I suppose not. But then it's always a bit confusing in battle. All those shots, all that screaming. Who's to say who fired first? I'd imagine twenty different men would have twenty different stories. I don't suppose I'd have much trouble getting my superiors to believe me."

He flicked his hand slightly, his forefinger upraised. At the signal, his troops lifted their muskets in one move, each selecting a target in the front lines of the colonial forces. The Americans raised their own weapons, determination steeling each man. They were untrained, but they had their families at their backs. There was no better incentive.

This couldn't be happening. Bennie felt a trickle of sweat slide between her shoulder blades. How could she be sweating, when she was so cold? Around her, women rushed to get their children into the fragile shelter of the buildings, but Bennie was rooted in place, unable to make herself move.

This could *not* be happening.

Rising to her tiptoes, she took a look over the heads of the men, suddenly grateful for her height. She could see only the back of her father's head and shoulders, so she moved to the side of the main body of colonists, oblivious of the fact that she was leaving herself an open target.

Silence. How could so many people make so little noise? There was no creak of leather boots, no rustle of cloth, not even the whisper of the wind through the trees. Just overwhelming, terrible silence.

A loud, squealing wail shattered the quiet. A fat pink pig from last spring's litter, not quite grown, bolted between the two groups of men. Splotched black with mud from the hollow, it shouldered its way through the tiny space between the captain and Cad, leaving dark streaks on the captain's white breeches and gaiters. He stumbled back, only at the last instant managing to regain his balance and avoid falling ignominiously on his rump.

The pig continued to dash wildly through the crowds, squealing loudly, as if a butcher was after it. It wove between the alert soldiers, pushing them out of formation, causing several to drop loaded muskets, which they frantically scrambled to grab before the weapons could accidentally go off.

It was chaos. Half the men stared agape at the unexpected intruder. The other half dodged to get out of its way.

"Somebody get that stupid pig!" the captain shouted, staring sadly at the soiled mess of his best dress breeches.

"I'll get it, Cap'n!" Jon charged through the men, his massive shoulders causing nearly as much commotion as the pig. He stumbled after it, diving and missing, only to jump to his feet and tumble after it again. He trailed in its wake, his arms spread wide as if ready to embrace a lover, not even noticing the havoc he wreaked.

At least half a dozen men, both colonial and British, were upended as Jon shoved his way after the frantic animal; they rose grumbling, nursing bruised posteriors.

"Almost got him!" Indeed, he did seem to be gaining slowly. The desperate animal took off at a dead run for its favorite mudhole. Reaching the hollow, it took a reckless leap into the dubious safety of its brethren, burrowing itself deeply in the sticky mud.

"I . . . got it!" Jon took a massive, rash dive. He landed with a splat, spread-eagled face down in the muck, sinking in at least a handspan with the force of his landing. Black clumps of mud flew, splattering the already grubby pigs.

Both arms wrapped around the wriggling, struggling pig, Jon rolled over to face the astonished spectators. His hat was gone, his mud-bedaubed hair stuck out in wet clumps, and he was black from top to bottom; his pale eyes showed light in his grime-covered face, as did his broad, triumphant grin.

"I got it!"

The crowd on the common was quiet with stunned disbelief. Cad and Captain Livingston cautiously approached the edge of the wallow, staring down at the pigs scrambling around the lieutenant.

"Well, Leighton, you certainly did get it," Livingston said calmly.

Laughter swept the clearing, ripsnorting, sidesplitting laughter. Laughter that swelled through both groups of men, an irresistible wave of gaiety.

Cad held on to his sides, trying to suppress his monstrous snorts. He glanced over at the captain, who was red-faced and nearly doubled over with amusement.

If the enemy found it funny, well then he couldn't. It was that simple. Cad straightened abruptly, fixing his face into severe lines. As soon as Livingston saw Cad's serious expression, he sobered too. The captain and Cad glared at each other, trying to impose the force of their wills.

And then the pig squealed again. The captain's mouth twitched. Cad's eyebrows wiggled. Gales of irrepressible laughter bubbled up in them both. Cad whooped. Livingston wiped watery eyes.

"Gawd, Livingston . . . you laugh . . . like a sick horse," Cad managed between guffaws.

"Me?" The captain struggled to gulp enough air. "You . . . stop this right now, Jones. This . . . have to be . . . serious. This is . . . a . . . military maneuver."

"I'm . . . serious." Cad snorted again.

"Not a military maneuver, Cap'n," Jon piped in happily, still clutching the wiggling animal. "It's a party."

"A party." Captain Livingston quieted immediately and looked speculatively around the common, taking in the assorted stands selling sweets and treats, the peddlers and their varied stock of wares, the obviously ample supplies of spirits. "A . . . festival, perhaps." It could be so easy. "Jones, would you say you were having a festival?"

"Well . . ." Cad said doubtfully.

Livingston gave him a significant look. "My commanding officer gave me orders to prevent any military action on the part of the colonists. He never said you could not have a festival."

"Oh, a festival." Cad pursed his lips. It went against his grain to compromise with a redcoat, to do anything but insist on their freedom to drill. But a chance to avoid the issue? To avoid putting anyone in danger? "Yes, certainly. A festival."

Livingston gave a relived sigh. "Good."

"But you know, if we had been having a 'military action,' we would have trounced you soundly."

"You most certainly would not have."

"A shame we won't have a chance to find out."

The captain lifted his eyebrows. His only desire had been to get out of the situation without bloodshed. But if there was the opportunity to gather a bit of information along the way, he was not one to overlook it. "Perhaps we could."

"Huh?"

"We could have a bit of a competition. That is, unless of course, our last contest put you off wagers entirely."

"That was a fluke. How was I to know you had the biggest ox around in your company? It had nothing to with skill or strategy, as a real battle does." Cad stroked the barrel of his trusty musket. "What did you have in mind?"

"Shooting. Knives. It matters little. I'm certain my men can both shoot and throw straighter than yours. After all, we are professional soldiers, not merely a collection of farmers who get together a few times a year to play make believe."

Cad's eyes narrowed. "A contest it is, then."

"Agreed."

"Ah, Captain?" At the question, Cad and Livingston turned to Jon. He was awkwardly struggling to his feet, sunk knee-deep in muck, his right arm still wrapped around the chubby body of the pig. "Can I let him go now?"

* * *

Waiting in line for his turn to shoot, Jon discreetly shook his rump, trying to dislodge the clammy leggings sticking to his private parts. After his disaster in the pig wallow, Sergeant Hitchcock, kind soul that he was, had taken pity on him and dumped two buckets of water over his head. It had washed away the worst of the mud, but it had left his clothes wet, clingy, and distinctly uncomfortable.

What a mess. He should be satisfied. Poking the pig and setting it on its wild run through the troops had been a last ditch effort to avert—or at least postpone—disaster. It had worked even better than he'd imagined, but it had made him, once again, look like a fool.

Why did it even matter? He'd always rather enjoyed his part, an actor whose stage was the world, and for whom a bad review could mean death. It had been a challenge, being continually on guard, fooling everyone, creating the illusion that allowed him to do his job.

An illusion. His gaze was drawn to Beth, standing quietly to one side of the meadow, watching as man after man shattered the bottles placed on the stone wall. She was serene, placid, a calm, still pool with nary a ripple showing on the surface. Why was he so sure it was an illusion?

It had been all he could manage to stay away from her all week, and he congratulated himself on his success. Well, near success. Once, unable to resist any longer, he'd followed her to her family's stable, staying out of sight, and listened to her play. Just listened.

He'd leaned outside the door, pushing it open a crack

so he could hear better, and closed his eyes. Her music had been different that day; muted, haunting, echoing . . . lonely. Almost desperate.

It called to his soul, a soul that had been buried so deep he wasn't even sure he still had one. But somehow she found it, dredged up the tattered remnants of it, and made him feel.

He hadn't seen her play then. He hadn't needed to.

Crack.

The sharp report of another musket brought him back to the matter at hand.

It was nearly Jon's turn to shoot. Another one of the Jones boys—what was this one's name?—was firing now. One of the middle brothers, Jon thought, but it didn't seem to make much difference; they all could shoot. They fired rapidly, with swaggering confidence and surprising accuracy—except for Brendan, who shot deliberately, almost contemplatively, but with even greater precision. He was quite possibly the best shot Jon had ever seen.

Another shot, and another bottle shattered. If there was any glassware left in the village after this afternoon it would be a miracle.

"These colonists are right fine shots." Sergeant Hitchcock stood near Jon, watching the competition with his captain. "Better'n I would've thought."

"Mmm." Captain Livingston rocked back on his heels and pursed his lips. He was growing weary of watching his soldiers getting outdone. They were supposed to be professionals, for God's sake. Why couldn't they shoot better than a bunch of bumpkin farmers? "It seems that we definitely need to step up our target practice."

"Hungry."

"Hmm?" The captain peered at Jon. "No, no, Jon, we'll get you something to eat later. When this is over."

"Not that." Jon jerked his thumb toward the colonial troops. "They shoot for food. Squirrels, rabbits." He waved his hands through the air, mimicking a tiny animal scurrying to escape its hunter. "Little animals. Fast. To feed their children. So, good shots."

"Ah." Livingston hadn't thought of that: the Americans had to be good shots, it meant food on their tables. After chasing small game, bottles were easy targets.

For his own men, shooting had simply become part of the job. It was up to him to impress upon his troops the fact that their lives would depend on their skill with their muskets. That should take care of the matter.

"Well." Hitchcock sucked his teeth. "I hope I don't end up 'cross a battlefield from 'em anytime soon."

Livingston sniffed. "I wouldn't be concerned about it, Sergeant. They have no discipline, no training. They elect their officers, for God's sake. How can an elected officer make the difficult, necessary decisions? He'll be too busy protecting his friends and family."

"Think it's goin' t'come to that, Cap'n?"

"Bah! They are like children, these colonists. They cannot hear the wisdom of their mother country. They can only hear the siren call of rebellion."

"Next!" a man bellowed. The bottles were being reset.

"Me!" Jon checked the loading and shouldered his musket.

Captain Livingston winced and took two rapid steps away. "Ah, Jon, could you try not to wing anybody this time? I wouldn't want you to accidentally start a war by killing someone."

"Not t'worry." Sergeant Hitchcock whacked Jon companionably on the back. "We been practicin', ain't we, Jon? He'll do just fine."

Jon bobbed his head. "No problem, sir."

The three bottles he was to shoot were carefully arrayed on a low stone fence at the far side of the pasture. They were perhaps seventy-five yards away, nearing the edge of a musket's accurate range. Off to his right was a stone barn; to his left, wrapping around the back of the fence, a tangled mass of thick forest.

Jon turned around, noting everyone's location. He didn't care to shoot anyone accidentally either. There were two clumps of people: the small, orderly, red-coated group that was his compatriots and the larger, disorganized, cheerful collection of colonists, women and children mingled among the militia.

Beth was still there, of course, in her green dress that looked like a piece of the forest. He'd nearly swallowed his tongue when he'd first seen her in it, looking so pretty he couldn't believe every unmarried man in the square wasn't clustered around her. When she noticed him looking at her, she smiled, like sunshine and light, all warmth and encouragement and pride. A smile like that could make a man want to beat the world.

Instead, she was going to see him look like an idiot. Again. Like he'd looked in that cold, stinking pig wallow. He wondered if she'd laughed at him, with everybody else. Somehow he was sure she hadn't.

If he was still Jonathan Schuyler Leighton, he could try to impress her. He could talk in words of more than one syllable, and he could walk without tripping over his gaiters. But he was Lieutenant Jon now, and he had to be a fool. He gritted his teeth and his jaw ached with the effort to keep that stupid grin on his face. He turned away abruptly, unable to watch her anymore.

"Sergeant? What do I do?"

"You jes' try t'shoot the bottles. Jes' like we practiced, Jon," Hitchcock said encouragingly. "Start with the left one."

Jon forced his face into an expression of blank bewilderment.

"Ah, the brown one, son. Over there."

"Yes." He lifted his musket and aimed at the brown bottle, perched temptingly on the fence across the meadow. And suddenly he was angry. Angry that he so seldom had a chance to test his skills at anything besides acting like an idiot. Angry that he couldn't go to a woman and smile at her without worrying if it would give him away. Angry that he couldn't allow himself to blow that damn bottle to smithereens.

He fired. The right bottle shattered.

"Lieutenant!" The sergeant whacked him on the back in exultation. "You did it! But, ah, I told you t'aim for the left one."

Jon tapped another ball into his musket. "I did."

"Oh." Hitchcock swallowed, his prominent Adam's apple bobbing. "Still, that weren't bad, son. Right height and all. Now all you gotta do is aim about six feet more to the left."

Jon lifted his weapon slowly, trying to appear as if he was taking careful aim, and frowned. At the last minute, he jerked, dropping his right shoulder. The dark iron rooster weather vane fixed to the top of the barn spun crazily, like a child's top gone amok.

"Cor!" the soldier behind him said in amazement. "Who coulda hit that if'n they tried?"

The devil was in him now. He was taking a terrible risk, leaving himself open to suspicion if anyone was alert enough to put it all together. Still, he didn't seem to be able to stop.

He reloaded and leveled his gun at the fence one more time.

The pine tree was a good fifteen paces beyond the fence. He fired. The top spike snapped off cleanly and tumbled merrily to earth.

And Jon hoped to God no one ever realized how good a shot he really was.

6

"*Thank ye, lieutenant.*" Pocketing his coins, the peddler flashed a gap-toothed smile.

And well he should smile, Jon thought. He's gotten at least double the going price. But Lieutenant Jon was a gullible fool, not a hard-nosed bargainer.

A fool. He *was* being a fool. Jon ran his fingers slowly over the strand of Job's tears. The seeds were hard, translucently white, and waxy, an inexpensive substitute for those who couldn't afford pearls.

Why had he bought them? It was frippery, a worthless frill. Foolishness. And he still wished they were pearls.

He shoved the necklace into the leather pouch attached to his belt, grimacing at the cold dampness. His clothes had, for the most part, dried out by now, but the leather remained moist. His shoes squished when he walked.

A gun boomed, the sound only partly muted by the distance. The common was nearly deserted; everyone was still out at the meadow, watching the shooting competition. Jon took advantage of the quiet to walk slowly through the town. Much as he needed to rejoin his company, he was strangely reluctant.

Was she still there? He'd looked at her after his final shot. She'd still been smiling at him, but not with encouragement and joy. With pity.

Pity, damn it! *See?* her eyes seemed to say. *That wasn't too bad. You almost did it. Next time you'll be closer.* It was probably the same way she looked at her favorite puppy when it pissed on her shoes. *That's all right, darling. Next time you'll get it right.*

He clenched his fists, his nails biting painfully into his palms. Somehow he had to rid himself of this compulsion about Beth. He was supposed to be gathering information. Plotting strategy. Looking for traitors. Not mooning around like a lovestruck adolescent in the grip of his first passion.

Jon slowed his steps by the hollow near the schoolhouse. The pigs were still wallowing away, grunting happily, munching on a pile of corn someone had given them, apparently to keep them out of the way for the day. They squealed merrily and twitched their mud-caked, spiral tails.

"Well, at least someone's having a good time," Jon mumbled under his breath, continuing on around the school. He paused when the sound of voices drifted to him; childish voices, taunting, calling, jeering. And one young voice desperately pleading. He slipped quietly around the corner, knowing it was none of his business but unable to help himself, remembering too well what it was like to be the one against many.

A slender young girl was surrounded by half a dozen

jumping and capering small boys. She was tall, gawky, with a mop of brilliantly red hair completely unrestrained by the two blue ribbons tied in it. Her nose was nearly the color of her hair, and Jon could tell she was on the verge of tears as she twisted and turned, trying to snatch something away from the nearest boy.

"Give her back!"

"You want her?" the boy, his own hair so blond it was almost white, jeered. "Then use those long sticks of arms and get her." He tossed a gray ball to the other side of the circle.

The girl nearly stumbled over her feet as she whirled and ran toward the boy who'd caught the ball.

"I hear cats always land on their feet." The second boy tossed the tiny puff of fur into the air again. "How high do ya think we can throw her before she don't make it?"

"Please, just give her back," the little girl pleaded, her voice choked.

"Yeah?" The boy held the kitten in one hand high above his head. "How you gonna make me, carrot?"

"Yeah," added the boy next to him. "She's a carrot. Long and skinny and *orange* . . ."

"I'm not orange! I just want Pickles. If you don't give her to me, I'll—"

"Hello."

The boys jumped abruptly, turning guilty faces toward the newcomer. They visibly relaxed when they saw it was Jon.

The towheaded boy, apparently the self-appointed leader of the gang, puffed out his small chest and stepped forward. "I know you."

"You do?" Jon said mildly.

"Yeah. You're that stupid lobsterback. The one who shot the tree."

"I'm Jon. What are you doing?"

"Aw, nothin'." He shuffled his feet. "Jes' playin'."

"Oh." Jon grinned. "That's good. Thought maybe you'd hurt the kitten."

"Naw," he said, an innocent look on his face. "We was just teasin'."

"Good." Jon crossed his arms over his chest, towering over the boys, who came barely to his hip. "Because, y'know, little kittens and girls and other things that are small and alone sometimes got big fathers and uncles and friends."

"Jimmy," whispered another little boy, poking the leader in his side. "What if'n her father finds out?"

"Her father, nothin'," said a third. "What about *Bennie*? . . ."

"Don't worry about it." Jimmy gave the little girl a hard glare. "She ain't gonna tell nobody. Are ya, Sarah?"

Sarah sniffled and wiped her sleeve across her eyes. "I want Pickles."

Jimmy frowned and dumped the tiny gray puff of fur into Sarah's waiting hands.

"Don't you boys think you'd better go back and find your parents?" Jon suggested.

"Huh," Jimmy said belligerently. "We ain't gotta do somethin' jes cause you say, you lousy redcoat! We—"

When Jon's hand clamped down on Jimmy's shoulder, he gulped. The man might be a stupid lobsterback, but he was a big stupid lobsterback. "We're goin'."

Once the boys had scrambled around the corner, Jon

knelt by Sarah, who was clutching her kitten to her chest. "Are you all right?"

She sniffed. "I think so."

"And Pickles?"

"I don't know." She cuddled the mewling kitten, not seeming to notice the sharp little claws digging into her skin, and looked up at him. "Please, mister, don't tell anyone."

"Why not?" he asked, wondering at the strange request.

"Oh, please," she begged, her eyes beginning to shimmer again. "You can't!"

Out of the corner of his eye, Jon caught a twitch of green coming around the corner of the school behind Sarah. Beth flew into his line of vision, her skirts clutched in both hands, her face set with grim determination. Anger and fierce protectiveness flashed in her eyes, and Jon could tell she was ready to lay into any little boy she got her hands on. This was not the quiet, controlled woman he'd seen in the tavern; here was the deep fire he'd sensed in her music.

Jon threw up his hand, motioning her to stop. When she did, he lifted a finger to his lips and jerked his head toward the wall. Beth frowned but stayed put, standing near the spot he'd indicated. She held her body tensely, as if ready to jump in at the first sign of trouble.

Jon returned his attention to Sarah, who stood holding her kitten to her cheek, her small shoulders still shaking.

"Can I see your cat?"

Sarah slowly lifted her face, her blue eyes swimming with tears. "Are you gonna hurt her, too?"

"No." Jon reached out a finger and tested the delicate,

smoke-colored tufts of fur on the kitten's back. "Did the boys hurt her?"

"I think so. They threw her up in the air an' let her fall, an' now she's cryin'."

"Let me see." He held out his hand, palm up.

Sarah studied his hand. He waited patiently, not moving. Finally, she gave a tentative smile and carefully deposited the kitten in his hand.

The kitten, so small it must barely be old enough to be away from her mother, gave one last yelp and quit mewling. She investigated her new perch, delicately tapping the pad of Jon's palm with her paw, her nose twitching, her tail swishing back and forth.

The kitten nuzzled Jon's skin, and Pickles's tiny pink tongue came out to daintily test the unfamiliar substance.

"She tickles."

Sarah gave a watery giggle. "She does, doesn't she?"

The kitten evidently decided Jon wasn't edible. Lifting her head, Pickles curled around and around on Jon's hand before settling down into a tight ball of fluff. She was the dark, smooth gray of a warm, cloudy autumn sky, and she looked ridiculously tiny in Jon's big palm. Jon felt a faint, gentle vibration as the kitten began to purr.

"She likes you," Sarah said.

"Do you think so?" With the forefinger of his other hand, Jon lightly stroked the kitten's back. "How about you, Sarah? Are you feeling better?"

"Some." She wiped her forearm across her nose and sniffled again.

"What's the matter? Are you hurt?"

"No." Her shoulders drooped. "But I cried."

"People cry when they're sad, Sarah."

Sarah scrunched up her freckled nose. "Do you?"

Jon's throat tightened as he fought the memory of when he'd been not much older than Sarah and it seemed as if he'd done nothing but cry. "Sometimes. Everybody cries sometimes."

"Not Bennie," Sarah asserted.

"Bennie?" Jon lifted his gaze to Beth. Leaning comfortably against the schoolhouse, she looked relaxed, her calm restored. At his questioning look, she shrugged. "Never?"

"Never," Sarah said with conviction.

"That why you didn't want anyone to know?"

"Yeah."

"I won't tell," he assured her. "Here." Jon deposited the kitten into Sara's hands. "Maybe you should find your mother now."

"Thank you, Mr. . . ."

"Jon."

"Mr. Jon." Sarah whirled and skipped awkwardly away, smiling brightly when she caught sight of Bennie. "Oh, hi, Auntie Bennie. This is my new friend. His name is Jon."

"Yes, I know, Sarah. He's a friend of mine too."

"Is he? I don't know why Grandpa always says the redcoats are bad men. Jon's nice. He's pretty, too, don't you think, Aunt Bennie?"

"Ah . . ." Bennie felt her cheeks heat. "Why, yes, he's pretty."

"I'm going back to the mustering. Are you coming?"

"Soon."

Bennie watched her niece run toward the meadow,

her kitten tucked in her arms. Although her brothers were proving every bit as good at producing boys as their father was, Adam had managed to have one girl in the midst of siring miniature versions of himself.

Sarah was Bennie's only niece, and she reminded Bennie so much of herself. Taller than the other children her age, with big hands and feet that Bennie was terribly afraid she would grow into, Sarah had the added disadvantage of having inherited her mother's blazing hair. Bennie knew too well what the next few years were going to be like for her niece and silently vowed to make them as easy for Sarah as she could.

"Hello, Beth." Jon's deep voice rumbled behind her. Bennie smoothed her hands over the wild mess of her hair, finding her quick run from the meadow had left it hopelessly tangled. She closed her eyes briefly—had he heard her call him pretty?—and turned.

She shouldn't have worried. He was grinning at her as always, openness shining from every beautiful plane of his face. "Ta-da!" he said triumphantly. "You came to rescue her?"

"Well, yes."

"How did you know?"

"To come?" He bobbed his head in response to her question. "Oh, Adam came to get me. He saw the boys bothering his sister and ran and found me."

"Why you?"

"Me? I'm a little protective, I guess. About my family. The boys have sort of gotten in the habit of coming to me, because, well, their fathers sort of expect them to handle things themselves."

He'd been walking toward her, all the time she was

talking, and now he was close to her; oh, so close to her. His chest filled her vision, and all she would have to do was reach out to touch him.

He braced an arm against the wall beside her head, nearly caging her in. He loomed over her, and if he had been anyone else, she might have been frightened.

But this was Jon, and she wasn't frightened, even if her heart was pounding just as if she were. She wondered at this compulsion to touch him; the memory of her arms around him by the creek was so clear and vivid she could still feel it.

It wasn't only that he was beautiful. It was his purity of spirit that drew her; Jon would never judge and find wanting. He would only like, and enjoy, and accept.

She lifted her face to his. She could see the rough, dark stubble on the elegant, defined planes of his chin, and the lush, straight fringe of mink-brown lashes. His eyes were pale, pale blue, like thick ice in the deepest part of winter, when spring is only a dream.

He brushed his knuckle under her eye, as if wiping away a tear, a touch so slow and gentle it felt as soft as that tear would, tracing down her skin. She tilted her head, seeking more of his touch.

"Beth." He moved his hand to her other cheek, slipping his finger along the lashes rimming her lower lid, but never in danger of coming too close to her eye. "You never cry?"

"Oh." There were tiny nicks marring the perfection of his chin. He'd hurt himself shaving, and she gave in to the impulse to smooth her fingers soothingly over the cuts. "I . . . not for a long time. My brothers used to have great fun seeing if they could make me wail. After a while, I learned not to show what I was feeling."

His skin was rough with the day's growth of beard; prickly, ticklish, masculine. The touch of her fingers became the touch of her palm; she cupped his cheek in her hand.

"Sometimes," he said, his voice rough and mesmerizing, "sometimes, it's good to let the feelings out."

There was a flash in his eyes, a bolt of spring sky in the winter ice. He dropped his hand abruptly and stepped back, a sudden, jarring motion.

"Are they done shooting?"

"What?" Bennie shook her head in confusion at the precipitate change of topic. "Oh, yes, I believe so."

"What's next?"

"Ah, knife throwing, I think."

"Good. I must go now. Coming?"

He turned and strode away, his long legs eating up the distance in great chunks. Bennie hurried along beside him, wondering when her gentle friend had become so enamored of sharp weapons.

Jon leaned against an old denuded oak tree, staring down at the blood flowing freely between his thumb and forefinger. Damn. He'd meant only to give himself a bit of a nick. Seems he'd gotten a bit overenthusiastic.

Back beside the school, he'd had to get away from Beth before he did something stupid. So he'd rushed off to the knife throwing competition, Beth trailing along in his wake. When they'd reached the meadow he'd immediately plunged into a group of soldiers, leaving Beth to join her family.

But then he'd seen some skinny little dark-haired fellow smile at her. And when that fellow had had his turn, he'd thrown his knife dead center into the middle of the target.

On Jon's own turn, he'd taken the sharp blade between his fingers and drawn back his arm, ready to hurl the weapon straight into the bull's-eye. That's when he'd known he was in real trouble.

He was coming damn close to letting everything he'd worked for the past six years get away, not to mention putting his own life in danger in the process. He'd let the knife slip, and it had bitten deeply into his skin.

Jon ripped a ragged piece of linen off the bottom of his shirt. Wadding it up, he pressed it against the wound, trying to staunch the flow of blood.

He'd run off into the woods after his "accident," not staying to hear the jeers of the spectators, not daring to glance at Beth. He couldn't.

He was going to have to do something about her. He couldn't stay away from her completely. It certainly hadn't worked the last time he'd tried it. His job was going to require running across her now and again, and the drought had made him crazier when he finally did see her.

Or he could spend as much time with her as possible, hoping proximity would blunt her allure. Maybe she wasn't as wonderful as he kept imagining. Not as strong, or sweet, or soft . . .

Soft. The skin beneath her eye had been tender, incredibly smooth, and he'd seen her shiver when he'd touched her.

Wonderful. He jammed the rag viciously against his hand, hoping the pain would bring him to his senses.

"You're going to make it worse."

She was there, slipping between the trees and taking his hand in hers, her warm brown eyes soft and concerned. She peeled away the cloth, wincing when she saw the gash in his skin.

"Does it hurt?"

Wordlessly, he nodded. It seemed he hadn't made a big enough fool of himself to get her to stay away from him yet. He should have known his helplessness would appeal to her protective instincts.

Suddenly he was terribly sure it would never be enough. Keeping away from her wasn't going to work. But trying to spend enough time with her so that the infatuation would wear off wasn't going to work either. Nothing was going to work, and he didn't know what he was going to do about it.

Her brow puckered in concern, she dabbed carefully at his wound. "This is going to need tending. Will you come back to the Dancing Eel with me?"

Bloody hell. He'd go anywhere she asked.

"Yes."

Bending low over Jon's hand, Bennie wound a strip of cloth around it one more time. Tying the rag securely, she tugged carefully, testing the knot.

"There. That should do it. Can you use it?"

She settled back onto the bench next to Jon. The tavern was empty; everyone was still out at the mustering. She was unused to the room like this, vacant and quiet; it seemed friendly, cozy, wrapping them in a quiet cocoon of warmth and welcome.

The tankard of ale she'd fetched Jon sat, still untasted, at his elbow. His clothes were rumpled and dirty, and there were dark brown splotches of blood on his breeches. His hair had come completely out of its club, hanging in a smooth, brown sweep to his shoulders.

He watched his hand as he flexed it slowly, opening and closing his fingers as if he wasn't quite sure they would follow his will. His head was down; he hadn't looked at her since she'd found him in the woods.

"Does it still hurt?"

"No."

His shoulders drooped, seeming as if all his energy had been washed out with his blood.

"What's the matter, then?"

"Clumsy."

"You're not clumsy."

"Yes!" he burst out. "Stupid Jon. Clumsy Jon. Always wrong. Always dumb. Always *clumsy*."

"No." She lifted his injured hand, palm up, cradling it in her own. "See this, Jon?"

He gave a small snort. "My hand."

"Yes, your hand." She brushed her fingers over the swells of his palm, tracing the small hills and valleys. "It's such a big hand. I saw you hold that kitten. You could have crushed it so easily. All you would have had to do is close your hand and squeeze."

His hand was hard, rough and callused from work. The flesh was unyielding, the texture fascinating to her fingertips.

"And what did the kitten do, Jon?"

"Purred." Bennie thought Jon's voice sounded oddly strained.

"Yes. She purred. Because she knew you wouldn't hurt her. Because she knew you were a gentle man."

Bennie twisted her wrist so her palm pressed against his, matching her fingers with his.

"You are such a big man, Jon. Big and strong. But you never hurt anyone, do you? You never hate anyone, and tell them that they're not pretty enough or smart enough or strong enough."

She pushed her hand closer yet, feeling his warmth seep through her skin.

"Never be sorry for what you are, Jon. Never be sorry you're not good with weapons."

"But I'm a soldier!" He looked so dejected, his eyes half closed, his head hanging. He needed someone to comfort him, someone to show him his value didn't depend on his ability to bury a knife in another human being.

She gave in to the impulse before she knew she had it. Sliding over on the bench, she wrapped her arms around him and laid his head on her shoulder.

"Shh," she said soothingly, her hands smoothing the scratchy fabric over his back. "Everything's going to be all right."

Oh, God. What had he done now? He had decided the safest recourse was to retreat as deeply as possible into his role. He would play the childlike fool so well she would find nothing in him to interest her, and she would never notice him again.

Instead, she was comforting him like a child. And he was reacting like a man.

His face was buried against the curve of her neck. Her skin was like warm, fine satin; he could feel her pulse beat against his cheek. Soft tendrils of her hair fell across his face, tickling his ear, tempting his touch.

She smelled like lavender. Faint, delicate, surprising. Completely feminine. He inhaled deeply, his blood quickening with the scent of this woman.

Her skin was in reach of his tongue. All he would have to do was open his mouth and he could taste her neck. All he would have to do was slide a bit over and down, and his face would be buried in her . . .

He would be taking shameless advantage.

"Beth," he murmured by way of apology. He slid over and down.

Her breasts were lush, a man's dream of tempting flesh. Even covered by the soft green wool, he could clearly imagine their texture, their smell.

"Lavender," he mumbled against her chest.

"What did you say, Jon? I couldn't hear you."

Her breasts trembled against him when she spoke. It took tremendous force of willpower to lift his head, finding his face only inches away from hers.

"I said . . ." He swallowed heavily. "Lavender. You smell like lavender."

"Oh." Her skin was flushed, a delicate pink blooming across the fine gold of her cheeks. "I use it in the coals, to clean my teeth."

Her teeth. His gaze dropped to her mouth, her glistening, tantalizing mouth. Then her breath would smell like lavender too. Would she taste sweet? He moved fractionally closer, until he could feel the warmth of her breath curl over his skin.

Closing his eyes, he tilted his head slightly. Their lips

were so close. Less than contact, but more than apart.
Temptation, anticipation.

What would it hurt? he asked himself. It would only
be a kiss.

Just a kiss.

7

In the end, he couldn't do it. Couldn't do the thing he knew was wrong. Couldn't move that tiny space that would bring his mouth to hers.

But he didn't have to. Because Beth did.

It was so easy. At first when she'd held him, she'd honestly thought of nothing but giving comfort, of soothing a bit of his pain. Then his scent had drifted to her nose and gone to her head. His warmth had seeped through her clothes and gone to her belly. His head had hovered over hers and his breath had tickled her lips and all thoughts of comfort had vanished.

She'd wanted to know what it would be like if he would close that small, significant gap and kiss her. Once, just once, she wanted to feel like every other girl whose sweetheart stole a kiss behind the stables. She wanted to know what it was like to be touched by a man whose mere presence made her heart do flips.

So she'd tilted her head that crucial little bit that brought their lips together.

His mouth was tender—there was no other word for it. It fit hers as well as her bow fit her hand. He was still, the contact between them the barest brush of skin.

Was there more? She had to know. Experimentally, she pressed her lips slightly harder against his.

She heard his breath catch, and then he began to rock his mouth against hers. The pressure changed, shifted, and changed again in a way that was wholly captivating.

If she had expected tentativeness, what she got was sureness. If she had expected warmth, what she got was heat. If she had expected friendship, what she got was something so much more.

What she got was magic. She felt him trace the seam of her mouth with his tongue, lingering at one corner as if he'd found a hidden cache of honey. It made her feel cherished, as if even that one tiny spot held the power to fascinate him. He seemed in no hurry to move on, content to savor.

She opened her mouth in wonder. His tongue slipped in, skimming the edges of her teeth, gliding over flesh she'd had no idea could be so sensitive.

This was a seduction she'd never known existed. And she wanted more.

She slid closer to him on the bench, close enough to press against his chest, and lifted her hands to his shoulders. He groaned, a rumble that reverberated through her mouth. He held himself away from her, his shoulders thrown back, as if he were trying to escape the contact. But that couldn't be, because his mouth clung to hers, his tongue exploring hidden recesses and seeking out secret places that made her shiver.

He tasted like the Eel's best whiskey, the stuff her da saved only for the most important customers. His flavor was dark, rich, smoky, and complex, hinting at subtleties that intrigued but couldn't be defined.

Enticed by the things he was doing to her, she wanted to try it herself. She tentatively rubbed her tongue against his. Would he like it as much as she did?

A tremor ran through him in response. She tried it again.

He groaned. The pressure of his mouth increased, but it wasn't demanding, it was tempting. He lured her in, stealing the strength from her body and the thoughts from her mind. His tongue played with hers; advance, retreat, advance, retreat. A stroke was madness. A glide, delight. Slide . . . rapture.

She felt his chest heave, as if he'd run miles. She moved her hands down his arms, feeling the hard, massive bulge of his biceps under the wool of his coat. Testing, she flexed her fingers; she couldn't even make a dent.

"Jon," she whispered. "Jon."

He jumped to his feet so abruptly she nearly tumbled forward. Bracing her arm against the now empty space on the bench, she opened her eyes, blinking away the haze of pleasure. Beneath her hand, she could still feel the warmed wood where his body had been. She wanted the warmth back.

"Jon?"

His body was rigid, and he paced away from her. His tension was undeniable; his fists were clenched, his eyes narrowed, his nostrils flared, his breathing ragged.

"Beth." His voice sounded strained. He stretched one

hand toward her, but the motion stopped halfway. He just stood there, his arm hanging in midair as if he didn't quite know what to do with it. "I'm . . . I'm sorry, Beth."

And he tore out of the tavern, slamming the door behind him.

Bennie stared at the door, not quite believing he was actually gone.

Dear Lord, what had she done?

Her hand shook as she raised it to her mouth. She'd kissed him. Kissed him, and he'd run away from her as if she were the entire Continental army and he was the only British soldier for miles.

She'd assumed that, because of his looks, women had probably been grabbing him and kissing him most of his life. But she was supposed to be his friend. She was supposed to understand that he probably didn't have the slightest clue what went on between a man and a woman—not that she did.

She was supposed to want nothing more than friendship from him. Instead, she'd acted like any other woman blinded by a pretty face and a whole lot of muscles. And she'd wanted . . . a lot.

She'd scared him. Bennie didn't doubt it for a minute. She was actually pretty good at scaring men; it was sometimes a rather useful skill, but she'd never meant to frighten Jon.

Long ago she'd come to terms with the way her life was going to be. There would be music, and there would be family. There wouldn't be sweethearts and kisses and babies. She'd known it for a long time.

She'd forgotten it just this once, and because of it,

she was going to lose a friend she wanted very much to keep.

Propping her elbow on the table next to the tankard of ale Jon hadn't even touched, Bennie dropped her forehead into her palm.

Dear God, what had he done?

He had done the worst possible thing he could do. Clomping along with the rest of the soldiers, Jon rolled his shoulders. His muscles ached vaguely from the amount of force he'd had to exert to keep his arms from going around Beth when she'd kissed him.

At least he'd managed that much. Unfortunately, his will hadn't been strong enough for him to keep his lips to himself as well.

What must she be thinking? More important, what the hell was he going to do now?

He could stay out of New Wexford as much as possible, but that wasn't going to get the job done. Today could have so easily degenerated into violence. Time was running out; both sides seemed set on confrontation, and the opportunities to change that were going to be severely limited.

The best thing he could do for his mission was to use her. If she liked him, well, there was no telling what information he could get out of her. Her family must know nearly everything that went on in the area.

It was a perfectly logical thing to do, but his conscience—what there was left of it—balked hard at that idea. Beth didn't deserve to be treated that way, and he wasn't entirely sure he could force himself to do it, no matter what the provocation.

Clearly, he'd been playing the idiot too long. He was becoming one himself.

Jon closed his mind to anything but the soothing, simple rhythm of the march.

Bennie was careful to stay in the shadows. The doorway led into the dark storeroom at the back of the Dancing Eel, and here she could watch and listen, safely out of her father's sight.

He knew, of course. He always did. But as long as he wasn't actually reminded of her presence, it seemed he could pretend she wasn't there. Bennie knew if she was out in the main room, where he was confronted by her, he'd probably order her out of the tavern.

A Sons of Liberty meeting was no place for a lady.

Bennie had known about the meetings for at least five years. After all, she was related to nearly a third of the men in the room. They were a loosely organized group in a small village that had never attracted much attention from the British, and they'd had little to do for the past few years but gather, drink, complain about the Crown, and read the information spread through the colonies by various committees of correspondence.

Bennie'd begun trying to talk her father into allowing her to attend the meetings as soon as she'd found out about them. She was as much a patriot as any of her brothers and was intrigued by the stories of protests and confrontations in Boston, New York, and Philadelphia.

Cad had been more than willing to let her come; all his other children were there. But Mary had told him in no uncertain terms that no daughter of hers was to be a member of a mob of big-talking patriots, and Cad was to send Elizabeth home whenever he found her there.

So Cad and Bennie had tacitly agreed that as long as he didn't see her, she could stay.

The crowd in the Dancing Eel this December night was unusually subdued. It was the regular monthly meeting, a full week after the mustering, and just that afternoon the first snow of the winter had begun to fall, cloaking the tavern in soft, frigid white. Inside, smoke floated around the quiet men. The glow of lanterns and candles was hazy, diffused, leaving much of the room in shadow.

"Now, that was a close one at the mustering, men. We were lucky to get the inspection finished before the redcoats showed up," Cad was saying, his silver hair shining pale in the dimness.

"What if they had come earlier?" a man from the front of the room yelled. "We could've taken 'em."

"Yeah, but at what cost?" Adam picked up the huge pewter tankard in front of him. "My children were there, Martin. So were yours."

"I think we all agree confrontation is inevitable," Cad said. "But there's no reason we can't pick the time and place to our advantage." He frowned. "I can't understand why the change of time didn't throw them off. It was enough of a coincidence that they showed up here last month a mere half-hour before we were due to meet, but to come early to the mustering—"

"It's perfectly obvious." Brendan leaned casually against a wall, almost invisible in the shadows. "Someone told them when to come."

"No!" Every man in the room mumbled the denial, then looked around at their friends, relatives, and neighbors. Surely no one here would betray them.

Brendan shrugged. "How else would they know our schedules so precisely? They're getting information from somewhere—very good information—and they're getting it fast. We'd only changed the time of the mustering two days before."

"Brendan," Cadwallader said, the warning clear in his voice. "I know every man in this room. As do you. No one here would ever turn against us."

"Perhaps not intentionally." Rufus adjusted his bridge spectacles. "But how many of us might have mentioned something in passing? To our wives, or our sweethearts? A peddler, or the barmaid at an inn we stopped at to pass an evening? There are any number of ways it could have gotten out."

Men shifted uneasily.

"Well, I don't know that it matters so much how they found out this time. No harm was done. What matters is that it never happen again." Cadwallader's gaze swept the room, carefully marking each man. "Now that there are British stationed in the area, it may be that the time for action has come. If any information reaches the British now, it could be dangerous—and we'll know it came from someone close."

"But what can we do?" one of the farmers asked.

"Maybe nothing. Maybe a lot." Cad stroked his

thumb down the side of his jaw. "You all know that the Sons in Boston have made it uncomfortable for the British for a long time. There's no reason we can't do the same."

"Father, what's the point? So they've managed to harass a few soldiers; so they've been able to get rid of a few minor taxes. The British are still here."

"The point, Brendan, is that this is our home. Our place. If they intend to govern us, to occupy us, without our permission, we don't have to make it easy for them."

"Yea! Let's go get rid of 'em!" Henry, Bennie's seventh brother, was only seventeen. He thrilled to the exploits of the Boston revolutionaries and was still unhappy he'd missed the excitement of the Tea Party and the Port Bill Riots, and he was completely convinced he could single-handedly drive a regiment of British soldiers out of the colonies. Bennie worried about George, Henry, and Isaac most of all; they had the energy and hotheadedness of young men, the size of all Joneses, and more patriotic fervor than they knew what do with. They didn't have wives and children to worry about, a worry that effectively kept most of her other brothers' tempers to a slow simmer, rather than a full, roiling boil.

"It's not time yet, Henry." Cadwallader smiled. "Let's wait and see for a little while. You'll get your chance."

The meeting broke up. Some men left to go home to their families; many stayed for an ale or two before heading out into the cold.

The heat and smoke in the tavern began to feel uncomfortably close. Needing some fresh air, Bennie pulled her cloak around her and slipped out the back door.

She leaned against the side of the tavern. Cold from the stone wall seeped through the fabric of her wrap. Bennie turned her face up to the sky. There was no moon, no stars, no clouds that she could see, just dense, impenetrable blackness. It seemed as if the snowflakes just appeared from the dark, floating lazily to earth.

She craved the quiet, the peace, the freedom. Peace was a quality that was rapidly slipping away from her life, and there seemed to be little she could do to restore it.

Her village was no longer peaceful. The proximity of the British left everyone tense and short-tempered, waiting for the explosion.

Her family, too, felt strained. The conflict between her father and Brendan, once sad but bearable, was becoming acutely painful. Her younger brothers were restless, eager to make their place in the world.

Then there was Bennie herself.

Snowflakes fell on her skin, tiny, brief dots of sensation where they melted. They clung to her lashes, blurring her vision and she ran her tongue over her lips to capture the few that fell there.

She'd thought she was content without passion, ready to settle for a life of quiet satisfaction. Yet even her own tongue sliding across her lips reminded her of the feel of his. The chill of the stones only served to make her wish for remembered heat.

She'd found that peace was no defense against fire.

*   *   *

It was back to business

Two weeks after the mustering, Jon marched into New Wexford. He'd put off going back as long as he could. He'd made sure, before he came, that his mind was filled with troop strength and strategies, not lavender and soft skin. The only secrets he was interested in were the ones that he'd been sent there to find out, not the secrets buried beneath the calm, beguiling surface of a woman.

He had traitors to find. If he had to use her in the process, then he would. That was his job. It was the only thing that mattered. If it had taken him two weeks to come to that conclusion, well, so be it. Every man was allowed one stupid, adolescent crush in his life. So what if his had come ten or fifteen years later than it was supposed to? He had it under control now.

The first thing he had to do was get the townspeople accustomed to seeing him around. He needed them to see him exactly as the rest of his company did—affable, clumsy, none too bright, a threat to no one. A careless word in his presence, a bit of conversation no one expected him to understand, and the job would be nearly done and he could move on to the next one.

Walking past the pig wallow, he grimaced. A good part of last week's snow had melted, leaving the rest dingy and ugly, and the pigs well supplied with mud. They squealed as he passed, as if in greeting.

"Can't stay and play today, boys," he muttered, hoping he'd never again be called on to bury himself in mud for his country. There were limits, after all.

"Hey, pig man!" A chunk of packed snow and dirt whacked into his right shoulder. Jon nearly groaned aloud. Not now! All he'd planned to do was go to the Dancing Eel, drink a little too much, and lose a good deal of money at cards. He'd heard harassment of the British troops had increased; they were often pelted with rocks and rotten vegetables if they so much as set foot in New Wexford. It seemed the young men and boys had learned quickly enough the soldiers were under orders not to retaliate.

He had no intention of getting into a wrangle with a bunch of bored little boys who thought he made an easy target. Damn. Why weren't they in school? So what if it was nearly suppertime? They should tuck the little brats safely away in boarding school, as he had been.

The tavern was only a few yards away. Jon quickened his pace. He was almost safely away.

Another chunk thunked off the back of his neck. Bloody hell, the buggers had pretty good aim.

Here we go, Jon thought, act two.

He stumbled over an imaginary rut in the path and landed face down in a pile of dirty snow.

Jon shoved himself over and rubbed at his face. The snow was granular, like tiny bits of ice, and stung as he wiped it off.

He was surrounded by a half dozen small boys. Right in front of him was a familiar, tow-headed boy, a smug smile on his face as he patted a handful of snow.

" 'Cor, you is the dumbest big bloke, ain't ya?"

"I remember you."

"Yeah?" Jimmy ran his sleeve under his red nose. "Well, I remember you too. An' you ain't gettin' rid of us so easy this time."

A withered apple core bounced off Jon's cheek. "Yeah?"

"Yeah. My pa says the lobsterbacks can't do nothin' to any of us Americans, no matter what. Not without, uh, auton . . ."

"Authority," another boy whispered.

"Yeah, authority. So the way I figures it, we can do pretty much what we want to you." He reached down and pulled Jon's nose.

Jon wondered if the little blighter had any idea of the insult he'd just delivered, but right now he was more concerned with the ball of hard-packed snow Jimmy was aiming at his face.

Jon dragged himself to his feet with every intention of finally heading into the Dancing Eel. With any luck, some of the patrons had seen the little scene he'd just created. He'd hate to think he'd pretended to be harmless for nothing.

The door to the tavern flew open. Beth rushed out in a swirl of navy blue cape. Her shoulders were set, her eyes narrowed in an expression of determination he'd seen once before—when she'd come to Sarah's rescue.

Except this time, she was going to rescue him.

He'd given up pride long ago—it was a luxury a man in his profession couldn't afford—but this was too much. A man shouldn't have to be saved from a pack of pint-size would-be soldiers by his woman.

He looked to heaven for help. Please, God, don't let her rescue me.

"Hey, boys! What are you doing there?"

He closed his eyes. Please God, no.

"Boys! You run on home before I tell your mothers!"

It was hopeless. When had God ever helped him when he'd asked for it?

He heard the boys scurrying away. One last snowball—Jimmy's parting shot, no doubt—struck his temple.

What else was a proper spy to do? Jon dropped to the ground, lay sprawled on his back, and waited for Beth.

8

Unmindful of the snow, Bennie fell to her knees next to Jon's prostrate form. He was still, his scarlet coat a vivid splash against the gray-white snow.

She'd spent two weeks berating herself for her foolish behavior after the mustering. Kissing him, for heaven's sake. She'd probably scared the man half to death. She'd told herself that the next time she saw him, she'd be friendly, but casual and controlled. She could manage this friendship as long as she kept her distance.

Then she'd seen the boys baiting him, and she'd rushed out without a second thought. She couldn't let them hurt him, even though she knew there was really little chance they could do him any actual physical harm. But she was afraid they'd hurt his feelings, and she'd been determined to stop them.

But now, as he lay too quiet and motionless on the cold ground, she wondered if they'd truly injured him after all. He seemed so strong and healthy; she hadn't suspected he was so vulnerable.

"Jon? Jon, are you all right?"

He opened his eyes slowly, blinking twice. "Wha . . . what happened?"

"You were hit with a snowball."

"Oh." He struggled to sit up.

"Wait." She rested her hands on his chest to keep him down. "Not so fast. Let me have a look at you first."

She lightly probed the red welt on his temple. He flinched a bit, but it didn't seem too serious. "Jon, can you see everything clearly?"

"Yes." His gaze held hers. "Very clearly." He reached up and took her hand, pressing her palm against his cheek. "No gloves, Beth. Shouldn't be out here. You'll get cold."

His fingers enfolded hers gently. "Hmm? Oh. I didn't stop to get any. Besides, you don't have any on."

He grinned. "I'm always warm."

He was. She could feel the heat from his hand, seeping into her chilled fingers. "You won't be if you keep lying here in the snow. We have to get you inside."

His eyes flashed blue. "I'd like to be inside."

If she knelt beside him any longer, she was going to kiss him again. Right out here in full sight of half the town. It wouldn't even matter that she would probably scare him out of his wits, just like last time. All she would care about was that his kiss had the power to warm her soul.

She jumped up and brushed off the snow clinging to her wet skirts. "Come on, then."

Jon pushed himself to his feet and trailed her into the Eel.

There were at least a dozen men in the tavern, clustered around the tables closest to the fire. When Jon entered, they turned to look at him. Although their eyes were narrowed in mistrust, several smiled with what appeared to be reluctant amusement.

Good, he thought. At least the show hadn't been for nothing. He plastered his idiot smile back on his face. "Hello."

Cadwallader hurried forward, wiping his hands on a limp swatch of linen. "Bennie, what is he doing here?"

Beth planted herself in front of Jon. Ah, damn, she was protecting him again.

"Da, he's cold. He just needs to be warmed up."

"We'll not be serving his kind here."

She moved closer to Jon, and his muscles tightened as he caught a faint, familiar whiff of lavender.

"He's not going to harm anyone, Da. It's just Jon."

Just Jon. His cheeks hurt as he forced himself to maintain the stupid smile.

Glowering fiercely at Jon, Cad flipped the rag over his shoulder. His expression softened when his gaze fell on Beth.

"All right, he can stay. Only for a bit, mind you." He returned his attention to Jon. "Cold, are you? No stamina, you redcoats. Never mind, I'll make you a flip. Warm you right up."

Jon choked. "A flip?"

A smile crinkled the corners of Cad's eyes. "Not a flip, eh? Well, maybe a little mulled cider."

Jon nodded enthusiastically.

Cad went off to fetch the drink. Jon settled himself at a table with Rufus, the shopkeeper, and one of Beth's brothers—Carter, he thought. The men glared as he sat down.

"Can I sit here?" Jon asked in his most innocent voice.

"Well . . ."

"Carter," Bennie said warningly.

"Oh, all right."

Bennie hovered around, her hands fluttering. She reached toward Jon, then withdrew her hand, her gaze sliding from Jon to Carter and back again.

"Bennie," Carter said.

She jumped. "What?"

"Would you stop flitting around like that? You're acting like a bee who can't find a flower to land on," Carter said. "I'm not going to hurt him. The lieutenant and I are just going to have a little chat. Why don't you go find something to do?"

Jon looked so eager, Bennie thought, as if he was delighted that somebody wanted to talk to him. Yet he was so alone here, surrounded by Americans, and she was the only one who cared whether he was hurt.

"Beth?" Jon's question was soft. "You sit, too?"

"You want me to join you?"

"Yes." Jon patted the bench next to him.

"Beth?" Carter was suddenly alert. "What's this about 'Beth'?"

"Bennie's a boy's name." Jon beamed up at her. "I like Beth."

A warm flush of pleasure flooded her, even though she knew he was talking about the name, not the woman.

Carter gave a brotherly snort. "Hmph. Bennie's always been a good enough name before."

Bennie plopped down on the bench. "I like Beth, too."

Jon's arm brushed hers. The last time she'd sat on a bench in the Dancing Eel with him, she'd kissed him. Was it her imagination, or had he slid a bit closer to her? Jon shifted his legs, and his thigh ended up resting against hers. Even through her skirts, she could feel the solid length of his muscle. The room was suddenly uncomfortably warm. Had someone built up the fire?

Cad had returned, and he slammed a tankard down on the table in front of Jon. Cider sloshed over the rim. "I hope nobody thinks I'm going to be renaming my only daughter after twenty-three years."

"I'm not asking you to, Da."

Cad grunted and left to see to his other customers.

"So, Lieutenant." Carter braced his elbows on the table and leaned forward. "What did you think of the mustering?"

"Jon," he said.

"Huh?" Carter looked taken aback.

"You can call me Jon."

"Oh. Well, then, Jon. What did you think of the mustering?"

"It was good. I liked it." Perfect teeth flashed in a perfect smile. What had his parents been like, Bennie wondered, to produce a son as handsome as Jon?

She looked at his big hand wrapped around the tankard. "Your hand? How is it?"

Jon held out his hand, palm up. A narrow red line cut across the thin skin between his thumb and forefinger. He flexed his fingers slowly.

"It's fine. Tough to fire my musket well, though. Still hurts a little. Makes me shoot bad."

Carter nearly choked on a mouthful of ale. "You shoot worse now?"

Jon nodded mournfully. "Yes, worse. And we have to practice all the time now too."

Rufus sat up straighter. "Practice?"

"Yes, practice." Now came the tricky part. He had to give them just the right amount of information—not too much, not too little. Too little didn't do any good; too much was dangerous. Years of this work had taught him the proper balance. "We must shoot every day now. Captain's orders. Fix fort and drill. That's all we ever do now."

Rufus and Carter exchanged glances. "Fix the fort?"

"Oh, yes." He made them wait a little while he gulped down the warm, sweet cider. The flavor burst in his mouth; the snap of apple blended with the sharpness of alcohol and spices. "It was all broken. No good to stay in. We had to sleep in tents."

"I'll bet that was uncomfortable," Rufus said encouragingly.

"Cold, too. But it's almost fixed now. We can move in after the new year, I think."

"That'll be much better, I'm sure." Carter gave him a friendly smile.

"Better." Jon tipped up the tankard and drained his cider. "Have to go back now."

"So soon? Let me get you another drink." Carter signaled Cad.

"No, no. Must go." Jon turned to Beth. "Good-bye, Beth."

"Do you have to go?"

She actually looked sorry to see him go, the warmth fading in her soft brown eyes. Little did she know how soon she'd see him again, he thought, and felt once more that unfamiliar pang of guilt.

He ignored it. Whatever pangs, urges, and other useless feelings his body insisted on coming up with were secondary to the job at hand. "Have work to do," he said.

With a snap of her wrist, Bennie spread the woolen blanket over a layer of hay. In the winter, when it was too cold to escape to the woods, this was where she came to play.

The stables behind the Dancing Eel were made of stone and spacious enough to accommodate both her family's own horses and those of the occasional travelers who stayed overnight at the tavern. The loft over the stables held a plentiful supply of fodder, and the thick stone walls kept out the worst of the cold; the only windows were small openings that let in a little light and not much else.

The loft smelled of sweet dried grasses and horses. It was snug and quiet, and nobody but Bennie ever came up here unless it was time to bed down the animals.

Bennie sat down on the blanket and pulled her violin case over to her. She'd managed to duck out of the tavern shortly after Jon had left, unable to satisfactorily explain to her father why she'd brought a British officer to the Eel.

Her explanation, that Jon was a friend, hadn't satisfied

him. He'd lowered his eyebrows at her and demanded
to know exactly how his daughter had gotten so friendly
with a redcoat, even such a harmless one as Jon seemed
to be. She'd mumbled something about seeing him at
the mustering, and something else about feeling sorry
for him. Her father had looked decidedly skeptical, and
Bennie was increasingly aware that the way she felt
about Jon wasn't quite friendship and had little to do
with pity.

So she'd slipped out at the first opportunity, fetched
her violin, and escaped to the stables. A thin beam of
late afternoon sun streamed through a tiny window;
particles of dust floated in the air. Bennie blew on her
chilled fingers and unlatched her case.

"Beth? Are you here?"

Her fingers stilled. "Jon?"

"Where are you?"

"I'm up in the loft."

"Stay there. I'm coming up."

His head poked up through the access hole in the far
corner of the floor. She could only make out the shadow
of his form in the dim light as he braced his hands on
either side of the opening and shoved himself upward.

Even if he hadn't spoken, Bennie would have known
immediately who it was; she would have recognized
those shoulders anywhere.

"What are you doing here? I thought you had to get
back to your company."

Jon scuffled through the loose hay, kicking up chaff
as he came toward her. He sat down cross-legged next
to her and coughed, waving a hand in front of his face.
"Dusty."

He pulled off his tricorn and tossed it aside. His club had come undone again, and his hair fell in a smooth, rich brown swath to his shoulders. "Didn't have to get back. Just didn't want to talk to them." His lids were lowered over his eyes, making him look relaxed and surprisingly sensual. "Wanted to talk to you. Alone."

"You did? What about?"

"Don't want to talk anymore."

She swayed toward him.

"I want to—"

"Yes?" she whispered.

"Listen."

Bennie stiffened. "Listen?"

"Yes." He smoothed a stray curl from her temple, his touch restrained and infinitely gentle. "Will you play for me again, Beth?"

His voice was a rough rumble. If he kept looking at her like that, she'd do nearly anything he asked. "Of course."

She wasn't sure how long she played, she only knew that the music came easier than it ever had. Light music, happy music, music that didn't speak of fear or loneliness. Music that was meant to be shared. And every time she glanced at him, he was smiling, watching her, his fingers lightly tapping his knees in time with the music. If his rhythm was sometimes off, who cared?

When her own fingers finally tired, she let the final note fade quietly away and slumped down onto the blanket next to Jon.

"Thank you," he said.

"For what?"

"For sharing your music with me."

"Thank you for letting me." She plucked idly on the strings. "I've never wanted to before."

"Never?"

"Never," she confessed softly.

There it was again, that flare of light in his eyes. Curiosity? Alertness? Intensity? It was too brief to identify. Yet it somehow made him unfamiliar, a hint of the man he must have been before his accident— perhaps, a bit of what he still could be, if someone was compassionate enough to look beyond his simple surface.

She was, suddenly, fiercely glad he was no longer that man. For that man, she was sure, would never have taken the time to sit in a stable loft and listen to a plain, overgrown woman play the violin. And that man would never have looked at her with such open appreciation and easy delight.

That man, a man with intelligence and determination to match his looks, would be too busy setting the world on fire. Too busy lighting another kind of fire in every beautiful woman he came across—lovely, delicate, feminine woman. He would never have had time for her.

Sick guilt assailed her. It was pure selfishness on her part, to wish this on him simply because she wanted him near. If she'd ever thought about it, she would have considered herself a relatively nice person. To find that she was glad of another's misfortune, because it gave her something she hadn't even realized she wanted so desperately, was a shock. But wishing it wasn't so didn't make it go away.

Jon watched the light go out of her eyes and her fine,

strong shoulders droop. She looked so sad. What had happened to change her mood? He scooped up a handful of hay and poured it over her head. It drifted down, sticking in the wild, golden curls of her hair, settling on her chest.

"Not scarecrow," he said. "Scare-woman."

"Oh, really?" Grabbing a handful, she tossed it at him.

He clutched at his heart and toppled over backward. "Oh-ho, you want to fight me, do you?" He stood up, his fists filled, and advanced on her steadily. "Couldn't beat me at arm wrestling. Think this is easier?"

Bennie jumped to her feet, swept up an entire arm load of hay and hurled it in his direction before she darted past him. Her laughter burbled on the air, as joyous to his ears as the music she had played earlier, because he had made her laugh.

Jon spun. She was no more than two steps away, lightly balanced on the balls of her feet, ready for motion. Her hair, the color of sunshine and earth and ripe crops, tumbled down around her shoulders. Her simple clothes were disarrayed, she was shedding hay with every movement, and she was the most enticing thing he had ever seen.

"You think you can catch me?" Bennie taunted. "My brothers never could." A quick slip and she was behind him again, raining torrents of dried grass and dust over his head.

He shook his head violently, sending the chaff flying, and turned. Her eyes were alight with mischief, her smile happy and free, and he wished he could make her look like that always.

He feinted left. She leaned right.

He darted right. She skipped left.

He let himself relax. "Hmm. Too fast for me." Then he dived.

The momentum of his jump carried them both down into a large pile of hay. Thrusting out his arms behind her, he took most of the impact of the fall, instinctively protecting her. Hay billowed around them, and laughter floated above them.

"I must be slowing down. I'm out of practice." She looked up into his face, and her laughter died.

Their faces were bare inches apart. And everywhere else, they weren't apart at all.

His chest and belly were pressed against hers. She was short of breath but doubted it was from the force of his weight, for he was propped on his elbows. His heaviness wasn't suffocating, it was . . . wonderful.

One of his legs rested between hers, and his thigh was pressed against a part of her she'd pretty much ignored most of her life but was now utterly aware of.

His hair was loose and brushed her cheek, its softness in complete contrast to the hard length of his body. His pale eyes no longer seemed cool and distant, and Bennie was reminded that only the hottest of flames burned blue.

Her arms slid around his waist as if of their own accord. "Jon," she whispered.

He jerked away from her as quickly as he would have removed his hand from a fire. Jumping to his feet, he strode over to the nearest window. Planting his feet apart, he crossed his arms over his chest and stared out into the fading light, his finely sculpted features set into implacable lines.

Dear Lord, she'd done it again. It was exactly like the last time. She'd been unable to keep herself from touching him, she'd said his name, and he'd left her.

He seemed willing to accept her companionship and her music. What he clearly didn't want was what her body kept trying to insist upon.

She didn't even know *why* she had this compulsion to touch him. Back when she'd been young enough and silly enough to have dreams, the man she'd dreamed of had been nothing like him—a beautiful man, yes, a kind man, and strong. But she'd dreamed of a man of intelligence and ambition, a dashing man who'd challenge the world and her.

Yet Jon was the only man who'd ever made her feel this way. It was absurd. It was ridiculous.

But it was.

She got up and walked slowly over to him. He was completely motionless, and she wondered what he was thinking as he looked down on the yard between the stables and the Dancing Eel.

"Jon," she said tentatively. "I didn't mean to frighten you. Or hurt you, either. I—"

"It's all right." He glanced at her over his shoulder. "We're friends. Friends hug. Friends kiss. Right?"

"Right." She swallowed; her throat was dry. Friends. As much as she wanted his friendship, it seemed such a bland, inadequate word.

He sighed heavily, and his forbidding posture relaxed. He turned to face her.

"Beth." Taking one of her hands, he turned the palm up and brought it to his mouth. He touched his lips to it, and even that small, tender brush made her wish for more. He lifted his head to look at her and enfolded her hand in both of his.

"Beth, I'm sorry. I can't . . . not anymore."

He couldn't. Although he had made up his mind to use their friendship as a convenient way to obtain information, he found he couldn't do this. It was one thing to listen to tidbits she'd picked up in the tavern or from the comings and goings of the townspeople. It was quite another to make love with her to do it.

Her hand tightened in his, squeezing gently. "What were you like before?"

"Before?"

"Before your accident. Do you remember anything?"

"Some." He dropped her hand and turned to stare back down into the shadowy yard. He'd never had any trouble before looking someone in the eye and lying to them. Why was it so hard now? "A little."

"What do you remember?"

More than curiosity, he heard concern in her question. He returned his gaze to her face. He would learn to face her and lie. He had little choice in the matter.

Not much light entered the loft now; shadows deepened under her strong cheekbones. Her eyes become dark—no color in them, just gleaming emotion.

"I was born here, in the colonies." That, at least, was the truth.

"You were?"

He nodded. "Mother married beneath her. Her father didn't approve."

She smiled slightly. "Mine too."

"They came here, to get away. Died in a carriage accident, when I was ten." Now came the hard part.

Now came the lies. "I don't remember them."

Images floated through his mind, clear and painfully sharp. His mother, small and blond and soft-voiced. His father, big, handsome, and loud. Both gone so suddenly the little boy he'd been had awakened every morning for months expecting to see his parents.

"I'm sorry." How had she ever thought Jon was simply, uncomplicatedly happy? His sadness was palpable in the room, burning the back of her eyes, tightening her throat. The one constant in her life had always been her family. Jon had been so young, and so completely alone. "What happened to you?"

"Sent to my aunt's. Back in England. She married an earl."

"Did you like it there?"

"Not so bad. Lots of room. Had eight children already. I was commoner nephew who was too big and clumsy." He shrugged. "Like now."

She knew what he didn't say. There'd been no one to tell a lonely, lost boy he wasn't alone. No one to hold him when he missed his mother. No one to teach him what his father would have.

"When I was old enough, they bought me a commission. After a while, sent me to Boston. Just before the massacre. There a year, the horse kicked me."

He thunked the side of his head. "When I woke up, like this." He spread his hands. "That's all."

That's all. It was so little. Yet it was too much.

Carefully, slowly, Bennie stepped closer to him and slipped her arms around him. She felt him shudder slightly and release a great breath.

This time, she wasn't yearning for more. This time,

she wasn't trying to do anything but give him a little bit of the affection he should have had all his life.

And this time, when she whispered "Jon," he didn't pull away.

9

Bennie scrubbed a table board in the main room of the Dancing Eel, wiping away the leavings of last night's customers. The yeasty, spicy scent of last night's beer and cider rose to her nose, mingling with the sharp tang of soap. Across the room, Henry sloshed water as he carelessly pushed a rag mop across the plank floor. Near the storeroom, George checked supplies and precisely arranged freshly washed tankards.

It was a clear, brilliantly cold winter day. Pale sunlight poured through the windows Isaac was polishing, setting the diamond-shaped panes asparkle.

Other than the Joneses, the Eel was empty. It nearly always was in the early morning, except for those rare days when a traveler was occupying one of the two bedrooms over the tavern that weren't being used by Bennie's unmarried brothers.

Bennie dropped her rag into the oaken bucket and moved on to the next table. It was calm and warm in the

Eel. She'd been helping clean the place since she was a little girl. The Dancing Eel was a family business, keeping it up was a family project, and the Joneses had always done it together. She enjoyed the quiet mornings when they worked together to clean the tavern before the customers arrived.

She didn't think her brothers felt the same way.

Henry shoved the mop over the floor. "I don't see why I always have to wash the floor," he grumbled. "Bennie should do it. It's woman's work."

"I'd be happy to do it," she said.

"You would?" His head popped up.

"Certainly. Of course, you'd have to scrub the tables instead."

His expression grew less eager. "Well . . . "

"I'm not entirely sure how you'd explain to Mercy Jernegan why your hands were all reddened like a scrub woman's, however."

George and Isaac snickered. A dusky flush spread over Henry's cheeks. "Mercy Jernegan? I don't know what you mean."

"Then you're not interested in her?" George said mildly. "She's a pretty little thing. If you're not going to court her, maybe I'll—"

The mop clattered as it hit the floor. Henry whirled on his brother. "You stay away from Mercy! Everybody knows you're all but engaged to Anne Beekman."

"Well, well." George grinned. "For someone who didn't know what Bennie meant, you certainly warned me off quickly enough."

Henry bent and scooped up the mop. "All right, maybe I'm a little bit interested."

"A little bit?" Bennie asked. "And I'm a little bit tall."

"Well, at least I don't have a stupid Brit whose brain is as small as the rest of him is big wandering around moon-faced after me."

Bennie planted her hands on her hips. "He's not moon-faced. And he's *not* stupid."

"Uh-huh. I'm just imagining that when he was in here last week he was following you around like a starved puppy."

"He was not." At least her brothers didn't know Jon had come to the stables later. That she'd hugged him, and afterward they'd sat and talked, and she'd taught him a few notes on her violin, and all the while he was so close to her their shoulders touched. They didn't know that when he'd left, he'd said he'd see her soon, and she'd believed him. And that although she hadn't seen him since, she still believed him. If they knew all that, she could only imagine what they'd say.

"Sure. And he didn't wag his tail every time you smiled at him." Henry swiveled his hips.

Bennie hurled her rag at his head. Henry ducked and the cloth missed, but it spattered a trail of dirty water in its wake.

"Why, you . . ." Henry raised his fists in mock threat and started toward Bennie.

Isaac clicked his tongue and shook his head. "Children, children. What am I going to do with you?"

"Children? I'm eight years older than you, young man, and I could still paddle your backside if the need arose," Bennie said.

Henry backhanded a wet streak off his chin. "I can't believe you actually threw it at me, Ben. You haven't done things like that since you were twelve."

"Don't think it hasn't been tough restraining myself, either. Lord knows you've needed it over the years."

"Still . . . " George left the supplies and strolled over to join them. "This attachment the lieutenant has formed for you could be rather useful. I don't think he exactly guards his tongue; no telling what he might let slip one way or another."

"That's true," Henry agreed. "You should be nice to him, Ben. Keep him hanging around."

"I couldn't do that."

"Sure you could. Just keep patting the poor thing on the head once in a while and he'll come trotting back for more."

"Henry, I'll do no such thing."

"What kind of a patriot are you? For the cause, and all that."

"At least we can use what we already know," Isaac put in eagerly.

"Isaac," George said warningly, inclining his head slightly toward Bennie.

She narrowed her eyes at her brothers. "What's going on?"

"Nothing, Ben." Henry tucked his hands behind his back. "What would be going on?"

She turned to Isaac. As the youngest, he had the least experience in trying to fool her—not that any of them, with the exception of Brendan, had ever been able to keep one of their schemes from her very long. She was simply more patient, more careful, and more observant than any of the other seven.

"Isaac, you may as well tell me."

He looked up, appearing to take the greatest interest in the ceiling rafters. "Nothing at all."

"Nothing at all," she repeated, unconvinced.

"Nothing."

"Well, then, I suppose you might as well all get back to work."

They didn't quite manage to disguise their sighs of relief as they scurried back to their tasks with considerably more enthusiasm than they had previously displayed.

They were certainly planning something, something they clearly didn't want her to know about, so it must be something that could get them into trouble—trouble she had every intention of preventing.

Bennie retrieved her rag and went back to scrubbing tables. She managed to get them all scrupulously clean and at the same time keep a curious, experienced eye on her three youngest brothers.

Although it must have been approaching midnight, it was nearly as bright as day out. White stars stood out brilliantly against an ebony sky. The full moon poured milky white light down on the equally pure snow, reflecting enough to clearly delineate the dark, skeletal trees twisting in the wind.

Bennie shivered and pulled the edges of her cloak tighter. The dark bulk of the Dancing Eel loomed in front of her; no light leaked from the tightly closed shutters. Should she go in? She could simply follow them and make certain they were safe. It would be easier.

But it really wasn't safe, and there was no way she could make it so. Although it would be better if she could keep them at home, Bennie had no illusions about the ease of deterring them from what they saw as their mission. She might as well try and stop winter from following fall.

Her father, Adam, and Carter combined might have been able to dissuade them. Unfortunately, they were as likely to join in, and then even more of her family would be involved in this foolishness.

No, she'd have to try and talk them out of it herself. If she couldn't, she'd simply have to go along. She'd make sure that hothead Henry wouldn't let himself get carried away, and that in his eagerness Isaac didn't do something thoughtless.

Bennie pushed open the door. George, Henry, and Isaac huddled around a table on which was a single lantern. Their heads were bent, and the light from the small flame burnished their hair to shining gold. Henry was gesturing wildly, talking in a loud but unintelligible whisper, and the other two were nodding agreement, their faces lit with excitement and anticipation.

She let the door slam shut behind her.

The young men jumped and turned, wariness and guilt etched on their handsome faces. When they saw who the intruder was, their expressions cleared.

"Oh, Ben, it's just you. Why'd you slam the door like that? You startled me." Like the other two, Henry was dressed in dark breeches, boots, and shirt, and his face showed pale above the black cloth.

"Who were you expecting?" Bennie crossed the room.

"Nobody, Bennie," George said patiently. "That's why we were startled. What are you doing here at this time of night?"

"I'm not going to let you do it, you know," she said.

"Do what?" Isaac's adolescent voice squeaked.

Bennie shook her head. "Whatever it is you have planned. Some raid on the British camp, I assume. It's too dangerous, and I'm not going to allow you to do it."

"But, Ben—" Henry protested.

"No, Henry. What are you outnumbered, twenty to one? It's sheer madness."

George leaned forward, bracing his hand on the table. "Bennie, this is the last opportunity we have to strike at them before they move into the fort and become nearly invulnerable."

"But why? What good do you think the three of you can do?"

"We're not taking any foolish chances," Henry said, his green-gold eyes glowing with anticipation. "And it's not so much a matter of doing a lot of damage. But we can bother them a bit, make them uncomfortable."

"If you're so sure this is the right thing to do, why haven't you told Da? Or the rest of the Sons of Liberty?"

Henry shifted uneasily and glanced at George for support.

"We're not going to be able to overpower them in any case," George said intently. "A smaller group will have a better chance of slipping in and out unseen."

"Not to mention the fact that Da might not agree with your approach to the situation," Bennie said.

George smiled. "That, too. Also, I'm not entirely sure Brendan wasn't right. I think there's a very good possibility that the British are getting information from somewhere, and I'm not taking any chances that they're going to be tipped off about this. That would be foolish."

"Well, then, I guess I'll just have to go with you."

"Oh, no you won't," Henry exploded.

"You said it was perfectly safe," she reminded him.

"Yes, but—"

"And you know I'd be able to keep up, Henry."

"I know, but—"

"Then I'm coming," she said firmly.

Once again, Henry appealed to his brother.

George rubbed his chin. "What did you have in mind, Bennie?"

"I promise I'll stay out of your way, George. I just want to keep an eye out. You know I'm more observant than you are."

"You can't really mean to let her come!" Henry protested.

"I could stand watch," Bennie suggested.

"All right," George agreed.

Isaac rubbed his hands together. "Let's get going then."

"So, is everybody ready to go on this mission?" A slender figure joined them, his shoes moving soundlessly on the wooden floor.

"Brendan," Henry groaned. "Is the whole bloody family going to be here before we're through?"

"What do you want, Brendan?" George asked.

"You didn't really think I was going to let you have this little adventure all by yourselves, did you? No telling what kind of a muck you'd make of it." He tossed a pile of black cloth on the table. "For one thing, those shiny tresses of yours will stand out like a beacon in the moonlight. Since, unlike me, you didn't have the good fortune to be born dark-haired, you'll have to tie those over your heads."

Picking up one of the swatches between his thumb and forefinger, Henry eyed it skeptically. "You don't seriously think this is necessary, do you, Brendan?"

"It certainly is." A bucket thudded as he set it on the table. He dipped his fingers into the pail and smeared a thick streak of soot across Henry's cheek. "And, you're going to have to cover up that pearly skin Mercy's so fond of."

Henry glared at Brendan, who smiled cheerfully.

"Well, come on, boys. Let's get to work."

Snow creaked beneath her feet as Bennie huddled a little closer to the ancient, dilapidated maple. The bark was rough against her back, even through the thick cloth of her cloak, but its trunk blocked the worst of the wind, and she hoped its dark shadows made her completely invisible.

The tree was on a small knoll, perhaps a hundred yards from the fort. Behind her, the woods were deep, thick, and black; in front of her, the massive bulk of the fort was limned with silver by the bright moon, now lowering in its nightly journey.

They had ridden their horses for only three of the four miles to the fort. A mile from camp, they had dismounted and tethered their mounts, preferring to creep on foot the last distance, ensuring no noise betrayed their arrival.

Brendan had insisted they each leave their horses in different places, hiding them as well as possible. That way, if one were discovered, no one could know how many others there were, nor would they lose all their horses at once.

He had been equally insistent that they would not meet up again after their mission. If one was captured, there was little the others could do anyway, and any attempt at rescuing him would only put the rest in danger. So no one would know until they returned to the Eel if everyone had made it back safely.

Brendan had stationed Bennie beside this tree with strict instructions that if things started to fall apart, she'd get herself out of there and back to safety as quickly as possible. Although the thought of leaving her brothers in the midst of the enemy made her feel vaguely ill, she had agreed, knowing their safety would be compromised even more if they had to worry about her.

Carefully, she scanned the camp that crouched on the narrow, flat strip of ground between the forest and the fort. A few dozen tents were scattered about, a couple much larger than the others. An occasional fire flared, adding a golden glow to the silver moonlight.

The camp seemed to be completely quiet. A handful of soldiers patrolled the outer perimeter or stood lackadaisically at their posts. They seemed inattentive, apparently sure that no one would challenge the might of the British army.

Bennie's heart thudded painfully. There was no indication that any of the guards were even the slightest bit suspicious, alert to possible intruders. If she saw any danger, she was to warn her brothers with an owl hoot. But could they hear her over this distance? And would it make any difference if they could? At that point, it would probably be too late for at least one of them; all she could do was hope and pray that the others got away safely.

She could detect no sign of her brothers. They had left fifteen—twenty?—minutes ago. It was impossible to judge the time, for each second seemed to drag by with agonizing slowness. There were no unusual movements in the camp, so either her brothers weren't there yet or they could move with much greater stealth than she'd given them credit for.

Another tiny glow appeared at the far side of the small encampment. Perhaps one of the guards had gotten cold on duty and had made a fire. Bennie shivered and thought longingly of the Eel's hot, spiced cider as the sharp wind whistled in the branches overhead.

The glow grew and brightened, looking warm and cheerful against the stark blue-white of the snow. And then she knew. It wasn't a simple campfire at all.

Brendan had done his job.

The shout sounded almost unreal when it shattered the stillness of the air. It must have taken the soldiers even longer to identify the alarm, for it was several more seconds before dark, human shapes began to stumble out of the tents.

There was no point in Bennie trying to warn her brothers now. By this time, surely they all knew the camp had been roused and were long gone—that, or it was too late to save them.

More shouts. More men running out of their tents, scrambling to the river with buckets. Perhaps they assumed that the fire was due to natural causes, for the guards didn't seem to be beginning a search; rather they rushed to join the others battling the fire.

The neighing of panicked horses joined the shouts. Although Bennie could not see them from her post, she knew the company's horses were fenced to the west of camp; her brothers had scouted the location well.

A faint rumble trembled under the other sounds, rhythmic and almost imperceptible. Hoofbeats—a lot of them. She smiled slightly. George had been as efficient as always.

The frantic scrambling in camp began to slow. Evidently someone had taken charge; one group of men still fought the fire, but individual troops were leaving camp in all directions, as if searching.

It was time to leave. If guards were going out, they knew someone had set the fires and released the horses. So far, none seemed to be heading toward her, but there was no way of knowing how long that beneficial state of affairs was going to last.

Bennie slipped along the edge of the forest, careful to stay in the shadows. If one didn't know it was there, the path she planned to take through the woods was almost impossible to find. Once she reached it, she would be safely away. Only a little further—

Boom!

Bennie clapped her hands over her ears as the sound of the explosion ripped through the clearing, loud enough to blot out all other sounds and shake small branches. Throwing herself behind the nearest tree, she looked back at the camp once more.

The fire must have made it to the powder magazine. Orange flames leapt upward and clouds of smoke billowed up, obscuring the clear sky.

Gingerly, she lifted her hands from her ears. Sounds were muted, as if her head was wrapped in soft cotton. She could hear faint pops as the fire reached smaller pockets of ammunition.

There was no doubt her brothers had succeeded beyond their expectations. It would take the British weeks to repair and replace what had been lost. But Bennie, as she watched in fascination the scene below her, could only worry that someone had been injured in the explosion.

She told herself her sudden trembling was due to the biting wind. Squinting, she began desperately searching the ground around the camp for some sign of a limp body. Particularly a large, familiar body.

What if he'd been too close to the fire? Surely they'd seen that it had been heading toward the ammunition supplies. But had he moved fast enough?

Bennie bit her lip until she tasted the metallic tang of blood. Why hadn't she found some way to warn him? Some way to make sure he was anywhere but here when this had happened?

Because she couldn't endanger her brothers. And because she really hadn't considered the possibility that someone would be injured. It had seemed somewhat harmless, a prank, like the Boston Tea Party, to be played on the too complacent British. She'd been sure the only risk had been to her family.

Now, too late, she'd realized she was wrong.

There was nothing to do. It was too dark and confused down in the camp to identify anyone, even one as big as Jon.

Bennie swore to herself that first thing tomorrow she'd find a way to check on Jon. At the moment she had no idea how she was going to manage that, but she'd think of something. If nothing else, she'd find some excuse to talk to that overfriendly Captain Livingston.

Reluctantly, fighting the urge to rush down into the midst of the madness and start hunting for Jon, she turned to leave.

The entrance to the path was cloaked by two large bayberry bushes. Bennie doubted that any of the British, even after several months of residence, had found it. But after nine children had spent their youth running all over the district, she doubted there was anyplace in the vicinity of New Wexford that the Joneses didn't know as well as they knew every board in the Dancing Eel.

Sucking in her stomach, Bennie pushed her way through the bushes. It wasn't easy; both she and the bushes had grown some since she'd done this as a child, and earlier tonight, she'd had her brothers clear the way, as several broken branches on either side attested.

Wouldn't be a hidden pathway much longer, she thought. In the daylight, any alert man would see the damage to the foliage and find the path. It wouldn't matter then; she doubted she'd ever have need of it again.

"Halt!"

10

Bennie's heart lurched. They'd found her.

She turned slowly, acutely conscious of the branches rustling around her.

He was no more than two long steps away from her—a soldier, the muzzle of his musket gaping at her midsection.

"Come out from there," he ordered. "Easy, now."

She could risk it, dive back through the bushes, try and make her way through the forest. She was faster than most men. But even thinking about it, she felt the flesh between her shoulder blades twitch. Her back would be exposed, vulnerable to a musket ball. Although it was dark, perhaps dark enough to provide cover, he was very near, and she had no faith in her ability to outrun a shot from that grotesquely oversize musket.

She hesitated for only an instant longer before pushing her way back out of the thicket. The soldier was young and vaguely familiar. Perhaps she had seen him at the

Eel, or the mustering. He must have already been on duty when the explosion occurred, because his uniform was faultlessly worn, unrumpled, not something that had been thrown on in the rush of the moment.

"Come on, now. Hurry up. The cap'n will be pleased to talk to you for sure." Moonlight, white and cold, glinted off the shiny blade of his bayonet.

Surely he wouldn't remember her. In black breeches and shirt, her hair braided and tucked down the back of her blouse, one of Brendan's black rags tied over her head, and soot smeared all over her face, she in no way resembled the woman he may have seen in New Wexford. Her cloak was navy blue and, as her mother had complained on many occasions, completely unfeminine. With Bennie's stature, as long as she didn't talk, perhaps he wouldn't perceive her sex.

She had to escape before he did realize she was a woman. If he knew her gender, it wouldn't take him long to identify her; every other woman in the area was at least a full head shorter than she.

If he discovered who she was, it would be very easy to guess who had raided the camp. There'd be little hope for any of the Joneses then. And, if there was as much destruction to the camp as she suspected, she doubted the redcoats would be inclined to be lenient.

"Come out now, I said, or I may have to shoot. The cap'n might want t'talk to you, but I'm sure I could wound you so's you'd last long enough so's he could question you."

Fear, sick and acidic, clogged her throat and churned in her stomach. There seemed to be nothing she could do. Every option she had endangered her life and her family. If only the guard would relax, just for an instant . . .

She was nearly out of the bushes now, almost completely visible. Still, there was no flicker of recognition on the guard's set features. A sharp tug on her cape stopped her. She pulled. Damn, she was caught on a sharp stick. Grabbing the fabric in both hands, she yanked hard.

She heard the fabric rip. The bushes on either side of her shook violently. Still, she was held fast.

"Got yerself caught there, have you? Well, I can't say that I care if you catch a bit of a chill."

Still training his gun on her carefully, the soldier reached forward and tore the cloak from her shoulders. Bennie registered the sudden cold in the fraction of a second before she realized her freedom.

There wasn't time to do anything about it. The redcoat grabbed her arm and yanked her out of the thicket.

The cloth could hide her hair. The soot could hide her features. Unfortunately, with her cloak gone, there was nothing to hide her breasts.

His mouth fell open.

"Bloody balls, you're a woman!"

His gaze was fixed on her chest, and the bore of his gun dropped a fraction.

It was all she needed. She shoved, the soldier stumbled backward, and she turned and flew into the forest.

"What the—Halt! Halt, I say!"

Sharp branches tore at her clothes and scratched her face. The cold air burned her chest. Her heart pounded so loudly she could scarcely hear the sounds of the man's pursuit.

"Stop! Damn it, stop!"

She kept running. The ground was uneven, rocky and

overgrown, and the path was almost impossible to follow in the dark while sprinting at high speed. She could only hope it was equally difficult for him.

Breaking into a small clearing, she pushed herself to run harder. The opening might give him the opportunity to get off a clear shot.

She gave no cry as she went down; there was only a muffled thud as she slammed into the snow-covered ground. Sharp pain stabbed up from her ankle to her calf. Had she stepped on a stone or in a hole, stumbled over a small ridge?

It didn't matter. It only mattered that she moved.

Her hands sank wrist-deep into the snow before she was able to force herself up. He was getting closer; she could hear him charging through the woods like a maddened bull.

Gritting her teeth against the pain, she tried a step. And went down again. Her ankle simply wouldn't hold her.

Perhaps she could crawl out of the clearing, hide herself in the undergrowth. Absurd to hope that he wouldn't find her, but—

"Stay right there."

She froze. He was advancing on her warily, his musket trained on her carefully. Clearly, he was taking no chances this time.

"Get up," he snapped.

"I can't."

His face registered the impact of her voice. "Dear God, you *are* a woman."

She grimaced. "Your captain said much the same thing to me once."

"The cap'n?" He bent, pulled the cloth off her head and tugged her hair out of its confinement. Grabbing her chin, he tilted her face up to the moonlight, turning her head from side to side as he studied her features. Bennie held her breath as the bayonet of the gun swept perilously close to her leg.

"I remember you," he said thoughtfully.

"That's most observant of you, soldier."

He smiled and straightened. "I think the cap'n is gonna be very happy to see you, miss."

"How lovely," she said tightly.

"Get up."

"I can't. I hurt my ankle."

"Well, I'm certainly not gonna carry you. You're too heavy. You'll just have to hop, won't you?"

"How gallant."

He poked her with the bayonet, not hard enough to pierce her skin but with enough force to show her she had better move or he might not be so gentle the next time.

Reluctantly, Bennie started to push herself up to her feet again. She heard a muffled thud and watched in disbelief as the soldier closed his eyes and sank slowly to the ground.

A hulking form loomed over her, dark, large, and shadowy—and completely nonthreatening, for she immediately recognized that bulk.

"Jon!"

"Hush." He knelt in the snow in front of her. "You all right?"

"What did you do?" she said in shock.

"Made him sleep."

"What did you hit him with?"

He shrugged and lifted one huge fist. "With this."

"But he's one of your own men," she protested.

Tentatively, tenderly, his fingers brushed her knee.

"He might have hurt you, Beth."

It was pure luck that had him stumbling upon the soldier chasing Beth into the woods. He'd been scouting the perimeter of the camp, gathering his own information and conclusions, when he'd heard the soldier holler "Halt!" Jon had caught only a glimpse of the soldier's quarry before both had disappeared into the woods, but that had been enough; Jon had recognized that fluid, controlled, sure way of moving and plunged into the woods to follow.

Luckily the soldier had been too intent on chasing down his prey to realize someone was quietly speeding along behind him. Jon had caught up with them when they'd reached the clearing and had been able to slip up behind them without either noticing his presence.

When the man had prodded Beth with that deadly silver blade, Jon hadn't thought; he'd only felt—rage, pure and blinding. The kind of rage that was fatal for a man in his profession, for spying required absolute, steady control. Before he'd had time to think about it, he'd whacked the hapless fellow over the head.

And he wasn't one bit sorry.

"Did he hurt you, Beth?"

"No. I fell, twisted my ankle on something. I can't seem to put any weight on it. Maybe if I try again—"

"Don't move." He touched her left foot. "This one?"

She nodded.

He lifted it to his lap. "First, we have to get your boot

off." His fingers probed gently around her calf, her ankle, the edge of her boot. "It's starting to swell."

He paused, looking at her intently. "It's going to hurt, Beth. Whatever you do, though, please don't yell. I don't know how many guards there are out here."

"I won't make a sound."

Her face, covered with dark streaks of soot, was composed, no telltale glimmer of silver dampness on her cheeks.

"Here we go."

He pulled steadily, putting the force of his massive strength behind it. He watched her carefully; she was calm. Not even a faint grimace crossed her features. The boot resisted, finally coming free with a sharp jerk.

He stripped off her woolen sock, rotating her foot carefully. Her ankle was puffing up rapidly, already showing faint signs of discoloration.

"You've earned a few tears, you know. A few moans, even."

"I'm fine," she said, only a small tightness in her voice betraying what he knew must be throbbing pain.

Her eyes were dark and bleak, the flat color of a night sky void of stars. "What happened back at camp?" she asked.

"Attacked. Set on fire. Small group snuck in." He didn't seem overly concerned. Perhaps it hadn't been as bad as she'd thought.

"Was anyone hurt?"

"No. Minor burns, a little smoke. That's all."

Had he made the connection? It would be so obvious to anyone else: her presence, the way she was dressed, and the attack on the British. But his mind didn't seem to run along the lines of deception and plotting and intrigue. Perhaps he wasn't suspicious of her presence. She didn't want to say, or ask, anything that would cause him to think about it too carefully. Yet she had to know.

"Did they catch whoever did it?" she asked carefully.

He continued examining her ankle, his attention absorbed by her injury. Although she studied his expression, she couldn't detect even a flicker of surprise or suspicion.

"No. Too slow. Were long gone."

Relief, sweet and seductive, flooded through her. Although she knew it was far from over, for the moment she had to believe that everything was going to be all right after all. If there were problems later, she'd address them then. For now, she surrendered to the silky night and the gentleness of the hands caressing her ankle.

Still cradling her foot in his lap, he reached up and began to strip off his shirt.

"Oh my Lord, what are you doing?"

He'd evidently tumbled right out of bed when the alarm had been given in camp, for all he was wearing was a dark pair of breeches, boots, and a rough linen shirt hanging loosely around his hips. Nothing else. He mustn't even have had time to grab a cape. He had to be freezing, running around with so little covering. What she couldn't imagine was why he seemed to be planning to wear even less.

"Going to pack your ankle in snow," he said matter-of-factly. "Have to wrap it in something."

"Oh."

Her pain receded abruptly as her brain became occupied with much more interesting things. Had there ever been a man like him? Moonlight and shadow danced over all those lovely bumps and ridges of muscle; they swelled and flexed as he pressed snow around her ankle with surprising deftness.

She didn't have enough air. She gulped in a breath.

He must have heard her, for he lifted his head at the sound. "Hurt?"

"Uh, no, not much."

"Good." He wrapped his shirt tightly around the snow and tied it securely. "There."

"What are we going to do about him?" She gestured at the still figure of the young soldier.

Jon reached over and placed his fingers against the soldier's neck.

"He's fine. He'll be waking up soon." He'd be waking up, he'd stagger his way back to camp, he'd tell the captain about the woman he'd found, and the captain would question Beth. Lord, what a mess. If only he'd gotten there before the soldier had recognized her.

Well, there was little he could do about now. Perhaps later he could find a way around the problem.

"Can you get up?" he asked

"I can try."

He bent down, slipped his arm around her shoulders, and helped her to her feet. Balanced on one leg, she was unsteady and leaned against him for support.

"Put a little weight on it."

She tested it gingerly, and almost immediately it gave out beneath her. She would have gone down again if Jon hadn't caught her.

"I'm sorry. It's just not going to hold me. If I can lean on you, maybe I can hop back."

He scooped her up quickly, holding her against his chest, one arm beneath her knees, another around her back.

"Jon! What are you doing? I'm too heavy," she protested.

"Heavy?" he scoffed, bouncing her in his arms. "Thistledown."

"Don't be ridiculous. I'm certainly not light. I'll hurt you."

He gazed down at her, his eyes reflecting silver in the moonlight. "Not heavy. Just a nice armful."

"You can't possibly carry me all the way back."

He ignored her objection. "Where's your horse?"

He really was going to carry her. It was unexpectedly nice, to be held securely against that broad, beautiful chest. Tentatively, she slipped one arm around his back; the flesh was smooth and resilient against her palm, the muscles bulging intriguingly as he shifted her in his arms.

"You're going to get cold without a shirt on."

The soft, seductive curve of her hip pressed against his belly; the gentle swell of the side of her breast rested against his chest. He could feel her hand stroking his back, gliding along his spine, and he wondered if she was even aware she was doing it. He certainly was.

"I think the soldier dropped my cloak at the beginning of the path," she continued. "We could go back and look for it."

"I'm plenty warm, Beth."

His voice was strained, almost harsh, and she frowned at him in concern.

"I *am* too heavy for you."

"We're going, Beth. Going to tell me where, or should I guess?"

She pointed to the far side of the clearing. "Through there. There's a path. My horse is a mile or so back that way."

"A mile?" He was supposed to carry her for a mile? Hold her that whole time, and not jiggle his arm down a bit and test the delectable curve of her backside? Not curl his wrist just a smidgen and find the tempting swell of her breast?

Cold. He needed cold.

"It's too far, Jon. Put me down now."

He didn't bother to answer, just took off across the clearing with big, long strides that ate up the distance and betrayed no hint that he was unduly burdened by the woman he carried.

How lovely, she thought. Her ankle still throbbed, but the ache was distant, unimportant. Her senses were filled with so many much more interesting things to concentrate on.

The rhythm of Jon's strides lulled her, like floating down a lazy river, lending a quality of unreality to the night. Occasional flashes of moonlight filtered through the branches, painting his face with odd, figured shadows. The only sounds were those of his steady, deep breathing and his footsteps crunching over the snow, and even that sound was so much softer than she would have thought it would be.

Her world narrowed down to him. She let her head fall against the curve of his shoulder; it nestled there so naturally. His skin was smooth and warm against her cheek, and she couldn't resist finding out if it would feel the same to her hand.

She placed her hand on his chest. His heart pounded against her palm, a vibration that thrummed through her hand and tingled up her arm. She wanted to explore, to find out if the rest of him felt as wonderful, as alive.

She could move her hand just a little, couldn't she? That wouldn't be entirely brazen. Just an inch or so.

She let her fingers creep a trifle to the side. She poked him a bit, just a little, so he wouldn't notice.

There was no give to his flesh at all. Just solid, hard, beautifully rounded muscle. He was so strong; his arms didn't betray the slightest tremor as he carried her along, and she was hardly a light little slip of a thing.

Lord, he was in trouble. He could smell her as she snuggled in his arms, that sweet drift of lavender melding with the crisp scent of cold and snow. Springtime in the dead of winter.

Her hand was resting on his chest. Those long, elegant fingers were spread out over his flesh, a fantasy he'd hardly dared have now coming true. Those fingers that were so quick and agile, then slow and seductive when she drew the music out of her instrument, and he wondered if they'd be just as nimble on him.

Her palm glided over his chest in tiny increments, agonizingly slow. Was he jiggling her as he walked, or was she doing it on purpose? He didn't know, and right at this minute he didn't much care. Just as long as it didn't stop.

Her fingers were barely an inch above his nipple

now. What would it be like if she dropped her hand that last little space and touched him there? He felt his nipple pucker abruptly at the thought.

It was just an inch. That wasn't so much to ask, was it? He pondered ways to get her to move her hand that crucial inch. He could nudge her that way, somehow. Maybe with his chin. No, that wouldn't work. His neck wasn't long enough.

With his hand? No good. He'd have to put her down, and he certainly wasn't going to do that. His own hands were better occupied where they were.

The ground dropped abruptly and he took a hard step down, jarring them both. Her hand slipped down an inch.

He stopped walking. His chest was going in and out like one of the bellows in Adam's smithy, and he was breathing like a horse that had been ridden too hard.

Poor man. She'd been floating along, having a nice, interesting ride, and here Jon's arms must be nearly ready to fall off.

"Put me down, Jon."

"Forget it," he said fiercely. "Which way?"

Bennie glanced around. He'd stopped where the trail split in two. A massive, barren oak tree stood proudly in front of them.

"The left one."

He strode off down the left path.

"You can stop pretending I'm not too heavy for you."

He glared at her. It was such an uncharacteristic expression for him she assumed it only proved the agony he must be in.

When he didn't answer her, she sighed and dropped her head back to its resting place.

"You can stop pretending you're not cold, either," she mumbled.

"What makes you think I'm cold?"

Darn. She hadn't really meant for him to hear her. Before she was able to stop herself, she glanced briefly at where her hand still rested against his chest.

His mouth quirked. "Doesn't just happen when you're cold, you know," he told her.

Heat flooded her cheeks. "No?" she squeaked.

"Happens when you're too hot, too."

"It does not."

He stopped and stared at her. His face was in shadow, but his eyes glittered brilliantly. "Guess you haven't ever been warm enough, then."

His breath misted in the night air, curling like smoke from between his lips, his breath drifting close to her, and she had the oddest urge to lean forward and breath it in herself.

"Is it much farther?" he asked.

"Ah, no. Just around the next bend."

She must have been mistaken, for as he set off again, she was almost sure she heard him mutter, "Damn."

Her horse was right where she'd said, tethered to a tree right around the next curve. He set her gently down, keeping one arm around her as she balanced unsteadily on her uninjured leg.

"Nice horse," he said, surveying the huge bay stallion nickering in welcome.

"Yes, Puffy's a good boy, aren't you," she crooned. The horse stamped and snorted in response.

"Puffy?"

"Puffy," she said defensively. "Anything wrong with that?"

"Puffy," he repeated, his voice laced with barely hidden laughter. "Yeah. Such a tiny, fluffy little pony."

"All right." She laughed. "When I got him, my brothers kept proposing names like Avenger and Demon. I rebelled a little."

"Just a little."

She rubbed the horse's nose companionably. "Well, Puff, let's see if you can get me home, huh?"

Jon grabbed her by the waist and tossed her up on the horse before she had time even to begin to worry about how she was going to mount. Jon tied the reins and handed them to her.

"Well . . ." She smiled down at him weakly. "I guess I'll be going, then." Her smile softened. "I don't really know how to thank you. What you did—"

"Move forward."

"What?"

"Too far back on the horse. Move forward."

"But I've always sat here." He frowned at her. "Oh, all right." After everything he'd done for her tonight, she could do this little thing. She scooted forward a bit.

He hopped easily up behind her.

"Jon!"

"Don't think I'll let you go home alone, do you? Late. Too dark."

"Jon, really, I can—"

He reached around her, plucked the reins from her fingers, and started the horse down the trail.

Really, sometimes he was the most annoying man. If

he wanted to do something, he just went right ahead and did it, not acknowledging her protests—perfectly legitimate protests at that—at all.

Although she had to admit, everything he'd gone right ahead and done so far had been actually rather pleasant. She was suddenly glad that she, fearing her brothers would take off without her, hadn't taken the time to saddle her horse but had ridden bareback instead. This wouldn't have been nearly as comfortable otherwise.

He held the reins in his left hand, and the inside of his upper arm rested against the side of her—well, she knew his arm shouldn't be there, but he was just making sure she was getting home safely, after all. The solid length of his legs pressed along hers, and she could feel his muscles tighten as he guided the horse.

His other hand was on his thigh; the back of his fingers rubbed against her own thigh with the swaying gait of the horse. She was safely supported from all directions, comfortable and protected. And since he was behind her now, she didn't have to battle the temptation to keep her hands and eyes off his bare chest.

It was almost too bad they were only three miles from New Wexford. She wriggled, settling back more comfortably into her perch.

He groaned loudly, as if he were in intense pain. Perhaps he'd been hurt back in the chaos at the camp after all, and she hadn't even noticed. How insensitive of her.

"Are you all right, Jon?"

No! He clamped his molars together before the word escaped. Lord, this was getting worse all the time. After carrying her all that way, her body jiggling against him with every step, he'd figured riding behind her on a horse had to be easy.

He'd figured wrong. She nestled so easily between his thighs, fitting him as no other woman ever had. He was acutely aware that he now had a free hand, a hand that could so easily slip up, down, over, around—any of those places sounded mighty good to him.

"I'm fine," he ground out. Fine, as long as she didn't start wondering what the hard lump against her lower back was. "Just a little, um . . ." *Stiff,* his mind supplied. "Tired," he said quickly.

She yawned. "Me, too. It's been a long night."

He slipped his arm around her waist. He could do that. It was pretty safe.

"Comfortable?"

"Mm-hm."

He tightened his hold on her. "Go to sleep, Beth. I won't let you fall."

11

"*Beth?*" *he whispered,* her soft curls stirring against his lips as he spoke. She'd been asleep for at least ten minutes. He'd immediately known when her body relaxed in his arms. The knowledge that she trusted him enough to keep her safe while she slept was curiously appealing. Now they'd reached their destination, and he was reluctant to disturb her.

They were in front of the Dancing Eel. The windows were shuttered and the place was quiet, as if all the occupants were peacefully sleeping—or were absent entirely. He would have been content to stay there with her, warming her with his body, letting her rest, but he knew he had to get back to the fort. In the madness that had reigned when he left, no one would notice his absence, but he didn't know how much longer that would be the case. It was equally necessary he get to Ben Walters, the young soldier he'd clocked on the head, before Ben's tale spread too far through the ranks.

He could count on Captain Livingston not to act precipitously. The captain wouldn't give orders based merely on a woolly-headed youngster's dubious identification of a woman he'd seen only briefly in the dark. Unfortunately, Jon wasn't quite as sure of some of his fellow soldiers. Those who'd been injured, discomfited, or downright insulted by the attack might find it necessary to investigate rather vigorously. Jon intended to dissuade them.

"Beth. It's time to get up now, Beth," he said more urgently.

"Mmm?" She arched sleepily, a sinuous stretch of muscle and limbs, like an elegant cat awakening from its afternoon nap. He ground his teeth together; the slow sway of her body against his with the rhythm of the horse had left him perilously close to the edge of his control. Now, her unconscious sensuality was nearly more than he could take.

"We're home."

"Home?" Apparently suddenly aware of the way she was snuggled up against him and of his body pressed against hers, she straightened her spine abruptly, putting as much distance between them as their positions on the horse allowed.

"Oh. Well, then." She started to swing her leg forward over the neck of the horse.

"Stay there."

He slipped easily off the back of the horse and scooped her into his arms before she had a chance to protest.

"Really, Jon, I'm sure I can stumble my way into the tavern. It's only a few steps."

He tightened his arms around her. "Not going to start arguing this again, are you?"

"No, of course not. It's simply that I've asked far too much of you already tonight, and—"

"Didn't ask. Now quiet."

"But Jon—"

"Arguing," he said warningly.

She shut her mouth. She wasn't stupid. If the man was going to insist on carting her around some more, who was she to object? Especially when he did it so competently. Since this was as close to a romantic gesture as any man was ever likely to make to her, she might as well enjoy it fully.

If only the door was just a little bit farther away.

When he reached the Eel, Jon turned, set his upper back to the door, and gave a shove. The door gave easily, opening smoothly on its oiled leather hinges, and he stepped inside.

The tavern was illuminated by a single lantern. Four of her brothers were there, slumped around a table staring glumly into their tankards. Looking bedraggled, worn, and worried, they swung their heads toward the new arrivals.

"Bennie! Thank God, it's Bennie!" One of them— one of the younger ones, Jon thought, although they all rather looked the same—jumped to his feet, toppling his chair in the process.

"Calm down, Henry. I'm fine. I take it you all are safe, too?"

Henry dragged a hand through the loose curls of his hair, which looked startlingly blond against the blackness of his smudged face. "Well, of course we are.

But you—it took you so long to get back! Where have you been?"

"Yes, Elizabeth. It might be rather interesting to hear, at that." The man's voice was laced with amusement. It was Brendan; this brother, slender and dark, Jon remembered, if only because he was so different than the other Joneses.

"Bennie," Henry repeated, this time with shock instead of relief. It was as if at first he'd been too relieved to see her safe and sound to register that she was wrapped up in Jon's arms. Now he had, and the veins in his neck bulged. Clenching his fists, he started for Jon. "Just what are you doing with my sister!"

"Oh, my word." She was abruptly, embarrassingly conscious of what it must look like. She was being carried into the tavern in the arms of a man, a big, strong, wonderful-looking man who was wearing nothing but boots and a pair of loosely buttoned breeches. Heavens! What were her brothers going to make of this? If the Lord were merciful, perhaps the other four wouldn't find out.

She wiggled a bit, trying to get her feet safely on the ground. Jon tightened his hold and spared her a brief frown. It was futile. She wasn't going anywhere.

"She's hurt." Jon carried her over to the nearest table and gently settled her on a bench, propping her injured leg up on the plank. His fingers skimmed lightly over her ankle, tucking in the edges of his makeshift bandage. He lifted his gaze to hers. "How is it?"

"It doesn't hurt too much. I'm sure it will be fine in a few days." She was warmed by his care of her and the tender concern in his eyes. She was used to being treated as capable, practical, and self-sufficient. Accustomed to being the caretaker, the protector, she'd underestimated the appeal of being on the receiving end of someone else's concern.

"Stay off it," he ordered.

"Yes, sir, Lieutenant." She saluted him smartly.

"Now see here." Henry shouldered his way past Jon to hover at Bennie's side. "Where the hell have you been? What did he do to you? Did he hurt you? And you—" He turned to face Jon. "Just where the bloody hell is your shirt?"

"Ankle."

Henry wrinkled his forehead in confusion. "What?"

"Put my shirt around her ankle."

"Bennie."

She smiled up at Henry brightly, in no hurry to disabuse him of either his worry or bafflement. After all, she knew right well the whole night had been his idea in the first place.

"Bennie, you tell me what happened or I'm going to beat it out of the lump over there."

"Uh-huh. I'm sure you'll be just as successful at that as you were at the arm-wrestling," she said sweetly.

"Bennie," he repeated, frustration clear in his voice.

"If you must know, I was captured."

"Captured!"

"Well, nearly. A soldier caught up with me right before I reached the path. I suppose I'd spent too long at the camp, watching to make sure you all didn't do something foolish."

"Ben—" Henry began apologetically.

"Guess it runs in the family, doesn't it? I should

have left earlier. Anyway, I'd nearly managed to escape the soldier, when I stepped in something—I don't know, a hole, a burrow, whatever—and turned my ankle."

"How did you get away?"

"Jon . . ." She stopped, turning from her brother to regard Jon soberly, the full impact of what he had done for her finally registering.

He had hit someone. One of his own men. It would certainly be considered treason, injuring a British soldier in order to help a colonial. It had undoubtedly gone against everything he'd spent the last several years doing and may well have put him in jeopardy besides.

And he had done it for her.

"Jon—"

"It will be fine," he said, as if he could read her concern. "He didn't see me."

"Are you sure?"

"Yes."

"Would someone please finish telling me what happened?" Henry's patience was long past the breaking point.

"Jon saved me."

"What? How?"

"I'm here, and I'm safe, Henry. That's all you need to know."

"But he's a . . . " Brit. Redcoat. Lobsterback. The enemy. Henry whirled to gape at Jon.

"Friend," Jon suggested.

"But—"

"Friend," Bennie agreed. He was more than that, she knew, but for now that would have to do.

"Shouldn't you be getting back before someone discovers your absence?" Despite the quiet pitch of Brendan's voice, it carried an impact that none of the others' shouts ever had.

Jon bobbed his head. "Yes. Long walk."

"Walk!" Bennie protested. "You're not walking all the way back. Take a horse."

"Can't take your horse."

"Exactly. He can't," Brendan agreed. "Besides, it's not that long a walk."

Jon glanced at Brendan. It was a quick look, not enough to raise suspicion, but after years of practice, Jon could gather a good deal of information with a minimal glance.

Brendan was calm, almost unnaturally so; he seemed completely unsurprised by the events of the evening. Jon wondered if that quiet demeanor was ever disturbed by anything, and if anyone ever really knew what went on beneath it. Perhaps with a bit of time and a little probing, Jon could catch a glimpse.

"You could come with me. Bring the horse back here after," Jon suggested.

Brendan smiled slightly, but his eyes were dark with calculating intelligence. This one, Jon knew, was going to be the toughest one to fool.

Brendan shook his head slowly. "No. If you just turn the horse loose and give him a slap, he'll find his way back. The question is, will you?"

"Brendan!" Bennie was shocked by his barb. Except for the occasional jab at members of his family, he rarely bothered to insult anyone and generally seemed to prefer to keep his opinions to himself.

Jon, however, seemed unpreturbed. "Oh, sure. Fine. It's bright out, and I remember the road. Been on it many times." Turning his back on Brendan and the others, Jon bent over to check her bandage once more. His big form filled her vision, blocking her view of her brothers and of the rest of the room. His fingers wandered above the wrapping, slowly rubbing her leg. After spending so much of the night pressed against his body, she was somewhat disconcerted to find that this small touch had a nearly identical effect on her.

He gently massaged the bottom of her calf, and the warmth of his fingers spread easily through her breeches. Her whole leg began to feel loose and floaty. She sighed. Pain? What pain?

"I'll send your shirt back," she said.

His smile was dazzling, amusement sparkling in his eyes. "Keep it. Yours now."

"What the hell happened!"

Sergeant Hitchcock winced as his captain's bellow resounded through the now quiet camp. The fact that the captain had hollered was an indication of just how upset he was; the captain always prided himself on his patrician, perfectly modulated tones. He might be in the army, but he was still Quality, and he wouldn't lower himself to such an unbecoming thing as shouting.

Unless, of course, his camp had nearly been destroyed by a raid.

Hitchcock warmed his fingers over a small campfire. It was still damn cold out, and he was unlikely to get warmer anytime soon. The worst of the blaze was finally out, but there was a lot more work to do before the night was over. Even then, there was hardly going to be a nice warm tent for him to crawl into.

He sighed; it was no use moaning over something that couldn't be helped. If there was one thing he'd learned in nearly thirty years in the army, it was to forget about the things that were done and past and get on with the job at hand.

"It must have been a small band, Cap'n. Any more, an' the sentries woulda noticed 'em."

"They should have 'noticed' them anyway."

"Yes."

"Why didn't they?"

"Gettin' soft, I guess, Cap'n. These younger ones ain't never been in a war, ain't never been in danger. Don't know how easy it is to die when you ain't payin' attention."

"It's your job to teach them, Sergeant."

Hitchcock straightened proudly. He'd never been one to flinch from his duty, or from his mistakes. "Yes, Cap'n."

"Double the watch, and the sentries' time on it. Perhaps they'll learn to be more alert."

"Yes, sir."

Livingston strolled slowly around the fire. Although they were out in the open, they were as good as alone; no one came within twenty yards of them. At least the men had enough sense to stay out of the captain's way just now.

"It's better than they deserve," Captain Livingston said. "I should discipline them more strictly." He watched the smoke curl up from the smoldering remains of fully half the camp's tents. He'd told his men, time and again, not to trust the deceptive quiet of the region. Colonials were unpredictable and reckless, given to violence and more than willing to put themselves in danger to inflict it. It was difficult for a calm, reasoned man to predict their actions.

He'd known from experience that sooner or later something was going to happen. He'd warned his troops, and they'd not had the wit to listen to him. Well, now their punishment would be the cold, the crowding, and the work necessary to make the fort comfortably habitable. That should prove enough incentive for them never to be so careless again.

"How much damage?"

"Not as much as it appears." Hitchcock ticked off his report on his fingers. "The horses were scattered, but all but a couple found their way back as soon as the fire died down. I expect the rest'll show up tomorrow. We lost lots of the soft goods—tents, blankets, an' stuff—but we can move into the fort immediately. It's not ready, but it's close enough. Ain't gonna be comfortable, but better'n a lotta places I've been stationed.

"They got into the food stores. Dumped a lot, poisoned a bunch more. Luckily, there weren't all that much there anyway. We're expectin' a new shipment next week. Worst of the lot was losin' so much powder. Nothin' for it 'cept order some new, an' who knows when that'll get here? We'll be short until then. No problem, unless war breaks out in the next few weeks."

Livingston reached up and clamped his hat more firmly on his head. He'd lost his wigs, damn it, and the hats just didn't fit quite right without a wig. Still, he didn't feel worthy of command without some sort of headwear. "Nothing to be done, then, but write a report for headquarters. If you would assemble a list of necessities, I will get it off first thing tomorrow."

"Yes, sir." Hitchcock paused, glancing around quickly to assure himself no one was near. "What do you think they'll do, Cap'n?"

"They'd better not do anything but send up new supplies. After all, they're the ones who are supposed to have such a bloody good source. Well, it wasn't good enough to tell us we were going to be assaulted in our sleep, was it?"

"No." It sounded reasonable enough. But, in Hitchcock's experience, command wasn't always entirely reasonable.

"Now then." Livingston turned to face his sergeant, and Hitchcock was struck by the uncharacteristic fire in his captain's eyes. 'Cor, the captain actually looked right pissed. In Hitchcock's mind, he had a right to be, but the sergeant really hadn't expected the captain to bother with getting mad.

"Any idea who it was, Hitchcock?"

"Well." The sergeant hesitated, unwilling to present anything he couldn't substantiate. Besides, he rather liked the girl.

"Out with it, man."

"One of the guards thought he saw somethin', before he got knocked over the head."

"What was it?"

"Who, Cap'n. He saw that girl."

"Girl?"

"The one from the tavern. The one you—"

"Ah, yes. The Jones girl. Did he see her do something?"

"No, sir. Jes' watchin', he said. He weren't none too clear—still a little knotty-headed, if you ask me."

Livingston picked up a long stick and poked at the fire. "Sergeant, what is your opinion about the action we should take in response to this unwarranted attack?"

"Well, sir, I guess ya got a coupla choices. Y'can go detain the girl, question her, try and find out what she knows. If'n we're forceful enough, mebbe she'll tell us somethin'. Then again, mebbe she doesn't know nothin'. She coulda jes' been meetin' a lover."

He sneaked a peek at Livingston, wondering if he'd react to that. The captain had sure seemed interested in the girl when he'd first met her. Would he use this opportunity to put a little pressure on her? In the sergeant's mind, it was unlikely it was going to do much good. These colonials stuck together, especially if they were family. And after all, you couldn't torture a woman, especially when you had no real evidence. Nope, they weren't going to get anything useful from her.

The captain continued calmly prodding the fire. "What else?"

"We could do nothin', for the time bein', anyway. Jes' keep our eyes and ears open, an' if anybody tries anythin' again, make sure we're waitin' for 'em this time."

"Yes." Livingston dropped his stick and straightened, brushing his hands together. "Then again, perhaps we have one more option."

"What's that?"

Livingston nodded grimly. "We know where their guns are." Determination flattened his voice.

The captain had a plan, Hitchcock realized. "But how—"

"Captain! Sergeant!" The eager voice interrupted them.

"Jon," the captain said. Lieutenant Leighton lumbered toward them, tripping several times in the dark. "Where have you been? I don't believe I've seen you in all the excitement."

"Was here when it started. Thought I saw something in the woods—"

"You saw something?" Livingston asked sharply.

"Thought so. Followed it."

"Who was it?"

"Don't know." Jon shrugged. "Disappeared in the woods. Spirit, maybe."

"A spirit," the captain repeated in disbelief.

Jon nodded. "Got lost then."

"You got lost." Livingston rubbed his temples, a habit he often adopted when he was trying to talk to Leighton.

"Yes. Couldn't find my way back for a long time."

The captain sighed. "I want you to think very carefully, Lieutenant. Did you see anything else beside your . . . spirit? One of the men—who was it, Hitchcock?"

"Walters."

"Walters was assaulted in the woods, and perhaps you saw something that could help us find his attacker."

"Walters? Was he hurt?"

"Not seriously."

Jon allowed himself to feel a brief moment of relief. He hadn't wanted to hurt the boy, not really, but if that was what it had taken to protect Beth, he would have done it. Not without a bit of regret, but that wouldn't have stopped him. He'd long ago learned to get past such trivialities as relief and regret.

"Didn't see anything. Must have been the spirit too."

"The spirit again. Jon, why don't you go ahead and go back to your—no, I don't think you have a tent anymore. Wherever you plan to spend the night."

"Maybe I'll go see Walters. See if spirit hurt him bad."

"Ah, he's in the medical tent, Jon. It wasn't damaged," Hitchcock said, ushering Jon in the proper direction. The sooner he was out of the captain's sight, the better.

"Why don't you do that, Jon," Livingston said tiredly. "You go tell ghost stories for a while."

"Yes, sir. I have a good story."

"I'm quite certain that you do."

Jon's big form faded into the darkness as he stumbled away.

The traitor had known about the little raid, of course. Had those boys really thought they could keep it a secret? Nothing that happened in New Wexford was ever a secret to him. All one had to do was watch, listen, and pay attention, and one could find out everything that was happening in this small village.

His contacts had no idea he'd known something he'd chosen not to tell them. What good would it have done? It wasn't important—boys just playing at war. And he hadn't gotten into this to put anyone he knew in danger; he was trying to stop the conflict from getting any worse. If he and his contacts didn't agree on the best way to do that, well, he'd always been able to make his own decisions. He wasn't planning on changing now.

Oh, they'd be upset if they found out he'd been withholding information. But what could they do? There was really no way they could ever know, and even if they did, they needed what he could give them.

So, this little bit of information, he'd kept to himself.

The sky was just beginning to show the faint paling that signified the approaching dawn as Jon ducked into the hospital tent. He made sure he conked his head on the frame as he entered, shaking the tent violently and earning himself a sharp rebuke.

"Hey, watch it! I don't want this coming down around our ears."

"Sorry." Jon spared an apologetic glance for the jowly medic.

Ben Walters was sprawled on a cot in one corner of the tent, holding a sack of ice to his temple. His nightshirt was tucked securely around him. His face was shadowed in the weak lantern light, and he looked a little sickly but not seriously hurt.

"Ben." Jon knelt beside the cot. "Heard you got hurt."

The young man opened one eye. "Somebody coshed me on the head."

"Who?"

"Dunno."

"Oh." So Ben hadn't seen him after all. Jon hadn't thought so, but he hadn't been entirely sure; there'd been a chance. He'd told Beth he was certain only because she would worry too much if she thought he might have been discovered. "Any ideas?"

"Some friend of that woman, most likely."

"Woman?"

"One of those Joneses, from town. Must o' been her and her brothers who set the fire."

"Saw them?"

"No. Only her."

"Oh. Tell Captain?"

"Yes, I told the cap'n. Didn't seem like he was goin' t'do much about it, though."

"Maybe not sure enough?" Jon suggested helpfully.

"I'm sure. Cap'n's just got kinda a weak spine, if you ask me. Well, they're not goin' t'get away with it, if I can help it."

"What you going to do?"

"Tell some o' my buddies. We'll make sure they're sorry for ever coming near our camp."

"Mm." Jon tapped his fingers on the rough blanket spread over the cot. "Tell 'em you caught a spy, huh?"

"Well." Ben winced and readjusted the sack of ice he held against his head. "Maybe she wasn't a spy, actually. But I caught her."

"Tell your friends you let girl get away, huh?"

"Maybe." Ben pondered that for a minute. "Didn't let her get away, exactly. I was attacked."

"Anybody see? Maybe girl hit you."

"She did not," he protested. "No girl could knock me out, not even that giant one."

"Yeah. Friends will understand."

"'Course they will."

"Sure. Cap'n won't mind you questionin' people without orders, either. Your head, after all."

"Yeah. He'd understand, wouldn't he?"

"Sure."

Ben frowned. "Maybe I'll just let it go for now, after all."

"Why? Got to punish girl who hurt you."

"Can't go around botherin' girls. She didn't do nothin' to me."

"Ah, a gentleman."

Ben closed his eyes. "I am, ain't I?"

Jon hastily left the tent before Ben could talk himself back into taking his revenge. More tired than he could recall being, Jon crawled into a nearby supply wagon, hoping to snatch a couple of hours of sleep before someone found him and set him to work hauling away the wreckage from the fire.

It had all worked, thank God. Beth was home, safe and sound, and it didn't look likely that she was going to be questioned anytime soon. It had been touch and go for a while, but he'd managed to pull it off, and one of the longest nights of his life was over.

And, damn it, it hadn't occurred to him until now that it was all completely unnecessary. If he'd been in his right mind, he would have stayed out of the whole thing. It wasn't any business of his; it had no bearing on the job he had to do. His task was simply to gather information, certainly not to endanger his cover by playing knight-errant to a colonial woman. He'd never, ever— not once since he'd begun this charade—let emotion get in the way of his job. He'd watched events unfold around him with a detached disinterest that was absolutely crucial to his effectiveness; he'd never felt even the slightest urge to help those who were unwittingly caught in the mess. Certainly, he'd never come close to acting on their behalf.

This time, he'd never once thought of doing anything else.

12

Jon heard the Jones house before he reached it. Children screamed, squawked, yelled, laughed, and generally sounded like they were either having a right good time or killing each other.

The next generation of Jones progeny certainly knew how to entertain each other. He picked his way through the children who tumbled and chased each other in the clearing in front of the house. They didn't seem at all concerned that a British officer was in their midst. They were too busy stuffing snow into each others' faces.

There couldn't be more than a half a dozen of them or so, although it certainly seemed like more as small arms and legs flailed in the snow and pint-size bodies rolled over his feet. Boys, every one of them, blond and healthy and red-cheeked. The single exception was a familiar carrot-topped little girl who was efficiently pelting one of the bigger boys with snowballs. Red curls bobbed from beneath her thick knit cap. She hurled another chunk with deadly accuracy. This time, however, the boy managed to duck quickly, and the snowball landed harmlessly at Jon's feet.

"Jon!" Her eyes shone as she scrambled over to him. "What are you doing here?"

He crouched down to bring himself to eye level. "Sarah. How is your kitten?"

"Oh, she's fine. Getting fat, though. Mama says I feed her too much milk." She smiled shyly. "Would you like to go see her?"

Jon glanced around. Somehow, in the time he'd been speaking to Sarah, the boys had managed to surround him, all six of them, with their stubborn little chins thrust out and thin arms crossed over skinny chests he was sure would someday take on the proportions of their fathers'. If they weren't outright hostile, they weren't exactly friendly, and he wondered what they thought they could do to him.

"Runs in the family, doesn't it?" he muttered under his breath.

"What?"

"Sorry, Sarah. Can't go see the kitty now. I came to—"

"See Bennie," she broke in decisively.

"How did you know?"

"Like her, don't you?" Sarah was bright and shiny as a new copper, and the knowing gleam in her eye made her seem much older than she was.

"I have to give her something," he told her.

"A present?"

"Well, yes."

"A Christmas present?" she asked happily.

"Yes."

She slipped her hand into his. "I'll take you to her."

"Thank you." They started for the door of the Jones house.

"Grandpa won't be happy to see you, you know."

"He won't?"

"No." She skipped along beside him, peeking up through her lashes. "He won't yell at you too much if I'm there, though."

She was right.

Inside the house, both the parlor to his left and the dining room to his right were filled with massive table-boards. Pristine white board clothes sprawled across the surfaces, topped with polished silver sugar pots, salt cellars, and creamy tapers waiting to be lit.

There were no women in sight; Jon assumed they were all back in the kitchen. But the parlor was filled with big blond men, who stopped sipping at their mugs and jumped to their feet the instant they spied Jon.

Not again, he nearly groaned aloud. He plastered on a grin.

"Hello. Happy Christmas to you."

"What are you doing here?" Cad thundered.

"Umm, visit Beth."

"Visit Beth? You most certainly will not. Isn't it enough you Brits must stick your noses into our business and our communities? You will not come into my home. You will not—"

"Uh, Dad?" George hesitated. "Maybe you should let him stay."

"What?" Cad rounded on his son. "Why would I be doing a thing like that?"

"Well, we sort of . . . owe him."

"What?" A deep flush crept up Cad's neck. "What are you owing a redcoat?"

"He, um, rescued Bennie," George said reluctantly.

"Rescued her! From what?"

"Well, the night she hurt her ankle."

"He was there that night? You fools! How could you be so careless," Cad bellowed. "You all could have—"

"Father," Brendan put in calmly. "Perhaps you should wait to discuss this until we no longer have visitors. It is a family matter, after all." He glanced meaningfully at Jon.

"Come on." Cad grabbed Jon by the arm and hustled him across the entryway into the dining room. "You can wait here." Cad disappeared into the back room and quickly reappeared carrying a huge black jack. "Here. Drink this." He shoved the large leather mug brimming with ale into Jon's hand. "I'll come and get you when we're ready." He turned on his heel and stomped back to the parlor to get the full story from his sons.

Jon was leaning against a wall and downing the last swallow of his drink when he heard Cad's words as he came to fetch him.

"I can't believe I'm gonna sit down to my Christmas dinner with a damn, stupid lobsterback," Cad was saying.

Cad entered, stopped, and glared at Jon. "You're staying for dinner," he ordered and stalked back to the parlor, leaving Jon to follow.

Jon didn't see Beth until they were ready to eat. He perched on a chair in the corner of the parlor and drank the fabulous beer they kept pressing on him. It was the best stuff he'd ever tasted. He figured owning a tavern had some decided advantages, if one could get supplies like this.

He felt oddly comfortable here. The furniture was huge, sturdy, built for big, heavy men. Nobody seemed to pay much attention to him, except when he knocked over a footstool. They argued among themselves over crops and guns and brewing and twice nearly came to blows. He had the definite impression they enjoyed it.

What an odd family. His task today would take only a moment or two, and though he'd planned on using the rest of the time to get a better handle on the Joneses, he found himself equally intrigued by what kind of a family had formed Beth.

It was a loving family, no doubt, but it was also demanding; members were expected to hold their own, to know their place and fill it. There seemed to be little room for individuality; for minor disagreements that got blown into entertaining arguments, yes, but not substantial philosophical differences.

He was somewhat surprised when they were called to dinner to find himself seated on a form next to Beth. She was wearing that green dress again, the one that made him think of deep forest glades and hidden treasures.

"Hello, Jon," she said softly, and he wondered why his name sounded different from her than when anyone else said it. "I'm sorry. They told me you were here, but Mother needed me in the kitchen. I couldn't get away until now."

"Don't worry."

"They were nice to you?" she asked anxiously.

He grinned. "Nice. Good beer."

She laughed lightly. "Yes, Da always has good beer." Her gaze dropped to the table. "I'm glad you're here."

"Me too. How's your ankle?"

Her face heated as she remembered him carrying her through the forest, caring for her, holding her against his bare chest. She could hardly believe he was here now, big and gorgeous beside her, and yet it seemed so strange to sit beside him and not touch him. "Better. I stayed off it for a couple of days, and it only bothers me now if I come down too hard on it." She looked up at him; his pale, sleepy blue eyes were filled with undisguised concern. "If it's fine, it's only because you took such good care of me. Thank you, Jon."

"My pleasure.

At the head of the table-board, Cad loudly thumped down his tankard. "Let's eat!"

Food covered every inch of the table board: huge pewter chargers of roast pork and duck, chicken pie, and stewed carp; puddings, breads, jellies, and a half dozen kinds of vegetables, including a whole stewed pumpkin. Enough food, it seemed to Jon, to feed half of his company, and he knew the same feast was spread out on the other two tables, where the rest of the family was seated.

Jon ate little and talked less, as he watched the Joneses manage to not only carry on a spirited conversation but with businesslike efficiency pack away every scrap of the food. Beth, although quieter than most of her family, delicately and with an unconscious, sensual enjoyment that nearly drove him crazy, ate as much as any of her brothers, with the exception of Adam. Adam ate more than Jon had ever seen any one person eat and still be able to walk, but it didn't seem to slow him down in the least, and no one so much as blinked at what was clearly a common occurrence.

The meal was followed by an equally large collection of creams, fools, trifles, floating islands, and syllabubs. Beth piled Jon's trencher with some of each, then gave herself full servings.

She took a careful bite of dried apple tart, closing her eyes in delight. Her tongue darted out to lick a crumb at the corner of her mouth, and Jon had to fight the urge to lean over and taste it himself. Why had he never known that watching someone eat could be so arousing? The expressions that moved across her face were ones he'd very much wished he'd caused himself. And the way her mouth moved—slow, easy, luscious, closing delicately around a spoon or gracefully nibbling a cake—Lord, it was so easy to imagine her doing that to him.

"Elizabeth," her mother said sharply. "You know a lady should eat only lightly."

Bennie put down her spoon. "I'm sorry, Mother." She'd known her mother had been keeping a careful eye on her; although she'd seemed to accept Cad's explanation of Jon's presence—he'd said they were trying to get information out of the man—Mary had been suspiciously attentive to Jon the entire meal. Bennie expected she'd hear about her "unsuitable friendship" later.

"Oh, Mary, let her eat," Cad said. "She's a healthy girl. She needs to keep up her strength."

"Good manners are good manners, Cad."

He shrugged. "So, Jon. How are things at the fort?"

Jon shoveled in a spoonful of trifle. "Pretty good. Moved into fort after fire. Lots of work, though."

Pushing his food around on his trencher, Cad asked casually, "Any idea what happened? Know who caused the fire?"

"No." Jon wiped a blob of cream off his chin. "Everybody too confused. Some thought they saw one thing, some another."

"So Captain Livingston isn't going to investigate any more?"

"Dunno. Just heard something about ammunition, that's all."

Cad's spoon clattered to the table and he leaned forward. "Ammunition?"

Jon nodded and tried to talk around a huge mouthful of sweets. "Ammunition, schoolhouse, guns, don't know. I think hide it better next time, maybe."

"Maybe." Cad sat back. "Maybe," he repeated thoughtfully.

Jon polished off the rest of his dessert. He wadded up his linen napkin, dropped it in the voider, and stood up.

"Good dinner, ma'am. Have to go now."

"I'll walk with you to the stables," Bennie offered.

"Elizabeth," Mary said warningly.

"I'll be right back, Mother." She scurried away for her wrap before her mother could object. Jon stopped to say good-bye to Sarah on his way out.

They walked quietly across the tavern yard to the stables. It was a bitterly cold day. The wind blew drifts of snow around their feet like shifting fog. Bennie huddled deeper into the new cloak she'd made to replace the one she'd lost the night of the raid.

The stable was warm, smelling of horses and hay. Grateful for its snugness, she lowered her hood as Jon followed her in. The wind whistled sharply outside; inside, it was quiet and dark.

"Brr. It's getting cold out there."

"Cold. Yes." He shifted awkwardly from foot to foot.

"Thank you for coming to check on me."

"Yes. Glad you're better."

He didn't seem to know quite what do with himself. He shuffled around, one hand clenched, looking first at her, then at the ceiling and back again at her.

"Well," she said. "You'd better get back before it gets colder."

"Yes," He made no move to ready his horse to leave. Finally he thrust out his fist. "Here."

"What?"

"For you."

"Me?" She cupped her hands beneath his, and he opened his fist. Beads poured out, continuous strands of sleek, glossy ivory that pooled in her palms. "What's this?"

"Present. For you."

A present. He'd bought her a present. Dumbfounded, she just stood there, the necklace in her hands, and stared up at him.

"Here." He lifted the strands and slipped them over her head. His movements were careful, with the rare, infinite gentleness that seemed as much a part of him as his overwhelming size and strength.

The beads were silky and warm against her skin, gliding easily if she moved her neck. "Why, they're warm."

"Well, uh, I wore them," he confessed.

"What?"

"Wouldn't lose them." He gestured to his own neck. "I wore them here."

"Oh."

She couldn't seem to move. Slowly, he reached to her, lifting the bottom of the necklace and slipping it underneath her neckline. His eyes were very blue, and she felt the beads slide down, pouring over the upper curves of her breasts and settling in the cleft between them.

"Like this," he whispered.

She swayed. She felt it, but she couldn't help herself. She was caught by the image of the same lustrous, milky spheres that rested against her skin glowing against the smooth bronze of his. He'd touched them, now they touched her.

Oh, God, he was in trouble. He'd done his duty. There was nothing else to learn here today. And yet he was still here, alone with her in this stable with the wind howling outside and her family only steps away. Instead of leaving, he was dreaming of beads resting under the soft green cloth of her bodice, gliding against her skin. Thinking of tracing them, sliding his fingers along the path they marked.

"They are a thank-you," he said with difficulty.

"For what? I'm the one who owes you."

"For the music."

The wind that screamed outside the stable became the lonesome wail of a violin. A violin that, he was sure, would sound painfully more alone after he was gone.

And he would be gone—he knew it, he felt it. He

regretted it, but it was enough to give him the strength to go without touching her. If only he could stay, stay longer than his orders, stay longer than his job. Longer than the month or two or three that it would take for everything to fall apart.

Longer than his life allowed.

"I have to go." He knew she thought he meant for the evening, and even that made the light in her shining brown eyes dim. He wondered how she'd look when he said good-bye for good, and he prayed he'd at least have the chance to when the time came.

"I suppose you must."

"Can I come back for the music?"

She smiled, the soft, enticing curve of her lips contrasting intriguingly with the sharp planes of her features. "Yes. For the music."

13

Two weeks after Christmas, the British marched into New Wexford.

Adam Jr., scouting for rabbits out by Skinny Creek, was the first to see them coming. He ran all the way back to town and shouted the news as he burst into his father's smithy.

Adam shoved the red-hot rod of iron he'd been shaping into a door latch into a tub of cool water. By the time the water stopped hissing, he was at the Dancing Eel, rousting out every man in the place who was old enough to shoot and young enough to walk.

The church bells pealed throughout town; loud, clanging, discordant bongs that didn't celebrate the worship of the Father but instead warned the townspeople, calling them to arms.

It worked. Before the British reached the common it was filled with colonists. They didn't have clean, matching uniforms. Their formations were raggedy and undisciplined, and some took up odd positions behind fences and trees and inside houses, poking their muskets through windows.

The day was white, one of those pure days of winter when sun glanced so brightly off clean snow it hurts the eyes. Captain Livingston called his men to an abrupt halt in the center of the square, facing the line of colonists that stretched from the schoolhouse to the church.

The captain, thin, tall, and very much in command, strolled slowly over to face Cadwallader Jones. His relaxed gait was in complete contrast to the alert readiness of his troops. Livingston's elaborate wig was powdered nearly as white as the snow, making his pale complexion look almost bleached. His red coat stood out vividly, a brutal slash of scarlet like a fresh puddle of blood on new snow.

He braced his feet apart and fisted his hands behind his back, rocking comfortably on his heels. "So, Captain Jones, we meet again."

Cad frowned. "I am captain no longer."

"Oh?" Livingston raised one eyebrow. "Lost the post, did you? What a shame."

"I retired. Voluntarily."

"Of course." The captain clucked understandingly. "Such a pity. However, I'm sure your wisdom will be invaluable. Thankfully, I have many years before I have outlived my usefulness."

Cad ground his molars together. "My son is captain now."

"My, so I'll be dealing with another one of you Joneses, then? How fortunate. Amazing how these children of yours keep popping up, isn't it?"

Cad studied the officer carefully. What had he meant by that? Cad had assumed that if his children were going to be arrested for the attack on the British camp, it would have happened by now. This captain was turning out to be entirely unpredictable.

"We are a large family," Cad said cautiously.

"Yes, indeed. Well, which one's, ah, in command now?"

"I am." Adam stepped forward, his huge shoulders squared.

"Of course. I should have known. You're the A one, right? Adam, I believe it is."

"You may address me as Captain Jones."

Livingston nodded in acknowledgment. "As you wish, Captain."

"What are you doing here?" Adam demanded.

"What are we doing here?" Livingston looked offended. "Why, this is my district. Have to keep an eye out, you know."

"With your full company?"

"There is that. Don't suppose you'd believe that I simply felt we needed a drill today, eh?"

"No." Adam crossed his massive arms over his chest.

"Well, then." Livingston gave a deep sigh. "I suppose you've heard we had a . . . bit of an inconvenience a few weeks ago."

Behind Adam, Henry and Isaac exchanged quick grins.

"I may have heard something about that," Adam allowed.

"I have no intention of letting it go unanswered."

"You're here to arrest someone? Because if you are, I

will not permit it without absolute proof." Adam gave him a look that usually caused men to clear out of his way like mice before a predatory screech owl.

But Livingston merely waved his hand carelessly. "No, no. Not at all. I'll not waste my time digging around to find someone who's essentially unimportant."

"What, then?"

"I will not allow illegal munitions to be stockpiled in my district."

"Illegal munitions?" Adam shook his head. "I have no knowledge of such a thing."

"Well, that's certainly a surprise, isn't it. Nevertheless, we will be searching the town."

"We will not permit you to search private property."

"Such a shame. I have instructed my men to be careful, of course. But we *will* search."

"You will not."

Tapping his fingers against his thigh, Livingston stared at Adam for a moment. "So that's the way it is to be, then?"

"Yes."

The captain gave a slight smile. "Very well." He stepped back and nodded to his sergeant.

"Up!" Sergeant Hitchcock called.

In one motion, every British soldier lifted his musket to his shoulder. The guns gleamed black and malevolent in the bright sunshine, their gaping maws seeming to aim directly at the chests of the colonists.

"Ready!"

"Wait!" Adam shouted as the men behind him scrambled to ready their own weapons. "You cannot mean to fight over searching our homes. It's foolishness."

"It is duty," Livingston said calmly.

"We could all die."

"We all *will* die, Jones. I'd just as soon it not be today, but that's up to you."

"These are our homes, man!" Adam said desperately. "We have a right to defend our homes!"

"Defense is unnecessary. We simply wish to look around. We are not attacking—yet."

Adam could feel the sweat begin to trickle down his back—and felt the fear and tension of his fellow colonists. He had to decide. He knew his men would fight, well and hard, if called upon. But there had been so little time to prepare, so little time to decide what was right. He wanted time! Time to think, time to talk to the other men, time to know what was right.

There was none.

"All right then. You can try to search, we'll stop you, and God help us all," he said quietly.

He felt a reassuring hand on his shoulder. His father. "Where do you want to search?" Cad asked.

"Does this matter?" Livingston asked.

"Perhaps if you left our homes alone, we could allow you to search . . . someplace. One place," Cad said slowly.

The colonists began to breathe again. There might be a chance after all.

"This is possible." Livingston nodded thoughtfully. "If I may choose freely, I might be satisfied."

Cad exchanged a quick glance with his son. "Choose," he ordered.

"All right." Very deliberately, Livingston turned in a circle, appearing to study the buildings that perched around the perimeter of the common.

Although the muskets aimed at their chests rendered it impossible to relax completely, the militia allowed themselves small smiles. There was no possibility Livingston would pick the correct place.

"The church."

The colonists' smiles vanished abruptly. How could he know? They had spend two full days just after Christmas transferring the stockpile from the school, where it had been for months, to the church, because Cad had claimed that the British might know about the cache. And here the redcoats were homing in on the supposedly safe, sacred hiding place.

"You can't!" Henry burst out, rushing to stand beside Adam. "You cannot defile the church!"

"Easy, Henry," Adam said soothingly.

"But they can't!"

"Well?" Captain Livingston cocked his head. "Shall we go? Or do you prefer to fight it out, after all?"

"They can't," Henry protested again.

Cadwallader stepped forward.

"Let them search."

The entire company of British soldiers, along with an equal number of colonists permitted to "keep an eye on them," barely fit into the First Congregational Church of New Wexford. The troops swarmed through the place, their red coats bright and almost cheerful against the mellow wood and whitewashed walls.

It was a simple church, small, snug, and properly respectful. The single stained glass window was the town's pride and joy. Sunlight streamed through the colored panes, casting brilliant blue, green, and red streaks across the burnished floor.

It was a good place to worship. A good place to follow God.

And now it was blasphemed by the presence of men and guns and hatred.

Cad whispered a silent prayer of thanks that his father-in-law was no longer alive to see what had invaded his church.

They were efficient, he'd give them that. The soldiers swarmed throughout the old church like ants on a drop of honey, poking under benches and behind the lectern, climbing up to check the bell tower. They were quiet, perhaps subdued by the setting, and not at all destructive, as Cad had expected searching soldiers to be. Instead, they were businesslike, restrained, and frighteningly determined.

It didn't take long. There weren't that many places to check.

"Cap'n?" A young soldier knelt on the floor, running his fingers along the edges of the floorboards.

"Yes?" Livingston and the sergeant strode over quickly.

"I've found something."

Livingston's triumphant gaze found Cad. "Let's get it up, then."

Sergeant Hitchcock rounded up tools and set three men to work. Within seconds they had pried up one of the boards.

"Cap'n, it's hollow under here. A large space, too, far as I can tell. Can't see the bottom."

"What's in there? Let's go men, get it up." Captain

Livingston peered into the dark hole that was rapidly being torn in the smooth polished floor of the church. A beam of sunlight spilled through a high window, shining directly into the black cavern like a ray from heaven lighting a follower's grave.

Hitchcock sat back on his heels. "It's empty, Cap'n."

"What?" Dropping to his knees, Livingston stuck his head down into the hole, nearly losing his wig in the process. "It can't be empty."

"It is."

The captain clapped a hand on his head to hold his wig in place and squatted back on his heels. "Empty," he repeated in disbelief.

Adam whistled as he strolled over to the stunned men. He poked at the pile of boards with his toe. "Finished here, gentleman? I'd like to get this place back in shape before the Sunday meeting."

Empty. The traitor still couldn't believe it. He'd had an opportunity to get rid of so many guns, so much ammunition—and it had failed.

His careful self-control had nearly given way when the floorboards of the church had been pried up and there'd been nothing—*nothing*—but dust and a couple of dead mice in the secret hold.

It had taken some careful work to get the information about the movement of the ammunition from the schoolhouse to the church to the proper people. Time had been short, and he'd had to take more risks than he cared to. But it would have been worth it, to take away so much potential death.

And then to find that Cad and Adam had spent every night the last week moving every ball and bit of powder to another location. They had done it all themselves, just the two of them. Adam had admitted it to the meeting of very relieved and startled men that had quickly gathered at the Dancing Eel after the British had marched back out of town.

But they wouldn't disclose *why* they had felt it necessary to shift the stores, nor had they been willing to disclose where the ammunition was stockpiled now.

They'd come into some disagreement over that one. The traitor had tried to argue that it was necessary for everyone to know the location. Otherwise, how were they to get to it when it was needed? Also, it was dangerous to have but two people who knew where it was; if something happened to those two, how would the others find it?

But he'd been overruled. The fact that the British had homed in on the church proved once and for all that they'd known too much, too quickly, to risk making the location widely known.

The colonists were worried. It made them nervous, and it made them careful.

His task had just gotten a great deal more difficult.

The colonies waited.

Four thousand British soldiers were stationed in Boston, straining the town of sixteen thousand at its seams. The soldiers drank and danced, drilled and patrolled, and waited.

Throughout New England, handpicked members of

the militia were organized into companies of fifty that were charged with being ready at a moment's notice. Old men and young boys were formed into alarm companies to defend their towns if the militia were elsewhere. They drank and farmed, kissed their women, drilled, and waited.

The Provincial Congress met illegally at Concord. They argued and wrote papers and waited.

In New Wexford, Bennie waited too. She waited for her life to become safe and comfortable again. She waited for her brothers to stop keeping their muskets oiled and close at hand, and for them to stop jumping every time a horse and rider clattered through town. Waited for her father to stop shaking his head and mumbling under his breath, for Henry to stop practicing shooting every day and Isaac to stop trying to badger their mother into letting him join the militia.

And she waited for Jon. Waited for those rare days he came to sit in the stables and listen to her play, those days where politics and war and freedom talk were very far away. Those days there was only the music and a handsome man who sat quietly and listened, and then smiled at her like she was a miracle sent just for him. Waited—in vain—for him to touch her again, and herself to stop wanting him to. For although he was simple, he was pure and good and strong—and he smiled at her like no one ever had.

The colonies waited.

Spring was nearly here.

And the storm was coming.

*   *   *

"Da!" Henry tumbled into the taproom. "They're marching!"

Cad, swabbing the floor after the last customer had—finally—gone home, glanced over his shoulder. "What?"

"The British! A messenger just came into town. They're marching on Concord."

The mop clattered to the floor. Trickles of dirty water spilled across the clean boards.

"Let's go."

Fog drifted through the common. The mist was insubstantial, quavering, a gray scarcely lighter than the bleak sky. Men hunched their shoulders against the April chill and murmured together in voices that were subdued, seemingly muted by the absorbing fog.

It was nearly dawn.

Women were there, too; women who buttoned their men's coats securely, ran their hands over beloved faces, and handed out sacks of food and pouches of musket balls. Women saying good-bye to their men.

"Cadwallader," Mary Jones said, her voice quiet and stern. "You're too old to go gallivanting around the country."

She smoothed his plain gray coat over his chest. He lifted her hand and enfolded it in his.

"Mary, my Mary. You know it's important for all the colonists to support each other. We have no other strength but our unity."

"There are others. Why must *you* go?"

"It will take all of us, Mary. You know that."

"Yes." She tilted back her neat dark head to look into the face of her husband towering over her. "But you mustn't let Isaac go, Cad. He's too young."

"Ma!" Isaac protested, clutching his musket.

"Hush, Isaac." Cad smiled gently down at his wife. The intensely tender expression on his face was one that any person who had never seen him with Mary would have sworn that grizzled face could never wear. "It's not a battle, Mary. We are simply showing support. We will help out where—and if—we can."

"But Cad—"

"We'll be back in a day or two. Three at most. I will keep him safe for you, Mary."

She closed her eyes and leaned against her husband. "Keep them all safe, Cad. All of them."

Bennie stood in the midst of her family and wondered why they all seemed so far away. The blotting presence of the fog blurred details and muffled sounds. It was as if her brothers and father were there but she couldn't quite grasp the whole of their forms, their voices.

The damp cold soaked through her clothes and cape in no time, chilling her flesh to the bone. Her stomach was clenched and empty, every muscle in her body tight, screaming to do something, fix something, do *anything*.

But there was nothing she could do. She could only stand, shivering and praying, in the bleak predawn, and let them go.

14

Bennie rubbed hard at the stubborn spot on the side of the simple pewter tankard, then swished it through a tub of warm water and inspected it again. The splotch was still there. Resolutely, she scraped at it with her thumbnail. If all she could do was make sure the Dancing Eel was kept the way her father expected it to be, she would do it.

Her father and brothers had been gone nearly two days. In town there'd been spotty reports of firing near Lexington, but little else. Her mother had spent the time drifting about, pale and composed, cooking abundant meals that were far too large for just the two of them. Bennie's sisters-in-law also wandered through, tense and uncertain, but they seemed somehow comforted just by being in the Jones' house.

Bennie had simply shouldered all her father's work, as well as George, Henry, and Isaac's. There were horses to be taken care of, supplies to be counted, and a tavern to be kept open. If it left her little time to sleep, what did it matter? Sleep was a solace that would have been all but denied her anyway, for she could only fall asleep when she was so exhausted her mind was too weary to worry about what might be happening on the road from Boston to Concord.

The only work she couldn't manage was Brendan's. Neither she—nor anyone else in New Wexford—had ever learned the printer's trade, so she'd had to go ahead and close up his shop. She avoided passing it whenever possible, for the sign reading *Closed*, neatly lettered in Brendan's precise hand, was a too visible reminder of a world spun out of her control.

"You shouldn't frown so, my Bennie. 'Tis only a cup. I wouldn't want you to wrinkle your lovely face over it."

Her hands stilled and she looked up at the bulky form filling the door.

"Da!" The tankard plopped into the basin, sending up a small geyser of dingy water, and Bennie hurled herself at her father's chest. "Da! You're safe! We heard rumors of fighting, but no one knew anything for certain."

"I'm fine." She felt his arms, sure and strong as always, close around her, and she sagged against him.

"Bennie, let me sit down. I'm feeling my age a bit more than usual."

"Sorry." She ushered him to the nearest bench. He sank onto it gratefully.

Cad's hair hung in wild, bedraggled silver tangles around his face. His clothes were dirty, rumpled, and torn, and one of his socks was missing. Bennie had never thought of her father as an old man; he'd always seemed too vital, too unconquerable, to be old. But now the creases in his weathered face seemed deeper; his shoulders drooped.

And she was, suddenly, very, very afraid.

"Da?" she asked tentatively. "Should I go get Mother? We should let her know you are back."

He shook his head. "I just came from the house, Bennie. She knows I'm home. Isaac's there too."

"And the rest of the boys?"

He looked up at her, his hazel eyes dulled with weariness. "They're fine, Bennie. You needn't worry about them." He sighed deeply. "But they're not coming home. At least not yet."

She groped behind her for the back of a chair and managed to find her way to the seat.

"Where are they?"

"Cambridge. At least, they're on their way there."

"What happened, Da?"

Leaning forward, Cad braced his elbows on his knees. "It started at Lexington, Bennie. It was over by the time we got there, so I don't really know how it all began." He looked down at his hands, curled into the massive fists that had served him so well all his life. "They killed ten minutemen."

"No," she gasped, and wrapped her arms around her middle.

"We made them sorry." He pounded one fist into his palm. "We stuck together, Ben! There were colonists all over. I don't even know where they all came from, lining the road from Concord all the way back to Boston. Behind fences, up in trees, hanging out of windows. Those damn redcoats were fired on every step of the return march."

"Oh my God," she whispered, but Cad went on as if he hadn't heard her.

"They must have seen it, Ben, seen that we could stick together, that we weren't afraid to fight. That we could stand up to their bullying and their brass and their damn royal rights! They lost men all the way as they scurried back to their holes."

She lifted her shaking hand to her mouth. "How many?"

"I don't know. Two, perhaps three hundred injured. I don't know how many were wounded seriously but the army was hurt badly—we hurt their pride, and their damn smug confidence, and their men! They'll never assume we're nothing but annoying little flies again."

"And next time, they'll be ready for you," she mumbled under her breath.

"What'd you say, Ben?"

"How many of ours were hurt, Da? What was the price?"

"Less than a third of what they lost, I'm sure of it."

She took a deep breath. "And us? You're certain they're safe?"

"Not a scratch. You should know the Joneses better than that. We took up behind a stone wall, and those lobsterbacks couldn't even come close to us." He snorted. "Not one of 'em can shoot even half so well as Isaac, much less the rest of us."

"Why didn't they all come home, then?"

"I told you, they went to Cambridge. The British are stuck back in Boston." He nodded firmly. "We aim to make sure they stay there."

"And you?" she asked quietly, hoping she'd kept the

fear out of her voice. If there was one thing Cadwallader Jones had no patience for, it was fear, especially in one of his children. "You and Isaac? Are you going too?"

"No." He frowned. "Not yet. Your mother and I are discussing it. She pointed out that the home guard needs someone to command it, just in case the British do decide to come this way, and, for now, I'm it—at least until I can get a competent replacement to take over from me. And she thinks your brother is too young, and I suppose she's right. He'll be sixteen soon enough, though, and there's no way we can keep him here after that."

"Oh." Bennie rose from her chair, hoping her legs would support her. It had happened. She'd known it was a possibility, had lain in her bed many nights trying to convince herself it wasn't going to happen, and yet had never understood the horrible reality of it.

They'd fired at her brothers, her father. Balls had probably whizzed over their heads and taken chinks out of the stone that protected them. Likely, the shots had come terribly close to ripping into all too vulnerable flesh.

She was a Jones, a member of a family that was famed throughout the district for being too big, too hard, and too tough to ever be hurt or beaten. But all those muscles were terribly fragile protection against ball and mortar.

And she knew they'd soon be fired on again.

Her knees wobbled; she could so easily crumple to the floor. She'd broken down in front of her father only one time, when she'd been a child and a boy at school had shoved her in the boy's privy, telling her that was obviously where she belonged; no real girl ever looked like she did. After she'd escaped, she'd run home to the Eel, only to have her father tell her that if she ever again cried in front of others, he'd lock her in the privy himself.

Being a Jones meant being strong. It meant never leaning on anyone else.

But for once, she wanted to be weak, just for a little while. It would be so easy. She wanted to be able to cry on somebody's shoulder, wanted to let someone else take care of her problems for a bit—wanted someone to at least *want* to take care of them. Or, perhaps, take on a bit of the burden, the worry. Maybe it wouldn't be so awful if it were shared.

Instead, she would deal with this the way a Jones always dealt with fear, or sadness, or hurt.

Alone.

She squared her shoulders and forced a smile. "I'm glad you're home, Da. I took care of everything for you."

He smiled proudly. "I knew you would, Bennie. We'll take care of everything while the boys are gone, won't we?"

"Of course. Now, I think I'll go practice while I can. It doesn't seem as if I'll have much time for a little while."

She made it through the door before she couldn't hold the smile any longer.

It was going to storm.

Jon glanced up at the sky. It was as dark as tarnished silver, and if he hadn't known it was late afternoon, he would have thought it was nearly nightfall. The wild, bitter wind whipped his hair across his face, and he shoved the strands out of his eyes.

The air smelled like rain, cool and metallic. He strode along rapidly, hoping to reach shelter before the storm unleashed its fury, even as he knew his destination was pure folly.

Any way he looked at it, he'd botched this job but good. He still hadn't caught whoever was passing information through New Wexford, and though he had a few ideas, well, ideas were cheap. Proving them was what was hard.

About all he'd managed to do here was get himself turned inside out by a woman whose eyes brimmed with suppressed life and whose music sounded answering chords in his soul. The first rule of espionage was to stay detached and objective, and he'd been doing that nearly his entire life without even trying. It came as naturally to him as the ability to walk through the woods without making a sound.

Yet for weeks his objectivity had been blown away as easily as a dandelion puff in the wind. Blown away by a woman whose loyalty mocked his, and whose own formidable control he longed to shatter too. Even knowing all that, even knowing it was wrong, useless, and downright stupid, he found himself walking down this trail one more time.

The stables were built of stone that matched the ground. The sky was even darker now, an unnatural lack of light that barely allowed him to make out the closed stable doors.

One window, high under the peak of the thatched roof, was open, and it was through this window the music came. Plaintive, low, streaming, it was nearly indistinguishable from the wailing of the wind. It raised bumps along the back of his neck and a rough ache in his chest.

Silently he opened the stable door and slipped inside, shutting it tightly behind him. The absence of the breath-stealing wind was abrupt, and he filled his lungs with the warm, steaming heat of horses.

In here, the call of the wind was muted, but the lure of the music was stronger. It sang of fear and loneliness, and all those dark corners that lurked in every human, corners most tried to deny. This music embraced them, gave them life and breath, and its power resonated in deep, shadowy corners of his own soul.

He could see nothing in the darkness. He brushed his hand along the wall, searching for the ladder that led to the loft. The stone was cool and rough under his palm.

It didn't take him long to find the ladder. One of his gifts was a memory that allowed him to recall places and things with absolute precision. The wood was smooth, polished from use, and he quickly climbed up to the source of the music. To Beth.

He didn't know how long he stood there, wrapped in the darkness and the song. He only knew that when the music became so beautiful it hurt, he had to get closer to her.

A board creaked under his foot, a sign of his carelessness. The music stopped.

"Who's there?"

"Just me."

Silence.

"Talk to me, Beth, so I can find you."

"I'm here, Jon." Her voice was a whisper, a seductive thread twining through the darkness. He scuffled through the hay to her. She was just under the window, a small opening that admitted no light, gave only a glimpse of the bruised, roiling sky.

He dropped down beside her onto a blanket that was thick and scratchy. The hay rustled and cracked with each motion.

"What are you doing here?" she asked.

"Hush." He didn't want to tell her yet; he just wanted to be there, to sense her closeness through the dark, to feel her warmth reach out to him, to catch beguiling drifts of lavender mingling with the hay.

"Play for me, Beth."

She was quiet for such a long time he was afraid she would say no.

"All right," she said finally.

It didn't really matter why he was there, she found; it was enough that he was. Before she had played of loneliness; now she played of fear, of mud and blood and anger, of a freedom that could only be bought at unbearable cost. Before she hadn't allowed herself to think of bodies lying, bleeding and abandoned in the road, of the acrid smell of powder and the sickening cry of pain.

And when she was done, she knew why he had come.

"You're leaving, aren't you?"

She heard him take a breath and slowly let it out through his teeth. "Yes."

"Where are you going?"

"Sent to Boston. Company will rejoin regiment."

She groped for his hand; when she found it, he laced his fingers with hers. His skin was callused, his touch infinitely tender, and she wondered if the same hands which could touch her so gently could pick up a rifle and fire on her countrymen, maybe even on her family.

"When?"

He slowly rubbed the back of her hand with his thumb.

"Tomorrow."

Her fingers tightened. "It's so soon."

"Yes."

Outside, the wind whirled in a world that was violent and frightening; inside, there was only the dark and a hand to hold.

"Teach me to play, Beth."

His voice seemed disembodied, a rumble that surrounded her and shimmered down her back. She nodded, knowing that, even if he couldn't see her, he would know her assent.

She found her way to him by touch alone and knelt behind him, her breasts nestled against his back, and braced the violin against his shoulder. She allowed her cheek to rest against the fine silk of his hair.

This time, she made no attempt to instruct him. His hands rested on hers, so lightly they didn't impede her playing. He merely followed the motion of her fingers, feeling them call the music from the instrument.

The loneliness was back. And this time, when she conjured up images of bodies lying in the mud, the body she saw was his, with dark, spreading stains spoiling the brilliant crimson of his coat. His rich, shiny hair was caked with mud and tangled around his pale face, his eyelids forever closed over those extraordinary pale eyes. All around him, the army marched, their steps sure and steady, undeterred by the body that lay in their path.

A flash of brilliant, piercing light; the sharp, ear-shattering crack of a musket fired at close range.

Bennie shrieked, dropped the violin, and collapsed against Jon's back, trembling. Her heart was pounding so hard she was sure he could feel it.

He turned and lifted her, settling her in his lap, and tucked her head firmly against his neck.

"Shh," he said. "Shh. It's only the storm."

The sky unleashed. She heard sheets of rain pouring down outside, pounding against the roof, running down the side of the stable. She burrowed closer to Jon, his big warm frame a bulwark against her fears.

He was stroking her back; up, down, easy, slow, the sensuous caresses turning her shivers of fear into shivers of something else entirely. She needed to touch him, needed to know that, at least for now, he was still safe and whole and alive. Her hands crept to his back, testing the solid muscle underneath the wool.

It was torture. She was kneading his back with a cautious thoroughness that made him want to beg her to explore other regions. With her head nestled underneath his chin, he could feel her breath flowing over his neck, a warm caress of air that was somehow more exciting than skin.

It was temptation. His neck was hot and smooth against her cheek, and warm, male musk filled her nostrils. And she knew she had only to reach out her tongue to taste the skin so tantalizingly close.

It was the smallest stroke; moist, textured tongue in

the hollow of his neck. He groaned, knowing that even that bare touch was more than he could take.

And suddenly he was tired of it all. Tired of spending so much time pretending to be someone else that he no longer had any idea who he really was. Tired of watching every word, expression, and action. Tired of living so close to the edge of death.

Tired of being utterly alone.

She hadn't thought; she had only known that dreaming of the taste of his skin was so much better than being tortured by images of death. She hadn't even realized she'd acted on her fantasy until she heard him moan.

She moved her mouth up, blindly searching, tracing her lips along the sharp line of his stubble-shadowed jaw. She knew so well what his features looked like in the bright, clean light of day. How much more interesting to discover what they felt like in the deep, intense blackness.

He grabbed her upper arms and held her away, his fingers biting painfully into her flesh.

"Beth," he said, his voice a harsh rumble. "You can't."

She went rigid, sure she had frightened him again. "Why not?"

"You don't know . . ."

She waited, holding her breath, for him to leave her again.

He didn't. "There are . . . some things . . . that I remember well," he said.

Lightning flashed a brief, brilliant instant that gave her a glimpse of his face, white in the brightness, his features bold and stunning. He was looking down at her with an almost violent yearning that so closely mirrored her own. Thunder rolled, a deep, baritone tremor that rippled down her spine.

"Good," she whispered.

"Beth—"

"I don't care anymore, Jon. I don't want to think anymore. I *can't* think anymore. I just want to feel."

He kissed her then, his mouth coming down with a hard force that pushed aside everything but the feel of his lips. Gone was the gentleness of every other time he had touched her, swept away by a greedy desperation that left no room for anything else.

He wasn't kind. He wound his hand in her hair to hold her head still, and the instant she leaned against him his tongue swept inside her mouth, demanding she give him everything. And she did.

When his tongue skated along the edge of her teeth, she prodded back. When he plundered the deepest recesses of her mouth, she forced her way into the darkest, sweetest corners of his. And when he swept his tongue along the inside of her lower lip, she sucked on it, hard, bringing it deeper.

Dimly, she knew this was wrong, knew she was using sensation, passion—*him*—to block out the fear. But she couldn't stop; the hot enchantment beat in her blood and lured her on, a seduction she didn't know how to deny.

He knew it was wrong, unforgivable, to take this from her when there were so many lies between them. But the pounding reality of war was too close, looming over his shoulder and waiting for the opportunity to strike. If he was to die, struck down in a barrage of gunpowder and blood on some nameless field, he needed it to be with her image burning clearly in his mind.

The scent of lavender and the warmth of her lips clouded his thoughts. He released her hair; she needed no encouragement to stay. He smoothed his hands down her back, exploring the clothing he couldn't see.

A blouse, buttoned down the back. Easy. The buttons popped open as easily as ripe summer berries dropping off a vine. He stopped only to squeeze her shoulders before shoving the clothes—her blouse, her chemise, one movement—down to her waist.

He drew back, intending to find somehow, some way, to slow down. Nature defeated him.

Lightning again. A flash of rich, round, pale breasts, and the dark, tight disks of her nipples. He bent his head to the unbearable sweetness of her breast in his mouth.

Nothing in her life had prepared her for this, for the intense wave of heat as he sucked at her nipple. For the greed, as she was helpless to do anything but clutch at his head and hold him closer.

She felt tight, ready to burst from her skin as his tongue rasped across the tip of her breast. She grabbed his jaw, urging him to the other side. A tug, a stroke, sent her mindlessly tumbling into pleasure.

He stopped, gasping, to stamp kisses along the curve of her neck, the slope of her shoulder. His hands were fervent and insistent, sweeping over her back and arms, curving around her waist.

Her lack of sight intensified her other senses. She was overwhelmed by the pounding of the rain and the harsh sigh of his breathing. She smelled spring and him, felt every ridge on his fingertips as he skimmed them over her nipple.

Lord, he thought, how long had it been? How long since he'd been enchanted by the silkiness of the skin over a woman's collarbone, been driven to madness by the taste of tender flesh inside an elbow?

Never.

She twisted in his arms, grabbing fistfuls of his shirt, tugging it from his breeches. And then she was touching him, kneading the muscles at the side of his waist, sliding her palms over his chest.

Heaven? Hell? Who cared?

He'd spent a lifetime being in control. Every time he'd touched a woman, he'd been cautious, careful, always conscious that his strength could easily bruise such fragile creatures. Yet here was a woman who met his strength, encouraged it, answered it with her own, and it destroyed every shred of control he'd ever owned.

The feel of his hands on the bare flesh of her thighs caused her to shiver. The brush of his chest against the sensitive tips of her breasts made heat flash through her body, quick and sharp as the lightning. He lifted her, turned her, planting her knees on either side of his thighs, then settled her against him. Her skirts were pushed up around her hips. The heavy pressure of him against her most intimate flesh made her shake.

There was nothing of romance here, sweet, gentle kisses in a meadow flushed with spring. This was a storm, unleashed in all its fury. Desperation, turbulence, greed, a violent need that bordered on insanity.

Rocking against him, she pressed herself closer, and

felt his answering shudder. He had one arm wrapped around her back, and he slid his other hand between them, down, down, and touched her.

He was deft, sure, wildly exciting. She felt heavy and hot. His fingers glided easily against her, touching some spot that sent a spasm of pure pleasure shooting through her. She sucked in her breath, and his fingers stilled.

"I . . . hurt you?"

"No!"

"Open wider," he urged, his gentle hands on her thighs telling her what he meant. She shifted, rising slightly to her knees, and did as he bade. He slipped one finger into her. The alien sensation made her clench her muscles.

"Easy," he whispered. "Easy."

The familiar rumble of his voice soothed her even as the smooth glide of his fingers sent her reeling. Music pulsed through her head. This was not the fluid, melodic notes of a single violin; this was an orchestra in full crescendo, clashing, building, a music that surrounded and swelled, lifted and filled. And all she could do was drop her head to his shoulder and hang on.

She barely managed to keep hold of a thread of reality, a thread that made her want to see if she could make him tremble too. The buttons on his breeches nearly defeated her clumsy fingers, but finally she freed him. Her hands were filled with heat, a thick, hard column spread with smooth, satiny skin, as solid and strong as the rest of him. Entranced, she closed her hand around it.

It was too much for him. He grasped her by the hips and lifted her. Her skirts billowed around his thighs. He probed lightly, but slipped away. The slide of her moist softness against him was incredible, but it wasn't what he wanted.

"Help me," he coaxed hoarsely.

Guided only by instinct, she took a firmer grip to hold him steady, and pushed herself down on his hardness. A bare inch of the tip filled her, stretching her tender flesh. Was it ecstasy? Agony? No matter; she only knew she wanted this, needed this, with an intensity that left no room for fear.

A low growl, and he surged up into her, entering her with a swiftness that stole her breath. A sharp pain, a spreading burn, and she collapsed against him.

He wouldn't allow it. Taking her face in his hands, he lifted it, kissing her with a slow thoroughness that soon had the warmth spreading through her veins again. He was all things forbidden, fire and thunder and sin.

She leaned back a bit, settling herself more fully, testing. Lightning flashed again, and she saw his face. Hard, perfect, all shadows and angles and strength. His eyes were burning, pale, holding their own bolt of lightning.

Experimentally, he flexed his hips once, and was rewarded with her gasp. Oh, Lord, he thought, if I have to die, let it be now.

It was too fast. He felt the steady, insistent throb of pleasure, and knew it would be too fast. There wouldn't be time to bring her with him.

He put his hand down between them, touching the place where his body joined hers, and felt himself glide even deeper into her. He stroked her, insistent, demanding.

"Sing, Beth," he urged. "Sing."

And she sang, flying to a place where the music had colors and textures and taste. "Come with me," she said.

He felt her shudder, felt her body close even more tightly around him. He thrust deeply, once, twice. Then the music took him too.

15

He lay on his back on the woolen blanket, Beth sprawled across him. Her cheek rested against his chest; her wild curls tickled his nose. Idly, he stroked her back, his fingers drifting over her fine, soft skin.

As much as he knew what he'd just done was wrong, he couldn't bring himself to regret it. Not yet. Not when her legs still tangled with his and her breasts were crushed against him. Not when the scent of lavender and lovemaking clung to his nostrils. Most of all, not when he was still joined with her.

"Have to go," he said reluctantly.

"I know." She pressed a kiss on him just above his right nipple.

An incredible languor had seeped through her. Moving didn't sound terribly appealing. Returning to reality sounded even worse. When he slipped out of the part of her that still tingled from their pleasure, she groaned in protest.

"Have to go," he repeated.

Reality came whether she wanted it to or not. She felt him move beside her, pushing himself to his feet. He was leaving—really leaving, not just returning to the fort. He was going away to shoot at people, and have them shoot back.

And she didn't know if she would ever see him again.

It shouldn't be so easy to get dressed again. All she had to do was slip her blouse back up over her shoulders and pull her skirts back down over her hips. All he had to do was button up his breeches and tuck in his shirt.

It made it seem as if it all had been so furtive, a quick, stolen fumbling in the dark. It had been nothing like that; it had been the most brilliantly beautiful thing that had ever happened to her.

Because it had made her *feel* beautiful. She'd felt like the woman she knew she wasn't: feminine, seductive, her emotions close to the surface. If nothing else, she was glad that just once in her life she'd felt like that.

"I can't fasten my buttons. Could you help me?"

He groped for her in the darkness, his hands grazing private places until he found the buttons he sought. He moved slowly, reluctant to close her blouse, the final symbol that the interlude was over. He couldn't resist trailing his lips up her spine as he slipped the smooth disks through their holes.

"Sorry, Beth. Some . . . gone. Tore off."

"That's all right."

He turned her around, wrapped his arms around her, settled her close, and held her. Just held her. Outside, the thunder and lightning had ended, leaving the steady rain that poured rhythmically from the dark skies.

"Didn't want to hurt you, Beth."

"You didn't hurt me." She clutched at his back, holding him closer. "You could never hurt me."

Finally, they could hold back the world no longer. He let her go and rose, stepping carefully to the corner where the ladder descended back to reality. She followed.

"Don't have to come. Can stay here," he said when she started down after him.

"I'll see you out."

Horses snuffled quietly in their stalls, oblivious to the storm without and the tension vibrating between the two people who passed. Jon slid open the door to the stable. Wind gusted through it, bringing the rain, cold, and darkness.

He paused, laying his palm along her cheek. Softly, tenderly, with the gentleness she was accustomed to from him. His thumb traced her cheekbone, delicate strokes that made her feel cherished.

Already, she missed the thunder.

"Too dark. Wish I could see you," he said huskily.

"Me, too." Unable to resist, she reached up, letting her fingertips see for her. Skimming her fingers over his face, she followed the familiar contours, memorizing the sharp angle of his jaw, the strong slope of his nose. Slowly, always slowly, she traced the firm curve of his mouth.

He opened his mouth and brought her fingers inside. Dark, warm, all too seductive. His tongue curled around her thumb, and she couldn't help remembering how that tongue felt gliding over her nipple and skating over her skin. Lord help her, she wanted it again.

"Sorry, Beth. For everything. Sorry."

Her throat threatened to close. "Don't be."

"Still sorry." He lowered his head to kiss her. His lips clung to hers, sweetly, delicately, a supple connection, his breath sighing into her mouth.

"Never forget you, Beth."

"I'll never forget you, either."

He brushed her mouth with his once more, then turned quickly and walked away. Bennie took a step, out into the rain and the wind. Her eyes strained, hoping for just one final glimpse of that large form walking away from her in the storm. There was only blackness and rain.

She blinked her eyes to clear them. It didn't matter; there was nothing to see. The rain had already soaked through her clothes, plastering them to her. The wind was strong, freezing, seeming to go through her skin as easily as it did the sodden cloth. She welcomed the cold. At least she could feel something. She needed to feel *something*.

She reached up, wiping the rain from her cheeks, and wondered how the moisture on her face had gotten so warm.

The days dragged by.

Cad prowled the Eel, his impatience to be with his sons clearly evident. He grabbed on to the tiniest scrap of news as if it were a precious jewel, but there was little news of any worth to be had. He drilled the alarm company, a ragged but dedicated group of old men and young boys, until their feet blistered in their boots.

Mary's serene countenance never seemed to waver, but she rarely smiled, going through the motions each day with calm detachment. She no longer seemed to notice Bennie's activities and only came to full awareness whenever Isaac proposed she should allow him to go off to join the army too. Then, suddenly alert, she brooked no disagreement. Isaac was staying in New Wexford.

Isaac mumbled and shuffled through his chores. His work was slapdash, and he complained loudly to all within earshot that a healthy young man should be fighting beside his fellow countrymen, not slopping the floors of a tavern. He knew precisely how many days there were to his sixteenth birthday—173.

Bennie worked. She scrubbed windows and counted barrels, polished silver and served drinks to the customers who passed through New Wexford on their way to Cambridge and the army. She took over Henry's responsibilities, caring for the horses and the stables. Inventory and stocking were George's duties, and she capably handled them, too.

There was little she could do to keep Brendan's press working, but at least one day a week she opened up the shop, aired it out, and scrubbed it from rafters to floor. While she was there, she managed to sell a few patent medicines and writing implements.

Whatever time she wasn't working she spent with her nephews and niece. Their mothers were overwhelmed, trying to keep the households going by themselves at the same time they worried over their husbands. The younger children couldn't understand why their fathers were gone and their mothers were always busy, and they welcomed the extra attention from their Aunt Bennie.

The older children understood far too well. It pained her to see their usually exuberant, playful personalities so subdued. Adam junior tried too hard to take on the responsibilities of the man he was too young to be. Sarah spent hours holding her cat close, sitting and watching spring push its way upon the land. All Bennie could do for either of them was hold them and hope she was there if they ever needed her.

No matter how much Bennie crammed into her daytime hours, it didn't seem to be enough. She tried to exhaust her body and her mind, hoping she'd fall asleep the instant she hit her mattress. It didn't work; she dreamed anyway, dark, disjointed dreams edged with smoke and blood. The only thing she remembered when she awoke, struggling for breath, was the image of Jon and her brothers smiling at each other—then lifting their muskets and blowing each other's chests away.

For the first time, she wasn't able to turn to her music; she couldn't seem to make it come out right. After years of it being her own private melody, she'd experienced the delight of sharing it, and she couldn't go back to the loneliness. The music seemed empty, echoing, as hollow as the yawning cavern in her chest where her heart should have been.

Brendan was back.

He strolled into the Dancing Eel the first day of June, leaned against the wall, and called for an ale.

"Brendan!" Bennie didn't bother to excuse herself

to the two old farmers she'd been waiting on. She fairly flew across the room and threw her arms around him.

"I can't believe you're really home," she said, her voice muffled against his shoulder. She gave him one more squeeze and stepped back. "What are you doing here?"

Before he had a chance to answer she hollered for her youngest brother. "Isaac! Dad went down to the mill to pick up some extra oats. Run and tell him to come home. Brendan's back! Stop at Adam's house and get Mother, too."

Isaac strode across the room, moving his lanky frame with the first eagerness Bennie had seen from him since he returned from Lexington. He grabbed his brother's hand and pumped it.

"Brendan. Can't wait to hear all about it. Shot many redcoats yet, huh?"

Brendan straightened. "No." He gave Isaac an even look. "You've grown again."

"Yeah."

"I think you've finally topped me, too."

"You think so?" Isaac's fine blond hair drifted around his bony face. "Don't know what good it'll do me. Mother still treats me like a child."

"Isaac, weren't you going to let Mother and Father know Brendan's here?" Bennie reminded him.

"Oh, right." He rushed out the door.

"What was that all about?"

Bennie sighed. "He wants to join you all in the army. Mother said no."

"I'm surprised Father didn't tell him he could go anyway."

"You know he never goes against Mother." She shoved her hands through her pocket slits and into the pockets that were tied around her waist with a tape. "He can leave when he's sixteen. Maybe it'll be all over by then."

"I wouldn't count on it, Elizabeth."

His quiet conviction was more than she could handle right then. She had to believe it was all going to be over soon, quickly, cleanly, and neatly.

"Let me look at you." She stepped back and surveyed him. His dark hair was shiny, neatly fastened in a bagwig at the nape of his neck. His clothes, though rough, were well mended and meticulously clean. He was thinner, having lost a little flesh he could ill afford to lose. But it was his eyes, as always, that stopped her. They were dark, shadowed, holding secrets and depths that even she couldn't read. In fact, she was sure she was the only one who saw the shadows at all.

She poked his stomach. "You haven't been eating enough."

"The food is not exactly appetizing."

"Then get some that is."

His eyes darkened. "It isn't that easy, Elizabeth."

She touched his arm gently. "Is it so terrible, then?"

"Not now." He shook his head. "I'll just have to tell it all over again when Father gets here. Later, Elizabeth, all right?"

"Well, then." She dropped the subject. Brendan was the one Jones she could never pry information out of, no matter how much she prodded. "I guess Mother and I will just have to feed you up. We'll have you back to normal in no time."

"I can't stay."

"What?"

"I'm going back tomorrow. I've only got two days' leave, and it takes a good part of it just getting here and back. I had to come and check on of all you, though. I promised the others I'll give them a full report when I return."

Cadwallader burst through the door of the Dancing Eel.

"There you are, my boy." He clapped Brendan on the back. "Isaac told me you were here. He went to get your mother. Might take a bit, though. Think she already headed out to Carter's place."

He grabbed a chair and practically tossed it at Brendan. "Sit, sit. A soldier should take a break when he can; never know when you'll get another one, do you? Bennie, go get us something to drink, will you?"

Brendan took the chair. His mouth quirked as Cad heaved his massive bulk onto a nearby bench.

"You don't change much, do you, Father?"

"Why should I change?" He clapped his hand on his knee. "Now then, tell me all about it. Seen much action?"

Brendan shook his head slightly. "Could we wait until Elizabeth gets back? I'm a bit thirsty."

"Of course, of course," Cad said, smiling genially. His boy was a soldier. It was a damn sight better than being a bookworm and a printer. Soldiering was man's work, a proper occupation for a Jones, and Cad could afford to be a bit patient now.

Bennie returned, clasping two huge tankards of beer in one hand, a smaller mug of cider in the other. She handed the tankards to the men and settled herself close to Brendan's side, wrapping both hands around the chilled mug of cider.

"Now then." Cad had been patient long enough. "The action?"

"There's no action to see. I'm sure you've heard that here."

"I know, I know," Cad said impatiently. "That's what the news is. But there had to be *something*. Certainly you could find it."

Brendan sipped his beer. "Very little. Oh, we pick off a British scout now and then. Nothing more."

Jon wasn't a scout. Bennie let her fingers relax around the cool, solid metal of her mug. He was safe, for now at least.

"Nothing." Cad slapped his thigh in disgust. "So the entire Continental army is just sitting around on its ass?"

"Pretty much."

"Damn. Knew they needed me there, but your mother keeps insisting it's foolishness for a man of my years to go chasing off after war. My years, indeed. I'm worth more than any of those young pups."

"We all know that, Da," Bennie said soothingly. "That's why we need you here. Someone has to protect New Wexford, in case the British decide to move in this direction again."

"Hmph." Cad downed half his beer, then leveled his gaze at Brendan. "Tell me the truth, Brendan. What's going on?"

"We've got them pretty much surrounded. We've got fifteen thousand men camped around Boston, from Cambridge through Brookline, all the way to Roxbury."

"And all we've managed to do with all those men is pick off a couple of worthless scouts?"

"It's not that easy, Da." Brendan leaned back comfortably in his chair. His tone was casual; he could have been discussing the quality of the latest batch of ale. "We've got three whole divisions running around. General Ward is in command, but none of the other generals really wants to report to him. And there are a whole slew of companies who don't want to report to anybody."

"Doesn't anybody know anythin' about military discipline around there? Nobody *wants* to report to nobody. You can't give 'em a choice."

"There's a group of Stockbridge Indians, and another of Mohawk warriors. They're certainly not going to take orders from any one of us, but they're better than the rest of us combined at slipping up on someone, or scouting out the enemy."

"Still, you gotta drill, drill, drill. Make an army out of 'em."

"Rations are short. Everybody's hungry. There's not nearly enough gunpowder."

"Gotta expect to make a few sacrifices."

"Pay is late. There's not much to do. People sit around drinking all day."

Cad slapped his huge palm on his knee. "Well, what's wrong with that?"

"They're not Joneses, Da. They can't all hold their spirits. We've had more men injured while fighting amongst themselves than in skirmishes with the British."

"Not men under your command, I hope. I expect better from you boys."

"No, not under my command." Brendan smiled wryly. "Nor any of ours. We've set our men mostly to cleaning. Keeps them busy, and Lord knows the camp could use it."

"Adam's idea, I expect. Boy always did have a good head for leadin'."

"No, actually, it was mine." Brendan drank deeply of his ale.

"Yours, huh? Wouldn'ta thought it. Know you got a good mind, course, but never seemed to have much of a practical bent."

Sipping at her ale, Bennie watched Brendan carefully. She didn't see so much as a flinch, and she wondered if he'd finally reached a point where their father no longer had the power to wound him. She wished she could recover the ability to close off her emotions, an ability that seemed to have melted away with the snow.

"Disease is running wild through the camps, Da. It's causing more damage than the British could ever do. I only hope to God they don't attack any time soon; half of our men will spend the entire battle looking for the nearest trench." Brendan smiled, the first genuine smile Bennie had seen from him since he returned. It lit up his eyes with the sudden, potent charm he so rarely displayed.

"Of course," he continued, "none of the Jones boys have had so much as a sneeze."

"Good breeding," Cad said.

Bennie laughed. Maybe it was all going to be all right after all.

"So that's it then?" she asked. "Everybody holds their ground?"

Brendan's smile faded as he turned to look at her. Her own new lightheartedness evaporated as soon as she saw the expression in his eyes.

If his eyes had been dark before, they were black now, but for once, she could catch glimpses of the emotions they usually shielded: desperation, and a soul-deep sorrow.

And she had her answer. It wasn't going to be all right after all.

Running the brush briskly down the horse's side, Bennie spoke softly.

"That's a good girl, Puffy. You stand so still and let me make your coat look nice."

Unseasonable heat had swept into New Wexford the day Brendan had ridden out. A week later, it was close and stuffy in the stable, warm enough that her light cotton dress was damp as she worked. She set down the brush and picked up a metal comb, starting to work the tangles out of the tan mane.

"'Scuse me, miss, are you Miss Beth?"

She froze. Beth? Only one person had ever called her Beth, but not in that cracked, quavery voice.

She turned to face an old man, spare and hunched as a sparrow. Faded blue eyes twinkled from either side of a beaky nose, and he had a huge pack slung over his slumped shoulder.

"What do you want?"

"Are you Beth?"

Idly, she turned the comb over and over. "Hardly anybody calls me that."

"But someone does?" he persisted.

She ran her hand down her horse's flank. "Yes."

Beaming, he dropped his pack, the gaps in his teeth somehow failing to diminish the contagious happiness of his smile. "I've got somethin' for you, miss."

"For me?" What could he possibly have for her? He'd yanked open the top of his sack and was now rummaging around inside, muttering under his breath as he poked and prodded. The sack bulged dangerously. "Who are you?"

His head bobbed up for an instant before he buried it in the opening again. "I'm a peddler, miss. Come from Boston."

"I don't want to buy anything."

"It's free, miss." Tossing a bulky wrapped package over his shoulder, he went on, mumbling under his breath. "Now where did I put that . . ."

Free? What kind of a peddler gave things away? For that matter, what kind showed up in the stables, knew her name, and starting unpacking his wares before she had a chance to get a word in edgewise?

"Now see here—" she began.

"Ah, here it is." He emerged from the depths of his sack, his face bright with triumph, waving a crumpled piece of paper. "I'd stuffed it in a gill cup, miss. Kept it safe for you."

Reaching out warily, she took the paper. It was folded in quarters. a mellow ivory square. On one side, in black ink, big, blocky letters spelled out *Beth*.

Closing her eyes, she pressed the letter to her chest. *Jon*. It had to be Jon. Who else would address a letter simply to Beth?

"Where did you get this?"

"Boston. I was tryin' to make a bit off those bloomin' British. Huh. Ain't interested in buying much but rum. Their womenfolk, now, they're good cust—"

"Who gave it to you?" she asked impatiently.

"Don't know. Big fellow. Not too swift in the upstairs, if you know what I mean. Paid me good, though, to get a letter to the tavern keeper's daughter in New Wexford an' not tell anyone else about it."

"Well, you found me."

"Ain't you gonna read it?"

She opened her eyes. The peddler hopped from foot to foot. She wanted to be rid of him, quickly. Although her first instinct was to open the letter immediately, it somehow seemed wrong to do so in front of someone else.

"Was there something else you wanted?"

"Well." He scrunched up his nose. "I thought mebbe you'd want to look at some of my wares. They're fine ones, that."

"No."

"Couldn't interest you in anythin'?" he wheedled.

"Perhaps. Are you going back to Boston soon? Could you get a reply through?"

Scratching at his gray-stubbled chin, he replied, "Naw. 'Tain't worth it. Gettin' dangerous around there, ain't ya heard?"

"Yes, I'd heard. Well, I won't keep you then. Thank you for your service."

"Pleasure, miss." It seemed to take him forever to repack his bag to his satisfaction, lift it to his shoulder, and shuffle his way out the door. She resisted the urge to hurry him on his way, suspecting it wouldn't do any good anyway.

Thank heavens. He was halfway out the door. Then he paused and turned back to her, deep creases crinkling around his eyes as he grinned cheerfully. "You enjoy that letter now, you hear?"

"I will." I hope, she thought. She didn't know why Jon would have gone to so much effort to get a letter to her. Trouble, perhaps? He was injured, he wanted to warn her—or her family—about something?

Rounding the corner of the Eel, the peddler was out of sight at last. Bennie scrambled up the ladder to the loft, not even thinking about why she sought out that place.

She'd been up in the loft several times since Jon left, getting fodder for the horses, but she'd never really looked at it. On those days, before the grass had grown long enough to sustain the horses, she'd simply thrown the hay down and gotten out as quickly as she could.

This time she stopped and took it in. How different it seemed now than it had that black, stormy April evening. Although it was dim, light poured through the open window, burnishing the hay to mellow gold. Dust motes floated lazily through the sunbeam.

Her violin was still there, packed away in its case where she'd left it, on one corner of the brown blanket that was still spread over a pile of hay. She hurried over and sat down.

Gently, she stroked the surface of the blanket. It was rough, scratchy, and yet it had never abraded her that night—because her bare skin had never touched it. Jon had protected her, had shielded her with his body, and she was, irrationally, positive he had meant to do so.

Their lovemaking had been desperate, frenzied, and brief. Despite how quickly it had ended, she remembered each instant with startling clarity, for she'd relived it again and again. Each night, when the terrible, terrifying blood and fire invaded her thoughts, she turned to him.

It no longer mattered to her whether it had been wrong. She'd needed it. She'd needed the feelings, she'd needed the thunder, and now she needed the memory.

Taking a deep breath, she unfolded the paper. The writing was sharp, angular, strong, and seemed perfectly suited to those big, powerful hands.

My drst. Beth,

I hope this finds You. I am not good with Words or Writing, so I paid a Printer here in Boston to write this Message for Me. He assures Me He will correct my Mistakes & make it sound Proper.

I wanted you to know I am well. Nearly half of the Citizens of this fair City have left, so we have ample Quarters. Ships from England bring steady Supplies. I have planted a small Garden in the Common, as have many of My Fellow Men. The Turnips & Radishes look very well, although the Beans are a bit slow.

I told You I am not good with Words. I wanted to tell You again that I am sorry for any Pain I have caused You. Your Friendship is My most cherished Possession.

I remain, always,

Your Devoted Servant,

Jon.

Bennie carefully folded the letter along its original creases and tucked it safely into her pocket. She reached for her violin and, for the first time in nearly two months, began to play.

16

God, he hated the smell of blood.

It clogged the back of his throat and filled his nostrils: sickeningly sweet, cloying, pungent. There was no getting away from it, no fresh breeze sweeping it away with the crisp warmth of early summer. It clung to him, making him feel sticky and dirty, and he knew there wasn't enough water in the world to wash it away.

Leaning wearily against a side-turned supply cart, Jon once more went through the motions of cleaning his weapon. To his right, the water glittered with deceptive cheerfulness, bright and gay with the late afternoon sun. To his left sprawled the line of stone fences, fortified rail fence, and redoubt that they'd spent the day trying to take.

Ahead of him lay the beach, a wide band that rimmed Charlestown, littered with the remains of a day of fighting—torn clothes and spent powder horns, crumpled bodies that lay like discarded rag dolls. Almost unbelievable that those loose, pale, disjointed corpses, dressed in red and stained with black, were real—except he could smell the blood.

Ramming the brush down the barrel of his musket, he methodically dragged it in and out. The cardinal rules of soldiering: head down, follow orders, keep your weapon clean.

Behind those fences the hill—Breed's? Bunker? Nobody seemed entirely sure which—swarmed with Americans. Hard to tell how many, but they'd dug in well over the night. The British command had determined that the colonists couldn't keep that high ground, which would give their cannon a clean shot down into the center of Boston where the British forces were clustered, and so this morning they'd begun the attempt to drive the rebels from Charlestown.

Sergeant Hitchcock dropped into the sand beside Jon. He pulled out a rumpled cloth and mopped his forehead.

"Damn rough one today," he said.

Jon glanced at the sergeant, who looked much too frail to withstand battle. Nevertheless, when they were engaged, he fought with precision, discipline, toughness, and rock-steady control.

"Yes," Jon agreed.

"You did good today, son."

"No. Scared." It had been near to impossible, trying to maintain the fiction that he couldn't shoot when all hell had been breaking loose around him. "You?"

"Naw. Only afterwards. That's when I start to shake. Still, ya done good. You're a big target. Kept your head down. Followed orders. I was proud of you," Sergeant Hitchcock insisted, clapping Jon on his shoulder.

Oh, God. Jon clenched his musket barrel. When was the last time someone had said that to him? Had anyone *ever* said that to him?

"Thanks."

"Ready to try it again?"

"Again?" They'd tried it twice today and been massacred both times. There were companies of fifty-nine men that had only a few members remaining. How could they possibly mount another assault with their depleted forces? It was suicide.

"Yep. Word just came down. We're gonna roust those mohairs or die trying."

Die trying. Those words echoed through Jon's head as the world exploded around him once again. He was bolstered behind a ridge of sand, which was, in his opinion, clearly inadequate protection.

The roar of artillery and muskets thundered so loudly in Jon's ears he could no longer tell if he was hearing the current fire or an echo of fire that was already gone. It was steady, pounding, bursting in sharp shards of pain inside his head.

Sweat trickled down his face, blurring his vision and tickling his upper lip. He longed to wipe it away, but he couldn't seemed to make himself release his rigid grip on his musket.

Fire. Pour in powder. Ram a ball down the barrel. Aim. Fire again.

There was a terrible, repetitive rhythm to his actions,

a rhythm that suspended time and submerged reality. Had ten minutes passed? An hour? Who knew? Just fire, reload, aim. Fire.

To his left, Sergeant Hitchcock, hunched low, scrambled across the beach like a hermit crab, scuttling along behind the ridge of sand. He ducked lower as a ball whined over his head and threw himself prone next to Jon.

"You doin' all right, son?" he hollered.

"Yeah." Jon fired again, at a beautiful indigo patch of sky a good five feet above the abutment.

"I'm going over."

"What?" Unable to hear above the thundering weapons, he turned to the sergeant. It was sometimes easier to understand when he could watch his lips and connect the movement to the snatches of words he managed to catch.

"I'm goin' over. Already told the cap'n. Want you and the rest of the company to cover me, then follow as quickly as ya can."

"Can't do that!" Jon protested. "Too dangerous."

"We sure as hell ain't gettin' nowhere down here." The sergeant scanned the ridge. "The firin's lighter, Jon. Ain't ya noticed, son?"

"Noticed."

"I figure some of 'em left, or they're gettin' low on shot. Maybe both. Best try and take 'em before reinforcements arrive."

"Maybe." And then again, maybe the Americans were setting them up, just waiting for the regulars to rush the barricades. They'd be pigs sitting in a fenced yard, waiting to be picked off. However, he didn't figure that scenario was one "Jon" should be clever enough to think of, so he bit his tongue and didn't object.

A small geyser of sand spewed no more than six inches from his thigh as a ball plowed into the beach. Then sudden, blessed silence, perhaps ten seconds' worth, so quiet after the thunder and firing that he almost didn't believe it.

"Now!" Hitchcock shouted, jumping to his feet and plunging forward. A hail of shot followed his ascent, all the gates of hell burst open at once, and his small, wiry body seemed pitifully fragile against the fury.

"No!" Jon's voice was lost against the volley of shots. He took careful aim this time, following the path the Sergeant was taking, trying to provide some cover. Swearing, he rushed after Hitchcock, trying to reload as he ran, only dimly aware that the rest of his company were fighting their way up the slope too.

He no longer flinched when a ball flew by his ear. It was useless; the fire was everywhere, anyway.

Hitchcock dived over the reinforced fence. Jon angled in that direction, keeping his gaze fixed on the spot where his sergeant had disappeared. Twenty yards, fifteen. Bushes whipped by in his peripheral vision; sand disappeared beneath his feet. Why, then, did it seem he was going so slowly, each second stretched to the limit of human tolerance?

Smoke, acrid and hot, stung his eyes and burned his nose. His ears rang with screams, shouts, and the crack of muskets; the sharp tang of battle filled his mouth. Ten . . . five. Bushes. Piles of hay and mud, clumps of timber and dirt. The fence.

He was over. He glanced around quickly for a barrel, a mound of earth, anything to provide some protection. A waist-high, naked bush made poor cover but he dived for it anyway. He crouched by the thin trunk and frantically gulped air. How long had it been since he'd breathed?

The Americans were in retreat. No uniforms, their lines ragged, but still fighting fiercely as they slipped back across the high ground. Returning fire, Jon wished, once again, for better cover. He was too big; too many pieces of his body—pieces he didn't care to lose—were exposed. Looking for a better position, he shrank closer to the bush and glanced around again,

Not far off a crumpled heap of red and dirty white lay on the ground—Sergeant Hitchcock.

Jon ducked his head and headed for Hitchcock. A sharp pang along his side was nothing; all his focus was on the body lying on the dusty ground.

No time for niceties. Jon grabbed a handful of coat and dragged Hitchcock back behind the bush, now grateful for the meager cover.

Jon shoved his rifle aside and rolled Hitchcock over, taking the sergeant's head in his lap. Hitchcock's face was pale and slack, his eyes closed. Jon groped along the loose folds of Hitchcock's neck, searching for a pulse. There. Unsteady, thin, but there.

Maybe there was still time. Jon jerked open Hitchcock's coat, shoving aside the powder bags and broken cross-straps.

Blood. Dark, sticky, thick, it covered Hitchcock's chest and belly. He peeled back the remains of the sergeant's shredded shirt, and sucked in his breath. God, it couldn't be all his, could it?

Jon stripped off his own jacket and shirt, vaguely surprised to find them stained with blood on the back as well as the front. He tore the shirt into long strips, grateful, for once, for his size. At least there was a lot of fabric. He was going to need a lot.

Lifting Hitchcock slightly, Jon ran his hands down the man's back, checking to see if wounds were there too. No exit holes. The balls must still be inside him, then, but all Jon could hope to do was keep the sergeant alive long enough to get him to the surgeon.

But he had to stop the bleeding. He packed the holes with wadded linen, pressing down hard as blood soaked through the fabric and covered his fingers. There wasn't even the slightest flinch from the sergeant when Jon pushed at his chest although the pain must have been excruciating. The man was out cold—or dead; Jon leaned over and put his ear close to Hitchcock's mouth.

Shallow breaths, too rapid, too weak, but breath. Jon straightened. Grabbing another handful of cloth strips, he carefully wound them tightly around the sergeant's chest.

He hadn't even noticed, while he'd been busy tending to Sergeant Hitchcock, that the hail of bullets around him seemed to have stopped. The colonials were in full retreat, out of his sight over the hill, and only the faintly muted sounds of firing reached him.

His company was going after them at full charge; they'd taken enough today and were determined not to let their tormentors get away unscathed. Unfortunately, it meant they were out of earshot; there was no one he could holler to for a medic.

Taking another rag, he reached for his canteen and tried to open it, but his fingers were slippery with blood, and he couldn't get a good grip on the canteen. He wiped his fingers on his breeches and tried again. The water was warm from the sun. He splashed it on the cloth and began to wipe the grime from the sergeant's face.

Perhaps the moisture and soothing strokes penetrated the injured man's stupor. The sergeant gave a low moan, and his eyelids fluttered open slightly.

"Lie still," Jon said quietly.

"Hurt," Hitchcock managed to rasp out.

"Yes."

"Bad?"

"Yes," he said simply, knowing his sergeant would accept nothing but the truth. "If you promise you'll be still, I'll try and go get a doctor."

"No matter." Hitchcock coughed, spewing out a stream of blood and foam.

Ah, damn. His lung. They'd hit his lung. And no doctor was going to get here soon enough to help.

"Hang on." And then there was the anger, hot and acid, against the useless, stupid, futility of it all. What would it change? What would it help for this man to die? A good man, a fair man, a man who had patience and tolerance with every soldier in his company, including a slow-witted lieutenant.

"Hang on," Jon said urgently. "I'll get help."

Hitchcock coughed again, his whole body shaking. "Soldier. Always knew . . . die . . . like a soldier."

His head rolled back limply. Jon couldn't have said how long he stayed there, staring, sitting by the sergeant's body as night swept in and obscured the horrible aftermath of battle. Quiet, blessed coolness; it was almost peaceful. Hard to believe that in the morning the sun would rise to illuminate again ground churned up by artillery fire and strewn with dead soldiers.

Jon's hand trembled as he reached over and finally closed Hitchcock's eyes. The body was already growing cool, acclimating itself to the temperature of the dead, not the living.

Slumping back against the bush, Jon dug the heels of his hands into his eyes, which stung from the smoke of the battle. He rubbed hard, painfully.

There was no escaping war. There was no escaping death.

And there was no escaping that this whole bloody carnage was his fault.

17

The moon stared down from the ebony sky like a malevolent, unblinking yellow eye. It illuminated the black, twisted shapes of the trees and limned the old abandoned fort in sickly yellow.

High summer night. Heat radiated from the ground; the air was heavy, close, so thick it felt to Jon as if he should be able to reach out and grab a fistful of it. It was a labor to draw a full breath.

Trying to let a little air get to his overheated skin, Jon tugged futilely at the thick padding that upholstered his waist, wincing at the pressure on the still-tender spot where the bullet had grazed his side. He hadn't discovered his wound until long after the battle, when his company had returned to find him still hunched beside the limp body of Sergeant Hitchcock.

It had taken nearly a week for him to return to full strength, a week in which he'd lain in bed and had too much time to think—far too much.

All he'd ever tried to do was the right thing.

He'd been so sure he'd known what it was. As a young lieutenant stationed in Boston, he'd been appalled at the Crown's treatment of those he still considered his own people. The massacre had been the last straw, and he'd begun feeding tidbits of information to Samuel Adams. Little had he known what it would lead to.

He'd been sure of who was right and wrong, who was enemy and who was friend. He'd been so confident, so damn self-righteous, absolutely certain he knew all the answers.

But the answers hadn't prepared him for the reality, and the reality was, people died. People who weren't his enemy, people who weren't evil or cruel or wrong. They were people just like him, doing their jobs, following orders, trying to do the right thing.

No matter how much he tried to cloak it in terms of honor and country, there was no getting around the fact that he'd provided the information that caused too many of those deaths. If he hadn't pulled the trigger, he wasn't sure that his culpability wasn't all the greater.

Worst of all, he saw no way out. He could only continue to do his job and pray that somehow the knowledge he gathered would hasten the end of the war. It didn't help that he knew neither side would surrender before they'd been beaten into the ground.

He could only cling to what he had left: duty, and the overwhelming loyalty that had led him down this path in the first place.

It would have to be enough. But in the dead of the night, when he remembered a dying man in his arms, it didn't seem like enough. Oh, not nearly enough.

He hunched his shoulders in the tight, rich brocade of his coat. The part he played tonight was a new one: a middle-aged Boston merchant who'd grown plump and lazy on his sales to the British soldiers stationed there. The merchant placed commerce above country but showed a bit of defiance in choice of his wig, which was heavily powdered and had thirteen curls trailing down the back, à la Independence. Just enough resistance to keep the British from suspecting more.

Jon rarely went to so much trouble just to deliver his information. But then, rarely was his information so important.

That was the reason, too, that rather than use his usual channels in Boston, he'd chosen to come here to pass on the packet of papers stuffed inside the padding that created his ample girth. He was taking no chances.

He'd spent months piecing it all together. In the last two weeks, once he'd been given a clean bill of health, he'd worked like a madman, day and night, driven by the possibility that, this time, it would be enough to end it. He had little else to hold on to.

There was no sign of movement down at the fort. All was still, the walls and rough structures skeletal in the humid air. The fort had been empty since his company had been sent back to Boston. Except for the length of the ride to get here, it was the perfect meeting site. No one would bother with the abandoned, useless place.

Shouldn't his contact have been here now? He'd made sure very few people knew about this drop, and he was using his best courier. But there was no sign of

the old peddler who'd been able to move in and out of
Boston and Cambridge without suspicion.

He carefully approached the perimeter of the fort.
His steps raised a swarm of insects, and he resisted the
urge to slap them away from his neck, knowing the
sound of his palm hitting his skin would stand out in the
quiet like a gunshot.

And it was quiet—too quiet, he thought. The only
sound he could pick up was the persistent buzzing of
mosquitoes. Not even a bird called, as if even they
couldn't bestir themselves in the oppressive heat.

Nerves prickled at the back of his neck. He reached
the outer wall of the fort and slid silently along it,
counting on the dark bulk to hide his presence.

What was that? He stilled, his ears straining. Nothing. Lord, even his own breathing sounded too loud to
him.

He squeezed through the open door and into the center
courtyard. Empty. He scanned the inner wall, looking
for the telltale rough outline of a man. He couldn't
make anything out. The ugly yellow glow cast by the
moon seemed to cloak as much as it illuminated.

"Halt." The order hung in the air, heavy and terrible.

They came from the walls of the building, emerging
from the blackness as if materializing right out of the
thick, dark heat.

Soldiers, at least half a dozen.

Jon went cold. They'd found him. Somehow they'd
known about the meeting.

Did they have the peddler already? Involuntarily, his
hand went to the place where he'd hidden the dispatches.

If they already had him, there was nothing he could

do for the peddler now, little to be gained and much to be lost by waiting around trying to find out.

Jon lifted his hands as if in surrender. He saw the soldiers relax almost imperceptibly and begin to walk toward their prisoner.

He turned and ran. Oblivious of the shouts behind him, he pelted across the barren clearing in front of the fort, heading for the woods. The heated air burned his lungs as he breathed.

Crack. A ball whined by his left ear. God, please let them be poor shots. Heart pounding painfully in his chest, he redoubled his effort, heading for the hidden entrance to the path where he'd once followed Beth and her soldier pursuer.

He knew he could more than likely outrun any soldier following him, but he seriously doubted he could outrun a musket ball.

The blow hit him behind his left shoulder. It sent him flying with its force. He slammed into the ground, tasting dirt. Pain exploded down his spine.

Clamping his jaws together, he sucked air in through his teeth and forced himself to his feet. He shuddered, just once, against the searing, stabbing heat in his shoulder. Pain was acceptable. Capture was not.

More sharp cracks rent the air behind him. He narrowed his focus to the edge of the forest. Thick with leaves and new growth, it looked very different than it had last winter. He selected a likely looking bush, hoped for the best, and plunged in.

Thank God. It was the right one. He ran on, branches scratching his face and scraping at the wound in his back. He staggered once when the pain ripped down his body, all the way to his knees.

All he had to do was get to his horse. They'd taken after him on foot, and by the time they realized he had a mount and went back for their own, he'd be long gone.

Lord, it hadn't seemed this far away when he'd set out. Sweat trickled into his eyes. Wiping it away with one forearm, he threw up his other to block a low-slung branch.

Damn, if only he could breathe. The trail was so narrow. He felt the edges of his world begin to close in.

Finally. As always, he hadn't tied his horse, just in case he needed to get away quickly. The huge, sturdy beast, his reins looped loosely over his neck, had been contentedly cropping the thick grass in a tiny clearing. He raised his head at the sound of Jon's arrival.

Jon reached to grab on to the saddle and pull himself up, and found his left arm didn't work. No time to worry about it. Hanging on with his right hand, he shoved his foot into the stirrup, and heaved, barely managing to swing his right leg over the horse.

God, he felt weak. His clothes were wet with sweat and blood, but he was shivering as if chilled. He knew it meant he'd lost too much blood already.

He tugged on the reins and banged his heels against the horse's sides, heading him down the trail before Jon slumped over his neck.

There was no way he was going to make it back to Boston. After tonight's fiasco, he didn't know who he could trust—on either side.

There was only one person he dared go to now. He had no right to ask, but he had little choice. Closing his

246 SUSAN KAY LAW

eyes briefly against the pounding in his brain, he hung on to his horse, praying he'd make it in time.

The sun was barely up. Why was it already so hot? Slipping into the stables, Bennie felt the light cotton of her simple blouse sticking to her back. She wasn't fond of getting up this early, but she'd wanted to get the worst of the work done before the heat became unbearable.

Inside the stable the heat seemed to hover, trapped, thick with the smell of horses and ripe grass. There were no overnight guests at the Dancing Eel and therefore no horses but the five her brothers hadn't ridden off to war.

Business had fallen off considerably since the outbreak of hostilities. No one wanted to travel unless it was absolutely necessary; conditions were simply too unstable. Bennie was grateful. The Eel had its regulars, who gathered everyday to jaw over the situation. There was enough income to take care of the few Joneses left in New Wexford, even though they helped out her sisters-in-law and their children. Any more work would have been more than they could manage.

It shouldn't take too long to herd the horses out to the pasture just beyond the woods. At least in the meadow there'd be the remote possibility they could catch a rare breeze.

She shoved impatiently at the stray curls corkscrewing at her temple. Knowing it would be too warm to stand even a few tresses plastered to her neck, she'd ruthlessly gathered every strand of hair into a disciplined knot this morning, nearly tugging out half of it in the process.

Useless. Less than an hour later, curls were springing out all over her head, as if they had minds of their own. She thought longingly of how neat her mother's smooth hair stayed no matter the humidity.

The horses' energy too seemed sapped by the temperature; they didn't even bother to rouse themselves at her entrance. They simply stood there, heads slung low, desultorily swishing their tales at the annoying flies swirling lazily around them.

Taking a handful of tack from the hook just inside the door, she approached Puffy first. Bennie ran her hands automatically over the horse's neck and withers, checking for depth and tone of muscle. Today, though, she was careful to stay at arm's length, avoiding the heat that radiated from the huge body. She slipped the halter over his head and led him out into the bright, hazy morning sunshine. Around the back of the stable, she looped the reins loosely over a post and returned for another horse.

"Easy there, Patience," she murmured to her father's big gray. The name was a complete misnomer; the horse was skittish, stubborn, and downright difficult to manage. Dancing away from her reach, his hoof struck the side of his stall with a resounding thud.

That couldn't be a groan, coming from the next, empty stall. She backed away from Patience as her heart began to pound. A cat, maybe.

Another moan, low, rumbly, decidedly human. A tramp, a vagrant? Maybe a deserter? Well, they didn't think they could just move into her stable, did they?

A weapon. She needed a weapon. Casting about for something suitable, her gaze fell on the pile of tools near the door. The ax Isaac used for chopping wood was propped up against the wall.

She tiptoed carefully over to it. There were no more sounds, but she had no intention of giving the intruder any indication she was doing anything more than caring for the horse.

The ax was large and heavy, its handle smooth from use. She lifted it easily, grateful, for once, that she wasn't as small as her mother, who never could have handled it. Raising it over her shoulder in preparation, she crept back to the stall.

"Jon!"

She dropped the ax, forgotten, to the floor. The empty stall was filled with broken tack and a small pile of straw left from the summer before. Jon was sprawled on the pile, resting on his right side. His right arm was flung over his head; his left rested loosely at his waist.

"Oh, Lord. Jon."

She flew across the stall and dropped to her knees. His hair was tangled and matted to his head, and he was wearing strange, rich clothes that were torn and stained.

"Oh, Lord." He was so still. She lightly touched his beard-shadowed cheek. "Jon," she repeated.

He opened his eyes slightly. Their beautiful, pale blue was glazed, washed of color.

"Beth," he said in a hoarse croak. "Found you."

"What happened to you?" His cheeks were hollow, and deep purple shadows looked like bruises under his eyes.

"Hurt."

"Don't move. I'll go get help."

"No." Weakly, he raised one finger, as if that small gesture could stop her. "Arrest . . . me."

They would. A wounded British officer would be a worthy prize to any colonial. He'd end up a prisoner of war, if a doctor could manage to save him.

He looked into her eyes, the plea in his own unmistakable. "Help . . . me."

Bennie twisted her hands together until the skin burned. "I don't know how."

"Take . . . ball . . . out."

Take the ball—oh, Lord, he'd been shot!

She couldn't do this. She had to go get help. Even if he got arrested, at least he'd be alive.

"I can't," she protested.

"Yes, can." He smiled slightly at her, a ghostly parody of his old grin. "Can do . . . anything, Beth." He closed his eyes as if the effort to both speak and keep them open was too great for him. "Can't . . . be arrested. Kill me."

"All right." What was she going to do? She needed . . . things. Bandages, scissors, water. What else?

"Hang on, Jon. I'll be right back. I have to get some supplies." He didn't respond, and she was suddenly afraid she'd lost him already. "Do you hear me, Jon?" she asked urgently. "Don't die while I'm gone." She raised her voice. "You can't die on me!"

"Yes . . . ma'am," he whispered.

Hesitating only a moment, she ran out of the stables. It was hardly the ideal place to leave him; anyone could stumble across him. But there didn't seem to be much choice. There was no way she could move him by herself, not when he was in this condition.

Patience snorted, reminding Bennie of his presence. She had to get the horses out to pasture before her father came wondering why they were still in the stable. At least the stall Jon was sprawled in wasn't visible from the door. If someone walked in a mere ten steps, however . . .

Thank goodness, neither her father nor Isaac were early risers. Her mother was certainly up, but she never came out to the stables. With any luck, Jon would be safe for at least a little while. Hurrying away, Bennie prayed for a little luck, and a whole lot of divine guidance.

She couldn't go back to the house; it was unlikely she'd be able to sneak what she needed right out from under her mother's nose. So she headed for Brendan's shop, hoping she could find what she needed.

Thankfully, she made it to Brendan's without running into anybody. The shop was stuffy and sweltering, filled with a stale, closed-up smell. She shoved everything she could think of in a large canvas sack and sped back to the stables.

"Bennie!"

The shout came when she had almost passed the Dancing Eel. Oh, Lord. Her father. She stopped cold, closing her eyes and breathing deeply.

Calm. She had to be calm. He didn't know anything about Jon. She just had to be calm. Taking one final gulp of air, she clutched the bag tightly and turned to face her father.

"Where have you been, my girl? I noticed Puffy still back of the stables. Thought you were taking them all out to the meadows."

"I am. Just haven't had time yet."

He jerked his chin in the direction she'd just come from. "And you were . . .?" he prodded.

"Brendan's," she said quickly.

"Brendan's?" He lifted one bushy silver eyebrow. "And what would you be needing at Brendan's so early this morn?"

She squeezed the sturdy muslin between her palms. Calm, she repeated to herself. "I . . . forgot a few things the last time I cleaned it. Went back to get them."

"That's what's in the bag, I suppose?"

"Yes," she said in relief.

"And what's so important you had to scurry down there first thing?"

The relief had come too soon. "Dust rags." Well, that was certainly important enough. She tried again. "Ah, I needed some . . . medicine."

He snorted. "Women's stuff, I suppose."

"Yes."

Narrowing his eyes, he peered at her closely. "That why you're so flushed and out of sorts? Never seemed to be like those weak, fluttery females before."

"I think it's just the heat, Da."

"There is that." He squinted at the sky, a cloudless, burning blue. "It'll be worse today, I think."

"Oh, no!" It would be impossibly warm inside the stables for Jon.

"Maybe you should take the day off, Ben. You've been working too hard."

"I think I will."

"Practice that violin of yours. Haven't had much time for doing that lately."

"I'd like that." Nobody bothered her when she was practicing. It would give her plenty of time to care for Jon undisturbed.

"I'll get Isaac to pasture the horses for you."

"No!"

He peered at her again.

"I–I mean," she stammered, "I . . . would like to take the horses out. I don't mind. I'll take the rest of the time off after that, I promise."

"Are you sure?"

"I'm sure." She scurried off before he could ask any more questions.

She dropped the bag just out of sight inside the stable door and ran around back of the house to the well, just barely managing to resist the urge to check on Jon. She would need the water in any case, and stopping to assure herself of his safety would take time she didn't think she could afford to waste.

The bucket banged against her leg as she hurried, and water sloshed over the side and soaked her skirt. She careened around the corner of the stall and stopped.

He was still there, sprawled across the golden-brown hay. Pale, silent, absolutely still.

And she was suddenly, terribly afraid that she was already too late.

18

Tentatively, afraid of what she might find, she laid her hand on his chest. Through the thin, tattered fabric of his shirt his flesh was still warm, and she could, just barely, detect the subtle rise and fall of his chest.

"Thank God."

"You're back," he whispered without opening his eyes.

"Yes." He was so white, so still, the skin stretched taut over the beautifully molded planes of his face. Who was she trying to fool? She was no healer, knew only the rudiments of dressing and tending wounds. If he never opened those wonderful, sleepy eyes again, she couldn't stand it if she were part of the reason.

"Jon. Are you sure there isn't someone I can summon? Somewhere I can take you? I don't know what to do."

"Trust . . . you." He tried to reach for her, winced, and let his hand drop back to the straw. "Trust . . . no one else."

She took a deep breath. "All right. What do I do?"

"Just . . . take out ball."

"Where is it?"

"Back."

His back. Oh, Lord. Not his arm or thigh, nothing simple. His back.

She could do it. She had to. Taking her bucket and supplies, she moved around to his other side, careful not to jar him in any way, and knelt behind him.

Her hand flew to her mouth to cover her gasp; she didn't want him to hear her distress. A fist-size hole had been torn in the back of the odd, fancy coat he was wearing. The hole was perhaps three quarters of the way up his left side. If the ball had gone deep, it was far too close to his heart for comfort.

But if it had hit his heart, he never would have gotten this far, so the ball had to have stayed fairly close to the surface. Beneath the hole, his coat was soaked with old, black blood. So much blood, but it looked as if the flow, if it hadn't stopped entirely, had at least slowed considerably.

First things first. She had to get that jacket off and she reached for her scissors.

"First I'm going to cut away your clothes so I can see what I'm dealing with, all right?"

She snipped the thick, heavily embroidered fabric and peeled the cloth away, letting out the breath she'd been holding. Step one done. Jon hadn't moved so much as a twitch the entire time.

"Jon?"

"Yes?"

"Just checking to see if you're still with me."

There was bulky padding wrapped around his waist. She wondered for a moment if he'd somehow already injured his lower back. But it wasn't a bandage, just a thick wrapping of batting and linen.

Time to worry about it later. She snipped through the strips of cloth and pushed them away.

Now his shirt. The linen yielded more easily to her scissors, but stripping it away was something else entirely. The blood had dried, causing the fabric to stick to his flesh. If she simply jerked it away, the pain would be awful; worse yet, he'd probably start bleeding again, and she wasn't sure how much more blood he could afford to lose.

She sat back on her heels for a moment, pondering her problem. Then she dug a clean rag out of her bag and dipped it into the bucket of water. When she'd drawn it from the well, the water had been blessedly, numbingly cold, but in the heat of the day, it had already warmed to nearly skin temperature.

"Now, I'm just going to put a damp cloth on your back. It shouldn't hurt."

As if her hands could ever cause him pain. He knew he was treading close to the edge of reality. His world was indistinct, shifting, and most of his surroundings escaped him. He'd vaguely recognized the stables when he'd gotten there last night. He hadn't even had enough strength left to go and call for Beth; he'd simply pitched over on the nearest pile of hay and let the blackness take him.

The blackness was still there, but he could focus clearly on one thing: Beth. On the gentle, soothing stroke of her fingers, on the soft, concerned music of her voice. Now she was doing something to his back that cooled the burning pain that had been there since . . . had it only been last night?

"There. Now I'm going to try and get the rest of this out of the way."

She peeled the shirt away slowly, tugging it away from his damaged shoulder. "Come on, come on," she repeated, as if she could urge it to come away with her voice.

"There," she said again. She swallowed heavily at the sight of his torn flesh. It wasn't that she had a weak stomach; her brothers had cured her of that at an early age. But she couldn't forget that this was Jon's back. Her gentle giant was incapable of hurting anyone, and he didn't deserve this pain.

She dampened the cloth again and dabbed at his wound, sponging away the gore and dried blood and hoping that the hole would be so shallow she would soon see the ball.

No such luck. His back was as clean as she could manage, and there was no sign of the ball that had torn him up. There was nothing left to do but hunt for it.

"I have some laudanum. Will you take it?"

He barely managed to shake his head.

"You can't move, or I might cut you deeper. And I'm not strong enough to hold you."

"No," he croaked. He really didn't think he'd feel anything. He hadn't felt much of what she'd been doing. His back was numb, the nerves apparently having had as much as they could take.

"All right," she agreed finally.

Catching her lower lip firmly in her teeth, she reached

for a blunt knife. She hadn't been able to find a proper probe; she would have to manage with this. She lifted it, and her hand shook.

That wouldn't do. She wished, desperately, that there was someone, anyone to help her.

"Beth."

That was all he said, but it was all he needed to say. With that one word, she remembered all the times he'd believed in her, all the times he'd looked at her with absolute approval in his eyes.

She poked at his flesh. He jerked once, then stilled.

"Jon?"

No response. But she could see his pulse, beating in the smooth patch of skin behind his ear. He must have blacked out.

Perhaps it was better this way. She bent to her task.

"Come on, come on. Where are you?"

There. The knife hit something hard. She leaned closer, blinking her eyes to clear them. The ball was black, misshapen, smooth. It hadn't gone in far—perhaps two inches. Either he'd been shot from some distance, or Jon's own heavy muscles had slowed its entrance. And she felt a new, vivid slash of anger at whoever had been so unscrupulous as to shoot him from behind.

Now to get it out.

Five minutes later she was still probing away with little success. "Damn, damn, damn," she swore. Giving up for the moment, she sat back and wiped at her eyes with her forearm, trying to rub away the stinging there.

This wasn't working. Her gaze fell on the pile of things she'd brought with her and dumped out on a square of ivory linen. What to do?

The scissors. Grabbing them, she bent over Jon's back once more. She found the ball again with the scissors. Amazing that such a tiny piece of metal could arouse such hatred in her. Opening the scissors just a bit, she closed them around the ball and prayed the grip would hold. Taking a deep breath, she tugged.

She was almost surprised when the scissors came out with the ball firmly between the blades. She violently swung the scissors in a wide arc, sending the ball flying against the wall, where it hit with a loud *thunk*.

Tossing the scissors back on the linen, she grabbed a large strip of cotton toweling and quickly folded it into a square pad. She laid it over Jon's wound and held it there. Then she tore a yellowed linen sheet into long, narrow strips, silently vowing to Brendan she'd replace the sheet she'd taken from a chest in his rooms over the printshop. When she had a sufficient pile of strips, she wrapped the padding securely in place.

Bennie's arms were trembling with fatigue by the time she finished. She slumped wearily against the side of the stall and looked with satisfaction at the neat bandage that covered Jon's upper back and chest. It would do.

She allowed herself only a moment of rest. She had to get the horses out to the pasture before her father came around to see why they were still stabled. After quickly slipping a harness over Patience's head—finding him cooperative for once—she let the other three horses out, too. They would follow Patience.

She mounted Puffy, leading Patience behind her, and set out for the meadow, the other three horses following behind. To her surprise, the sun still wasn't all that high in the sky. Although it seemed as if she'd been at it for days, it probably hadn't been more than a couple of hours since she'd found Jon in the stables.

She couldn't help wondering what had happened to him. Such odd clothes, and the padding around his middle. If he'd been wounded in battle, wouldn't he have had his uniform on? Except for the night he'd rescued her in the woods, she'd never seen him out of uniform. And if he'd been in a battle, where was the rest of his company? Why hadn't they taken care of him?

Bennie turned the horses, their hides gleaming in the hot, brilliant sun, free in the meadow. Lifting her skirts, she took off back to the stables at a dead run. Though she'd removed the ball, Jon hadn't stirred again before she'd left. There was still no guarantee that he was going to live.

She stumbled into the stable and knelt at his side.

So far, so good. He was still breathing. Spreading a blanket next to his prostrate body, she settled into watching over him. His breathing was a little shallow, but it was steady; she could see the expansion and contraction of his massive chest.

Cautiously, not wanting to wake him, she laid a palm on his forehead. Warm. Too warm? Hard to tell if the cause was from fever or the oppressive, sweltering air.

It had been months since she'd seen him. He was injured, pale, dirty, and sweaty, and still she marveled at the perfection of his features. Flawlessly balanced, finely sculpted, nearly too handsome to be real. It almost seemed as if perhaps the accident that had damaged his mental faculties had been meant to balance things a bit; nature needed to offset his exceptional features with a flaw or two.

But she had never really considered his slowness a flaw. It had given him that gentleness and acceptance that was so rare, had left him quick to offer the friendship she gratefully accepted. For although she had family in abundance, she had never really had a friend.

The last few months mustn't have been easy for him. He looked thinner. She let her gaze trace his length. Corded muscles still bulged from his arms and chest which tapered abruptly to his stomach. But along his side was a vicious, shiny pink scar.

He'd been injured. She thought back; it had been dark in the woods when he'd carried her through it, and she hadn't gotten a close look at his side. Had he had the scar then?

She reached out and skimmed her hand over the scar. It was smooth, almost waxy, beneath her fingers. If she hadn't seen him that time above the stables, she had touched him, had slid her hands over his body, again and again. She would have felt this.

Then he'd been hurt since he'd left. So much pain, another flaw put into that beautiful body. And she wished she'd been there to care for him that time, too.

She couldn't have said how long she sat there, watching him. Sweat trickled down her back, the straw scratched her legs, and the hot air was heavy in her lungs. Still, there was an odd contentment being there with him, knowing, at least for this brief time, that he was safe. Hearing him breathe, and being able to reach out and occasionally touch his damp skin.

"Bennie!"

The bellow from outside the stable brought her up sharply. Da! What was he doing here?

"What?" Jon mumbled groggily and opened his eyes a crack.

"Shh. Quiet. Don't move," she said frantically.

"Bennie!"

"Just a minute, Da, I'm coming!" she called back. She leaned over and spoke into Jon's ear. "Don't move. Don't make a noise. I'll be right back."

She scrambled to her feet and hurried out of the stables, meeting her father just as he was coming in the door.

"There you are, my girl. What was keeping you?"

"I was . . . in the loft. Practicing."

"Ben, it's far too hot in there to be practicin' in the stables. Why don't you go out by the creek?"

"It's fine. Quiet. I like it there."

"Look at you! You'll be keeling over from the heat in no time."

"I'm fine," she said, a bit too sharply.

"Well, then." He frowned at her. "Make sure you clean up a bit before your mother sees you."

"Yes, sir. Why were you looking for me?"

"Oh, that." He brightened. "We have customers."

"Customers?"

"Passing through on their way to Cambridge," he said happily.

"Oh. You need me to help serve?"

"No, Ben. I promised you the day off. But their horses have to be stabled."

"Their horses? Here?" She shoved the damp curls off her forehead. "But you can't!"

"Why not? That's why we have the bloody stables."

"But . . . I—I haven't mucked them out yet. Can't put customers' horses in dirty stalls."

"Well, I guess not."

"Of course not." She turned him around and headed him back toward the tavern. "You go give them a drink. I'll get the stables mucked out and then I'll get their horses."

"Fine. But make sure you get them clean, mind. They'll be in and out, checking on their horses. Right fond of their mounts, these fellows."

"They'll be spotless."

"I know." Whistling over the prospect of paying customers—ones who might have news, at that—he strolled back to the Dancing Eel.

Bennie put one hand over her rapidly beating heart, willing her pulse to return to normal. They hadn't been found out—yet.

She hurried back to the stall and stood over Jon. Where to put him? There was always Brendan's. But she wasn't sure no one would comment on her going there as frequently as she would need to to tend Jon. Nor could she figure out a way to get him over there, through the middle of town, in broad daylight.

Well, there was no hope for it. It would have to be the loft. He'd be both close at hand and out of sight. But how on earth could she get him up there?

She dropped to her knees. "Come on now, Jon. Time to get up."

Eyes still closed, he smiled crookedly. "Don't want to."

She shook his shoulder. "You have to get out of here, Jon, or they're going to find you. Jon? Come on, Jon."

He blinked his eyes open. His irises were dilated and unfocused. "Find me?"

"Yes. We've got to get you up to the loft, do you understand me? They won't find you there."

"Go to loft," he repeated, slurring the words.

She grabbed his right arm and tried to tug him to his feet. "Come on, I'll help you."

"Always help me, Beth."

"Yes." Lord, he was big. He managed to get to his feet, but he had to lean heavily on her shoulder. His movements were slow and uncoordinated, and if she hadn't known he'd had nothing, she would have thought that perhaps he'd been drugged after all.

"Come on. Let's get you to the ladder."

Pushing, pulling, Bennie half dragged him across the stable, where she propped him against the wall. She stood trying to muster her strength, and looked up at the hole in the ceiling. She'd never realized how high it was.

There was no way she was going to get him up that ladder by herself. The morning had already sapped her strength, but even if it hadn't, he was simply too large. He was going to have to help her.

"Jon," she said urgently. "Jon!"

His head rolled on his neck, but he managed to look down at her. "Beth?"

"Jon, we have to get you up the ladder. I can't do it for you. You're going to have to climb up yourself."

He swung his head to look at the ladder. "Can't. Tired . . . so tired."

"Jon," she said sharply. She grabbed his head in her hands and looked into his eyes, trying to find some spark of understanding. "You have to. For me."

She could see him straighten, gathering himself, finding some hidden reserve of strength. "For you." He grasped the ladder and lifted his foot to the lowest rung.

It was laborious going, inching up with the slow motions that seemed to be the only ones he could manage. Once he stopped and clung to the ladder, marshaling his strength so he could move again. Finally, he pulled himself through the hole and collapsed on the loft floor.

19

Yellow moonlight, nearly as warm and golden as the sun, streamed through her window. Bennie's sheets were tangled around her legs, her night rail damp and clinging to her too warm flesh.

It must be nearing the middle of the night, she thought, yet it was still so hot. She'd tossed and dozed, then turned again, trying to capture just a hint of coolness. It had to be nearly unbearable in the stable loft.

After Jon had managed to make his way up the ladder, she'd rapidly dragged up the rest of the supplies and made a pallet for him. He'd crawled onto the bedding and collapsed on his stomach, out like a candle snuffed by a brisk October wind.

Bennie had stabled the customers' horses and spent most of the afternoon with Jon, watching over him, as if that would somehow assure his health. He'd slept the rest of the day away. Near evening, she'd managed to awaken him and get a few swallows of thin broth down him, but he'd been unfocused and nearly incoherent.

She had to go check on him again. The combination of heat and worry was making sleep impossible anyway. Snatching a thin, dark cape, she tossed it around her shoulders, more to cover the bright white of her gown than for any need of its warmth.

Her bare feet glided over the smooth wood of the stairs, making no noise as she descended and slipped out the front door. The scent of the summer night was heavy in the still, hot air, thick with growing herbs, fermenting ale, and the heady fragrance of vibrant blooms.

Dry grasses prickled the soles of her feet, and she wondered when this unusually warm, dry spell would finally end. Opening the door to the stables wide, she let in a bit of the moonlight, enough to make out the dark, familiar shapes. A horse snuffled quietly. Just inside the entrance, tucked along the wall, they kept a lantern, and she scooped it up before heading for the loft.

Jon's breathing was harsh and labored. Filled with sudden, icy trepidation, she ran to him. She fumbled with the flint and steel before managing to light the lantern; dangerous to do in the loft, where a spark could ignite the dry hay, but at this moment that wasn't her primary concern. She set the lantern down close enough to Jon so she could see him clearly, the golden light illuminating the sharp angles and hollows of his face.

He moaned, moving restlessly, his features twisted into fierce agony. Oh, God. Was he in so much pain?

"Damn . . . don't die!" he muttered hoarsely. "Hang on!"

A nightmare, she thought, wondering what nightmares he'd been through since the last time she'd seen him.

He'd obviously been shot twice. What else had happened to him? Something to cause this kind of anguish. He groaned again, and she reached for his shoulder to shake him awake. At a touch, she snatched her hand back.

He was blazingly hot, far too warm to attribute it simply to the temperature in the loft.

She laid her palm against his brow, hoping to find it moist with sweat, but his skin was bone dry, hot as metal left out in the noon sun, and she knew he hadn't just been having a nightmare. He was in the grip of a raging fever.

A sick ache settled into her belly. Lifting the lantern high, she edged up the bandage covering his back and peered under it. The skin around his wound was puffy, mottled with dark splotches that she knew in the full light of day would prove to be angry red.

There wasn't time to think. Bennie worked quickly, pawing through the jumble of patent medicines she'd taken from Brendan's shop. She tilted bottles towards the lantern, trying to read their labels.

ELIXIR VITRIOL. She vaguely recalled her mother giving that to her brothers when they'd had various fevers. But how was she going to get it down Jon's throat?

"Jon."

No response.

"Jon. Wake up!" she said sharply into his ear, hoping that once again she could get through to him for just a moment or two. His condition was so much worse than it had been the past morning.

"Beth?" he murmured groggily.

"I've got something for you to drink."

He grimaced. "Flip?"

"No, no flip. Medicine. You have to take it." He was still sprawled on his belly, and it made administering the elixir more difficult. She couldn't just prop him up into a sitting position.

His face was turned toward her. She pried his mouth open, and poured a good swig of the liquid into his cheek. "Swallow!"

She watched his throat until she saw his Adam's apple slide up and down. She got another swallow into him, eyeing the length of his body. He was so big. Once more, for good measure.

Waiting for the medicine to take effect, she stroked his face, feeling the sharp rasp of his unshaven beard. Unable to resist, she slid her hand to the strong hollow of his throat and over the curve of his uninjured shoulder. Despite the temporary weakness caused by his illness, it was so easy to feel the strength contained in his body. He was made of solid muscle and thick sinew wrapped in smooth, polished skin, and she couldn't quite suppress the glimmer of heat that rippled through her at the pleasure of touching him.

He began to shiver, and she realized that despite the almost overpowering heat in the loft, he was chilled. The medicine hadn't done its job; the fever was still rising. As much as she wanted to give in to the temptation to warm him and make him comfortable, she knew it was more important to get the fever down.

She ran from the stables to the well and hauled up a bucket of water. In the quiet night, the creaking of the rope seemed unusually loud, and water poured back into the depths of the well.

She filled her own bucket, the small bits of metal that held the oak slats together cooling almost instantly as it was filled with the cold water. Their well was deep, one of the coldest in town.

When she returned to Jon's side, she dunked a rag in the water and began to wipe him down. He jerked away from her touch, mumbling under his breath; to him, it must feel as if he were being stroked with ice. The toweling quickly grew lukewarm, and she plunged it in the bucket again, grateful for the water's smooth coolness against her wrists.

She wiped every part of him that was bare; his forehead, his cheekbones, the smooth column of his neck, the broad panes of his back. The moisture didn't evaporate into the humid air, so his skin glistened with it, reflecting the rich, golden light from the lamp.

He began to talk again, feverish murmurings that made no sense, fragmented snippets of battle, senseless splinters of his childhood.

Again and again, she ran the cold cloth over him, twice returning for a fresh bucket of water when the one she had became too warm. The night took on a rhythm of its own, as she glided the cloth repeatedly over his heated skin. Her back began to ache, but she kept on, doing the only thing she could, the steady back-and-forth motion soothing her, and, she hoped, him. His restless stirring diminished slightly, and she watched shiny beads of water run down the swells of his back and settle in the hollow at the base of his spine.

His ramblings were more coherent now, no longer jumbled by the violent shudders of his body. He spewed out a long row of sentences.

270 SUSAN KAY LAW

Bennie frowned. It made no sense. He was feverish, perhaps delusional. And yet . . .

She leaned closer, listening carefully to the words tumbling from his mouth. As her hands continued to cool him, her brow furrowed in concentration.

Finally, so slowly she at first thought she'd imagined it because she was so hoping for it, his body began to cool. When she touched the back of her hand to his forehead, it no longer felt as if it would burn her own skin.

Wearily, she tossed the rag into the bucket. Through the tiny window, she could see the first graying of the sky. She'd been at it half the night, but if she'd been asked, she might have thought it days; the hours had all run together, a seamless blur of his skin under her hands.

Unfolding a fresh linen sheet over Jon's legs, her own limbs felt drained of all energy. Climbing down that ladder once again seemed like an almost overwhelming task.

Her cloak was spread out beside her and, with a sigh, she lay down on it, slipping her hands under her cheek. She needed to rest, just for a moment, needed to gather her strength. She could scarcely even manage to think. There was something she was supposed to be thinking about, she remembered vaguely, but she couldn't quite manage to catch hold of the thoughts.

Why was he so hot? Jon swam dizzily through vicious, heated blackness. Slowly, he became aware of bits of reality: the scratching of a rough blanket beneath his cheek, the damp stickiness of sweat on his body, and a steady, strong ache in his upper back.

Struggling to recall what had happened to him, he tried to force his eyes open. His thoughts were fuzzy, and it frustrated him that he couldn't think with his usual clarity.

The light that met his eyes was dim and diffuse, thick with dust and humidity. A bit of straw tickled his nose, and he huffed it away.

Beth. Not more than three feet from him, resting peacefully on her side, looking like an innocent child, her hands tucked underneath the smooth curve of her cheek. For a moment, he stopped struggling to make sense of it all and allowed himself the pure pleasure of looking at her.

Her skin was flushed with the heat and sheened with perspiration; her hair was a wild tumble of curls the color of the straw and sunlight that surrounded her. He realized he'd never before seen her with her hair completely free.

She was wearing a voluminous night rail that was made of a fabric thin enough to flow and dip over her wonderful soft curves. It was twisted around her body, tight over her breasts, and he wondered whether in enough sunlight the gauzy cloth would hint at the dark tips of her nipples.

She frowned in her sleep, her high forehead furrowing. What worries disturbed her rest? He shouldn't let her have any worries.

And she was much too special to be sleeping in hay. What was she doing here? He managed to take his eyes off her long enough to look around at his surroundings.

Familiar. It was the loft where they'd . . .

Oh, hell. He remembered going to the rendezvous,

only to find it had all gone bad. Somehow, his enemies had been there waiting for him. He'd made a run for it, and then there had been that fiery pain in his back.

He'd weakened so quickly. He'd had no place to go, no one he could turn to. He remembered reaching the stable and pitching head first onto the nearest pile of straw. The memories were fragmented after that, oddly distorted. There was a ladder and the awful, impossible task of climbing it. Beth had been there, twisting in and out of his memories, her hands cool and soothing upon him, her voice penetrating the fog in his head.

And there'd been nightmares. He couldn't really remember them, but he knew he'd had them. There was only a residual blackness; emptiness, violence, and the terrible certainty that, somehow, it was all his responsibility.

Her eyelids fluttered open, sable lashes sweeping up over eyes an even richer brown. Hazy awareness settled into them.

"Morning, Beth."

"Jon." Her lips curved into a sleepy smile, and he felt a sharp pang of regret that he'd never seen her awaken before. She was unconsciously sensual, settling slowly into wakefulness with an easy, natural stretch of her limbs. What would it be like, if he had the right to reach for her, making love to her in the morning when her body was still lethargic and damp with sleep? He imagined himself entering her slowly, while she leisurely arched beneath him and rubbed her cheek against the rasp of his morning beard.

He watched consciousness come over her. She sat up and pushed her hair back, the motion tightening her gown across her breasts, and he couldn't help watching the play of cloth over skin.

He dragged his gaze back to her face. The welcoming look she'd given him upon wakening had been replaced with distance and alert wariness. Her eyes were dark, the color of the best, freshly made coffee, liquid and shimmering—and impossible to fathom.

He'd spent a lot of time learning to look beneath the surface, trying to read the emotions she hid so well. He'd gotten quite good at it, but now, he found, he couldn't see anything at all. She was closed to him.

Well, why not? he berated himself. He was her enemy. In all likelihood, he'd shot at some of her family. He was lucky she hadn't killed him herself.

"How are you feeling?" she said slowly, as if choosing her words with great care.

He flexed his left arm experimentally, relieved to find it still functioned. The movement sent sharp pains shooting through his shoulder and down his back, and he ground his molars together against a groan. So it hurt. At least it worked.

"Hurts . . . a little. Not bad."

"You had a fever." She frowned a bit, then knelt beside him, tucking her gown between her knees, and dropped a hand to his forehead. "It seems to be gone now. Are you hungry?"

"A little."

"I'll bring you something later." She stared at him, her expression carefully controlled, showing no emotion at all. He was oddly piqued, just a bit. He'd have thought she'd be at least slightly happy at his recovery.

"Feel sticky," he said, conscious of the sweat and dirt

clinging to him. He didn't want to be soiled in her company, at least not on the outside. He couldn't do much for the inside.

"I'll wash you." She fetched a white enameled washbasin, filling it with a steady stream of water poured from the wooden bucket. As always, her motions were competent, graceful in their confidence and strength. This wasn't a woman who fumbled.

She dipped a cloth in the water, wringing it out with a strong twist of her wrists. He sighed in pleasure as she began to wash him, welcoming the cool cleansing, but her touch was distant and impersonal, as if she was simply a hired nurse caring for a tolerated patient.

"What happened?" she asked.

"Battle. Got shot."

"I didn't hear about any battles near here."

"Small one."

"Small one," she repeated slowly, her hands stilling on his back. "That's all?"

"All I remember." He tried a smile on her. This time, she didn't smile back.

Her hand went back to the pan, wetting the rag again. She was watching him intently.

"Don't you want to tell me anything else?" she asked flatly.

She was certainly acting odd. She had the right to be angry with him, considering what had happened between them. Yet, he didn't think that was the problem. There was something else, something that made her wary of him in a way she'd never been before. He saw another emotion, carefully hidden but simmering just beneath the surface. What was it?

"What?" he asked carefully.

"Oh, I was wondering what you've been doing since you've been gone."

"Missed you?" he tried.

He didn't see it coming. Water cascaded over his head, filling his open mouth, sluicing over his shoulders, soaking his bandage, pouring onto the blanket under him.

She'd actually dumped the wash water over him! Sputtering, he shook his head to clear his eyes. With his good arm, he pushed himself up slightly and stared at her.

It was anger. She towered over him, her gown swirling around her calves. Her eyes snapped with fire.

"You . . . you . . . How could you? How *could* you, you lying, deceptive, unprincipled—you're no more of an idiot than I am. No, *I'm* the idiot, for never having seen it in the first place!"

His tongue felt too big for his mouth. Damn! He'd spent three years in this role, and no one had ever seemed to catch even a glimmer of the truth. Now it was shot to hell, all because he'd done what he'd *known* from the beginning—oh, yes, he'd known—he shouldn't do: get involved with this woman.

Her foot was already on the first rung of the ladder.

"Where are you going?"

She glared at him. "To turn you in!"

He lifted an eyebrow. It was almost a relief, not to have to control every gesture. "In your nightgown?"

She glanced down, as if she'd forgotten what she was wearing. "Lord," she muttered, and her head disappeared below the floor of the loft.

She popped up again a moment later. "The horse is still there."

Bennie strode across the loft, chaff flying around her, and stopped in front of the window, mumbling under her breath something he couldn't quite catch.

"What horse?"

"My mother's."

"So?"

Pursing her lips, she spared him another searing glance. If she were a man, she'd make one hell of an army officer; all she'd need was that look and insubordinates would cower before her.

"So she's still here. So she hasn't left for Adam's yet. So *I* can't go back to the house or she'll see me like this."

"Oh." The strain on his shoulder was beginning to tell, and he lowered himself back to the blanket.

She wasn't leaving him yet.

20

She wanted to kill him. She'd spent a whole day and night, slaving away to save his worthless hide, and right now she felt fully capable of stripping it from him, inch by miserable inch.

How had she missed it? She took a quick peek at him; his eyes were blazing with intelligence and intensity. How could she not have seen it? All the vagueness was gone from his face, replaced with absolute control and concentration.

There was only one explanation. She'd been blinded, too bedazzled by that gorgeous face and body to bother with looking deeper. There'd been hints—oh, yes, there had been, and she'd ignored them. She'd pushed them away, writing them off as her imagination, or bits of the "past Jon" showing through, because she'd liked him as he was, now accessible and accepting.

He'd always been gorgeous, even with that deceptive vagueness on his face. Now, with his features sharpened, his eyes alight, he was absolutely devastating. And he looked entirely too calm.

"If you're going to be here awhile, you may as well sit down," he suggested.

"You really don't want me too close to you right now."

"I trust you." His grin was dazzling, almost enough to blunt the edges of her anger.

"You might want to rethink that." She sat down and leaned up against the stone wall beneath the window. It wouldn't do to get too close. Even if she didn't kill him, she was afraid his nearness would be enough to weaken her judgment again. This time, she was thinking clearly, no matter what.

"How did you know?"

"You had nightmares, with the fever. You talked a lot."

His eyes went gray, filled with a terrible bleakness that, irrationally, made her want to comfort him.

"Yes," he said, his voice strained. "And you know everything."

She shook her head. "I don't know who you work for."

She waited for his answer. Damn him, he wasn't going to tell her!

"Who?"

"It's not safe for me to tell you. It's better you don't know."

It had to be the Americans. It was the only thing that made sense, and it was a small balm to her wounds to believe that if she'd been duped and used, it had at least been for a good cause.

But if it was the Americans, why wouldn't he tell her? It was possible, she supposed, that he was working for British command, ferreting out spies among his own ranks.

"Better for whom? Tell me," she demanded.

"No."

"You owe me that much."

He simply shook his head.

"I'll turn you in!" she threatened.

He looked vaguely amused. "To who?"

Beneath them, the door to the stable creaked open.

"Hush," she whispered.

Your mother? he mouthed. She nodded.

They listened, the air in the loft crackling with tension, just as the atmosphere sometimes did before a violent storm. They could hear Mary preparing her horse, speaking softly to her mare in a sweet, modulated voice. When she'd led the mare out and closed the door behind her, Beth stood and peered out the window. Jon heard the thud of hooves on hard-packed earth, and she headed for the ladder.

"Beth? Are you coming back?"

That look again, the one that said she'd be more than willing to put a few more holes in him. Then she was gone without a word.

She did come back, when the sun was high overhead and heating up the loft like an oven prepared for the weekly baking.

Wearing a flowing ivory blouse and an earth-colored skirt, she had a bottle tucked underneath her arm and carried a covered basket that smelled of fresh, yeasty bread. Her hair was twisted into a thick braid, but wild curls sprang out around her temples.

Her hair was so like her. She tried hard to keep it all

in, keep it neatly contained, but little pieces kept finding their way free.

"For me?"

She handed him the food without speaking and turned to go.

He glanced at the label on the bottle and nearly strangled. "Dr. Walker's Jesuit Drops? Beth, I assure you—"

"It's cider." Her face flushed red. "I needed a bottle, so I just washed it out and used this one."

"I was afraid you were trying to tell me something," he said, giving her a lopsided smile, hoping the humor would cause her veneer to crack, just a little bit.

She continued on her way, but he didn't want her to go, not yet. "Beth," he said quietly. "I'm sorry."

She wasn't ready to hear it. She was gone before he could say any more.

Two days passed like that. Bennie came twice a day, bringing food, and left as quickly as she could, unable to bear being in the same room with him.

She was angry; oh yes, she was angry. He'd lied to her, had let her believe he was something he wasn't. Had let her learn to care for—to lie with—a man who didn't exist.

And yet, there was more to it. If her soul had been soothed and warmed by Jon, this stranger in her loft intrigued her. He radiated tangible power and exceptional intensity. As his body healed, she would have thought such a big man would get restless. He didn't. He was still, absorbed, perfectly controlled.

More than his body was in pain. She would watch him out of the corner of her eye, when she knew he wasn't looking. He stared off into the distance, his eyes fixed on some unknown point, his expression one of agony—she knew no other word for that extreme emotion.

What had happened to him? Even though he'd expertly deceived her about so much, she still felt that, somehow, she would have sensed it if he'd been in so much pain all along. It was as if his soul had been bruised and had never begun to heal, but rather had been pounded again and again until the wound was excruciating.

On the morning of the third day, Bennie came up to the loft with a bag slung over one shoulder, a bucket of fresh water hooked carefully over one hand.

The heat had yet to break. Although Jon surely would have given anything for a breath of fresh air, he'd never complained. Since the day his fever had turned, in fact, he'd never said anything, apparently respecting her wish for silence. It was as if it were his way of apologizing.

She glanced over at his motionless form. He was still asleep; he seemed to sleep most of the time, giving his body the rest it needed to heal. There'd been no recurrence of the fever, and his skin now glowed with a healthy bronze color, his former pallor gone.

Her heart gave a lurch—just a little one. Despite his injury, despite her justifiable anger, he was as gorgeous as ever. Every day when she made her brief visits, he lay there, clad only in a pair of breeches and his bandage, which exposed far too much of his body for her peace of mind. And some tiny, traitorous corner of her mind— and a slightly more demanding part of her body—insisted on remembering that the blanket he lay on was the one they had shared.

Squaring her shoulders against the roil of emotions, she marched over to him and nudged him with her toe.

"Jon."

His eyelids snapped open. "Jonathan," he answered sharply.

"What?" she asked, confused.

"Jonathan Schuyler Leighton. That's my name. Not Jon." His jaw was set, his mouth a harsh line.

"Jonathan, then." She slammed the bucket down, splattering a bit of water over the side, and dug into the sack. "Here. These pants belonged to one of my brothers. They should fit you."

His features softened. "You're talking to me."

"Only because I have to."

"Thank you." He plucked at the dirty, stained breeches he wore. "These are a little worse for the wear."

"I noticed."

A bit of a twinkle lit his blue eyes. "You did?"

Dropping the sack, she turned away abruptly.

"Leaving already?"

"No." She glanced at him over her shoulder. "I'll empty the other bucket later."

"Oh." Amazingly, a bright red flush crept up his neck. He'd been forced to use a bucket as a bedpan. Bennie had frequently helped nurse her brothers, and she was constantly surprised at how a man who was utterly crude around other men could become completely flustered over a simple bodily function when it was mentioned by a woman.

She clamped down on the smile that threatened to

emerge; she would not be charmed by a display of boyish modesty. Not after what he'd done to her.

"I'll change your bandage today," she said, and began laying out the things she would need. She looked up to find him watching her. Watching her, and smiling.

There was the man she remembered, the one she thought didn't exist. His eyes glowing with pale blue fire, he was smiling at her with that absolute acceptance, more, *approval,* that he always had. With that beautiful smile that made her feel like the most special woman on the face of the earth. And she remembered why she'd trusted him, and begun to care for him, so easily in the first place.

"Stop that!"

The bleak expression returned abruptly as the smile vanished. Bennie felt a pang of loss at its disappearance, even knowing she was the one who'd caused it.

"Do you miss the idiot so much?"

"Yes!" she cried.

His expression grew shuttered. "Change the bandage."

"Lie on your belly." He rolled over, propping his chin on his hands. She caught her breath, for even in such a simple motion the extent of his strength was evident. Muscles flexed and stretched, sliding and bunching easily under his skin. And she wondered, as she had once before, what had formed a man like this.

Taking her scissors, she knelt close against his side, where his breadth tapered abruptly to his waist. For a moment, she could only look. There was beauty in his body, not the cool, lifeless beauty of a sculpture, but the live, physical beauty of a champion stallion, running free in the breeze. It was the beauty of sweat and muscle and tendon, a beauty that moved, that worked, that touched.

He lifted his head slightly to look back at her. "Beth?"

"Oh. Yes." She slipped the tip of the scissors under the strips of cloth and snipped through them. Then she pushed them aside and carefully peeled off the padding, holding her breath, hoping the wound had begun to heal.

It looked better. The wound itself was still an angry red, but the skin around looked healthy. It was no longer swollen, nor marked with the telltale red of poisoning.

She prodded it gently, and his shoulder twitched.

"Does that hurt?"

"Only a little."

She continued to knead his shoulder, checking for tenderness or any softness that might indicate swelling. It seemed to be healing well. She pulled her hand away, her fingers brushing lightly down his back, and she heard his breath catch slightly.

"I'll wrap it up again now. Can you sit up?"

He was obviously stiff and sore. His movements were strained when he sat up, but even so, she could see the difference from the way he'd moved when he'd been playing the idiot. Now there was no awkwardness, no fumbling, no uncoordinated motion that would cause him to knock over glasses and bump into tables. He was a man clearly at ease in his body, graceful, in absolute control of his strength.

"Careful. You've been lying a long time. You're bound to be weak."

"Don't I know it." He laughed low, the familiar throaty rumble, but now with a distinct note of mockery. "My head doesn't seem to want to be vertical."

"It'll be better soon." She moved behind him. With a quick twist of her wrist she opened a tin of salve, and a pungent herbal odor filled the air. She dabbed the sticky substance on his wound, then covered it with fresh padding.

"I'll use strips of cloth to hold it in place again. It would help if you could lift your arms a bit."

He complied. "How did you ever manage this when I was out?"

"It wasn't easy." It wasn't this time, either; it caused her to be far closer to him than she wanted to be. She was on her knees at his back and had to stretch to wrap the strips around him. Her arms went over his shoulder and around his side again and again as she wound the bandage around his chest. Now matter how careful she was, her palms whispered over his flesh, and she couldn't help but remember how his body had felt when she'd really touched him.

She smelled summery herbs and male warmth. Her movements slowed, and she couldn't keep her breasts from brushing his back when she leaned forward to reach around him. She wondered for a moment if she was catching his fever, and shook her head to clear it.

"There." She tied the last strip neatly. "All done."

She didn't really have to move, did she? His head was bent, his hair falling forward. The strong column of his neck merged into the breadth of his shoulders in the most intriguing way. Her gaze traced down his back to where the scar she'd noticed before creased his side.

"What happened?"

"When?" He twisted to look over his shoulder at her.

"There. The scar on your side."

His eyes closed for a minute. When he opened them again, they were cool and pale, and she knew he was shielding something from her.

"Bunker Hill," he said curtly.

"Oh." She couldn't seem to stop her hand. Slowly, so slowly, she traced the line of the scar, trailing her fingers around along the edge of his ribs. Even this body, which seemed so mighty and impervious, was vulnerable to those little pieces of metal. And despite it all, she was fiercely glad he'd survived.

"Beth."

"Yes?" She looked up at him, her hand resting motionless on his side. His eyes were intent, his voice strained.

"Go."

Bewildered, she asked, "What?"

He lowered his gaze to her hand on him, and a muscle twitched in his jaw.

"Go! Now!"

Embarrassment flashed through her, and she snatched her hand back. Oh, God. Even now, she couldn't seem to keep her hands to herself. How shameless he must think her. She jumped up and fled the stables, ignoring him as he called her name.

She didn't come back that evening to bring his supper, as she usually did. He heard her mother return the mare to her stall, heard some man whose voice he couldn't identify—a customer, probably—come and fetch his own horse. Now and then he heard Cad's bellow across the yard, and Isaac's answering holler. Evening came, and although the temperature didn't drop one whit, he thought he caught the faint, distant scent of coolness. Perhaps the heat would finally break.

Still he waited, lying alone on his makeshift bed, sweating and calling himself a bastard in every language and form he could think of. Well, that was no surprise. One would think he'd be getting used to it by now. Yet he tasted the sharp tang of regret, for he knew that this time he'd had other choices.

He hadn't needed to be sharp with her. He could have shifted quietly away so she wouldn't have noticed. He could have feigned dizziness and lay down. He could have pretended her touch on his scar hurt.

But his brain had rapidly progressed beyond rational thought, clouded by the exceptional feel of her hand on him. If he hadn't chased her away, if it had lasted just one second longer, he would have reached for her. And after all he'd done to her and taken from her already, that was the last thing he had any right to do.

So he'd hurt her, once again, this time with his words and his tone of voice. He lay there, listening to mice scurry in the corners and the slight stirring of the heavy air in the leaves outside, and he pondered how something begun for all the right reasons could go so wrong.

21

He was on his feet. And he'd washed himself.

The next morning, when Bennie came up into the loft, Jon was standing, his forearm braced above the open window, staring out at the softness of the warm morning.

His hair was loose, clean, hanging in a smooth, rich brown sweep to his shoulders. He was wearing only the breeches she'd given him the day before, his shoulders bare and impossibly broad, and he was bathed in the buttery morning light. Her breath caught before she could steel herself to the sight of him.

As if any woman could ever manage that.

"Jon," she said softly.

"Jonathan," he said without turning around.

"Jonathan." A basket of fresh rolls swinging over her arm, she strolled over to him. "You're up."

"It's about time."

"And you were outside."

"Last night." His lips quirked wryly. "I couldn't stand to smell myself anymore. I went down very late, when no one would see me, and washed off at the well." He glanced down at her. "You have a very cold well."

A quick bubble of laughter escaped before she could hold it in. "I know." She had to tilt her head to look up at him. "How do you feel?"

"Weak. Nearly didn't make it back up that damn ladder. But in a day or two I should be ready to leave."

A day or two. She should be thrilled to get rid of him. Yet her heart sank at his words. "I can't get used to hearing so many words coming out of your mouth."

He grinned suddenly. "I don't usually talk so much. But then, I do a lot of things around you I don't usually do."

He didn't mean anything by that—he couldn't, and she'd be a fool if she allowed herself to believe he might. But she wanted to, oh, how she wanted to.

He glanced back out the window. "Smells like rain."

Forcing her wayward thoughts into line, she leaned closer to the window and sniffed. "I think you're right. Maybe it'll cool off some."

He smiled down at her, a quick glint of blue in his eyes. "I doubt it."

He was amused about something. Puzzled, she made no attempt to understand the workings of what was clearly a very convoluted mind. She lifted the basket. "I brought you some breakfast."

"You didn't have to."

"You must be hungry. I'm sorry that I didn't bring you any food last night."

He shrugged. "You're the last person in the world who owes me an apology. You probably saved my life."

"Then we're even." Their gazes caught, and she was lost in the pale blue depths of his eyes. She knew she spoke the truth. No matter what devious actions he was involved in, the night he'd saved her in the forest had been real. It had happened too fast, too unpredictably, to be something staged for her benefit. She'd seen how hard he'd hit that soldier.

"You don't know how many times I've tried to convince myself how stupid that was," he said quietly.

"Really?" Sunlight warmed her shoulders and shone off his hair. The fragrant smells of yeast and cinnamon rose to her nostrils.

"I don't regret it," he said, his voice a rich rumble.

Helplessly, she let her gaze wander over his chest. It had been as close to heaven as she'd ever expected to get in this lifetime, being carried through the cold winter night, held close against that brawny, warm chest. Later, of course, in this very loft, she'd reached heaven itself.

He cleared his throat and stepped back. "Uh, would you like to stay and eat with me?"

How did he always know, whenever her thoughts turned wanton? Then he would pull away, clearly uncomfortable with her attentions. And why wouldn't he be? She was only Bennie. Certainly not the kind of woman he'd choose under normal circumstances.

She shook her head. "I shouldn't."

"Just for a little while." There was a plea in eyes, along with an apology and something that looked like . . . loneliness?

"All right."

They sat down on the blankets, and she handed

him a bun, sticky with honey and currants. He ate half of it in one bite. It was lucky she was well acquainted with the appetites of big, hungry men. She'd brought plenty.

He grinned in appreciation of the delectable treat. "How do you keep managing to smuggle so much food to me without anyone noticing?"

"My mother's gone a lot."

"I noticed. Where does she go?"

"Out to Adam's place. My sister-in-law isn't feeling well."

"Is she seriously ill?"

"No." She smiled. "It seems Adam was busy again before he left for Cambridge."

He raised an eyebrow in question.

"I'm going to have another nephew."

"You're so sure it's a nephew?"

Bennie licked a drop of honey off her thumb. "She's sick."

"From what I hear, that's not uncommon."

"My mother was very ill for five months with each of my brothers." She tapped her chest. "With me, nary a day. So far, it's been the same with every one of my sisters-in-law. None of them felt well, except when Hannah carried Sarah."

"I've never heard of such a thing."

"Hannah says that Jones men bedevil women from the beginning."

"But doesn't your mother ever notice how much food is missing?"

Bennie grimaced. "She's used to my appetite."

"Your appetite?"

"Mother's despaired of ever teaching me to eat like a lady."

"Why would you want to? Picking at your food, wasting away like you've got some dread disease. I've never figured out why women put up with it."

"Why do women do any silly thing? To catch a husband."

The glint in his eyes was wicked and satisfied. "There's something to be said for a woman who can enjoy life and food in full measure."

She grinned and sank her teeth into her bun.

"You have honey by your mouth."

"Where?" She stuck her tongue out to one side, attempting to get it. "Here?"

"No. Here." It caught her completely by surprise. He leaned forward in a motion so natural and casual she thought he merely meant to point it out. But then he licked her, his tongue sliding quickly across the corner of her mouth and just along the edge of her upper lip. He sat back before she had a chance to respond.

"Mmm. Sweet."

Openmouthed, she stared at him.

"It's gone," he said cheerfully.

Snapping her mouth shut, she scrambled to her knees. "I have to go."

He put his hand on her arm to stop her. "Why?"

Outside, the soft patter of falling raindrops began. A crisp wind blew in through the window, finally sweeping away the heavy, heated air, bringing the fresh, metallic scent of rain.

He glanced out at the sky, and when he returned his

gaze to her, his eyes were dark and intent. "No thunder this time," he said softly.

She was caught, held motionless by the velvet in his voice and the gentle warmth of his hand on her arm. *No*, she mouthed.

"I miss the thunder."

Oh, Lord. If only she could be sure that the thunder was all he wanted. If only she was completely convinced he was not her enemy. And if only she had the faintest idea how to handle a man like him.

"I have to go!" She jerked her arm away and jumped to her feet.

"Why?" His voice rose, his frustration clearly evident. He got up and planted himself in her way. "Why? Why do you miss the idiot so much? I would think most women would be happy to find out the man they slept with wasn't simpleminded!"

He blocked her path, his big form seeming to take up even more space than it usually did. Why did she never seem to remember the overwhelming impact of his physical presence? And why did she, who was so used to large, powerful men, seem completely unable to accustom herself to this one?

The refreshing breeze cooled the back of her neck, rustling the fine hairs there. It lifted Jon's hair away from his face, leaving the beautifully sculpted features clearly evident—the straight nose, the jutting jaw, those strange pale eyes, now lit with fierce intelligence. There was nothing fine or thin about his face; it was all strength and forceful masculinity.

"Lord, you're so beautiful," she whispered helplessly.

"So what!" He gestured to his face. "So some accident

of nature gave me these features. What does it matter?"

"Women must throw themselves at your feet."

"It's not generally been my desire to have women at my feet."

"I'm sure they'd be happy to throw themselves at other parts of your anatomy too."

"So maybe they threw. That doesn't mean I caught."

She gave a small snort of disbelief and made a move to go around him. He sidestepped quickly to stop her.

"Beth." His voice was barely more than a whisper. He cupped her cheek in his palm. If so much about Jon—Jonathan—had changed, his touch was the same: reverent, tender, almost heartbreakingly gentle. "There have been very few women."

"You can't expect me to believe that."

His thumb swept down, barely touching the corner of her mouth. "I learned very early that the act, without any affection, any understanding, was empty, brought no more lasting satisfaction than any other bodily function. No more important than a sneeze. But my job has left very little time for any affection to grow. And, since I began this charade, there's been no way to allow any woman to get close to me at all."

"I don't know who you are."

He rubbed lightly, tempting her to turn her head and take his thumb into her mouth. "You know me better than you realize."

Jon, Jonathan—one was as bad as the other. In any role, he made her weak, wanton, prone to forget anything but the way he made her feel. There was no denying the heat in his eyes when he looked at her, and it made her feel pretty and seductive and utterly feminine. It was a heady temptation.

She tried again. "I have to go."

"It's raining. You'll get wet."

"I've been wet before."

He leaned closer, breaching the distance she'd put between them. "I know."

Heat flashed through her, as sudden and sharp as lightning. One more inch, one more second, and she'd be lost. Dashing to one side, she tried to flee this man she seemed unable to resist.

He caught her, hauling her up against his body, holding her softly but securely to him. "What is it?" he ground out. "You liked the simpleminded lout? You thought you could handle him? You don't know what to do with a man who can match you?"

"Yes! He was simple and uncomplicated and easy to be with. He didn't keep secrets and hatch plots and twist me up until I don't know what's right or wrong! And he didn't hurt me!"

The light in his eyes went flat, his shoulders drooped, and he let her go so abruptly she stumbled. Stepping aside, he allowed her to pass.

She hitched up her skirts and fairly slid down the ladder. Rain splattered in her face when she tugged open the door, but she paid no mind. The chilly water soaked quickly through her thin summer clothes and ran down her temples. She splashed through the puddles in the yard, but still she ran, heading toward home—heading toward safety.

* * *

The rain had only lasted an hour or two, but it had washed the air clean of dust and stench and suffocating heat. The leaves on the trees shone wet, bright green. Birds hopped around on the ground, snatching at bugs and tugging at earthworms.

And Bennie stood in the middle of the muddy yard, staring up at the window in the loft.

There was no excuse for it. There'd been enough food in the basket she'd brought that morning to keep him fed the rest of the day. His wound needed the minimum of care. He was completely out of danger.

The only possible reason for her going up there was simply that she wished to see him again. It was silly, it was foolish, it was quite probably downright stupid— and she was going to do it.

He was by the window again, all stillness and power. The new sunlight bathed his naked chest in gold. Bennie took one look at him and knew she was lost.

"Hello," she ventured when she reached him. He had his hair pulled back, knotted with a piece of twine, and his brooding profile faced out the window.

He wouldn't look at her, he'd decided. He'd watched her striding across the wet ground. She moved like no woman he'd ever seen, sure, decisive. And he knew that if she came up to the loft, he couldn't look at her. For every time he did, he did things he'd promised himself he wouldn't; he forgot every lesson he'd ever learned about restraint and self-preservation and control.

But as soon as she got close to him, he caught a whiff of lavender, underlain with the faintest hint of womanly skin. He hadn't counted on that. He still wouldn't look at her, for his sake as well as her own. For when she'd said that he had hurt her, he'd felt the sickness in his gut; it was like taking a punch he hadn't known was coming. He couldn't do that to her again.

He felt her fingers lightly following the scar on his side, his badge of honor—hah! his badge of shame— from the battle that had taken Sergeant Hitchcock's life.

"Was it so terrible? The battle, I mean?" she asked.

When he looked down at her, Bennie saw it again: that terrible, bleak despair that glazed his eyes.

"Yes."

She rubbed the scar, as if smoothing away the hurt. "My brothers were there. None were hurt, though. Henry has been back here since, on leave. He said it was glorious."

"It's not." He turned away from her. "I was like him when I was young. You get into something, sure you're doing the right thing for honor and glory and country." He shut his eyes and leaned his forehead against the fist braced over the window. "Then you're in this situation, and every choice you can make is wrong, and you don't know how you're going to live with the one you choose."

"How do you?"

"You don't. You just hang on to the only thing you have left."

"Which is?" she whispered, unable to bear his pain, unsure she wanted to know the answer, but compelled to try and understand this man.

"Loyalty."

He was no more than a foot from her, but he was suddenly so far away, closed into himself.

"Will you bring me some more clothes tomorrow? A shirt?" he asked.

Her throat closed. "You're leaving?"

He nodded.

"All right," she agreed, knowing it would be useless to protest. "Is there anything else you need?"

You! he wanted to shout. But there was no way he could drag her into the darkness with him. She belonged in the sunshine, with the wind tangling those wild curls and her music lifting to the sky. "No."

"I'll leave you alone, then," she said, and turned to go.

Surely he could give himself this much. He could have one simple afternoon of sunshine to take with him, back to the cold.

"Stay," he said softly.

Her eyes were wide and wary; she was like a forest creature confronting a man for the first time, drawn by curiosity, repelled by danger. Finally she nodded her agreement.

Carefully avoiding touching each other, they settled back down on the blankets. Bennie smoothed her skirt —she'd changed into a dark green one after her soaking that morning—over her knees and tried to think of a relatively harmless topic of conversation.

The silence between them seemed awkward. She felt nervous, and unsure. He was watching her, she knew, but she couldn't chance looking up and getting lost in his eyes again. When he'd been only Jon, silence between them had been easy and companionable. Now it seemed empty, and she searched for something to fill it.

But nothing she could think of seemed harmless. The hell with it, she thought recklessly. She squared her shoulders and forced her gaze up to meet his.

"How did you end up here?"

One corner of his mouth lifted. "I rode a horse."

"No, I meant—" She stopped. "What happened to your horse, anyway?"

"I turned him loose. He'll find his way back to Boston. Someone in the company will take care of him."

"But how will you get back?"

"I'll manage." One knee was bent, his forearm propped on it, his hand dangling loosely. "You were about to ask me something?"

"I meant, how did you end up here? At this place in your life?

"Playing this role, do you mean?"

"Yes."

He picked up a long piece of hay and began to methodically break it into pieces. "Most of what I told you was true. I did go live with my aunt and her husband after my parents died. And they weren't particularly interested in me. They had several children of their own, and I was simply a reminder of their "common" relatives. It didn't seem to help that they had a son my own age, and I was always bigger than he, and could run faster, and the tutors thought I was easier to teach, and I was . . ."

"Better-looking?" she suggested.

"Yes." He cleared his throat. "Well, as soon as I was old enough, they bought me a commission. No cavalry for me, of course. Something slightly less expensive. Still, it was probably the best thing they ever did for me."

His voice was calm, carefully modulated. Yet, he snapped the bit of straw with more and more force. There was still some of that boy inside him, she realized, that growing man who had been so young and unwanted.

"I learned early on that I had a talent for . . . solving puzzles, I guess you might say. Taking snippets of information, things that nobody else seemed to notice, and putting them together. My superiors soon made use of it."

"And so you became involved in spying."

"Yes." He crushed the last piece of the hay in his palm. He opened his hand, and chaff and dust drifted down to the floor. "I really did get kicked by a horse, you know. Three years ago. When I came to, I was . . . muddled. Couldn't make the words come out properly. I was like that for several days.

"But I noticed, when I was like that, that no one paid very much attention to me. Because I didn't make any sense when I spoke, they assumed I couldn't understand much either. They didn't guard their tongues carefully around me, and I found out things it might have taken me weeks to discover otherwise."

He was brilliant, she realized. Enough so to carry on such a masquerade for three years and have no one ever suspect.

"So you decided to continue the ruse."

"Yes. It was quite simple, really."

Simple. To spend all that time, making his graceful body move clumsily. To veil the sparkling intelligence in his eyes under sleepy, half closed lids. To soften the lines of his face and wander around with that good-natured grin. And what must have been worst of all, to completely bury his pride, to end up in pig wallows and snowbanks, to take all the taunts and the condescension and the outright cruelty, knowing all the while he could outthink any one of them. The force of will and the concentration it must have taken was amazing.

"How did you ever manage it?"

"I thought it was the right thing to do."

She would have given a lot to be able to wipe the bleakness from his eyes. All the arguments she'd given herself to leave him the day before suddenly seemed much less important.

"Enough of that." He picked up another piece of hay and stroked her cheek with it. It tickled and she laughed lightly. "What about you?"

"What about me?"

"How did you get here?"

"I've always been here."

Had she? he wondered. Had she always been this fascinating person, unlike any other woman he'd ever met? What had made her so serene and controlled on the surface, so strong and yet so giving underneath?

"And do you always want to stay here?"

"Yes, I think so."

"You told me once that all you wanted was your family and your music."

Her mouth opened slightly, and he wanted nothing more than to see if it was as sweet as he remembered.

"You remembered," she said, clearly surprised.

"Yes. Was it true? Surely there's more. A family of your own, perhaps?"

"That's not something I could ever really have." Color bloomed on her cheeks, a delicate, honey-hued rose that made her eyes look all the darker. "I want . . . someone to look at me and see me." She laughed self-consciously and dropped her head. Wild, loose curls fell around her face, each a different hue, gold and tan and brown, the colors of harvest and plenty. "See me, not just another Jones offspring like all the others, or a woman who can't quite manage to be a lady like her mother, or the one who towered over them in school and still does. I want someone to see just . . . me."

"Beth." He placed his knuckle under her chin and gently tipped her head back up, urging her to look him in the eye. Her own eyes were luminous, shimmering with emotion, and he knew that once again she was allowing him to glimpse beneath the surface. He was grateful for the gift, but he asked for still more. "Would you play for me again, Beth?"

22

She kept her violin in the loft now. The extremes of humidity and temperature weren't good for the instrument, but it was simpler than forever trying to sneak it out of the house past her mother. And for some reason, it seemed to belong here.

She undid the leather clasps; the violin was snuggled safely in its case. The smooth wood gleamed richly, winking at her like an old friend. She lifted it out and tucked it under her chin.

He loved her concentration, the almost sensual way she took pleasure in the look and feel of her instrument. Her fingers trailed over the surface the way they had once stroked him.

Strands of hair curled tightly at her temples; the rest tumbled down her back in a luxurious cascade. The dark, shining wood of the instrument was nearly the same color as her eyes, sparkling in anticipation and enjoyment.

She tuned the instrument, frowning as she plucked strings, tightened them, and tested the tone again. Finally, she gave a brisk nod and began to play.

Before, when she'd played for him, he'd often closed his eyes, preferring to let the music wash over him without the distraction of his other senses. And too, he'd been afraid that something would show in his eyes, that she would catch a glimpse of how the music moved him, would see too much of the man beneath the role.

Now, he watched. Her fingers were strong and supple, nimble as they plucked at strings, fluid as they pulled the bow. She was totally absorbed, often closing her eyes or swaying from side to side. All the passion and emotion in her music were also clearly evident on her face. She was stripped of her surface control, all the fascinating layers of her soul laid bare.

Her music had changed again, he realized. It had lost the surface veneer of smoothness. Now there was only emotion, raw and exposed. Sometimes it was quick, fragmented, light little sparkles of joy; and then there was pain, turbulent, harsh, violent.

She played until her back ached and her fingers were sore. She was only peripherally aware of Jon's eyes on her, but she felt him, deep down inside, as she played. Oh, yes, it was better when the music was shared. Yet she somehow knew there was no one else who would share it like he did, not with just sympathy or appreciation, but empathy. He *felt* her music, and she knew it. If she would never have this opportunity again, then she would use it to the fullest.

Finally, exhausted and breathless, she collapsed on the blanket. He clapped slowly in appreciation.

Flushed but pleased, she put a finger to her lips. "Shh. Someone might hear you, and I'd have to pretend I was applauding myself."

"Sorry. I forgot." He had. While he had only to watch and listen to her play, he had forgotten where he was and how he'd gotten there. He'd forgotten all the things he'd done, and all the things he had yet to do.

It had been blissful. But it was over.

The smile faded quickly from his face, she noticed, and she was tempted to lift the violin again and play something light and airy that would bring it back. He had such a wonderful smile, one that made her feel as if she were bathed in sunlight.

But his face hardened with a new, cold determination, and she doubted she could bring the smile back, no matter how well she played. She reverently laid the violin back in its case, stowed it away, and turned to face him.

"You will remember the clothes?" he asked.

Her heart tumbled to the vicinity of her knees.

"Yes. Tomorrow."

She brought him the clothes in the morning, when she delivered his breakfast, and came back again at noon with more food. But their conversation was stilted and awkward. What could they say? There was nothing more he could tell her. And there was nothing more she dared ask. She promised to return near dusk, bringing a few supplies that he could take with him when he left.

The evening was still and pleasantly warm. Crickets chirped in the grass, freshly green after the recent rains.

The sun dropped below the trees in the west, edging them in brilliant gold.

Bennie clambered up to the loft one more time. Jonathan was bending over, fastening the leather latchets on Henry's new low-heeled shoes. Someday it was going to be interesting explaining to her brothers what had happened to their clothes while they were away.

He waved a greeting at her and straightened. She stopped, and her heart skipped a beat.

As a simpleminded soldier in a scarlet and white uniform, he'd been beautiful. As a wounded man in breeches and a too-revealing bandage, he'd been compelling. But dressed in simple clothes, he was downright stunning.

The ivory linen shirt, its sleeves loose and flowing, fit his massive shoulders well. He wore thick woolen stockings, full, dark brown breeches, and a plain leather jerkin. He stood tall and straight, his hair tied neatly in a scrap of ribbon. His presence was nearly overpowering, and he was every inch the image of a proud American man. She knew her brothers, who were quite proud of their own good looks, would be roundly jealous of the way this man looked in the clothes they'd unknowingly donated.

"Beth." He came to stand near to her—as close as he dared, but farther than he wanted to be. Standing in the middle of the nearly empty loft, surrounded by drifts of hay, she was tall and proud and absolutely striking. She'd brought the supplies she'd promised him in a sack slung over one shoulder, and she was unsmiling, her eyes dark and remote.

He'd spent the afternoon very inexpertly sewing the

crucial packet into the lining of his jerkin. The instant he'd become coherent he'd looked for it. To his immense relief, it had still been securely bundled into the padding he had wrapped around his waist. The whole mess— bloody padding, shirt, jacket—had been dumped in a corner of the loft. Obviously, Beth hadn't had time to worry about finding another place to dispose of it.

The entire time, while he jabbed his fingers with the needle he'd taken from the bag of supplies Beth had left and made long, clumsy stitches, he'd tried to think of a reason—even the weakest of ones—to stay here another day or two. It wasn't difficult; he wasn't strong enough; another day added to his absence would make no difference; he needed time to make better plans.

None were any more than what he knew them to be—excuses. He simply wanted to look on her face a few more times. But there were no real excuses. He had information that still had to be delivered, and he had to somehow discover what had gone wrong the other evening at the fort.

He had a job to return to. If it was a job that had turned out to be infinitely uglier than he had known when he began, it was still his duty. He had little else.

As he looked down at her, admiring the prominent curve of her cheekbones and the lush lashes that were shades darker than her hair, he knew there was yet another reason to leave now. For if he stayed, there was no guarantee that he wouldn't try to take more from her than he already had. And he had already taken far too much.

"Here." She dropped the sack at his feet. "There should be enough food for two days or so. How are you going to get back? I suppose we could pretend a horse was stolen, but—"

"No. I'll manage. I hardly look much like any Lieutenant Leighton now." The risk was greater than she suspected; there was always the possibility he'd been recognized the night he'd been shot. But he had little choice; there was no other way to get the information through, no other way to begin to find out why the ambush had been set in the first place. It was becoming increasingly clear that the other side had an agent of their own, one both dedicated and clever.

He could only trust that his disguise had been enough to prevent recognition. If not, it was quite likely too late for him anyway.

"I won't take anything else from you, Beth." Unable to resist, he brushed a stray curl off her temple. "There is one thing I want you to know. I never, never, meant to do you any harm." He rubbed the strand of hair between his forefinger and thumb, savoring its softness. "I tried to tell you in the letter, but—"

"The letter?" Her eyes widened.

"Didn't you get it?"

"Yes." She put her hand in her pocket, feeling the square of paper she always kept there. The paper was soft, the edges fuzzy from constant handling. "You wrote that, didn't you? There was no merchant you paid."

"Yes."

She should have known. The bold, angular handwriting. It was so much like him. Who else could have written it?

"I tried to tell you in the letter, but I was afraid

someone else might read it. And, well, I didn't know how to tell you . . . the proper way."

He seemed at a loss for words. It was a trait familiar in Jon but one she hadn't seen since he'd dropped his charade.

She felt his pain, sharp and acute, as if it were her own. The urge to comfort, to lay her hands on him and soothe him, was almost overwhelming. It was as if she had some old, powerful connection with him. She'd felt it from the beginning, and the feeling had only increased since he'd ceased to play his role. It was more than sympathy, more than understanding. It was a basic, almost elemental . . . oneness.

And yet, he could very well be her enemy. If only she knew who—and what—he really was. He'd fooled her completely once. There was no guarantee he wasn't doing it again, and, if he was, she was sending a British soldier—worse, a British spy—back into battle against her countrymen and family.

"Tell me who you're working for," she demanded.

He merely looked at her, his expression unreadable.

"Tell me!" She grabbed his jerkin in both fists, as if she could shake it out of him. "You owe me that much!"

He couldn't tell her. It would serve no purpose—save his own—and could possibly put her in danger. His mind recoiled at the thought. It was one more thing to hate himself for, the idea that he might have exposed her to harm simply by coming here; he couldn't compound that, especially since the only reason for doing so would be to make her smile at him again.

She realized he wasn't going to tell her. "Damn you!"

she cried, pounding on his chest. He caught her wrists to stop her, his grip painless but firm.

"Even if I told you, why would you believe me?"

The impact of his words sent her thoughts reeling. *He had lied to her.* Still, she had never completely *felt* it, had never truly believed that he was fully prepared to lie to her again.

"It would be so easy," he said slowly. "I could tell you that I work for the Americans. Why not? It would make you happy, and you would believe me, wouldn't you?"

Damn him. She *would* have believed, would have accepted his allegiance without a second thought.

"God damn you!" Heat flashed in her chest and scorched behind her eyes. "You liar!" She twisted her arms violently to free them, and the skin on her wrists burned. Blindly, she ran toward the ladder and escape.

"Yes!" He caught her easily, grabbing her from behind and pushing her up against the wall under the high peaked roof of the loft. He held her there, caged by his big body and the thick arms planted on either side of her head. "I lied."

His eyes were fiery blue, brimming with unleashed violence. So many times she'd looked into those eyes, and all she'd ever seen was gentleness. Why hadn't she ever seen the capacity for ruthlessness, for fury?

Still, she felt no fear. If there was one thing she knew, with a soul-deep certainty that seemed grounded in her bones, it was that his violence would never be turned on her. Even as his body held hers against the wall, it touched her softly, with no hint of a threat. His gaze roamed over her face, and she felt as if his fingers whispered over her features. His warmth crept through her clothes, and, suddenly, she felt more cradled than caged.

"That's what I do, Beth. I lie." The smooth rumble of his voice was harsh now, singed with anguish. "To you, to everyone . . . even to myself."

He was close now, so close she could feel the motion of his chest as he breathed. "Don't ever believe what I tell you, Beth." He dropped his head, his lips hovering inches from hers. "Even when I tell you I love you."

His lips brushed hers when he spoke, and she began to tremble, quaking between the hard stone at her back and the warm man at her front.

"Especially when I say I love you."

He kissed her then; his lips were hard, searching, demanding almost to the point of desperation. Her senses clouded, filled with Jonathan. His chest was hard against her breasts, and her nostrils filled with the sweet, earthy scents of hay and skin. The sound of his exhalation sighed past her ear; tiny points of lights, like drunken stars, whirled behind her closed lids.

And her heart believed. Despite it all, despite all the evidence, despite his self-condemnation, and despite the logic of her own brain, her heart and body believed him.

The force of will that had made it possible for him to deceive every person he came in contact with for three years, the will that propelled him, injured and nearly insensate, to this stable, was the only thing that allowed him to wrench his lips from hers. Even so, he felt the loss of her mouth so acutely it was nearly painful.

Her eyes were wide, dark, and beautiful, like those of a wild doe caught unaware, unsure if there was danger. And he knew, with terrible certainty, that *he* was the danger.

He tried to force himself to push away, tried so hard his arms shook with the effort. The feel of her was so exquisitely lovely he couldn't bring himself to do it.

But the last time he had touched her, it had been in this stable, too. He had taken her—he couldn't make it sound better by calling it something else, for he had taken—he had done so in a matter of minutes, without even bothering to remove her clothes. He had done it in the loft of a stable, as if she were a barmaid or domestic servant, a setting so fabled it was cliché. A roll in the hay. And he had let her—no, seduced her into making love with a man who didn't exist.

She deserved better than straw and fumbles, rapidity and lies. She deserved snowy sheets and a fresh, downy mattress tick, whispered endearments and genuine promises.

She deserved honor. He had given her none.

Remorse worked where guilt had failed. He let her go, moving back and turning away, unable to look at the revulsion and betrayal he was sure must be etched on her angular features.

His was a job that depended on expediency and left very little room for honor; he found one remaining shred, and he clutched it. The demands of his body, heavy and swollen, were nearly impossible to subdue. Rubbing a palm over his face, he conjured up the image of the battlefield, letting the dirt, gore, and ugliness remind him of all the reasons he must not touch her again.

There was the rustle of straw, and he knew she was leaving. He prayed it would be quickly, before the last battered shards of his integrity wore out.

And then he felt her touch.

His back had been to her, his head bowed, his shoulders hunched. She had known—she had *felt*—his despair, and she had realized one thing: she could not leave him like this. She came to stand before him and placed her hand on his chest, spreading her fingers wide to touch as much of him as possible. Heat seeped through the fine linen shirt, warming her palm, and she felt the accelerating rhythm of his heart.

He lifted his head, and his eyes were dark and wild.

"Oh, God, Beth." His throat worked convulsively. "When I close my eyes, all I see is blood. But when I touch you, all I see is you."

She took his hand and placed it over her heart. His big hand rested there, motionless, the long fingers spreading over the upper swell of her breast, and her own heartbeat quickened.

"Then touch me," she whispered.

23

For a moment, she thought he wasn't going to do it. Then he placed his hand over hers where it rested on his chest, pressing it to him. He stepped closer and, slowly—far, far too slowly—lowered his head.

He brushed his mouth over her face, over her temple, her cheek, her eyelids, her chin, with delicate little touches that left her yearning for more, and she wondered if each place he kissed glowed. It certainly felt like it.

He kissed the spot where her jaw met her neck, and the tip of her nose, then let his lips roam along the edge of her hairline. And finally, his mouth found hers. His lips were supple and mobile, playing lightly, drawing subtle little sighs from her, coming back for more. His tongue traced the edges of her lips, lingering here, exploring there, as if there were all the time in the world, and skated along the seam of her mouth.

He gave a harsh sigh, put his palm on the back of her head, and drew her close. His other arm came around her back, he tucked her head under his chin, and held her. Just held her.

They stood there, bodies pressed together, slowly rocking back and forth. Tentatively, she slipped her arms around his neck and found the ribbon binding his hair. A single, sharp yank and his hair was free, spilling down around his shoulders and over her hands. Sliding her fingers through it, she marveled at the silky texture.

"Oh, Beth." He rubbed his cheek against the top of her head. "For the rest of my life, every time I smell lavender, I think I'll get hard."

He thrust his hips, just once, just enough so she could feel him, and her cheeks burned. She buried her face against his shoulder.

"Beth." He sounded lighthearted, and her own heart swelled with joy. He bent, catching her behind the knees, and swept her into his arms.

His eyes gleamed with a note of wickedness, and he grinned. "If you only knew . . ."

He carried her easily over to his makeshift pallet, muttering under his breath as he tried, with his toe, to kick it into some semblance of order. He looked down at the jumbled blankets, and regarded her seriously.

"I'm sorry, Beth. You deserve better."

"Shh." She stopped his words with her mouth. He resisted for a moment, then yielded, his lips twisting over hers, becoming more insistent. He lowered her to the blanket without breaking the contact of their bodies, following her down.

Once she'd thought his kiss was magic. Now she knew it was something stronger than that, darker, an enchantment she didn't want to resist. He slid his tongue wetly along the inside of her lower lip, and she opened her mouth, silently beckoning him deeper.

His tongue flirted with hers, teasing, probing the depths of her mouth. She lifted her head, trying to get closer, and he obliged, deepening the kiss until her head reeled as if she'd sampled far too much of her father's supplies.

He drew back, propping himself on an elbow, one leg resting intimately between hers. Her regarded her with absolute concentration, and she knew he thought of nothing else but her and was glad of it.

Her thick braid lay over one shoulder, and he ran his hand down the length of it. The back of his hand brushed her breast along the way, and she caught her breath at the abrupt tightening of her nipple.

"May I?" he asked, holding up the end of her braid, which was wrapped with a length of string.

"Of course."

He worked the twine free, then slowly undid the braid, completely absorbed in his task. "There are so many colors in your hair. Sunshine and moonbeams, ripe wheat and fresh earth." He let a strand curl in his palm. "So vibrant. Alive." He smiled at her, his teeth flashing white through the dimness in the loft. "Like you."

"Jonathan," she protested, unused to such praise.

"Hush now. I'm busy."

With a single-minded sense of purpose, he set himself to divesting her of her clothes, seemingly undeterred by the flush of embarrassment she felt heating her cheeks.

Her blouse was over her head nearly before she realized it had been unbuttoned. She was distracted, her head muddled from his intoxicating kisses and the caresses he dropped on exposed portions of her body. Her skirt followed, tossed over his shoulder, and he flashed a grin that should have belonged to a storied pirate.

His fingers were deft, and he dealt with her corset with one pull on the single string. With a slight grimace, he flipped it, too, somewhere in the gloom behind him.

"I wouldn't have thought you would wear one of those."

"It comforts Mother."

"Still . . ." His hands circled her waist, rubbing with gentle care. "You certainly don't need one."

"I'm hardly small, Jonathan."

"Compared to me . . ."

"Compared to you, Goliath was small."

"Perhaps." His gaze traced over her slowly, and the flash of blue in his eyes told her how much he liked what he saw. "Do you know what a pleasure it is, not to have to worry about a woman's fragility or my clumsiness?"

The snug waistband of her petticoats suddenly loosened, and she knew he'd already untied the tapes. "You are never clumsy unless you intend it."

"Lift up." She complied, and the fine cambric whispered over her skin as he slipped her chemise over her head. She was sensitized by his touch and his kisses, and the slight friction of the fabric felt nothing like it ever had before. It was no longer innocuous and everyday; now it hinted of caresses and hidden pleasures.

Her shoes and stockings were the work of a moment. He paid no attention to her hesitation and stripped off her petticoats and pocket tapes.

His obvious approval left little room for modesty.

She lay there, sprawled naked against the scratchy blanket, and his gaze was almost a touch.

As stunning as the time before had been, with the thunder and impenetrable blackness, the addition of sight seemed to sharpen her other senses. It was arousing simply to watch the play of emotions on his face, to see his nostrils flare, his eyes darken, and his features sharpen, and to know that she had caused it.

He was beautiful, lit with fire and passion. But he wore far too many clothes.

She sat up and reached for the neck of his shirt. He caught her hands and stopped her.

"Why?" she asked.

"Beth . . ." There was a flicker of something disturbing in his eyes.

"Please. I want to see you."

His jaw twitched and he nearly ripped off the leather jerkin. He yanked the shirt over his head and balled it up, hurling it almost violently against the sharply slanting roof of the loft.

The wrappings of the bandage slashed white across his chest, drawing her attention. It seemed almost sacrilegious to scar that sculpted perfection, yet it had happened twice.

His muscles bulged as he stretched out beside her, and once more his gaze swept her body.

"You still wear the beads." His voice held a note of wonder.

She swallowed. "Always."

He traced them, his fingers circling the base of her neck, sliding over the swell of her breast, grazing her nipple, then trailing along the underside.

"I never thought . . ." His finger rounded the curve

and began to follow the beads up the other side. "They are just cheap seeds. Yet, against your skin, they glow like pearls."

She quivered as his hand passed over her other nipple.

"Here, let me," he murmured.

She lifted her head slightly and he slipped the beads over it, gently disentangling the necklace from her hair. Holding on to one end of the strand, he pooled it on her belly. The beads, smooth and rounded, were warm from her skin. He trailed them over her, drawing them through the valley between her breasts, then letting them slide over her nipple. Over and over, he caressed her with the necklace.

The touch was almost too much, yet not nearly enough. The seeds skated over her skin, a fluid, sinuous strand, like the purling of water. He dribbled it across the line of her hip and drew it over her waist. She shifted restlessly, needing more.

"Open your legs."

Unable to think clearly enough to do anything else, mesmerized by the husky rumble of his voice, she let her thighs part.

"So beautiful," he whispered. The beads slid easily against her flesh. Tiny darts of sensation shot through her.

"Jonathan . . . please."

And instead of the beads, there was his hands and his mouth. His touch was reverent, whispering over her skin. He tasted her breasts, and his hands explored her inner arms. He licked the hollow of her throat and stroked her ribs. He nipped her shoulder, and his palms polished her hips.

His touch poured over her, drowning her in sensation. And his words poured over her too.

The difference stunned her. The first time had been hushed, their silence broken only by the sound of thunder and their breathing. Now he spoke softly, continuously, telling her she was lovely, how feminine the curve of her belly was, how womanly her thighs. The silky swath of his hair swept over her with the equally smooth sweep of his tongue. Each part he touched, he tasted. And each part he tasted, he praised.

Heat shimmered along her skin, and need quivered within her. She was overwhelmed, almost frightened.

"Jonathan, please," she said again, desperately.

"Yes."

His hair brushed her stomach, and she felt his hands slip under her to cup the curve of her buttocks. The heat of his breath shocked her; the touch of his tongue nearly made her cry. She tried to protest, tried to say stop, but she couldn't get her mouth to form his name, only an incoherent moan.

The pleasure was excruciating, just shy of too much. His tongue was gentle velvet, but the stubble of his beard rasped the soft flesh inside her thigh. She felt herself tightening, felt the beginning clench of pleasure . . . and she was unbearably, achingly empty.

"No!" Sitting up, she tugged on his hair to pull him up to her. "Jonathan, no."

He settled himself next to her then, and with fingers that shook ever so slightly, brushed damp tendrils of hair from her temples. "What's wrong?" he asked quietly.

"I'm so . . . empty."

He stared at her for a moment, his expression harsh,

and for an instant she wondered if she'd done something unforgivable in stopping him. Then he smiled gently and slipped his hand down her body.

His middle finger slid deeply, naturally into her body. She gasped, and the pleasure began to spiral through her again.

But it wasn't enough.

She pushed his hand away.

"Please," she repeated. Hesitantly, she brushed her knuckles over his hardness. He sucked in his breath, and she reached for the buttons on his breeches.

He grabbed her hand and flattened it against his hip.

"I can't."

"Why?" she asked, unable to keep the quaver from her voice. His gaze sought hers, and his eyes were clouded, unreadable. Sweat beaded on his forehead, and a muscle in his jaw bulged.

Finally, he swore and jerked to his feet. He ripped at the fastening of his breeches, and Bennie was distantly surprised when one tore. He yanked his drawers and breeches off in one motion and dropped them aside.

He towered over her, his feet spread, his hands planted on his hips. His chest heaved, his hair lay loose on his shoulders, his erection jutted boldly from his body, and he was every mythic god come to vital, vivid flesh.

He dropped to his knees between her thighs, slipping his arm around her hips and lifting her to meet him. She felt him slide into her slowly, and she was empty no longer.

Levering down, he brought his stomach flush with hers, but kept his weight from her by propping himself up with his elbows.

But she wanted his weight. Digging her nails into his shoulders, she brought him closer. He gave a strangled sigh and went still. She waited for the wonderful rhythm to begin, but he didn't move.

Unable to wait any longer, she tilted her hips to deepen the contact.

"Oh, God," he whispered, and began to move, stroking deep and long and slow.

She kept her eyes open, watching his face above her. Even with the lines of his face sharpened by strain, his eyes nearly closed, and his teeth clenched, he was beautiful, all male power and sexuality.

"God, Beth . . . I can't . . . please . . ." he said urgently.

She'd been nearly there before; now, pleasure burst through her, suddenly and without warning. Closing her eyes at last, she threw back her head and let go.

Maybe he was going to be able to manage it. Beth was shuddering beneath him, her face exquisitely lovely in ecstasy. He ground his molars together with such force his jaw ached. He purposely put more weight on his left shoulder, welcoming the pain that shot down from his wound. It was the only thing that kept him from his own release.

She was calming now, giving soft sobs of pleasure he found unbearably sweet. He thrust once more, and was rewarded by her small convulsion. Finally, he pulled out and fell to one side. She was still shaking, and he gathered her close, soothingly sweeping his hand down the soft curve of her back.

She stirred slightly.

"Don't move." Her lush form nestled against him was

nearly driving him to madness, but he couldn't deny himself at least that much pleasure.

She sat up and, with a characteristic gesture, shoved her tumbled curls away from her face. Her eyes blazed.

"What the hell was that about?"

"Uh, what do you mean?"

"You know very well what I mean!" She glared accusingly at his still-erect member.

"Beth . . ."

"Just your way of saying thank you? Well, no thank you!"

She was gorgeous, all fiery and outraged. And she was too far away.

He held out his arms. "Come here."

Her eyes widened in disbelief. "You can't be serious."

"I'll try and explain it to you. If I can. I'd rather hold you while I'm doing it."

She bit her lip, then gave in, nestling against him as if she belonged there. He gave a sigh of satisfaction and threaded his fingers through the luxuriant length of her hair.

"You are so beautiful."

"That's hardly a reason to stop when you did."

He gave a small laugh—no easy feat, considering the condition of his lower body. "No." He found her hand and twined his fingers with hers. "What I did to you before, Beth. It was unforgivable."

"Jonathan—"

"Quiet. How am I supposed to explain when you insist on interrupting me?" He squeezed her hand lightly. "It was bad enough that I made love to you, pretending to be something I wasn't. But did you ever consider that you might have gotten pregnant?"

He felt her sudden stillness. "Yes."

"That was the worst thing I did, Beth. I might have been leaving you to bear a child alone and unmarried. I won't—I *can't*—take that chance again."

"Jonathan," she said crisply. "Two of my four sisters-in-law had babies less than seven months after their weddings. It's hardly unheard of."

"It's not that simple." He allowed himself to drop a kiss on the top of her head. Surely that wouldn't strain his still-insistent passions. "They did get married, after all. I had—*have*—no idea if I'll ever be back. And even if I do come back I couldn't marry you. There is no way I could do that and maintain the illusion of Lieutenant Jon. You would be left alone, to bear the child of an enemy. You could probably never marry. Would your family stand by you then?"

He took her silence as her answer.

"I can't take your family from you too. I've already taken far too much."

She disengaged her hand. He'd convinced her, he thought, even as vicious regret pierced him.

And then she touched him. He was still slick from her, and her palm slipped easily over him, circling, gliding, stroking. Despite himself, he arched up into her hand.

"Beth . . ." he protested weakly.

"Don't I have any choice in this, you foolish man?"

Let her, his body demanded. Although he deserved the frustration, was there so much honor in sacrifice? This was safe. This wouldn't cause her any real harm. She couldn't get pregnant.

He *was* a foolish man, she thought. He didn't know the Joneses at all if he thought her family wouldn't stand by her. And in all likelihood, she would never marry anyway. She would take what fate gave her. It was her choice.

He was hot, hard, and silky beneath her hand, vibrantly alive. His eyes were closed now, his breath coming in sharp gasps, and he jerked slightly with each stroke of her hand.

She moved swiftly, straddling him.

"No, Beth!"

"Yes," she said. "Tell me you don't want this and I'll stop."

He couldn't answer, could only think of the feel of her soft, hot flesh closing around him.

"Yes," she repeated with satisfaction. "It's my decision too, Jonathan."

She sank down on him, and he filled her even more completely than he had before. Tiny, unexpected bursts of pleasure tingled down her spine.

He shuddered and threw back his head. With a hoarse shout, his back bowed up, and she felt his warmth flood her.

24

She lay sprawled across his chest. He smoothed her hair, and his fingers followed the line of her spine with exceptionally slow, languorous movements.

"Oh, Jonathan," she whispered, turning her head with tremendous effort to press a kiss into the hollow of his throat. "It felt as if you were pouring your soul into me."

"God, I hope so." He cradled her face, lifting it so she could look into his eyes, eyes that were filled with churning emotion. "It's certainly better off in your hands than mine."

"You're not angry?"

He raised his head and brought her mouth to his. There was no passion in this kiss; the touch of their lips was a communion, a vow.

He leaned back and brushed his fingers down the line of her jaw. "I promised myself I wasn't going to do that to you again."

"You didn't do anything *to* me." He could find no regret in her eyes, in her voice, and the sharp tang of his own guilt was muted. "You did something *with* me," she finished softly.

He regarded her seriously. "Promise me you won't be sorry."

"I won't be," she said, and the glow in the warm brown depths of her eyes reassured him. "Life is so . . . fragile right now. I don't think it's wrong for us to take a little joy where we can find it."

"I'll try to be in touch with you regularly. If you should find yourself . . . " He paused, swallowing the sudden thickness in his throat. "With child, send for me, and I will find a way to come to you."

"It's too dangerous."

"Promise me," he demanded, command ringing in his voice, and she suddenly realized, that along with his talents as an agent, here was a man who would be extraordinarily skilled at leading others.

"All right," she agreed.

"I may not be able to see you myself," he warned her.

"How will I know if someone comes from you?"

"He—or she—will say . . . " He grinned suddenly, with a roguish, mischievous bent that warmed her heart. What a charmer he would be, she thought, if he were free of the demands of battling nations. "'Job's tears.'"

Heat flashed through her, and she lowered her lashes.

He chuckled and rolled her beneath him. His weight was heavy and delicious, settling comfortably between her thighs, and he kissed her with a complete thoroughness that quickly turned embarrassment into abandon.

Regretfully, he broke away. The skin beneath her ear tempted him, and he licked it slowly. How could any skin be so soft, he thought hazily?

"It's dark," he mumbled. "I should go."

Her fingers raked through his hair, and her voice was laced with amusement. "How long could it take?"

He laughed and moved farther down her body.

"Not long."

The darkness was thick, nearly impenetrable. She was glad of it, because she didn't want him to see her face.

She knew this man so little, knew nothing of what drove him, what shaped him, what he thought. But she knew one thing—he was a man who'd shouldered more than his share of guilt and regret. And she knew too that for him to see her sadness would only add to his burden.

"Do you want me to walk you back to the house?" he asked, hoping to prolong the torture just a bit. If he'd known how much it would hurt to leave her, would he ever have come to her in the first place? But then he felt her body come close to his, her arms wrap around his waist, her head settle on his chest, and he knew the question was absurd.

Of course he would have.

"No," she said, her voice muffled against his chest. "I'll stay here and pack up a bit."

"Fine."

He smelled so good, and his chest was hard and smooth beneath the softness of the linen shirt. She rubbed her cheek against it. "You will be careful, won't you?"

"I promise."

She squeezed her eyes tightly against the sting. "You'd better. I'll come and make sure you'll regret it if you aren't."

His laughter was strained. "You will, will you?"

"Yes. Joneses are notorious for taking their revenge if someone breaks a promise to them, you know. No telling what I might do to you."

"Well, I'd better take care, then." His arms closed around her, belying the lightness in his tone. "Beth, I'm s—"

"If you're going to apologize again, I'm going to hurt you worse than that ball you took in your shoulder did," she said fiercely.

"Only if you promise to nurse me back to health."

He could stand there and hold her forever. In fact, how easy it would be never to go back. He could stay here and love her the way she deserved to be loved. Instead of death and betrayal, his days and nights would be filled with lavender and sunshine.

But if he didn't return, all the terrible, haunting things he'd done already would be for naught. They— *he*—only held value in the completion of his task. And he knew that even Beth wouldn't be enough to keep the memories at bay.

"Good-bye."

He was gone with only a whisper of sound, so soft it could have been the sighing of an errant breeze. She didn't know how he managed, in the absolute darkness, to find the ladder and make his way down it without

fumbling, but she wasn't surprised. His senses seemed
beyond those of ordinary mortals, and she'd discovered
that moving with utter silence was as natural to him as
breathing was to lesser men.

She stood there, frozen, fighting the trembling that
threatened to overtake her. The darkness cloaked her,
welcoming, mysterious, vaguely comforting, and a
single, desolate melody played through her mind.

Jon trudged through the narrow streets of Boston. He
grimaced, reaching down to tug at his stockings. The
shoes Beth had given him were a shade too tight and
had rubbed the skin at the back of his heel raw.

Brick buildings crowded the street from both sides,
shadowing it from the midmorning sun. It always made
him feel confined, as if the pathway was too narrow for
his shoulders. He seemed too big for the place.

Slumping into Jon's characteristic slouch, he continued
on his way. He passed an empty milliner's shop, its window festooned with faded ribbons and bedraggled
feathers. A tobacco shop perfumed the air with the
earthy scents of pipe tobacco and chocolate.

Boston was quiet, so different from the bustling city
he'd found when he'd first come there. Now many of
the shops were closed, their owners having escaped the
volatile situation in the city at the first opportunity. Still
he shuffled along, finding returning to his dimwit role
more difficult than he'd imagined.

There was no sense in taking any chances that someone
would see him acting too alert. But after only a few days
as himself—or at least, as close to it as he was likely to

manage—he was loath to become the idiot once more.

He turned a sharp corner and plodded on. When he'd first begun playing the role, it had amused him. People were so easily deceived, too lazy to look beneath the obvious. They always saw what they expected to see, what was easiest to believe, and he'd taken full advantage of their blindness.

Now, he felt a chill as he forced the idiot grin back on his face. He had the terrible, absurd premonition that, if he hid behind the facade of Lieutenant Jon again, he might never find his way back to Jonathan.

His ears picked up the distant throb of steady drumming. Troops were drilling in the common.

It was nearly thirty-six hours since he'd left Beth. He'd been slowed by his injury and recent inactivity more than he'd expected and had made it only a third of the way back to Boston the first night. He'd spent the day in a tumbledown barn, dozing and satisfying his suddenly sharp appetite from the generous store of food Beth had given him.

He was dressed as a colonial and, if the pinch came, he assumed he could pass for one. But he'd just as soon not take the chance of traveling through the daylight hours; the only weapon he had was the sharp knife he'd found in Beth's supplies, and if he'd been seen, he'd more than likely have had to answer questions about why a young, apparently healthy man wasn't with the Continental army in Cambridge. It had been simpler just to stay out of sight.

He'd made better time last night, slipping easily past both American and British sentries and into Boston. Then he caught a few hours of rest in the empty lean-to behind an abandoned blacksmith's shop, waiting for day and the appropriate time to go find his captain.

One more turn and he was approaching the subdued red brick building three blocks from the common that Captain Livingston had commandeered shortly after they'd been stationed in Boston. Two soldiers, polished and stiff in their bright crimson coats, guarded the door, their bayonets gleaming silver. The captain never forgot the proprieties.

Jonathan took a deep breath, and the muscles near his wound twitched. He felt completely exposed and longed for his musket, a sword, anything. If he'd been recognized the night of the fiasco at the fort, he'd be arrested the instant he identified himself to the guards—arrested, tried, and shot.

Then again, there was always the possibility they would attempt to use him, turn him as a double agent, or simply follow him closely, trying to flush out his contacts. He might not know his fate so quickly after all.

He ruthlessly shut down his emotions, forcing the rigid control that had served him so well for so long. He'd not allowed himself to feel for so many years it had become second nature, and it had no longer been an effort. Now, it was becoming more and more difficult to submerge his feelings and find that place of cold, automatic duty.

He lowered his eyelids, as if he couldn't quite wake up, and let his features go slack. Acutely aware of the careful attention of the guards, he ambled up to the door.

"Halt!" Two bayonets snapped down, crossing in

front of the entrance and effectively stopping his advance.

"Identify yourself," one of the guards said sharply.

Jon studied the soldiers through his lashes. He didn't recognize either of them. They were young, enthusiastic, and more than a bit edgy, the kind who were always a bit too quick to fire. His muscles tightened, but he made himself relax.

"Hello," he said in his most friendly tone.

"Who are you?"

"Lieutenant Leighton."

"Lieutenant . . . Lieutenant Leighton, did you say?" The guard narrowed his eyes and glared at Jon.

"Yes."

The guard who'd asked the questions redirected his bayonet. It hovered slightly above Jon's waist.

"You've been missing for nearly a week."

"That long?"

"What happened to you?" the guard demanded.

Jon grinned casually. "Tell Cap'n."

"Tell me where you were."

"Tell Cap'n," Jon repeated. The bayonet was just a little too close for comfort, and it took all the self-control Jon could muster not to reach out and relieve the guard of his weapon. It would be simple enough; the young man's grip was too loose.

The guard hesitated, then glanced at the other guard and jerked his head toward Jon. "Watch him." He snapped open the door of the building and disappeared inside.

Jon turned his attention to the other guard, who, so far, hadn't uttered a word. "Hello. I'm Jon."

This one blinked and fingered the stock of his musket. "Quiet," he ordered.

"Your name?" Jon asked.

The guard simply stared at him. This one took his job just as seriously, it seemed. Jon had hoped to strike up a bit of a conversation and find out if he'd missed much while he was gone. With any luck, he also would have gotten a hint of what his disappearance had been attributed to, but it didn't look as if he was going to get much out of this man.

Jon smiled, slouched, and settled in to wait.

Captain Livingston frowned down at the dispatch. He shuffled the papers, then tapped irritably on the polished, gleaming dark wood of the desktop.

A traitor. By God, they thought there was a traitor, in *his* company! It was patently absurd. All his men were loyal.

He straightened his wig and settled back into the blood red leather chair. He looked around the familiar room that served as his office. Furnished in leather and dark wood, accented with brass and a few really lovely carpets, it was an adequate office for a captain, he supposed. A bit small, but it would suffice. Certainly it was a tremendous improvement over the pitiful conditions at that awful fort. Thank heavens his superiors had the good sense to call him back to the city where he belonged. Although Boston barely deserved the title of city, being unable to hold a wick, much less a candle, to London, he could work here. He knew his duty.

And now there was the affront of this dispatch.

They'd been investigating his company for months now—months!—and they hadn't told him. It had taken them that long to verify that he himself wasn't the traitor. He would have laughed at the absurdity of it if it hadn't been so insulting. They'd told him they had an agent working in his company, but they wouldn't tell him who it was. Only that the captain had been cleared, and the agent would continue to work to uncover the traitor. Complete effrontery!

The entire thing was almost beyond bearing. He realigned the inkpot, quill, and papers until his desk satisfied his sense of order. The entire task in the colonies had been bungled almost from the beginning. The politicians in Britain clearly had no idea how to deal with the rebels.

He had plenty of ideas, by God. These colonists were simply waiting to be led. But prodding them and giving them ultimatums merely fueled their rebelliousness.

Yes, if he'd been consulted, there wouldn't have been the awful, humiliating slaughter at Bunker Hill. It didn't matter that they had ultimately won the hill and the day; their losses were too great for any but one who hadn't been there to claim victory.

And now they were penned in this town, surrounded on all sides by a force of vastly superior numbers, if completely inferior character and training. He'd lost the best sergeant he'd ever had, and the replacement troops were raw and ill-prepared. And that idiot lieutenant had somehow managed to get himself lost in the bargain!

Sighing, he rose from his chair, clasping his hands behind his back, and began to pace. There had to be a way to bring the new troops up to scratch more quickly.

A sharp knock interrupted his thoughts. Heavens, he hated it when he was disturbed. Didn't people know when he was contemplating?

"Enter," he called sharply.

The door creaked open and a head popped around it. It was one of those new ones—Herrington? Something like that. The boy was anxious to please, but he had the most confounded difficulty remembering orders. Livingston had set him to guarding the front door. That much, he'd thought, the private would be able to handle.

"What is it?"

The soldier's round face flushed. "Ah, there's a man, sir. At the door." His voice rose to a squeak. "He, ah, he says he's Lieutenant Leighton, sir."

"Lieutenant Leighton? Well, is it, man?"

"I don't know, sir. He's, ah, he's rather large, sir."

"That's him! What's his explanation of his absence?"

The young private cleared his throat. "All he'll say, sir, is 'Tell Cap'n.'"

"That sounds like him." Captain Livingston allowed himself a small smile. "Well, then, send him in."

"Yes, sir." The soldier gave a quick bob of his head and disappeared.

Livingston tugged his cuffs and smoothed his coat as he waited for Leighton. With any other soldier, he could have assumed one of two things: the soldier had deserted or had been captured. With Leighton, however, there were endless possibilities. His horse may have run away with him. He could have fallen into a well. He might have been chasing butterflies. The captain rather found himself looking forward to the Lieutenant's explanation.

A brief knock, and the young private popped in again. "Lieutenant Leighton, sir," he announced.

"Lieutenant Leighton," Livingston said with what he felt was the proper note of joviality. Leighton shuffled in, followed by the young private who, clearly curious, hovered in the background.

"You are dismissed, soldier." Livingston gave the young man a stern look.

"Yes, sir." The private lowered his eyes sheepishly and backed out of the room.

"Now, then." Livingston clapped Jon on the back and indicated a nearby chair. "Sit down, sit down." He seated himself behind the desk, braced his arms on the top, and leaned forward, frowning. "You're out of uniform, Lieutenant."

"Yes, sir." Jon fiddled with the bottom of his leather jerkin.

"I hope you have an explanation."

"Yes, sir."

Livingston furrowed his brow. "Let's have it, then."

"Got shot."

"Shot? Again?" Dubious, the captain looked Jon up and down. The lieutenant looked healthy enough, but then again, he'd always had the constitution of a draft horse.

"On free night, was walking. Got lost."

Lost again. Clearly he needed to assign a keeper to Leighton, although he hardly had the manpower to spare anyone. Still, it might be a good job for that Herrington fellow.

"Ran into American sentries. Told me to stop." Jon pursed his lips. "Didn't want to get captured."

"Of course not."

"So I ran. Shot me."

"So they captured you, then? How'd you get away?" He wouldn't have thought Leighton could have managed an escape. More likely, the Americans let him go after he'd destroyed half of their camp. Probably thought it would make a more effective weapon to turn him back on the British.

"Didn't catch me." Jon grinned widely. "Run fast."

"Where have you been? You've been gone nearly a week."

"A week?" The lieutenant looked confused. Too difficult a concept for him, obviously. "Didn't know. Was sick some, I guess."

"Have you had a doctor look at your injury, Leighton?"

"Not yet. Took good care of me."

"Who?"

"Tories. Found me, took care of me till ready to come back." He shrugged. "Better. Come back."

"Yes." Livingston was vaguely disappointed. He'd expected the tale to be slightly more entertaining. "That's it, then? Nothing else?"

"No." Jon looked crestfallen. "Sorry."

"No matter. Who were the people who cared for you? We must thank them properly."

"They were, ah, Williams? Wilson? Ah, Winston?" Jon's shoulders slumped in defeat. "Wilkins?"

"Never mind. Certainly you remember where they lived?"

Jon brightened. "That way." He waved west. "Somewhere."

Livingston sighed. "Perhaps you'd best go have your wound attended to before we continue this conversation."

"Yes, sir." Jon jumped to his feet, bumping the nearest table and rattling the fine porcelain tea set displayed on it. He quickly skittered aside and backed toward the door. "Sorry, sir. Go see doctor now, Cap'n."

Livingston closed his eyes gratefully when Leighton slammed the door behind him. He must remember not to interview Jon in his office again. He had no desire to see the place wrecked.

Nearly a week, and the man could only remember the slightest bits about where he'd been. But then, he didn't seem to know where he was half the time.

Livingston sat up sharply. It wasn't the first time Leighton had disappeared and no one had known where he'd gone to. It had only been for brief periods of time before, and they'd all simply assumed he'd wandered off and gotten lost again. But what if there was more to it? What if he was meeting someone?

It was completely ridiculous. The man didn't have the mental capacity of a field mouse. More, he'd found Jon on the battlefield, holding the body of Sergeant Hitchcock. His grief had been genuine; Livingston was sure of that much. He'd seen enough grief in his years as a soldier to know it at a glance. That look—the shock and emptiness—in Leighton's eyes couldn't be faked. It certainly wasn't the triumph of a man who'd witnessed the death of an enemy.

Livingston hadn't known Jon before his accident. He'd heard how intelligent and clever Jon had been before he'd had his brains bashed in by a horse, but Livingston had always assumed that that "brilliance" was only in contrast to what Jon was now. But what if he'd been truly ingenious? Enough to pull off a ruse like this?

It was utterly, absolutely absurd.

But so, then, was having a spy in his company.

25

"*Excuse me, sir,* but would you be Jon?"

Jon bit down an oath and turned to the woman who'd followed him from the potter's. He'd spent more time than he had to spare in the shop, feigning an interest in dishes, mugs, and bean pots, all the while trying to delicately probe for any information about the peddler. This was his last contact, damn it, and he'd come up empty again. He didn't have the time nor the patience to listen to this little bird of a woman, whose hands fluttered in the air like a hummingbird's wings.

It was getting more and more difficult to keep the grin plastered on his face. "Yeah," he replied.

She peered at him carefully, her bright little eyes peeking out from under a snowy cap and a fringe of equally white hair.

"The peddler told me to expect you."

"The peddler?" he asked cautiously.

She nodded.

342   SUSAN KAY LAW

"You know the peddler. Why didn't you say anything inside?"

"I know the peddler. I didn't say me husband did."

"But—"

"No one pays much attention to a frail old lady, sir."

He looked at her more closely, noting the glint of determination in her eyes. "It could be useful, I suppose."

"Yes." She patted her lacy cap. "He left you a message."

"A message?"

"Yes. Said he thought he was being watched. Thought it was best to get out of town, quickly."

"Yes," Jon said thoughtfully. "I'm sure he was right."

She peered at him. "Something you might consider yourself, sir."

"Perhaps I should. However, it's not something I'm able to do just yet."

She straightened her spine, and her air of fragility disappeared. "Yes, sir. Some of us have more work to do, don't we?"

He tipped his tricorn. "That we do."

After the little woman had disappeared back inside the shop, he began the trek back to the common.

Damn, *damn*! The peddler had been his last hope. All his contacts had evaporated as if they'd never even existed.

The intelligence operation was completely compartmentalized: if someone was caught, the number of others that agent could identify was severely limited. Unfortunately, it also meant that in this situation Jon had no idea whom to contact. He knew only the limited number of people he'd worked directly with, and they'd all disappeared.

That left him few options. He had information that *had* to get through, and the only way to be sure it got into the proper hands was to deliver it directly to Washington, who'd recently been appointed to head the colonial troops.

How? Now there was a problem. There was simply no disguise he could think of that would allow him to slip through two lines of sentries, through an entire camp, into the general's headquarters, and back out again without being detected. Even *he* wasn't that good.

Jon absently kicked a rotting apple out of his way and turned into a quiet side street, taking the long way to return to the common. He needed the walk, the time to think, before he had to be back on his guard when he returned to his company.

A bank of clouds had rolled in, blotting out the sun, and the narrow street was dim and cool, hedged with buildings and smelling of horses. He consciously slowed his steps to a shuffle.

There had to be a way to get the information through, there just had to be. And he would find it—but not before he'd attached a small additional note of his own.

Nibbling on a bit of cheese and the fresh bread she'd baked that morning, Bennie watched the small creek meander by. Its surface was dappled with the sunlight that filtered through the lush leaves of the trees, and dragonflies lazily flitted from reed to reed in the marshy area by the opposite bank.

She leaned back, letting the breeze caress her face. It was quiet here, as if the lush vegetation absorbed superfluous sound. She enjoyed the calm, something that had been so absent from her life for too long. The tension and the worry that surrounded the Eel and New Wexford frazzled her nerves and left her inexplicably convinced that something even worse was going to happen at any minute.

Her only respite was out here, in Finnigan's Wood. She knew the peace was an illusion, but the sound of the water soothed her, and the vibrant life made the presence of the dread that lurked over her shoulder seem a little less pressing. The sick, heavy feeling in her stomach eased a bit.

She took another mouthful of the tangy cheese and chewy, hard-crusted bread. A copper-colored squirrel skittered down a nearby oak and perched on its hind legs, chattering at her.

"Hungry, are you, little one?" She tore off a chunk of bread and tossed it at the animal. The squirrel stopped scolding her, its tiny nose quivering. Then it whirled, gave a disdainful flick of its tail, and scampered back up the tree, leaving the bread on the grass.

She laughed. "Ungrateful little creature. I'm not that bad a cook."

"Really, Beth, you must learn to control this regrettable tendency to care for helpless creatures."

The familiar voice rumbled up her spine. She turned and looked over her shoulder. "Like you, I suppose?"

"Of course."

Then she dropped any pretense of casualness. The bread and cheese fell to the ground unnoticed. She sprang to her feet and hurled herself into his arms.

"Jonathan!"

He closed his arms around her and shut his eyes. God, how had he forgotten? She felt even better than he'd remembered—and what he'd remembered had been pretty damn good.

"I didn't think you'd be able to come yourself."

He couldn't do this. He couldn't tell her that he had any reason for being here except to see her. And he couldn't—God, he *couldn't*—ask her to do this.

"I wasn't sure I'd be able to," he muttered, breathing in the fresh, clean scents of summer and lavender rising from her hair.

"How are you?" She tenderly probed his shoulder. "Does that hurt?"

"No. I'm fine." She didn't ask why he was here, didn't demand explanations or wonder why it had taken him so long to get in touch with her. She just worried about him. Even after all he'd done to her—and, despite her protests, he didn't believe he could ever make up for the deception—all she was concerned about was his well-being. He didn't deserve it. Especially not now.

But first, he would kiss her. He'd take advantage of her welcome, and he'd give himself just one more memory to take with him. Because after he asked her this, he promised himself he'd never ask her another thing.

There was something wrong. She knew it. She could hear the strain in his voice, feel it in his slight hesitation, but right now, lost in the wonder of seeing him well, whole, and alive, she was going to hang onto the happiness as long as she could. Let the darkness come when it would.

But then his mouth was on hers, and everything was

right. His kiss was tender and sweet, but flavored with an edge of desperation that told her exactly how much he missed her.

He lifted his head, and she smiled up at him.

He didn't smile back, and there was a gray bleakness in his eyes. "Beth, I have to talk to you."

A sudden chill froze in her chest. "What is it?"

He lifted a hand to her face, but when she tilted her head in anticipation of his touch, he clenched his hand into a fist and let it drop. "Can we sit down? This might take a while."

"Certainly." She didn't want to hear this, she knew it. She sat down on the creek bank, wishing she'd worn skirts instead of breeches. She was unable to decide what to do with her hands; at least she could have fussed with the fabric of skirts. Instead, she smoothed the leather over her knees and fiddled with the long weeds growing luxuriantly along the brook. He captured one of her hands, lacing her fingers with his, and brought it to his lap.

She turned to look at him then, at his absolute stillness, at his cool, hooded eyes watching the water flowing away.

"You're not in uniform."

"No. That red coat seems to be an invitation to fire in these parts. I'd just as soon not be a moving target again if I can help it." He continued gazing at the creek, a muscle working in his jaw.

"What is it?" she asked finally.

He took in a breath. His features hardened, sharpened, and suddenly he was a man who could do what he had to without showing a flicker of hesitation or remorse.

"I know I promised you I wouldn't ask anything else from you. Sometimes, though, there are things that are more important than promises."

She squeezed his hand. "Go on."

"I've been working for the Americans—"

"I knew it!" Thank God, they were on the same side after all. He wasn't her enemy. "I knew you weren't—"

"Stop it." The command, though soft, was clear and sharp. He withdrew his fingers from hers and shoved her hand away from him.

"But we—"

"Don't make me out to be some kind of hero. It's nothing like that."

"But you are," she protested. "The information you've been gathering—"

"Is getting people killed." He picked up a twig and began to strip it of its leaves and bark with precise, careful movements. "Let me tell you what it's like, Beth. I found out that the British were planning a possible assault on colonial headquarters and the supply depot at Cambridge. We were going to land at Dorchester Point, then march on through Roxbury. I passed on the information, just as I always do."

With such abrupt violence Bennie jumped, he hurled the naked twig into the water and watched it float slowly downstream. "They decided to fortify the hills above Charlestown."

"Bunker Hill," she said softly.

"Yes." He turned to look at her then. His eyes were stark, bleak, filled with dark despair. His features were taut, and for a moment she was sure that if she touched him, he would shatter.

"All those men, Beth. They died. They died because of me. Because I'm so damn good at my job."

"Oh, Jonathan." She did reach out to touch him then, and he jerked away from her. She could feel him curling up, closing down, trying to ruthlessly stamp out any sign of emotion or regret. "They were soldiers. They knew what might happen," she said.

"Yes, they were soldiers. That's all. Just men and boys like me, trying to do what they thought was right. They weren't my enemies. My *enemies* are back in England, stuffed in velvet-draped halls and gilded rooms. But they're not the ones dying, are they?"

If he'd let her touch him, she thought, he'd be cold. His flesh would be chilled, as if he'd sat out in a late November rain.

"You had no choice."

"Choice!" He gave a harsh laugh. "We always have choices. Except sometimes all of them are bad." His voice became remote, utterly expressionless. "It's living with yourself after you make them that's the trick."

"Jon," she said, her throat raw and aching. She wanted to curl herself around him and warm him, to grab the darkness in both fists and shove it away, revealing the man she'd known.

But she had never known him, had she?

He allowed himself to touch her then, just one little stroke along her temple. He would have given much if he didn't have to ask her this, but there was no way he could get to Washington himself without being recognized. He could get through once, but he'd never be able to go back to his post with the British, and he had to return; he was more vital than ever now.

Lord, she was lovely, fine glowing skin over strong, clean features. Nothing delicate or dainty, no fragile flower that would wilt with the first sign of age or difficulty. No, she was a woman, a woman who could stand with a man, work with him, build a life with him.

And he wished—more than he'd ever wished for anything, even when he was a child and wanted his parents back—that he'd never gotten embroiled in the plots of kings and countries. That he could have met her at church, courted her slowly with flowers and walks through the square, and taken her home to his house and made love to her among lacy sheets and feather pillows. That they could have children and laugh and grow old quietly, without ever being touched by things like war and duty and the damn bloody job.

Instead, the job was all he had.

"I wouldn't ask you this if I didn't think it was imperative. Even then, I wouldn't ask if I wasn't sure you would be perfectly safe."

"It doesn't matter. Who is completely safe these days, anyway?"

"True." If only there was some other way . . . but if there was, he couldn't see it. "I gathered some information. It has to be gotten through to Washington."

The breeze blew a strand of hair across her lips, and she tucked it behind her ear. "Important?"

"Yes. I was trying to make contact the night I was shot."

He heard her quick intake of breath. "They caught you?"

"Almost. I don't think I was recognized. At least, there's been no indication of that so far. But they obviously knew

when and where the meeting was to be. There's someone feeding information back to the British, someone
who's very good at it."

"Who is it?"

"I don't know—yet. But they've done an absolutely
complete job of eliminating all of my contacts. I've been
trying for weeks to find someone to get the information
through, but every one is either dead or has disappeared
entirely."

She paled. "Dead?"

"Yes," he said brutally, unwilling to pretty it up for
her, half hoping she'd get frightened and refuse.

"Why don't you take it through yourself?"

"There'd be no way I could return to my company. And,
at least until we identify the traitor in the American
ranks, I'm needed on this side."

"You want me to deliver it." She was calm now, her
voice steady. She would make a very good spy herself,
he thought in admiration; she too had the ability to
present a very different face to the world.

"There's no one else I can trust, Beth."

She considered briefly. "All right. Where is it?"

He felt a sickening thud in his gut. She was going to do
it. He wanted her here, tucked away safe and sound. "It
shouldn't be any problem. You don't have to cross any
British lines at all. All you'd need is a legitimate reason
to enter camp."

"I have seven brothers in that camp, Jonathan. As
you say, it shouldn't be a problem."

"Fine," he said, more sharply than he'd intended. She
was being very businesslike and accepting about the
entire thing—and he was finding it completely impossible

to treat her the way he would any other compatriot.

He yanked off the jerkin she'd given him, folding it inside out. He removed the small, deadly dagger he always kept in his boot—sometimes, guns were too noisy—quickly slit the fabric of the lining and pulled out a bundle of papers.

"Here." He held them out. The papers were white and pure in the sun, tied with a black ribbon, and looked utterly innocuous. Yet he knew as he handed them to her that he was giving her something equally as dangerous as a poisonous asp.

She took the packet and tapped it against her thigh. "What is this?"

He simply stared at her, his face stony. "It's better if you don't know."

She tucked her tongue in her cheek. "I suppose I could always open it and read it."

"If you're not going to take this seriously, you're not doing it." He snatched the packet from her hand.

"Really, Jonathan. I'm taking it seriously. But I can't imagine how there could be any danger. I'll just go visit my brothers, drop these off, and go home."

"You don't understand, do you?" Still clutching the packet, he grabbed her by her shoulders and pulled her toward him. "There's somebody in that camp that doesn't want this information to get through. Somebody who has, more than likely, already killed to prevent it. And God help me if something happened to you."

She saw the ice in his eyes, heard the despair in his voice, and knew it was true. If something happened to her, something he could have prevented, it would be the final blow, the thing that sent him hurtling over the

352 SUSAN KAY LAW

edge of the abyss into blackness. He was treading very close to it, as it was.

"Jonathan," she said quietly. "Nothing's going to happen to me."

"You're right. Because unless you promise me you can follow instructions exactly, you are not doing this," he said savagely.

She nodded, and he loosened his grip on her. He rubbed her upper arms as if in apology for any pain he'd caused her. "When I get inside the camp, what do I do?" she asked.

"You'll have to find Washington. It shouldn't be too difficult."

"Fine. What then? I can't simply ask to see him."

"No. Talk to the guards, have them use the name Goliath. He'll see you. By now, he should have been briefed about me."

"Goliath?" She grinned. "How appropriate."

"Yes, well, all it took was one little rock, didn't it?"

She sobered. It might take more than a stone, but one more ball, a little closer to the heart this time, or a knife between his ribs was all that would be needed. She realized he lived every day, every minute, among people who, if he slipped up once, would consider it their duty to rid the world of the traitor in their midst. Despite the warmth of the sun, she couldn't suppress a small shiver.

"Goliath. I'll remember."

"Good. There's something else. You can't tell anyone about this. I mean it, Beth. Not *anyone*."

"Of course not."

"Promise me!"

She nodded, slightly bewildered by his vehemence. "I wouldn't. I rarely talk to anyone but my family, anyway, and—"

"No!" He jumped to his feet, roughly hauling her up with him. "Not your family!"

"But Jonathan . . ." His eyes were pale, cold, unreadable. Her throat closed in dread. "You suspect one of them."

He didn't answer, merely looked at her, as immovable and unreachable as a granite statue. His silence was all the confirmation she needed.

"No!" she shouted, pounding him on the chest with her fists. "It's not one of my family!"

Jerking away from him, she went to stand by the bank, her face a frozen blank as she stared out over the water.

He went over to her. "Beth—"

"What happens to him?"

"Who?"

"The traitor. When you catch him." She wrapped her arms around her middle, and her gaze didn't waver from the slowly meandering water, but he wondered if she saw anything at all. "What happens to him?"

"The same thing that happens to all traitors."

He sounded so cold, she thought, cold, emotionless, ruthless. She turned back to him then, and his features were set, his eyes pale and icy. There was no warmth in him, no softening, no acceptance.

"The same thing that would happen to me if I were caught," he continued. Not even a flicker of emotion crossed his face. This was not the man she thought she knew. Here was a man, she realized, who could kill, and go on to do his job, detached and remorseless. Any trace of the gentleness she'd always seen in him was gone.

Which was the real man? Had every bit of warmth and tenderness he'd ever shown her been carefully planned, just his way of manipulating her into doing his bidding? If that hadn't worked, was this the man she'd have seen? Dangerous, unfeeling, untouched by any reality but that of his duty?

"It's not one of them," she repeated.

"If you say so," he said coldly. Her eyes were dark, glazed with hurt and fear, and he wanted nothing more than to take her in his arms and tell her it would all be all right. But that was something he couldn't promise, and he found himself unwilling to outright lie to her again. He refused to give her false hope.

He saw her square her shoulders and lift her chin, the classic Jones posture: let the world try and come get me. He prayed the Joneses were all as invulnerable as they believed themselves to be.

"Give me the papers," she said, steel threading her voice.

"Not until you promise me you won't say anything to anyone. Including, *especially* your family—not them."

"Then I want to know what they are."

"Beth, it's safer if you don't know."

"I want to know," she said, and he knew she wouldn't relent.

"Every British asset in the colonies."

He saw a brief flicker of surprise in her eyes before she extinguished it. "Every one?"

"Yes. Troops, artillery, ships, everything."

"I can see why it's so important." Her words were clipped. "Anything else?"

God, would it never end? Once again, he found himself unable to tell her the entire truth. "Contingency plans if the colonials attack Boston. Defense and escape plans."

She thrust her hand out. "Give them to me."

He reached to put the packet in her hand, then paused, the papers hovering a bare inch above her palm. Once he gave it to her, there'd be no going back. He'd have embroiled her in danger, in these deadly games of war she had no place in.

But there was the job. He'd spent years putting the job first, above everything and everyone. He could do it one more time.

The paper, pristine and unwrinkled, nearly gleamed in the bright sun. He wondered irrelevantly why it still looked so untouched after all the hiding and carrying around it had been subjected to in the last few weeks.

"You won't tell anyone?" he asked one more time.

"I'll follow instructions, sir." He dropped the packet into her hand. She tucked it into her pocket. Her voice became rich with intensity, heavy with repulsion. "But don't ever, *ever* ask another thing of me."

She turned and walked away, her strides sure and swift. At the edge of the clearing, underneath a huge, twisted oak, she paused to look back at him. Her skin was pale, her eyes huge and dark.

"It's not one of us."

26

Bennie was not particularly impressed with the army camp. It was smelly, crowded, dirty, and it seemed the men spent a great deal of time digging what to her appeared to be utterly useless holes.

Well, so much for military discipline, she thought as she strode around yet another group of men playing cards. When she'd reached the first line of encampments, the occasional soldier had tried to stop her, assuming that a female could be entering camp for only one reason. One glare took care of most of them, although she had to admit that the fact that it was delivered from a vantage point half a head taller than their own had to help. The rest were dispensed with by the simple expedient of mentioning who she was there to visit. Her brothers, it seemed, had been cutting rather a wide swath through the place.

To her surprise, sentries stopped her only briefly. As soon as they ascertained that she was indeed there to visit her brothers, they'd simply bid her a good day and pointed her in the direction of her brothers' regiment. She'd expected the camp to be better patrolled. But then, there was little damage a lone woman could do to fifteen thousand soldiers.

She slipped her hand in her pocket to check the safety of the packet she carried. She'd repeatedly done so since she'd gotten it; it seemed somehow dangerous to simply carry it around in her pocket as she would a handkerchief or a ball of thread, but she hadn't been able to think of any better place to hide it. If she'd been taken and her captors had been determined to find it, it wouldn't have mattered where she'd hidden it.

Her father had seemed somewhat perplexed when she'd announced she was going to Cambridge to visit her brothers. She'd managed to convince him that she'd been utterly dissatisfied with the assurances they'd given on their brief visits home. She simply had to see for herself that they were taking proper care of themselves.

Her mother, oddly enough, had seemed to think it was a fairly good idea. Bennie suspected her mother cherished a secret hope that she would be swept off her feet by a handsome young officer.

Well, she'd tried that once, and it wasn't an experience she planned to repeat anytime soon. She wasn't sure she'd survive it again.

Bennie realized she was clutching the packet in her pocket, nearly crumpling the papers. She forced her fingers to uncurl; the information must remain undamaged. That was the only thing that mattered now.

So she'd been sent off with a bag stuffed with new shirts, underclothes, and stockings that her mother and her sisters-in-law had been making for the Jones men. How convenient, they'd all thought, that Bennie'd volunteered to take the things to them. Who knew when any of the men would get a chance to come back to New Wexford again?

Her brothers turned out to be surprisingly easy to locate. All of them, it seemed, were camped within Cambridge itself, near the headquarters, not in one of the outlying areas.

She'd already found Henry. He'd been delighted to see her—after he'd gotten over the fact that she'd been wandering alone through thousands of men. She'd finally gotten him to admit that no man was likely to bother her; first, because she could take care of herself, and second, because he was her brother. He'd seemed somewhat gratified by the thought that he was a deterrent.

He been equally happy with the clothes that her mother had made. Although Bennie'd never quite managed the delicacy necessary for small, tight needlework, Mary was an expert seamstress, and the clothes she made her men always fit better than anything from the finest tailor shop. Henry's clothes had been hard-used, he admitted, and the camp laundress didn't exactly clean and mend up to the standards he was used to.

Then he'd finagled two of the currant tarts she'd brought along for herself, claiming they certainly didn't know how to properly feed a Jones around here. He'd been so enthusiastic about showing her the camp, he'd pointed out General Washington's offices before she'd even had to ask. Then he promised he'd take care of Puffy for her while she visited with the others, gave her one final hug, and took off, leading her horse.

Bennie smiled fondly, shaking her head. The army had certainly not dimmed Henry's enthusiasm.

Taking a deep breath, she turned to face the plain, whitewashed frame building that served as Washington's quarters. To her surprise, it was only lightly guarded. Then again, one had to go through the entire encampment to get to it.

All at once her heart was pounding painfully in her chest. She was going to meet the new commander of the entire Continental army. By all accounts, Washington was an exceptional man, tall, handsome, and brilliant. He was also said to be quite stern, and with his new position, he was undeniably powerful.

She was suddenly afraid that they wouldn't let her in to see him after all. Why should they?

Because Jonathan had said they would. Whatever else he was—and wasn't—she was certain he was absolutely perfect at his job. And much as she hated the things he'd become in order to do it, she wanted him to succeed. The only safety her family had lay in the war's ending as quickly as possible.

Once more, for reassurance, she groped for the packet in her pocket. The sharp, clean folded edges and the thin smoothness of the ribbon gave her courage, and she started for the headquarters.

"Bennie!"

"Adam!" She laughed as he swept her up and twirled her around in the air. When she'd been very small and Adam had been a sturdy youth too big for his age, he'd often thrown her into the air until she'd been helpless with laughter. Even now, she knew he was the one who felt most responsible for her.

He put her down. "At first, I wasn't sure if that was you I saw walking across camp. But then I realized, no other woman covers ground the way my sister does."

She frowned at him. "Watch it, Adam, or I won't give you any of the things I brought you."

"What are you doing here?" His happiness at seeing her faded quickly, and concern darkened his hazel eyes. "It's not . . . everything's all right with Hannah, isn't it?"

"Yes, of course," she hurried to reassure him. "She's still losing her breakfast, but that's nothing new."

"Lord." He dragged a hand through his dark blond curls. "If I could do it for her, I would, you know?"

She snorted in disbelief. "Sure you would."

"I would." The corner of his mouth twitched, and then a wide grin spread over his face. "All right, maybe I wouldn't. I wish I was there with her, though."

"Mother's taking good care of her."

"I'm sure she is."

"Besides, when has a Jones ever married a woman who wasn't strong enough to stand up to him? She'll be fine."

"I suppose." He gave a deep sigh. "What brings you here, then?"

"I come bearing gifts." She plopped her satchel down on the ground and opened it up. She plowed through the assortment of items until she found the ones intended for him. "Here. Two new shirts and three new pairs of socks. Hannah said you go through socks in no time at all."

"It's my toe," he protested.

"Uh-huh."

"It is. It sticks up, sorta, and goes through the sock, and—" He stopped when he saw her laughing at him. "All right. I give up." He took the bundle she handed him. "My thanks."

"You're welcome."

"You have quite a load there, Bennie. Did you bring things for everyone?"

"Yes. I've already seen Henry."

"Oh, no."

"Yes. He's enjoying himself thoroughly, isn't he?"

"Yes. But then, he hasn't seen much action yet, either. We kept him well away from the front lines at Bunker Hill."

Shading her eyes from the sun, she squinted up at him. "How about you?"

A brief shadow of pain darkened his eyes, but he shrugged. "Not now, Ben."

"All right."

"When you get home, will you . . . tell . . ." He stopped, a red flush creeping up his neck. "Tell her that I love her," he said in a rush.

"I will," she said softly.

He swallowed. "Thanks."

"Now, can you tell me where I can find the rest of the crew? I'd like to lighten this satchel a bit more."

He glanced around quickly. "David, I think, is off digging barricades today. Everyone else is still in my company, so they should be around somewhere."

"What is all this digging for anyway? This place looks like its been overtaken by giant gophers."

Adam laughed, a rich, rolling sound that boomed

throughout the camp. "Washington believes it's better that they have something to do, and I have to agree with him. We were having far too many men injured by their fellow soldiers. When the men have nothing better to do, they fight."

"Sounds familiar," she said, shaking her head.

"Doesn't it, though? The general hasn't had an easy time of it, trying to shape a regular army. We started out with forty or so odd-size regiments, and he wanted us in twenty-eight uniform ones. Many men didn't take well to being reassigned."

Bennie appraised the confusion and disorder that surrounded her. This was an improvement? "Tell me honestly, Adam. Do we have any chance?"

"I have to believe that we do." He crossed his massive arms over his chest. "We have good command now. And we have one huge advantage: we are fighting for our homes. They are simply following orders."

"And we have the Jones family, right?"

"Right. The one you should really ask, though, is Brendan. Now that he's been assigned to Washington's staff—"

"Brendan's been reassigned?" she broke in.

"Yes. Someone decided he was too brilliant to waste slogging through the mud."

"Good for them. I wonder what Da will think of it?"

Adam frowned. "He'll think that the only real soldier is one that is belly-deep in the muck."

She sighed. "You're probably right."

"You should give it up. After all this time, I doubt there's anything you—or anyone else—can do to change the way it is between them."

She crossed her arms in unconscious imitation of his belligerent stance. "I never give up."

Sunlight glinted off his dark blond curls as he threw back his head and laughed.

Bennie slanted a curious glance at the headquarters building. So Brendan worked for Washington now, did he? How useful. If worse came to worst, and she found it impossible to get in, she could go to Brendan. He was sure to be able to find a way to get her an audience with the general.

And if she had to, she'd tell Brendan why. She considered getting the information in Washington's hands her primary goal; following Jonathan's instructions was a secondary consideration.

After all, she'd already broken one promise to Jonathan.

"Ben? Are you with me, Ben?"

"Huh? Oh Adam, I'm sorry. I was thinking about something."

"Now why would you want to do that?"

She swatted him playfully. "It was wonderful to see you, too."

His expression grew serious. "You will keep an eye on my family for me, won't you?"

"You know I will."

He reached for her hand and squeezed it, nearly crushing her bones in the process. "Thanks."

"It really *was* wonderful to see you, Adam. I think I'll go see if I can find Brendan."

"I'm not sure he's on duty right now. You might want to ask around for his quarters."

"I'll find him."

"Good." He pressed her fingers again. "Take care, Ben."

"I will."

Watching him stride away, head and shoulders above every man in camp, Bennie felt a quick swelling of pride. She waited until he was out of sight, unwilling to take the chance that he would turn and see her heading for Washington's quarters. She wasn't sure she was up to answering any questions right now.

As casually as she could manage, she strolled over to the whitewashed building. The soldiers who guarded it were unsmiling, utterly serious about their jobs. Unlike most of the men in camp, they were in uniform—plain and dark blue, but clean and neatly turned out. Their black boots shone, a gleam only rivaled by that of their weapons.

Bennie swallowed heavily, set her shoulders, and approached the nearest guard.

"Excuse me, sir. I'd like to see General Washington."

His gaze flicked over her dismissively, resting for the briefest moment on her breasts. She wondered if he could see her heart knocking against her chest.

"Are you expected, ma'am?" he asked stiffly.

"No, but—"

"Then I'm afraid it will not be possible."

"I know it's irregular, but I have to see him. It's important."

"I'm sure it is, ma'am," he said with just a trace of condescension. "However, the general is a busy man."

"I'm aware of that."

"Excuse me." He turned on his heel and began to march across to the other side of the building. Another soldier was high-stepping toward them; the dead grass was worn thin in criss-crossing lines that they followed precisely.

"Wait!" She hurried to go after him. She wasn't used to being dismissed.

He stopped and turned impatiently when she reached him. "Ma'am, I'm sorry, but if you don't leave I'll have to get someone to escort you away."

She checked quickly to see if anyone was in earshot. "Tell him it's about Goliath."

The young soldier wrinkled his brow. "Excuse me?"

"It's important," she insisted.

"Goliath?"

"Just tell him!" she said, glaring down at the soldier, grateful, not for the first time, that she'd had plenty of experience in quelling recalcitrant young men.

"If I do, and he won't see you, will you leave quietly?"

"Yes," she said, impatiently shoving back stray curls. Why would her hair never stay where it belonged?

The soldier marched crisply to the plain structure and up the steps. He opened the wooden door, then turned and looked at her, his eyebrows raised questioningly, as if giving her one final chance to back out. She nodded forcefully, and he disappeared inside.

Bennie waited, fingering the papers in her pocket. She swallowed, licked her dry lips, and wondered if she'd be able to get any words out when the time came. Maybe words wouldn't be necessary. She could just give the general the packet and get out of there.

The general! Oh, Lord. The impact of what she was doing struck her forcefully. What she was carrying in her pocket could make the difference between life and death for thousands of men.

She looked around quickly. No one seemed to be paying any attention to her at all. Thank God.

The young soldier stuck his head out the door. He was frowning, and she braced herself to be told to leave.

It would be all right. She'd find Brendan, and he'd listen to her, and he'd find a way to get the information to Washington. Yes, it would be all right. It had to be.

"Follow me," he said.

"Excuse me?"

"He's waiting for you. This way ma'am."

She managed to gulp down a full breath of air, straightened her spine, and went to meet General Washington.

The traitor mopped the sweat from his brow and looked around him in disgust. Two soldiers were sprawled to his left, drinking rum straight from a common bottle and exchanging stories about the whore they'd shared the night before. To his right, one man shouted and four others groaned as each lost half a crown on the turn of a card.

It stunk. A haze that smelled of unwashed, sweaty male bodies and spoiling food clung to the camp. The sanitary conditions were deplorable, the food was worse, and soldiers were dropping like flies—not from battle wounds but from illness.

It was a complete waste. It was disgusting. And nothing he'd done to try and prevent it had amounted to a damn thing.

There'd been precious little information to be discovered in the last few months. Both sides seemed content to sit on their hands and wait.

He sighed in disgust and rose from the crate he'd been sitting on. Perhaps a turn about camp would help. He needed to stretch his legs anyway.

The gamblers hailed him and invited him to join their game. They needed fresh blood—and fresh coin. He declined. He had better things to do, both with his money and his time.

Neatly sidestepping the drunks, he strolled across the camp, automatically noting and cataloguing every thing he saw. One never knew when something crucial would drop into one's lap.

A woman was standing in front of the General's quarters, staring at the door and impatiently tapping her foot. That was unusual enough to catch his interest, but there was also something very familiar about the figure. He slowly ambled closer.

Bennie! What in the world was she doing there?

Before he had time to make up his mind whether to approach her, a young soldier appeared in the doorway and beckoned her in.

It made no sense. There was absolutely no reason she would be expected in the headquarters of the Continental army.

He wondered if it was worth trying to find out what business she could have with the general. Crossing his arms, he waited, unmoving, oblivious to the bustle around him. After nearly a half-hour had passed she still hadn't come out.

Well, his decision was made. He would have to satisfy his curiosity.

27

Dark clouds scudded across the black sky, blotting out the moon. The light was gone, and darkness settled like mist over a swamp.

That was fine with Jonathan. He saw well in the dark.

He couldn't have said why he'd chosen to come back here. He put little stock in superstition or luck, so coming back to this place didn't bother him. Instead, it seemed fitting somehow, to close the circle where it had begun—in New Wexford.

The outlines of the old fort were a mere impression in the darkness. The eye was easily fooled by outlines, in any case. He watched for texture, for movement, and listened for any sound that was manmade.

He knew there would be no repeat of what had happened the last time. The instructions to Washington that he'd attached to the end of the troop information had been clear. They were to seal off every possible exit from Boston, throwing a tight, impenetrable line around the city. There was no possibility that even a small force of British troops could have made it through.

The almost imperceptible swish of a bat in flight stirred the air over his head. He hoped the creature had good hunting tonight. He certainly intended to.

If only the traitor had taken the bait. He'd suggested that Washington have the information leaked. It was a lure Jonathan was sure would be irresistible; Jon was supposed to be meeting with the highest-ranking American spy to have infiltrated the British army, a person whose existence had only been rumored until now.

A person who didn't exist. Jonathan had created him. There was no way the traitor would pass up the opportunity to identify—perhaps to capture—both of them.

There was no sign of anyone else. He would have thought he was completely alone, but he knew his target was there. He felt it somehow, a disturbance in the air, a tang of anticipation.

His prey was careful; there was little doubt about that. It appeared Jon would have to expose himself in order to draw the traitor out.

That was fine, too. Tall, broad, completely unprotected, he strolled across the empty space in front of the fort. Anyone would have a clear shot at him.

He wasn't afraid. Felt little, in fact, not even nervousness or a sense of impending triumph. He'd felt almost nothing since the day Beth had left him in the woods. It was as if all his emotions had retreated into some gray, cold corner where they couldn't reach him anymore. He no longer noticed them in any but the vaguest of ways—a clinical acknowledgment of their presence, but he didn't really *feel* them.

The wind was off the river, bringing with it a hint of coolness. He filled his lungs and emptied his mind. Action was easier when unaccompanied by thought.

He was sure that the traitor didn't want to shoot him—not yet, anyway. Why kill him, when a bigger fish was soon to arrive? Wouldn't do to scare off the prize.

Jon silently crept up on the fort. He backed up against the solid bulk of the outer wall and let out a slow, even breath. He listened. Still nothing. Either he was alone, or the traitor was every bit as quiet as he was.

Jon was betting on the latter.

He slipped along the wall. It smelled of damp and rotting wood. He hugged it tightly, counting on its black flatness to hide both his motion and his form.

He moved slowly. Speed was almost impossible without accompanying sound, and right now, stealth was much more crucial than quickness.

The old gate was open, sagging slightly on one side. It was one of the things the captain hadn't had time to repair. Jon edged around the gate just enough to give himself a quick peek, then slipped inside the fort. The empty central yard was dark and deserted. No shadows, no light, no sound. Only an increase in intensity, a slight thickening in the blackness, indicated where the various buildings stood.

Choices now were a delicate matter. Somehow he needed to flush the traitor out into the open. In order to capture him, Jon had to find him.

Conscious of his audience, Jon turned around restlessly and stamped his feet as if he were growing impatient waiting for his contact. He was acutely aware of the heavy, comforting weight of the flintlock pistol tucked at the small of his back underneath his jerkin, and the cold familiar steel of the blade slipped into his right boot.

Not much protection against a musket or rifle— particularly if the shooter was who Jon suspected it was, for there was only one person in New Wexford who had the access to information, the intelligence, and the temperament to carry this off.

All right, all the traitor needed was a place from which to watch and listen. Safely, comfortably tucked away, all he had to do was hear and see.

There was no place to hide along the inside of the fort. The flat wall provided no cover other than the barest shadow cast by the overhang—

The overhang. Jon looked up at the walkway that rimmed the top of the wall. It was there that British soldiers had stood and fired on attacking French and Indian troops. Narrow, roughly bulwarked with thick wood, it provided rudimentary if fragile protection.

It could also, quite easily, hide a person. A person who from that position would have no trouble hearing and seeing what was happening in the yard below.

A faint prickle lifted the hairs on the back of Jon's neck. He was being watched. How was he ever going to climb to the walkway and sneak up on the traitor without being seen?

Glancing around him once more, he gave a loud, theatrically exasperated sigh. Striding wearily over to the wall, he slumped against it like a man who was tired of waiting. He whacked the wood loudly. Loud enough to be heard above, he hoped.

He was now out of sight to anyone on the ledge directly above him, though still exposed to a watcher on the walkway along the other three sides of the wall, but he had to assume the traitor was here, close enough to see clearly anyone who entered the fort and near enough to hear any conversations held just inside the entrance.

Jon moved soundlessly along the wall. Not even the packed earth and spare grass beneath his feet whispered his passing. Some way from the gate, a crude, broken ladder led to a small opening in the ledge above.

His senses focused on that access hole. He was no longer aware of the coolness of the air, the feel of his clothes, or the sounds of the forest night. He was sharply, acutely conscious only of the task in front of him, and what waited above him on the narrow walkway.

Reaching high above him, almost two thirds of the way up the ladder, he closed his hands slowly around one of the few rungs that seemed still sound. He carefully placed his foot on the fourth rung from the bottom, easing his weight onto it, testing it as much as possible.

The wood was sturdy beneath his boot. He let out a long, even breath, and moved upward.

The old wood creaked beneath his weight. He froze, clinging to the ladder, mentally cursing the sound and his completely vulnerable position.

He could detect no movement above him. No muffled footsteps crept along the ledge toward him. Perhaps the traitor wasn't up there after all, although Jon doubted it. He'd spent six years in this profession, and every shard of instinct and experience he had told him his prey was here.

Maybe the traitor hadn't heard the sound or had written it off as the noise of an old, settling structure.

Once Jon emerged through the hole, there was no going back, no making any other, safer choices.

He wanted this job over. He wanted to wash as much of the blood off his hands as possible, to bury the memories of a special, vibrant woman and her family as deeply as he could manage and go on with his empty, cold life.

He reached for the edges of the hole. The rough, splintery wood cut into his palms, as he shoved himself through the opening.

The musket was black, almost indistinguishable in the darkness. It was also no more than two feet away and pointed directly at Jon's head.

He was still for only a moment, before he finished climbing through the hole. He stood easily, comfortably balanced on the narrow walkway.

"Hello, Brendan," he said calmly. "You're very good, you know. I didn't hear you move."

The clouds blew away from the moon, and they were bathed in cold, silver light. Brendan was dressed in black, blending subtly into the night, and his face was completely composed and emotionless.

"No more so than you. I wouldn't have heard you if the ladder hadn't creaked." He gave a tiny, chilling smile. "Sometimes there are advantages in weighing somewhat less than an ox."

"Yes."

"Raise your hands where I can see them."

Jon complied, careful to make no threatening moves.

His gaze flicked quickly over Brendan, evaluating, looking for an opening.

There were none obvious. His opponent betrayed no telltale tremble of nerves, no tiny lapses of concentration that would give Jon the advantage he needed.

"Now what?" Jon asked.

"A bit of a problem, isn't it? If only you hadn't taken it upon yourself to look for me up here. It would have made things so much simpler."

Jon inched forward. "It would have?" Keep him talking. It was a time-honored tactic. Get someone to talk enough, eventually he gave something away. It was one huge advantage when he played the idiot; he hadn't had to do much talking.

"Yes." Brendan's grip on his weapon was steady, relaxed, familiar. His body was absolutely still; no wasted motion, no excess energy. "I could have simply identified you both and passed it along to the appropriate people. Now things are somewhat more complex."

"Really?" Jon lowered his hands slightly. Easy, easy, he told himself.

"Now you'll have to go back down, wait for your contact, and act like nothing is wrong. Wouldn't want the other party to suspect anything. Of course, pretending won't be much of a problem for you, will it?"

"No."

"You were really quite good. Stupidity puts most people right off. One rarely bothers to look below the surface if the water seems so obviously shallow. Even I wasn't certain until right now."

Jon bowed slightly. "And if I won't do it?"

"Well." Brendan's eyes narrowed. "One way or

another, you will never return to your company."

"Ah." Jon studied Brendan thoughtfully. Did he really have it in him to murder a man in cold blood for no other reason than they were on opposite sides of the war? He had no doubts about Brendan's ability to kill in battle. But an apparently unarmed opponent? Surely despite all, there was too much Jones in him for that.

But shooting Jon here really wouldn't be necessary. All Brendan would have to do would be to make his way safely back to the British. Jon's life would be forfeit if he ever got anywhere near British troops again.

Then again, Jon could do the same thing to Brendan.

Jon narrowed his eyes and focused all his concentration on the man in front of him. This might well be his only opportunity. "Brendan, I'm meeting no one, you know."

There was the barest glimmer of surprise in Brendan's dark eyes. "What?"

"I'm here for only one purpose. To capture you," Jon said evenly.

Brendan started for only an instant, glancing briefly toward the entrance to the fort.

He lowered his guard for scarcely a moment—but it was the only moment Jon had.

Slashing at the musket with his left hand, Jon dived for Brendan's midsection. Brendan's reaction was rapid; he stepped back, trying to bring the musket around so he could get off a shot. It was too late.

The musket went flying off into the darkness as the two hurtled over the edge of the walkway.

The men let go of each other as they fell, twisting in the air to limit any damage from the fall. Jon hit the packed earth with a muffled thud, pain shooting up through his knees and up his back. He ignored it, spinning toward Brendan, and sprang again.

The musket boomed, going off as it slammed into the ground several feet away. As the echoes of the shot faded, he heard the falling tones of a woman's scream.

A familiar scream. Yet he had no time to attend to it. He'd expected Brendan to go down as soon as he'd hit him, but the man had stood his ground, bracing himself for the blow, then clipping Jon behind the knees.

Jon grabbed Brendan's arms and brought him down with him, grappling for a secure hold, but Brendan was like a cat, quick, fluid, graceful, and surprisingly strong. Fully occupied with preventing Brendan from escaping his grasp and reaching his musket, Jon had no time to reach for the knife in his boot.

As they rolled over each other, Jon felt the hard mass of his gun digging painfully into his lower back. Little good it did him there. He swore as he took a heavy blow to his stomach, then barely managed to deflect Brendan's forearm whipping up under his chin.

Damn, he was out of practice. He'd always had a distinct advantage in a fight; his opponents mistakenly figured that the movements of a man his size would be cumbersome and slow, and he'd usually been able to overtake them quickly.

But now he faced an opponent whose quickness was perhaps greater than his. Brendan was as slippery as an eel, and twice he managed to slip through just as Jon was certain he'd gotten a solid hold.

"Stop it. Stop it now!" Jon ignored Beth's frantic demands. Unfortunately, so did Brendan.

Another musket blast, loud and extremely close, shocked him. The ball kicked up a tower of dirt not more than two feet from his head.

"Stop it, I said," Beth shouted. "Or I'll shoot again!"

It slowed Brendan for just an instant. Jon caught him under the chin, digging powerful fingers into his neck, and lifted Brendan off him. Throwing his heavy body over Brendan's, he ripped the pistol from his back and pressed it into the soft skin of Brendan's temple.

"Don't move," he said quietly. "Do you agree?"

Brendan went very still, swallowed heavily, and gave a tiny nod.

"Oh, God." Jon heard her tortured gasp and spared a quick glance at Beth before he returned his attention to Brendan. Her face was white, as pale as the moonlight that turned her tumbled curls to silver, and her eyes were wide with shock and terrible pain. The eyes of an animal that had just been shot but was unable to comprehend its fate.

"Get out of here, Beth," he said, although he knew it was hopeless. It was too late to spare her.

"No," she whispered, a single, tortured syllable that barely managed to make it out of her throat.

"Just go, Elizabeth," Brendan said, his words precise and utterly without inflection.

"No," she repeated, more strongly this time. Jon heard the tap of a ball being tamped down the barrel of her musket. "Let him go, Jon."

"Put the gun down, Beth."

"I mean it, Jon. Let him go." Her voice quavered.

"I can't do that, Beth, and you know it."

"Do it!" she said desperately.

"No. You're not going to shoot me, Beth, and we both know it. Put the gun down."

She gave a soft sob, an inarticulate sound of despair. Out of the corner of his eye, he saw her lower the gun.

"Good." For emphasis, he screwed his pistol tighter against Brendan's head. "Now, I'm going to let you up. But be careful. No sudden moves. Be assured I can shoot nearly as well as you can. Understand?"

"Yes." Brendan's agreement was flat and unemotional.

Jon got slowly to his feet and backed away, keeping the pistol aimed carefully at Brendan. He wanted to turn to Beth, to comfort her, but he couldn't allow his attention to wander.

"Slowly, now," Jon ordered.

Brendan rose carefully, rippling to his feet like a hunting cougar slipping through high grass. His eyes were focused on the gun.

"Stay there," Jon said. He stepped a little farther back, putting himself safely beyond reach. He saw Brendan give a deep sigh of surrender.

"Now then," Brendan said, and turned his gaze to Beth.

"Oh, God, Brendan. Why?" Her voice was low but brittle, as though she kept herself from shattering only by great force of will.

Although her brother's voice was controlled, the sorrow in his dark eyes was brutally clear. "It's all such a waste, Elizabeth. I had to try and stop it any way I could."

"But you couldn't stop it!"

"No, I learned that. But then, I thought perhaps I could help end it more quickly. And finally it was too late to do anything else."

"Oh, Brendan," Beth said in a hoarse, thick voice. She straightened her shoulders and turned to Jon. He could see the shimmer of anguish and moisture in her eyes, and his own burned. "What happens to him now? Exactly."

"Beth . . ." Never had he hated his job—and himself—so much. There was family, and there was country. There was honor, and there was love. And there was what there had always been—loyalty. "He's a traitor, Beth."

She closed her eyes. Her throat worked, and a faint tremor shook her body. "Jonathan," she whispered desperately. Her agony pierced him, a razor-sharp, vicious pain that twisted in his belly and made breathing difficult.

He turned his attention back to Brendan. "Go," he said curtly.

"What?" Brendan said, bewilderment breaking through his rigid control.

"Go. Go, I said, before I change my mind."

Brendan hesitated. "You can't mean this."

"Yes, I do," he ground out. "I'd suggest heading west, following the river, and then north. You're less likely to run into patrols that way."

"I'll manage."

"Getting through to the British might be a bit of a trick."

"I'm not going to the British."

Jon raised one eyebrow in question. "Then where?"

"I don't know." Brendan shrugged slightly. "Somewhere far to the west. Or perhaps Canada. Somewhere quiet."

"Good."

Brendan turned to his sister. Moonlight highlighted his features: elegant, patrician, unsmiling. He swallowed convulsively. "Elizabeth—" He broke off, as if unable to find the words for what he wished to say. Taking a great breath, he forced himself to continue. "Tell them . . . I'm sorry." His voice dropped until it was barely audible. "And tell them I loved you all."

He reached for her then, and when she came to him he crushed her tightly in his arms. They were almost of a height, light hair against dark; brother and sister, so different on the outside. Inside . . . who knew what shaped a person to make the choices he made?

"Well." He pushed her from him and stepped back, allowing himself to touch her cheek one last time. "I'll miss you most of all, you know. Good-bye, Elizabeth."

Brendan squared his shoulders and lifted his chin, the familiar gesture Jon had seen Beth make many times.

"Would you tell me one thing, Jon?" he asked. "Why? Why would you let me go?"

Jon looked down at the pistol he still held in his hand, then tucked it away in the waist of his breeches. "We're not so different, you and I." He set his jaw. "We're both traitors, after all."

Brendan stared at him. The corner of his mouth lifted slightly. "And we both love her."

A silky night breeze swept through the clearing. Its keening was low as soft as it flowed around the wooden corners of the old fort. In the distance, a lonely owl hooted to its absent mate.

"Yes."

"Good." Brendan nodded his satisfaction. "Take care of her, Jon."

He started away, then paused and turned back. "Oh, and Jon? I wouldn't go back to your company after this. I told them about the meeting tonight, and with your absence . . . "

Then he was gone, fading quickly into the night, his black clothes and dark hair blending into the shadows.

Bennie watched her brother dissolve into the blackness and felt the same, cold darkness invade her soul. Her family was broken, and there was nothing she could do to make it whole again. Brendan was going away, alone and beyond her reach.

But he had always been alone, she realized. He had his life, and perhaps, somewhere, he would be able to find some measure of peace.

And now, there was Jon. He had said he loved her. *He loved her!* Miraculous joy suffused her, pushing away the bleakness.

She turned to him. He was kneeling on the ground, his shoulders slumped tiredly, his head buried in his hands. He looked weary, all the strength and sense of purpose she associated with him sapped from his body. Defeated.

Once he had told her that when everything else was gone, all there was left to hold on to was loyalty. Without family, without plans, without future, the one thing he had left was allegiance to his country.

She had begged for the life of her brother, and he had given it to her. Had she asked too much?

She went to him and laid a tentative hand on his shoulder. He shuddered in response.

"Jon?" she asked softly.

His shoulders heaved once, then he stood and turned to her. The expression on his face was stony and remote—unreadable. When his gaze met hers his eyes were cool, glazed, a perfect, shallow reflection of the silver moonlight. They revealed nothing.

"What are you doing here?" he asked, the rough rumble of his voice unemotional and atonal.

"I read the letters before I delivered them to Washington."

"You read the letters." He shook his head. "I should have known."

"You suspected my family!" she said defensively. "I didn't know what you'd written there! I only knew what you'd told me."

"But I said nothing about who I suspected."

"True." She bit her lower lip. "But you requested that you come here tonight alone, completely without backup."

"I always work alone, Beth. I really am quite competent, you know."

"And last time you tried that you were shot and ended up nearly bleeding to death in our stables!" she protested.

"So you thought you'd come to my rescue again." A faint, brief glint of amusement sparkled in his eyes, and her heart swelled slightly.

"Well . . . yes."

Then the tentative spark faded, and once again the starkness filled his eyes. She could feel him becoming detached from her, retreating into that place inside himself where there was no warmth, no emotion, no pain. The part that maintained a role and valued a job above all. She nearly cried for the absence of his life and warmth.

"Jonathan." Carefully slipping her arms around his waist, she lay her head against his chest. He made no move to return her embrace, but neither did he shrink away.

The familiar warmth of his body seeped through her clothes. The thudding of his heart was steady and strong beneath her ear. Try as he might, he was not inhuman, could not be free of painful things like emotion and wants and desires. She would not allow it.

"You're not a traitor, Jonathan."

"The British wouldn't agree with you," he said flatly.

"You but did your job."

His body went rigid. "That wasn't the real betrayal. It was . . . all those men who died, Beth. Oh, God!" Anguish seeped into his voice, breaking through the toneless control. "All those men!"

Her arms tightened around him. "And how many did you save, Jonathan?" she asked fiercely. "Do you count those too?"

"Beth!" The word seemed torn from him, coming from some place hidden deep in his soul. His arms came around her then, crushing her wildly, almost savagely against him, but she welcomed his fervent embrace. She knew then that everything was going to be all right.

She held him while he shook in her arms like a great oak buffeted by a mighty storm. Finally, his arms relaxed their grip. He cradled her head, touching her with a gentleness that bordered on reverence, and lifted her face.

"Beth," he said urgently. "I've played a role so long

that even I am not sure what is underneath. I think it's time I found out. I'd like to do that with you."

"Yes."

He smiled at the speed of her answer. "Wait a minute. Once we strip away the layers, there may not be much left underneath. And it probably isn't pretty," he warned her.

"I know what's beneath."

"You do?"

"Yes." She reached up to touch his face, lightly trailing her fingers down the clean, powerful line of his jaw. "The man I love."

"God, Beth!" There was no hesitation in his kiss, no hint of restraint or subterfuge or shadow. There was only passion and gentleness and fresh, clean emotion.

There was only love.

When he raised his head, all the coldness had left his eyes. They gleamed, alight with fire and intensity. "I do love you, Beth."

Her smile was as powerful and warming as the sun on the first true day of summer.

"Come on, soldier. Let's go home."

28

Cadwallader and Mary Jones were somewhat surprised to see who their daughter brought home.

It was well after midnight by the time Beth and Jon arrived. No welcoming light glowed from the dark windows of the quiet house. It looked peaceful and homey, and Jon was suddenly reluctant to disturb the hushed tranquillity, unwilling to bring the untidy and painful currents of war into Beth's home.

Beth reached out to open the door, but Jon put his hand on hers. "Maybe we should wait until morning," he suggested softly.

"Why?"

"Your parents probably need their rest. We shouldn't disrupt their sleep. The morning's soon enough."

She studied him quizzically for a moment, and then grinned. "You're not afraid to face my father, are you?"

"Well, I am bringing home his only daughter in the

middle of the night. I don't want every male in your family to come after me at once."

She gave him a mock scowl. "Are you trying to tell me your intentions aren't honorable?"

"It would probably be a lot more honorable to let you go." He tenderly brushed the curve of her cheek. "My intentions are to love you for the rest of your life."

"Oh, Jonathan." She lifted her face to kiss him, her lips feathering over his, a kiss that had little to do with heat and everything to do with warmth.

He angled his head and opened his mouth, tracing the delectable curve of her lips with his tongue. What extravagance, to be able to kiss her without urgency, to explore slowly and without greed, knowing that there would be other times and other kisses. He'd never before had that heady luxury with her.

The snarl could have come from an angry bear or rabid dog; the only certainty was that it was a creature lost in the grip of fury or madness. Jon whirled and shoved Beth behind his back for safety, his hand automatically groping for his pistol as he readied himself to face the wild beast.

Her father thundered across the yard between the tavern and his house. His eyes were wide, dark, and snapping with rage, his fists clenched. He charged Jon, slamming him up against the side of the house next to the front door.

"Just what the bloody hell are you doing with my daughter!"

Slowly, trying to be as unthreatening as possible, Jon lifted his hands. There was no conceivable way he was going to do anything that might possibly injure Beth's father. If he got the tar beaten out of him, well, he figured he probably deserved at least that much.

He looked steadily down at Cadwallader. "It's not what you think." That wasn't precisely true, either, but there was certainly more to it than Jones undoubtedly thought there was.

Cad's beefy forearms were crossed over Jon's chest, one just under his neck, keeping him solidly pushed against the rough stone wall. Then Beth wriggled between them, pushing her father away and ordering him to back off. Spreading her arms wide protectively, she planted herself in front of Jon.

Oh, God. She was rescuing him again. He was really going to have to do something about this particular penchant of hers.

"Now, Da," she said soothingly. "We've got a lot to tell—"

"What is going on out here?" Mary Jones's voice was unruffled, as soft and musical as if she were asking a neighbor in to tea.

"Mary, it's that idiot redcoat again," Cad shouted. "And this time, he's put his hands on our Bennie!"

Mary had a white shawl drawn securely over her voluminous nightrobe, and a lacy little cap was perched daintily over her smooth braids. She seemed completely unconcerned about both her attire and the scene in front of her house. "Elizabeth?" she asked.

"It's rather complicated, Mother."

Mary smiled slightly. "I'd imagine so. Well, you all may as well come in. No need to discuss it out in the yard."

"But, Mary, my love—"

"Come along, Cadwallader."

The whale oil lamp Mary lit in the parlor cast eerie, dancing shadows against the walls. Jon perched uneasily on an upholstered settee, and Cad forcibly hustled Bennie to the chair farthest away from where Jon sat. Mary glided over to sit next to Jon, while Cad took up pacing back and forth across the room. His footsteps thundered on the polished wood floor.

"Now then, Ben, give me one good reason why I shouldn't call the regulars and have him arrested right this moment."

Bennie quickly glanced over at Jon. At his small nod, she straightened her shoulders and looked steadily at her father. "Because he's been working for the Americans all along."

"Oh, Bennie." He shook his head sadly. "You don't truly expect me to believe that, do you?"

"Beth is quite correct, sir. I was born in the colonies, in Philadelphia, and lived there until I was ten, and I have always considered this my home. I have only tried to help in any way I could."

Cad spun around, his jaw agape in shock. "You talked!"

"I believe you have heard me speak before, sir," Jon said in his most respectful voice.

"But—" Cad clamped his mouth shut and studied Jon carefully.

Superficially, he certainly looked like the man Cad remembered. His clothes were rumpled and torn, streaked with dirt and what looked suspiciously like blood. He'd seen Jon's clothes in that state many times, although before he'd always worn a British uniform.

But there the resemblance ended. This man was taller, his head held proudly and his posture perfect. He radiated indefinable but absolutely tangible power, the kind of power that led men and accomplished impossible things. His eyes, alert and assessing, sparked with exceptional intelligence. And, when his gaze fell on Bennie, they softened with equally uncommon tenderness.

"So," Cad said slowly, trying to reconcile the man who'd stumbled into the Eel with the one who sat in front of him now. "No stupidity?"

Jon's mouth quirked in amusement. "Well, sir, your daughter might choose to disagree with that."

"All right." Cad stopped his pacing, crossed his arms, and glared at Jon. "That explains why I shouldn't turn you in to the militia. But considering what I saw outside my own front door, can you give me one good reason I shouldn't grab my musket and haul you both off to the nearest man of the cloth?"

Jon met Cad's gaze squarely. "Sir, there's nothing I'd like more."

Cad's mouth popped open again.

Mary took over. "Elizabeth! How wonderful!" Beaming at her daughter, she rose, her nightrobe settling gracefully around her feet. "I knew you didn't mean it when you said you never wished to get married."

Cad was still standing in the middle of the room, his stunned gaze darting back and forth from his daughter to Jon and back to Bennie again.

"Sit down, Cad," Mary said briskly. "We need to celebrate. I'll just go and fetch—"

"Mother, I really think you should sit down too."

The serious note in Bennie's voice must have alerted

Mary. She glanced uncertainly from her daughter to Cad, then slowly complied.

"Now then." Beth swallowed heavily, her eyes nearly black with pain. She lifted her shoulders, preparing herself, and determinedly plunged in. "There's something else we have to tell you—"

"It can wait," Jon broke in. Beth looked at him questioningly, and he nodded. Perhaps her parents need never know their son had been a traitor. He could ask Washington to keep it quiet, to let them all believe Brendan had simply deserted. Maybe this much, at least, he could spare them. He could certainly spare Beth the burden of telling them. "It can wait," he repeated implacably. "We're all tired. We should get some rest. The morning will be here soon enough."

Beth felt the tightness in her chest ease. Not completely—just a notch—but enough so that it was bearable. He meant to help her, she realized. This she didn't have to handle alone. Although she found the pain didn't dim, the pressure had lessened. The responsibility, the duty to stand completely alone was gone. Now there was someone to share it.

Now there was Jonathan.

"Well." Cad slapped his hands on his thighs and stood up, a signal to the others to rise also. "I guess you're right. No reason to be sitting around hashing it out in the middle of the night when there are perfectly good beds upstairs. Jon, I'll show you a room over to the Eel you can stay in."

"The Eel?" Jon said in a strangled voice. He looked at Beth, and she could see the yearning in his eyes, his reluctance to leave her, and even a little disbelief that he had to, and she had to work to stifle her laughter. "You want me to sleep in the tavern?"

"Of course," Cad said jovially. "That's where my boys sleep. You'll be perfectly comfortable, I promise. And Isaac doesn't really snore all that loudly."

Cad had Jonathan halfway out the door by this time. Jonathan planted his feet, bracing his hands against the door frame, and turned to look back at Beth. "Beth?" he asked plaintively.

She knew her amusement showed in her voice. "I'll see you in the morning, Jonathan."

"Yes." Mary tucked an invisible hair back beneath her cap. "It will be a busy day tomorrow. We'll have to start planning the wedding. If we get right to work, I'm certain we could have it in no more than a month."

Jon's shoulders sagged. "Beth," he begged. She smiled at him innocently.

"Now then," Mary was going on, "I believe I saw just the fabric for a wedding dress over at Rupert's store. Beth, do you want to go see it tomorrow? A month will be plenty of time to make something truly stun—"

"A week," Jon said sternly.

"What?" Distracted from her plans, Mary focused on her prospective son-in-law. "We can't possibly be ready in a week. I've waited for so long—"

"A week," Jon repeated, his jaw set.

Cad looked Jon up and down once before shoving him out the door. "I'll tell you one thing, Mary my love," he called as he left. "What grandchildren these two are going to give us!"

*   *   *

Jonathan and Beth were married a week later in the First Congregational Church of New Wexford, the church where her grandfather had presided for so many years and where Cadwallader had first laid eyes on the prettiest, most feminine bit of woman he'd ever seen. It was the church where her parents were married, and where four of her brothers had wed.

Since the young minister who'd replaced Mary's father had gone off to do his duty to country as well as God, they'd had to fetch the elderly reverend from Middleton to perform the ceremony. In Mary's opinion, he'd managed things adequately, if not exceptionally well.

There'd been no new dress after all. Jon had spent most of the week in Cambridge, giving his report to General Washington, but he'd stayed around long enough to decree that Beth should wear the forest green dress he liked so much. And Mary, who'd spent a lifetime moving large, immovable people, found she'd finally run into one she couldn't budge. Amazingly, she seemed to like him even more for it. Or perhaps it was just that her daughter was finally getting married. She was willing to yield the battle, for she'd already won the war.

Cad and Mary had taken the news that their second son had deserted with surprising equanimity. Cad, although shamed, had also declared he'd always known the boy hadn't the stomach for war. Mary had paled and turned in on herself, saying little. Bennie suspected her mother had always realized she'd lose Brendan someday and also thought Mary was perhaps a bit relieved to have at least one of her children out of harm's way.

Sometimes, when Mary went very quiet, Bennie wondered if her mother knew more about Brendan's disappearance than Jon had told her.

Now, after every scrap of food her mother and all her brother's wives had spent each and every minute of the past week preparing had been devoured, after her father's private stock had been seriously depleted, and after they'd finally been able to roust the last of the guests from the tavern, the house, and the yard between, she sat on the bed in the room she'd had as a child, waiting for her husband.

She smoothed the fine lawn of the nightgown Hannah, Adam's wife, had given her, fingering the delicate white lace her sister-in-law was famous for tatting, and wondered if a bride had ever been less nervous on her wedding night.

There was no room for trepidation when she was so completely overwhelmed with anticipation. She'd spent the week docilely doing whatever her mother told her to do, lost in dreams of what it was going to be like to have Jonathan beside her the whole night long. When her mother had, with calm detachment and absolute precision that was belied by the dreamy gleam in her dark eyes, informed Elizabeth what to expect on her wedding night, it had been all Bennie could do not to burst out giggling—and she *never* giggled.

And when they'd stood in the front of the church, Jon had looked down at her and quoted his vows in a voice that fairly vibrated with strength and commitment. If she had never before known that he loved her, she would have believed it absolutely at that moment. Sunlight had streamed through the high stained glass window, painting him with jeweled tones of sapphire and emerald and ruby light that glowed and sparkled like gems too precious to be real. But his eyes had shone even brighter, gleaming with satisfaction and exultation and love, emotions that reverberated in her own heart like the purest note she'd ever imagined.

So where was he? She bounced off the bed and began to pace the room impatiently, the hem of her new gown whispering around her ankles. There was sensual pleasure in the feel of the fine cloth against her naked skin, and she realized her skin was primed, anticipating a touch of another sort.

The door slammed open and Jon rushed in. He shoved the door closed and weakly leaned against, his eyes brimming with light and humor.

"God, Beth, why didn't you warn me?"

She crossed her arms over her chest and gave him a mock frown. "Where have you been?"

"I've been getting lectures. From your father, from that pipsqueak of a little brother of yours, and from that old storekeeper. Not to mention your mother, bless her dainty little steel-edged soul, as well as all the ones I got from your other brothers when I was in Cambridge." He loosened his collar, exposing a wedge of smooth tawny skin. "Why didn't you tell me what I was getting into?"

"I thought you didn't want me to rescue you anymore."

He grinned and threw his arms wide. "Come here and rescue me, Beth. I have a most desperate need to hold you."

She flowed against him with a sigh of pleasure, fitting her curves automatically to his planes. His arms came around her securely, and beneath her ear she heard his heartbeat quicken. His hands began to roam, sweeping her back, and she discovered the thin cloth of her night-dress was little barrier to his warmth.

"God, Beth, it's been too long."

She leaned back to look up at him and gave a teasing smile. "You could have tried a bit harder, you know."

"Are you serious?" He looked aghast. "Your mother is a regular Tartar when she puts her mind to something. There was no possibility I was putting my hands anywhere near her precious, innocent, defenseless Elizabeth before the vows were spoken."

"Well, thank God you already had."

He slid one hand around to caress her belly, massaging her softly through the wispy fabric. "You never got in touch with me after I'd left. Should I take that to mean we're not expecting?"

She nodded.

"Damn!" He grinned roguishly. "Well, I guess we'll have to get to work on that."

"I imagine so." She leaned against him, letting her breasts press against the solid wall of his chest, watching with satisfaction as his features began to sharpen. "My father's quite looking forward to the grandsons we're going to give him."

"I rather like the idea of daughters myself." He closed his eyes as she slipped her hand inside the opening of his shirt and began to explore. "Damn, Beth, you'd better stop that."

"Why?" She found a place that intrigued her, right where the bulge of his pectorals segued into the ripple of his ribs, and traced it with her fingertips.

"Because your parents are right next door, that's why."

"So?"

"So you're noisy."

"What? I am not," she protested. "As if you're quiet!"

"I'm the soul of discretion." He swooped, lifting her in his arms, and tossed her onto the bed. The rope frame creaked and she laughed loudly, "See what I mean? Noisy."

He grabbed her ankle and sent his fingers wandering up her calf, slowly stroking the back of her knee until her eyes began to darken. "Remember, after you were hurt, and I brought you back to the Eel, and I checked your ankle before I left?"

She nodded mutely, unable to think clearly enough to form words when his hands worked their magic on her skin.

"I got so hard I was terrified one of your brothers was going to notice and I would never get out of there alive. I had a hell of a time sidling out of the place sideways," he said, and she felt a tiny catch in her heart at the thought that she could affect him so much.

Grinning, he lay himself down on the bed, settling his big body on hers comfortably, and all amusement vanished.

His gaze traced her face slowly, lingering on each feature as if he were trying to imprint it in his mind. He lifted a lock of her hair, watching in apparent fascination as it curled around his finger. The light blue of his eyes was vivid, shining, like the color of the sky on a brilliant winter day reflecting off pure, gleaming, fresh snow.

"God, Beth," he whispered, his voice vibrating with emotion. "I do love you."

His kiss was slow, gentle, a meeting of lips and breath and souls, almost delicate in its reverence. But Beth could feel the low, impending rumble of thunder.

The first time he'd touched her, she'd called him Jon. The second, he'd been Jonathan.

This time, he was simply her husband.

A single tallow candle guttered on the nightstand next to Beth's bed. The mellow, dancing light played over the angles and hollows of her face. The thick golden-brown crescent of her lashes lay against the creamy skin under her eyes.

Jon tightened his arms around his wife and watched her sleep. Outside, the sky was beginning to pearl into the gray just before dawn, but he had yet to close his own eyes.

He couldn't bring himself to waste a moment in sleep.

She sighed and shifted closer to him, as if seeking his warmth, and he found himself unaccountably proud that even in her sleep she turned to him. One naked thigh, curved, soft, womanly, but hiding, he knew, exceptional strength—much like Beth herself—slipped between his own, and he felt himself begin to harden yet again.

Again! He feared he'd exhausted her completely before he'd finally allowed her to drift off to sleep, well into the depths of the night. He was disgracefully grateful that his bride wasn't a virgin on their wedding night, or he would have felt extremely guilty about demanding his husbandly rights three times.

Of course, in all honesty, Beth had really been the demanding one.

Her cheek rubbed against his arm, the curly strands of her hair tickling him. He couldn't resist sliding his fingers through the soft, golden strands, combing through the entire, heavy length. Her eyelids fluttered open; she looked up at him and smiled. A sleepy, content, womanly smile, a flirty little grin that rushed through his veins and went to his head faster than even Cad's most potent brew.

"Hello," she said softly. "You're awake."

"I haven't slept yet."

"No?" She stretched, all suppleness and skin, sliding over him in a way that made him groan out loud. "I'm ashamed. And here I'd thought I'd tired you out thoroughly."

He ran his forefinger down the narrow slope of her nose and dropped a kiss at the corner of her eye. "I wasn't going to waste a single moment of the first time I finally get the chance to hold you all night long. God, Beth, do you know how many times I've dreamed of this?"

"No more than I have." Contentment. Happiness. Satisfaction. Love. How had she ever thought she'd known the meanings of those words? Now she knew that her understanding of them had had everything to do with the surface and almost nothing to do with those deep, swelling feelings that started way down inside.

She studied him in the darkness. Most of his face was hidden in shadow, but his pale eyes shone, gleaming

light and bright in the darkness. Why hadn't she been
able to read them before? How difficult it must have
been for him to shield all his emotions from the world
with those clear eyes that went all the way to his soul.
There was burgeoning passion and open happiness,
total approval and unshakable love. And, behind them
all, almost hidden, there were deep, swirling shadows of
. . . disquiet. Disquiet?

"No!" she said sharply, pushing herself out of his
embrace and sitting up in bed. "You're not going back,
Jonathan."

Surprise flashed for only an instant. He sat up too,
the sheets falling away from him and pooling around his
bare hips. "I have to, Beth."

A sick heaviness settled in the region of her heart,
and she felt the burn of tears. She tried to blink them
away, forcing herself to sound teasing. "I'm really getting very weary of this. Every time we lie together, you
run off to war. It's enough to make a woman wonder."

The words came out bare, heavy, not at all as she
intended. She saw pain streak through his eyes like
summer lightning, then his jaw hardened in determination. "It's my duty, Beth."

"You think I give a damn about duty?" She'd heard
about men who, unable to live with the acts they'd
committed in the name of war, became careless with
their own lives, taking outrageous chances, as if seeking their own punishment. She was shaking, nearly ill
with the fear that Jon would follow that path. She'd
thought he'd come to terms with what he'd done, had
settled in his own mind that he'd had no other choice.
But what if she'd been wrong? What if he was driven

to atone for the wrongs he was convinced he'd done?

He would drag her down to hell with him, for his loss would be her own damnation.

"Beth," he said helplessly. He couldn't talk to her when she was so far away. He took her into his lap, grateful that at least she didn't resist him, and rested his chin on the top of her head. "Am I wrong in thinking we want a family?"

She sniffed slightly. "'Twill be difficult to manage if you're not around to impregnate me."

He sighed. This was more than he'd ever expected to have out of life, the soft weight of her nestled against him, the stir of her breath against his skin. He would have given every bit of wealth he'd ever have to stay right here forever. But there were some things he couldn't surrender.

"I want our children raised in freedom. In a country where they are valued, where what they can achieve is limited only by their own talents and determination. If I must fight for that, then I will."

She made a strangled sound, then slipped her arms around him, hugging him tight. "I'm so afraid."

"I am too." He closed his eyes, fighting the suspicious wetness that gathered there. "But it's even more important to me now, Beth. Before, I fought only for country. Now I'll fight for us and our future. And I'll be able to do it openly this time."

She burrowed against him, as if she were trying to be absorbed through his skin, an idea that held a certain appeal. "But it's more dangerous for you now," she mumbled in a broken voice. "If you are captured, you wouldn't just be a prisoner of war."

"I'd be a traitor," he said, his voice even and edged with steel. "I guess I'll just have to make sure I'm not captured, then."

"You'd better," she choked out.

He lifted his hands to cradle her face, tipping her head up so he could search her eyes. "You don't honestly think that I'm really going to leave you for good, do you? After waiting this long to find you? After we've come through so much already?" He hoped she would see it in his eyes, feel it in his touch. He knew he had to do this, but he also knew he was coming back to her. Not even the most horrendous demons hell could unleash could keep him from her; certainly neither a tiny bit of lead nor the British forces could do it. He wouldn't let it happen.

"I want you to say it, Beth," he said, his voice harsh with intensity. "I want you to tell me you believe I'm coming back."

She smiled at him then, the light of certainty in her eyes shining behind the shimmer of unshed tears. She reached up, tracing the bones of his face with a touch that was both light and absolutely sure.

"You are coming back to me."

Epilogue

It was the spring of 1783, and Colonel Jonathan Schuyler Leighton was finally coming home from war.

The road he trudged down, just outside of New Wexford, was rutted and frozen. He didn't notice. His eyes, his attention, his entire being was focused on one thing: the modest, whitewashed frame house settled prettily among bare, towering maples at the edge of Finnigan's Wood.

The windows of the house, like the door, were oversize, slightly out of proportion. He liked that; the house seemed to suit its occupants.

The house was bathed in silver light from a narrow crescent moon. Branches rubbed and squeaked together in the chill wind that seemed to have forgotten spring was on its way.

But Jon wasn't cold. In one of the upper windows, through diamond panes polished to startling clarity, a single candle glowed. He could nearly feel its warmth from here. The flame was small, steady, burning with golden light. Burning for him.

He knew that small blaze had been glowing there for more than eight years, night and day. It had been there, never wavering, never fading, every time he'd been able to come home on leave, a symbol of the belief that he would indeed come home.

He was nearly there, and the bone-deep, soul-searing weariness of so many years of war began to lift, replaced by a burgeoning, swelling joy. For this time he didn't have to leave again.

Quietly, unwilling to wake the occupants of the house, he pushed open the front door. Once inside, he just stood there, absorbing the soft sounds of a resting house and breathing in the scents of beeswax and cooking spices that meant home.

He mounted up the center stairs that swept up in front of him, his footsteps light. His hand slid easily over the glossy surface of the handrail, and he remembered the day he had spent rubbing it to that fine-grained finish. He'd only been able to work on bits of the house himself; his father-in-law had built most of it, helped occasionally by whichever Jones male had been home on leave, and with more assistance from Beth than she probably should have been giving. But he was glad that there were parts of the house that bore his mark, that showed the labor of his hands and the care he'd put into it.

He paused at the first bedroom to the right. Two small beds, dressed in frilly white, were filled. His girls. He didn't know how long he stood there, noting all the changes, how much they'd grown since he'd seen them last.

Six and four years old! God, where had it all gone? His eyes stung as he thought of what he'd missed, all the things he'd never get to see. The times when their white, baby-fine curls had turned to thick, gold sunshine; when their chubby little bodies had begun to slim and lengthen into childhood. It was nearly beyond his strength not to scoop them right into his arms and hold them close. They'd squeal then, he knew; when he came back after he'd been away, he always squeezed them just a little too tight.

He let them sleep. In the next room, milky moonlight pouring through the window illuminated a small tester bed. Cadwallader Leighton was the pride of his grandfather, who, after two girls that he adored, had all but given up hope that his daughter would produce a grandson, and who had nearly burst his buttons when he heard his newest grandchild's name.

The Jones men had not been impervious to war after all. They'd lost David at Valley Forge, and his widow and child had moved in with Cad and Mary.

And, of course, they'd also lost Brendan, who was never mentioned in the Jones house. Jon knew Beth received occasional letters from her brother, who was in Montreal and had found work cataloguing the library for a community of monks. Brendan seemed content with the books and the silence.

Henry had lost a leg at Princeton and had come home bitter and angry, drained of every bit of exuberance and joy.

Little Cadwallader was nearly a year old now, his head covered with swirls of fine, light brown hair that gleamed almost white in the moonlight. His skin was smooth, flawless, and Jon couldn't resist running the back of one finger over the plump curve of his cheek. His eyes were closed, outrageously long lashes resting gently against his cheek. Jon knew those eyes were big and brown and shiny with the wonder of the world and the knowledge that he was loved.

Jon shuddered slightly and felt a drop of moisture slip out of the corner of his eye. He hadn't seen his son for nearly eight months and had never been there when one of his children was born. But he felt a deep satisfaction that they would grow up in a place where freedom was more than a word.

He stepped out in to the hall and heard the faint whisper of bare feet on the polished wood floor.

"Jonathan?" she said uncertainly.

She was standing in the doorway of their bedroom, the place she'd slept far too many nights alone. The rich spill of her curls tumbled down her back, and the pale sweep of her nightdress swirled around her lush, strong body.

"Jonathan!" she cried.

He didn't remember how she got there, he only knew that suddenly she was in his arms, clutching him tightly around the neck, trembling as he held her.

"Can you stay this time?" she asked, her voice muffled against his chest.

"Yes," he said hoarsely. "This time, I'm home for good."

And then he found her mouth, a kiss flavored with desperation and emotion and feelings pent up over far too much time. His lips slanted and his tongue swirled with hers, going deeper, farther, more. He had to have more.

He wrapped his arms around her waist and lifted her clear of the floor, walking her back into the bedroom without breaking the contact. He leaned over the bed, bracing himself with one arm while holding her with the other, and lowered her to it, still without ever moving his mouth from hers.

There was no time for preliminaries. He was quick, nearly crazed, as he kept his lips firmly on hers while he shoved her nightdress up to her waist and fumbled with the fastenings of his breeches.

He touched her once, briefly, to assure himself he wouldn't hurt her. Then he thrust inside her, quickly, one strong flex of his hips and he was buried as deeply as he could go.

He went still. There was no longer any necessity for speed, for he was where he needed to be. Now there was time for caressing and stroking and touches, time for sliding his tongue along her collarbone and kissing the place where her pulse beat in the hollow of her throat. Time for gentleness, time for tenderness. For now he was with Beth, in her, surrounded by her.

For now, at last, he was home.

It was over. Finally, completely over. No more would her husband leave her after only a few days of heaven. No more waking up in the middle of the night, trembling and drenched with sweat after living through dreams that were drenched with blood. No more standing watching their children sleep and wondering if they were going to grow up without a father. No more rumors of battle that obliterated anything but icy fear.

It was over at last. Jonathan had come home to her.

She placed her hand along the slope of his jaw. The

stubble rasped against her palm as he turned his head to gently place a kiss there.

Beth looked up at the man who lay over her in the dark, whose body filled hers and whose presence filled her heart. His face was illuminated by moonlight and the wavering flame of the solitary candle. His features were sharpened, made even more handsome by the hardships of war and command. There was strength there, and harshness, and an aching, extraordinary tenderness.

He was the most beautiful man in the world.

And he was hers.

AVAILABLE NOW

CHEYENNE AMBER by Catherine Anderson

From the bestselling author of the Comanche Trilogy and *Coming Up Roses* comes a dramatic western set in the Colorado Territory. Under normal circumstances, Laura Cheney would never have fallen in love with a rough-edged tracker. But when her infant son was kidnapped by Comancheros, she had no choice but to hire Deke Sheridan. "*Cheyenne Amber* is vivid, unforgettable, and thoroughly marvelous."—Elizabeth Lowell

MOMENTS by Georgia Bockoven

A heartwarming new novel from the author of *A Marriage of Convenience* and *The Way It Should Have Been*. Elizabeth and Amado Montoyas' happy marriage is short-lived when she inexplicably begins to pull away from her. Hurt and bewildered, she turns to Michael Logan, a man Amado thinks of as a son. Now Elizabeth is torn between two men she loves—and hiding a secret that could destroy her world forever.

TRAITOROUS HEARTS by Susan Kay Law

As the American Revolution erupted around them, Elizabeth "Bennie" Jones, the patriotic daughter of a colonial tavern owner, and Jon Leighton, a British soldier, fell desperately in love, in spite of their differences. But when Jon began to question the loyalties of her family, Bennie was torn between duty and family, honor and passion.

THE VOW by Mary Spencer

A medieval love story of a damsel in distress and her questionable knight in shining armor. Beautiful Lady Margot le Brun, the daughter of a well-landed lord, had loved Sir Eric Stavelot, a famed knight of the realm, ever since she was a child and was determined to marry him. But Eric would have none of her, fearing that secrets regarding his birth would ultimately destroy them.

MANTRAP by Louise Titchener

When Sally Dunphy's ex-boyfriend kills himself, she is convinced that there was foul play involved. She teams up with a gorgeous police detective, Duke Spikowski, and discovers suspicious goings-on surprisingly close to home. An exciting, new romantic suspense from the bestselling author of *Homebody*.

GHOSTLY ENCHANTMENT by Angie Ray

With a touch of magic, a dash of humor, and a lot of romance, an enchanting ghost story about a proper miss, her nerdy fiancé, and a debonair ghost. When Margaret Westbourne met Phillip Eglinton, she never realized a man could be so exciting, so dashing, and so . . . dead. For the first time, Margaret began to question whether she should listen to her heart and look for love instead of marrying dull, insect-loving Bernard.

COMING NEXT MONTH

THE COURT OF THREE SISTERS by Marianne Willman
An enthralling historical romance from the award-winning author of *Yesterday's Shadows* and *Silver Shadows*. The Court of Three Sisters was a hauntingly beautiful Italian villa where a prominent archaeologist took his three daughters: Thea, Summer, and Fanny. Into their circle came Col McCallum, who was determined to discover the real story behind the mysterious death of his mentor. Soon Col and Summer, in a race to unearth the fabulous ancient treasure that lay buried on the island, found the meaning of true love.

OUTRAGEOUS by Christina Dodd
The flamboyant Lady Marian Wenthaven, who cared nothing for the opinions of society, proudly claimed two-year-old Lionel as her illegitimate son. When she learned that Sir Griffith ap Powel, who came to visit her father's manor, was actually a spy sent by King Henry VII to watch her, she took Lionel and fled. But there was no escaping from Griffith and the powerful attraction between them.

CRAZY FOR LOVIN' YOU by Lisa G. Brown
The acclaimed author of *Billy Bob Walker Got Married* spins a tale of life and love in a small Tennessee town. After four years of exile, Terrill Carroll returns home when she learns of her mother's serious illness. Clashing with her stepfather, grieving over her mother, and trying to find a place in her family again, she turns to Jubal Kane, a man from the opposite side of the tracks who has a prison record, a bad reputation, and the face of a dark angel.

TAMING MARIAH by Lee Scofield
When Mariah kissed a stranger at the train station, everyone in the small town of Mead, Colorado, called her a hellion, but her grandfather knew she only needed to meet the right man. The black sheep son of a titled English family, Hank had come to the American West seeking adventure . . . until he kissed Mariah.

FLASH AND FIRE by Marie Ferrarella
Amanda Foster, who has learned the hard way how to make it on her own, finally lands the coveted anchor position on the five o'clock news. But when she falls for Pierce Alexander, the station's resident womanizer, is she ready to trust love again?

INDISCRETIONS by Penelope Thomas
The spellbinding story of a murder, a ghost, and a love that conquered all. During a visit to the home of enigmatic Edmund Llewelyn, Hilary Carewe uncovered a decade-old murder through rousing the spirit of Edmund's stepmother, Lily Llewelyn. As Edmund and Hilary were drawn together, the spirit grew stronger and more vindictive. No one was more affected by her presence than Hilary, whom Lily seemed determined to possess.

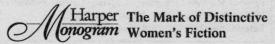 **Harper Monogram** **The Mark of Distinctive Women's Fiction**